GREEN LORELEI
Francis John Thornton

June of 1898 was one of the hottest months on record—and one of the deadliest. For rich playboys were turning up dead all over gaslit Philadelphia. With no hope of solving the case, the police turned to former Scotland Yard pathologist Dr. Ian Blakeley for assistance. Only Blakeley, with his unparalleled powers of deduction, could track down the mysterious woman in green who lured men to their deaths—and then disappeared as if she'd never existed.

Other *Leisure Books* by Francis John Thornton:
CEREMONY IN SCARLET

FRANCIS JOHN THORNTON

GREEN LORELEI

LEISURE BOOKS NEW YORK CITY

A LEISURE BOOK®

September 1992

Published by

Dorchester Publishing Co., Inc.
276 Fifth Avenue
New York, NY 10001

This one's for Buffy.

Chapter One

It was always chilly in the morgue—damp and clammy, no matter how merciless the heat in Philadelphia. And June, 1898, would be one of the hottest months on record, which was already apparent even though it was only the seventh. The morgue was quiet, too, like a tomb. In the midst of this sepulchral silence, a tall, portly man of middle age and another, younger man examined a corpse that had been mutilated almost beyond recognition. Although the two men spoke in solemn tones—partly out of deference to the dead man, partly out of habit—their voices seemed to echo through the hall.

The elder gentleman—Dr. Ian Blakeley, late of Scotland Yard—used his pen to direct Nathan McBride's attention to the triangular spots on the corneas and inner sides of the corpse's eyes. One eye was half closed, the other bulged up at them in red-netted horror.

"See there, Nathan? *La tache noire de la scléro-*

tique. Those little dots can only come from sheer, paralyzing terror."

Nathan nodded. A detective sergeant with the Philadelphia Police Department, he'd seen dead bodies before, but he would never get used to examining them, especially not when he had to do it first thing in the morning.

Blakeley removed his monocle, fogged it, and wiped it on the linen apron he wore over his light summer suit. Nathan wore an apron too. It was a courtesy granted them by the morgue staff that they gladly accepted since they had no desire to smell of death for the rest of the day.

"You look a bit ashen, dear boy," Blakeley said, his voice much too cheery for the surroundings.

Nathan ran a handkerchief across his forehead and smiled lamely. "I missed breakfast."

"One should never miss breakfast," Blakeley chided.

"Right." There was a catch in Nathan's voice, the result of having swallowed too much air while fighting nausea.

"Terrible way to make an exit," he said when he had overcome the wave of nausea.

"I've rarely seen worse," Blakeley said. He replaced his monocle and measured the width of a deep wound that ran across the lower abdomen. The shredded blob on the table had been Louis Paul Hazleton, financier, socialite, art patron and iconoclast. Blakeley paused in his examination for a moment, rubbed his well-groomed Vandyke, then said, "One has to wonder if the punishment could possibly fit the crime. Did you know him, Nathan?"

"Only by reputation," Nathan answered, forcing himself to look at the corpse.

"From what I gather," Blakeley said, "there was much to despise about poor Hazleton. He was contemptuous of everything and everyone. I cannot say

I had the displeasure of dealing with him often, but I do recall one occasion when he wanted me to use my family ties in southern Africa to help him secure a contract with some mining interests in Natal. He floated up the Schuylkill on that flamboyant yacht of his, docked at my estate, disembarked with all the flair of visiting royalty, and presented himself. One would have thought Cleopatra's barge had arrived. I told him that those Portuguese chaps with whom he was doing business in Matamini were, as far as I could see, little more than filthy slave traders and therefore dismissed his proposal on the spot. He had a hard time accepting my response. He even threatened in that high, piping voice of his to call on some friends in Washington to have me deported. But I was adamant. Civil, of course, but adamant. After that our meetings were mercifully infrequent."

Nathan had had enough of the bulging eye. He turned his attention to the grim details Blakeley had jotted in his note pad. The young detective didn't pretend to have any expertise in forensic pathology. But in the months he'd worked closely with Blakeley—who was happy to lend his expertise to the Philadelphia Police Department and to undertake an investigation whenever it struck his particular fancy—Nathan had absorbed much more knowledge than even he realized. Blakeley put more faith in this young man than he ever extended to the stuffy professionals in his field. Owing to Blakeley's vote of confidence, Nathan felt free to think aloud.

"Your mentioning Africa just brought something to mind," he said. "Do you remember when John L. Sullivan used to walk around with a lion on a leash? That's still in fashion, I hear."

"You think one escaped, do you, Nathan?"

"Either one escaped or Hazleton owned one that

attacked him. I wouldn't put it past a character like Hazleton to think he could buy anything he wanted."

"Yes," Blakeley said, nodding, "Hazleton was the sort of chap to keep such a pet."

"It attracted attention," Nathan said.

"Quite." Blakeley concluded his measurements, jotted another note, and put his pad away. "That is a good idea, Nathan, except there was not one hint of fur, parasites, or animal saliva either on the body or in the stateroom where it was found or, for that matter, anywhere on the yacht. The laboratory fellows went over it with combs and magnifying glasses."

"The lab people have their good days and bad days. Evidence has been known to get lost or destroyed in the past," Nathan said, speaking clandestinely because a morgue attendant was seated at a desk not far away.

"There is that possibility, Nathan," Blakeley said, lowering, his voice too. "Perhaps a quiet check on the laboratory would be advisable." Blakeley put the rest of his materials away, pinched the bridge of his nose for a moment, and sighed. "Unfortunately, all we know for certain is that Louis Paul Hazleton was lying on his back when attacked. The perpetrator—man, beast, or otherwise, singular or plural—tore at his body with one hand while gripping his jaw with the other." He demonstrated what he believed to be the killer's method, then gestured again at the face of the corpse. "That accounts for the right eye being open and the other half closed."

Nathan forced himself once again to look at the body. "I remember an uneven tension of the neck structure. I've noticed it in hangings."

"Very good," Blakeley said like a satisfied schoolmaster.

Nathan was pensive. "A grappling hook could

have done that. I think I'll check out the waterfront too."

"Eh? Yes, I suppose it's worth a look." Blakeley started to remove his linen apron. "Well, do you think you've seen all you care to see, Nathan?"

Nathan was halfway out of his apron before he said, "If you think so, I think so."

Blakeley signaled the attendant to return the body to a slab. "Let's have a look at the suspect then."

Outside, the sun was high and hostile in a graying sky that promised rain, but was probably only teasing. The weather had been the same for the past two weeks, so neither Blakeley nor Nathan mentioned it. The sun beat down mercilessly on the hood of Blakeley's cabriolet, but as long as the carriage was moving, a pleasant breeze cooled the men. The refreshing wind was important to Nathan, whose stomach was settling very slowly as they bounced along the cobbled roadway. The horse, a muscular black mare named Hecuba, was glossy with sweat after only a quarter mile.

Blakeley and Nathan rode in silence for a while, as they headed north on Monument into the Eleventh Precinct. Trolleys and horse-drawn wagons crisscrossed the street, and pedestrians on their way to work in the shops and offices downtown meandered through the traffic and crowded the trolley islands. Because of the early morning heat, several people had gathered near the ice wagons parked outside the saloons and ice-cream parlors. Blakeley grunted irritably as he maneuvered through the pedestrians; finally he decided to take a detour through a shaded, less-traveled road.

When the danger of vomiting no longer threatened him, and his cheeks had become more pink than green, Nathan took the reins and gave Blakeley a chance to sit back. The young policeman was not the sort to become nauseated easily. He still had the trim body of an athlete, very little having changed since the years when he boxed his way through college, never losing a bout. He wore his bargain-sale suits in a way that tricked the eye into thinking they cost more than a policeman's salary would allow. And until most people knew him well, it was almost inevitable that they would misjudge him, because he had the kind of brooding good looks that ladies liked so much, but that kept strangers at a distance. Yet those same humorless Celtic poet's eyes, which darkened at the sight of a fool or pierced like a hot knife when facing an enemy, could just as easily twinkle like a blue sea at twilight. A less generous man than Blakeley could easily resent him.

"He wasn't entirely bad, you know," Blakeley said, fanning himself with his bowler as Nathan slowed down to take advantage of a cool, elm-lined stretch.

"Hazleton?"

"Yes. I know one person who'll miss him. He was a big help to my wife when she put together the masquerade ball last year. You know, that benefit for the charity hospitals? Poor Sophia is working feverishly on it even as we speak. I suppose the idea of dressing up in royal finery and having four strong fellows carry him in on a sedan chair was appealing. In any case, he used to contribute large sums for the privilege. No matter what he may have done to others, Hazleton always treated Sophia kindly. He used to call her *La Sophia*."

Blakeley smiled. He always smiled when he spoke about Sophia and her projects. The Restoration Ball, held annually at the end of June to commemorate the founding of Philadelphia, had been Sophia Blakeley's idea. She'd convinced her friends in the

Tuesday Ladies that it was a perfect motif, one certain to gather great quantities of money for the hospitals. For one night, the revelers could shed the prim, confining fashions of the day and dress in the sumptuous clothing of that glittery period long ago when King Charles decided that life on Earth was too short to be spent worrying about the next one. It was all within the bounds of good taste, of course; Sophia would never suggest otherwise. No doxies or vizards or bedchamber politics were tolerated, just courtly costumes, convivial feasting, and the stately music of the time. For a generous donation, one might be Mistress Gwyn or the poet Dryden or, for an even higher fee, the King himself. It was a rare inspiration, everyone agreed. Not one Tuesday Lady in the entire Delaware Valley was unwilling to sing the praises of Sophia Blakeley and her vision. But one by one the Tuesday Ladies always pleaded they had other, more pressing, matters to attend to, until the planning of the Restoration Ball fell into Sophia's small if capable hands.

"She's quite frazzled with her preparations this year, I fear," Blakeley said, still smiling.

Nathan smiled too. "I'd be frazzled now if it weren't for you. Lt. Hudson was happier than I've seen him in a month when he found out you agreed to take this case. The hot weather has us swamped with drunks and family squabbles."

"It came at a good time," Blakeley said, his smile quickly fading. "I'm thoroughly frustrated with the Beecham business. Good intentions gone to the devil, I'm afraid."

"Oh, that explains it," Nathan said.

"Explains what?"

"Your mood for the past two weeks."

Blakeley frowned. "I wasn't aware that it showed," he said, then fell silent as his mind filled

13

with thoughts of the maddest man he had ever encountered.

Christopher Beecham had murdered his own mother in a fit of sexual pique and would have escaped unpunished if Blakeley had not stepped in when he saw the district attorney's office was about to lose the case. But before Beecham was hanged for his crime, Blakeley intervened again. Although the dead woman had been a close friend, and the entire affair appalling, Blakeley asked the governor, William Stone, to commute the just sentence to life imprisonment. He wanted to study Beecham's mind, to look into the mysteries of the Oedipal impulse, he had told the governor. And the governor, an admirer of Blakeley and his psychological studies, had reluctantly agreed.

Blakeley, however, had reaped no scientific rewards from his efforts because Beecham refused to do anything except rant about Blakeley's meddling and promise revenge. At such times, the madman would howl like an animal, foam at the mouth, and force Blakeley to have him restrained.

The only thing that had ever seemed to calm Beecham down was his weekly visit from a minister, who would read passages from the Bible. Blakeley marveled at Beecham's strange behavior for he had previously regarded religion with great disdain, professing interest only in the Greek god Eros.

Blakeley had tried several times to approach the minister. But the strange little man was at first shy and then downright rude when Blakeley asked him to discuss their common interest. After all, he had said to the minister, had he intended Beecham any harm, he'd hardly be there tolerating all of his abuse, would he? But the minister had let it be known, through Beecham, that he had no intention of cooperating. Blakeley, he was reported to have said, had no Christian purpose.

"He thinks you're a charlatan, Blakeley," Beecham had said with a sardonic smile. "He wants me to inform you that his world and yours are far apart and never the twain shall meet."

Then he had laughed in Blakeley's face until he had once again had to be restrained.

The memory of the maniac's laughing face made Blakeley painfully aware that there were many more people awaiting the opportunity to call him a fool.

"Well, even if I'm wasting my time, at least I won't have to travel so far," Blakeley mused aloud as Nathan steered the carriage off the shaded detour and reentered the blistering avenue.

"Sorry?" Nathan said, glancing at him.

"The Hospital for the Insane."

"Oh."

Blakeley smiled again, this time at himself. "Please forgive my rambling, Nathan. There's talk of transferring Beecham from Graterford Prison to the Hospital for the Insane on Haverford Road."

"I think it would be good for you to take a vacation from Beecham, Dr. Blakeley," Nathan said, raising an eyebrow.

"True, Nathan, I should do so before I too am committed to the same place."

The surface of Monument Avenue was rough, creating a din under the wheels and making conversation difficult. So they lapsed into silence once more as they continued toward the station house.

The Eleventh Precinct was an unusual jurisdiction. Running eastward from the Pennsylvania Railroad tracks at Fifty-fourth Street, it encompassed the crowded northwest, some graceful acres north of Fairmount Park, and the bustling streets across the Schuylkill south of the Reading tracks. Looking at the precinct for the first time on a map behind Nathan's desk, Blakeley had thought it seemed an amorphous mess devised by a mad or at least whimsical, geographer. In reality, the precinct had been mapped out long before the city had seen wave after wave of immigrants coming to man the mills and sweatshops. Although it should have been carved up into three separate precincts, no such wisdom prevailed.

The station house stood in the heart of the precinct. The neighborhoods surrounding the station house were a cross section of immigrant life. Everywhere the smells and idioms of the Old World gradually melded with the smut and slickness of the New World.

The streets there were less crowded than in the center of the city, but Nathan had to jerk the carriage to a stop when a neighborhood drunkard named Bummy Rummel stumbled into their path. For a moment, Nathan watched the drunk's progress as he crossed to the other side and trudged along the sidewalk in no apparent direction. Bummy teetered and tottered and did figure eights but never fell, a feat that could not have been easy on a pavement that tilted and buckled and sometimes disappeared entirely. Everyone knew Bummy as a harmless old sot who became annoying only when the polka-dotted snakes bit his ankles or the pink and purple elephants danced in his head.

At last, the drunk disappeared into an alley, where he was probably relieving himself. Peeing in public was a misdemeanor, but Nathan was much too hot to climb down, take Bummy by the collar, and run him in to the lockup.

"Tell me about the suspect," Blakeley said, as Nathan prodded Hecuba onward. "Have you seen anything to suggest he's capable of doing what we've just seen in the morgue?"

"No," Nathan said flatly. "But we found him on the yacht, and we know he was closely acquainted with the victim. There had been a serious disagreement between them and reported threats. So we're holding the suspect until something better turns up."

"Is he cooperating?" Blakeley asked.

"No again. He's scared, sometimes I think out of his wits, but he isn't cooperating."

They passed a vacant lot on the corner of Monument and Falls Road where some youngsters were playing stickball, turned right onto Falls, paused again to permit two nuns from St. Canicus's convent to cross the street, then eased the carriage into a shady spot near the old brick-and-mortar precinct house.

Some of the youngsters hurried away from their stickball game and offered to look after Hecuba for a fee. Blakeley watched them exchanging worldly glances and decided which one was the leader. One of the the boys was taller and husky with a nononsense-you cast to his eyes, but he kept glancing at a shorter, somewhat emaciated boy with a dark, inscrutable look, as if he needed the little boy's approval. Blakeley thought of a young Napoleon. He handed each of the boys a penny and promised young Napoleon another when he returned, provided Hecuba was watered and cooled off by then.

"Good choice," Nathan said on the way into the building. He knew the boys well because they were part of his first alma mater, Sacred Heart Orphanage.

"One wonders where the capitalist ends and the extortionist begins," Blakeley mumbled.

Inside the precinct house, they passed the main desk. A sergeant was booking big Rosie Gilhooly, who ran a disorderly house four blocks west in Friday's Alley. The men of the Eleventh called her Holy Gilhooly after her habit of carrying rosary beads wherever she went. She was fingering them and muttering prayers as the desk sergeant struggled with his typewriter.

When Rosie saw Nathan, she sneered. "Well, if it ain't every girl's fantasy."

"Keeping busy, Rosie?" Nathan asked.

"Go bugger yerself, McBride."

"Business before pleasure, Rosie." He winked at Blakeley as they went on to find Lt. Hudson. "One of the many friends I made when I was walking a beat," he said, as they arrived at Hudson's office. "She prays for my death."

Inside, Hudson was in shirtsleeves, sitting back with his feet on his desk, fanning himself with a newspaper. His collar was open, his tie undone, and his sparse white hair clung tightly to his forehead. Hudson was a tough, wiry welterweight who had lied about his age to get into the Civil War and out of Camden. Wilted in the heat, he resembled an aging terrier.

Hudson pointed to the idle overhead fans and said, "Goddamned things aren't working. This place will be an oven by noontime."

"You'd almost think you were in Cuba," Nathan quipped and was relieved, when Hudson grinned.

Only those on good terms with Hudson got away with such a line, especially under present circumstances. Hudson's reactivated ulcer testified clearly to the kind of stress the war with Spain had put on the Eleventh. Most of his able-bodied and mentally sound men were serving in the military at a time when the heat was drawing lunatics out of the walls like termites.

The only thing keeping Hudson from losing Nathan as well was a knee injury that the young officer had suffered chasing a mass-murder suspect a few months earlier. And when his knee was almost healed, Nathan had reinjured it when he tried to wrestle a crazed, bear-like felon a few weeks later.

18

Nathan's inability to fight in the war with Spain was a sore spot that his friends avoided at all costs.

Despite the heat and everything else, Blakeley's willingness to assist in the investigation of Hazleton's death kept both Hudson and Nathan in good spirits.

"I can't tell you how glad I am to see you, Dr. Blakeley," Hudson said, sitting up and pouring two glasses of cool water from a pitcher.

"I can well imagine, Lieutenant," Blakeley said, taking one of the glasses and sipping from it. "I'm only glad I can be of help."

"So am I," Hudson said. "It's a nasty business. I wish to God it hadn't happened in my precinct. But with the likes of Hazleton, it was bound to happen somewhere."

Hudson hated the Louis Paul Hazletons of the world—all the blue bloods, as he called them. He had decided when he had gone upstate as a young man to search for work in the coal mines and found instead a new form of slavery that the world would be better off without them. He hated the rich even more because he firmly believed, with good reason, that the war with Spain was their war. For it provided them a chance to puff up their portfolios with sugar and rubber and, above all, cheap labor. So the idea that someone would want to turn the rich bastards into bloody coleslaw was perfectly all right with Hudson, just as long as the dead men's stuffings weren't spread all over the Eleventh Precinct.

Since the particular blue blood in question had connections in all of the high places, Hudson had had no difficulty in convincing the commissioner to call for Blakeley. And the commissioner, who kowtowed to the city's rich as if they were titled royalty, hadn't even balked when Blakeley asked that Nathan be relieved of his other duties in order to assist him.

"Were you surprised when the commissioner honored my request?" Blakeley asked, slightly taken aback by Hudson's bitterness.

"If you catch the old bastard at the right time, he says yes without thinking. Must have been counting his payoffs," Hudson said, reaching into his desk and pulling out a folder. "Here's the file on the suspect. There isn't much to it because he hasn't been in town for long. Came all the way from New Orleans to be with us."

Blakeley opened the folder and frowned as he perused its contents. While he was occupied, Hudson and Nathan traded impish smiles. When Blakeley looked up, Nathan was gulping down his glass of water.

"Pretty strange guy, huh?" Hudson said.

"Yes. Yes indeed, Lieutenant," Blakeley agreed.

Nathan noticed Blakeley's eyes moving across the top of the second page and knew what must be going through Blakeley's mind. At first, he had merely forgotten to fill Blakeley in on the details about the suspect. Then he had decided to wait for Blakeley's reaction. Precinct-house humor was of a gallows nature.

"Ready?" Nathan asked, when Blakeley finished reading and frowned again. He was a little disappointed that Blakeley didn't react more strongly to the report. "Lead on, Nathan."

Hudson whistled and officer Bones Fatzinger came from the back room. The policeman had a loping, manure-dodging stride. In his hand was a sandwich that Hudson thought smelled like limburger and onions, but its contents could have been something even stronger and unpronounceable. Fatzinger was typical of the men Hudson had to keep because of the wartime shortage. It was a daily challenge for him to find something Fatzinger could do without causing any permanent damage.

When he saw Fatzinger, Hudson felt his ulcer begin to burn. That morning, he had ordered Fatzinger to clean out the few cells in the lockup that were still unoccupied. As a result of his exertions, Fatzinger's tunic was off and his suspenders hung loosely over a faded red undershirt, which was rolled up at the sleeves. Hudson didn't mind Fatzinger being out of uniform; it was the paper daffodil in the officer's helmet that bothered him.

"I thought I told you to get that damn thing off your helmet!"

"Cheez, Lootenant, it's chust fer nice," Fatzinger grumbled, then turned to Blakeley and beamed proudly. "Up in der widow Schmeck's barnyard I vunn it at Hausknecht's picnic. Dey bet me I couldn't ten shoofly pies eadt."

Hudson stared at his desk and counted to ten. When he was sure he wouldn't leap from behind his desk and throttle Fatzinger, he said, "Take McBride and Dr. Blakeley back to see the suspect in the Hazleton murder."

Fatzinger stuffed the rest of the sandwich into his mouth and gestured for them to follow. "We keep diss here turkey's neck in insulation," he said and giggled, his mouth still full of food.

He led the two men past the row of cells that held the night's catch. Nathan knew all the prisoners. There was a smelly, foulmouthed drunk named Fricko Kilroy sitting up on his bunk. Just coming out of a two-week binge, he cursed at shadows and imaginary visitors. There was a snoring wife beater named Zavos, who may have gone a step too far in his last assault. Hudson was holding him until he got the word that the woman had made it. Next to Zavos was a little round man known as Dr. Happiness. He had been arrested for selling worthless drugs that were supposed to keep men's sexual powers alive forever, in addition to curing constipation, insomnia, foot fungi, gout, and halitosis. Then there was a dapper if silly old man whose name was Wallace Wetstone, but who was known around the precinct as the Lordly Lilywaver because he terrorized just about every unwary maiden who strolled past any of his favorite bushes. He was the regular occupant of cell number six.

Fatzinger, Blakeley, and Nathan turned a corner, passed two vacant cells, then reached the suspect in the last one.

"Good heavens," Blakeley said under his breath.

Nathan smiled—that was the reaction he had expected.

The suspect, Richard Petticord, was pacing the floor. He was a pathetic sight in his soiled, wrinkled gown and silk-stockinged feet. His lip rouge and other makeup had faded. Sweat and tear rivulets ran down his cheeks over the thin layer of rice powder that remained. A blue-black stubble covered his chin. His blond wig, summer bonnet, and high-buttoned shoes lay in a small pile near a slop bucket.

Fatzinger was still giggling as he opened the cell and let the other men in. "I call him der nanny goat. Mit hairs on der chin like dott I never seen vun lady before."

Petticord stopped pacing and put his hands on his hips. A New Orleans accent was immediately apparent in his speech, though it was not thick. "And just who the hell are you?"

"My name is Blakeley, Mr. Petticord, and this is—"

"I know him." Petticord waved Blakeley off in midsentence. "McSomething-or-other, one more barbarian with a badge. And you say you're Blakeley? *The* Blakeley?" He drifted closer and inspected Blakeley as if he were pricing a show horse. "I suppose you could be. One could hardly mistake that shape or the Vandyke. Don't you know, Dr. Blakeley, Vandykes are going out of fashion?"

"Something else I forgot to tell you," Nathan said out of the side of his mouth. "He's very easy to dislike."

"Do tell," Blakeley said under his breath.

"It's impolite to whisper," Richard Petticord snapped.

"Yes. Terribly sorry, Mr. Petticord," Blakeley replied. "Poor form."

"It certainly is."

Easy to dislike was putting it mildly, Blakeley decided. Richard Petticord had the peevish, sullen, ingrained scorn of a harridan, which was all the more irksome coming from such a ridiculous-looking fellow. Men like him, however, were not new to Blakeley. He had often come across Oscar Wilde and his bizarre entourage while living in London.

"Blakeley in person," Petticord said. "Wouldn't Lulu be impressed?"

"Lulu?"

"Louis Paul Hazleton. It was his pet name. Obviously."

"I shall strive to be quicker," Blakeley said in mock apology.

"And how about you, Petticord?" Nathan asked. "Do you have a cute little name, too?"

Petticord had been trying to ignore Nathan, but now he turned and scowled. "And what do you do, Sgt. McSomething? Beat people up for Dr. Blakeley?"

"Sounds like fun," Nathan said.

"Nathan, please," Blakeley said.

Fatzinger could hardly contain himself. Up in Ebenezersville, a cow pasture 50 miles north of the city where he had grown up, the most exotic sight he had ever encountered was a grown woman under 200 pounds.

"What do you want, Blakeley?" Petticord asked wearily.

"To talk to you about Mr. Hazleton," Blakeley said. "I hope you don't think we came here for fashion advice."

Petticord's eyes flashed his contempt for Blakeley, but he hesitated before saying anything. "I'm not altogether certain I should speak to you without my attorney present," he said at last.

"Who is your attorney, Mr. Petticord?"

Petticord bit his lip. "I'm not sure yet. That is, I haven't made up my mind. New in town and all that."

"Have you narrowed it down to three or four yet?" Blakeley asked.

Petticord started to bite his thumbnail. He walked away and sat on the edge of his bunk.

Blakeley gave him some time to speak up, then said, "It must be rather difficult to find an attorney willing to take on the Hazleton family."

When Petticord held his silence, Blakeley turned to Nathan. "Do you get the feeling, as I do, Sgt. McBride, that Mr. Petticord is in a terrible fix?"

Nathan shook his head. "No, not at all Dr. Blakeley. There must have been at least a hundred other gentlemen dressed like Mr. Petticord sleeping on Mr. Hazleton's remains this morning. And all of them picked up a dagger last night and told the world they were going off to settle matters once and for all. Good Lord, Dr. Blakeley, it was a veritable suspects' convention."

"Give me a cigarette," Petticord demanded.

"I smoke a pipe and an occasional cigar. Sorry," Blakeley said and looked at Nathan.

"Trying to quit," Nathan said.

24

"I'm not going to waste one syllable on you unless I have a cigarette," Petticord insisted.

"Very well," Blakeley said. "Officer Fatzinger, please get Mr. Petticord a cigarette."

Fatzinger left, shaking his head. "Ladies mit real manners don't shmoke der cigarettes."

There was an awkward silence while they waited for Fatzinger to return. Petticord got up, folded his arms, and gazed through the window. The cell looked out on an alley where sun-light occasionally made its way overhead and cast a grudging ray through the bars. The suspect could hear the noises of the street—the shouts and curses of the stickball game, the rumbling of wagons on the brick road, an argument over the price of something between a vendor and a customer, the distant clanging of a trolley. Petticord's eyes focused on the pigeon droppings that coated the outside of his window and winced.

Blakeley and Nathan could only shrug at each other. Hard as it was to like their suspect, it wasn't difficult to feel sympathy. Petticord reminded Blakeley of a bad little boy who had gotten carried away with his mischievousness and wound up in a school for boys much worse than he.

Nathan had a far less charitable view of the man. "He's like an otter in a crocodile pool." Nathan was thinking when Fatzinger returned with a cigarette.

The moment Petticord saw Fatzinger, he snatched the cigarette out of his hand, puffed on it, and faced the window again, ignoring the pigeon droppings. Suddenly he stopped puffing and threw down the cigarette, gagging and squeezing his throat.

"Yeck! It tastes like stinkweed!"

"Dott's from der limburger," Fatzinger said, burping. "Good shtuff, too."

Petticord was appalled. "You lit it yourself?" He

turned to Blakeley and pointed at Fatzinger. "Must he remain in my cell? I don't like him."

Nathan tapped Fatzinger on the shoulder. "Bones, go see if you can sober Fricko Kilroy up. We'll probably need his cell in a few hours."

Fatzinger left, slamming the door with a loud clack. "Shidt." ·

"I can't believe you'd let him light a cigarette for me," Petticord said when Fatzinger was out of the cell. "He's the sort who'd have me burned at the stake or something."

Tired of Petticord's peevishness, Nathan was ready to box his ears for making such an unfair allegation. Whatever his other failings, Wilmer P. Fatzinger didn't have a mean bone in his body. But Nathan was anxious to get on with the interrogation, and taking his aggression out on the pathetic man before him wouldn't help at all.

"Why exactly were you on Mr. Hazleton's yacht?" Nathan asked, doing his best to control his temper.

Although Nathan asked the question, Petticord looked only at Blakeley when he responded. "I was hoping to mend some fences."

"With a carving knife?" Nathan asked.

Petticord suffered the question in silence.

"I would like to hear you answer that, Mr. Petticord," Blakeley said.

"If I tell my side of it, will you listen?"

"If it isn't too outlandish," Blakeley said.

"And if I do, Dr. Blakeley," Petticord said, "will you represent me? Rumor has it you're a fairly competent lawyer. No William Jennings Bryan, but good within your sphere. Of course, I don't wish to pay a large fee."

"I doubt I'd be worthy of you," Blakeley said bluntly. "Do go on, please."

Petticord sulked for a moment, collecting his thoughts. "For some time I'd been his favorite," he said deliberately, "but Lulu was a difficult person. He enjoyed humiliating me, and his hangers-on used to guffaw whenever he made me the goat. And he did it for no reason, mind you, simply out of caprice. For example, he used to like to imitate my way of speaking. I'm sure you are aware of my origins. I come from New Orleans, as any fool who isn't tone deaf can plainly tell."

"What made you leave New Orleans?" Nathan asked.

"Please do not interrupt me. I'm trying to reconstruct the evening in my mind and my mind isn't too clear."

"Continue then," Blakeley said.

"If you must know, I left New Orleans because I ran up a pile of gambling debts, and some big hairy gentlemen from the French Quarter were threatening to cut off my crocus," Petticord said. "Not that it's anyone's damned business."

"Thank you," Blakeley said. "I hate loose ends."

"It was the most wretched period of my life," Petticord said.

"No doubt," Nathan interjected.

"Not that," Petticord said irritably. "I'm talking about Lulu. Though, come to think of it, there's a connection. I'd met him, you see, a few months previous in the French Quarter. At a place called Bonnefoy's where—" he struggled for a euphemism "—people of my sort congregate. He liked me, I knew. And so when I made my hasty retreat northward, I looked him up. It was wonderful at first, all that attention, and I even enjoyed the jealous little snipes I'd get from those he'd cast off. Then suddenly, for no apparent reason, he started to treat me like something he'd dragged in on the sole of his shoe."

"Have you any idea why?" Blakeley asked.

Petticord sought an answer, found none, and shook his head.

Then a voice from a cell around the corner spoke up. The man had the foggy, croaking voice of a drunkard, but he did his best to imitate Petticord's unmistakably prissy voice. "Probly wanted to dump ya fer a real blond."

Petticord cupped his hands over his ears and screamed, "I hate this place! I'll cut my throat if I have to stay here."

Nathan shouted through the bars, "Bones, I told you to get Fricko out of here. Do it!"

"Chust ass soon ass he puts der pants on, Sarge," Fatzinger said in the near distance, then shouted at Fricko Kilroy in Pennsylvania Dutch. Fricko mumbled something gutteral in reply.

The events of the morning were beginning to tire Blakeley. He started to massage his temples and said, "Continue, please."

Petticord took several deep breaths before going on in a shaky voice. "Lulu had driven me practically insane with his taunts. Finally, I had to act. We said some things we shouldn't have. One word led to another and he told me go to hell. He said he wished to find another squaw. That's what he called me, his squaw. That was a few days ago. and as far as I was concerned he could go to hell too. But then the day before yesterday, I got to pondering my future. I decided I couldn't let him simply dismiss me as if I were a mosquito or something."

"You were afraid you'd be left out of his will, right?" Nathan asked.

"I told you not to interrupt me," Petticord said, looking directly at Nathan for the first time. "I don't know about a will and I don't care about a will." He turned his back to his interrogators for a moment, wishing he had a real cigarette. Then he faced the others again and spoke more evenly. "Well, after

all, being one's favorite is something of an invest-
ment, isn't it?"

"That's much better, Mr. Petticord. Expelling the
truth is an excellent moral purgative," Blakeley
said, then added almost apologetically, "Now,
about the yacht?"

Petticord sighed. "I got dressed. Lulu always
liked silk. But it's so damned expensive and just
look at the condition of this dress. I made the rounds
of our familiar places, but I was unable to find him.
I'm sure my anger showed. And no doubt the more
drinks I had the more vocal I became. Then someone at the Outside Inn—gloating, naturally—told
me he'd seen Lulu in the company of a woman
and—"

Blakeley started in surprise.

"I know, I know," Petticord said quickly. "But he
did that from to time. He was free spirited."

"I see. Do you know who she was?" Blakeley
asked.

"How the hell should I know? Some floozie. I
went on to his other haunts, intending to put the
floozie straight. The knife was just for show, like a
theatrical prop. I'd never have used it. I can't stand
the sight of blood! Then finally, Oscar, the steward
at The Rod and Gun, told me he'd heard Lulu offering that woman a nightcap on his yacht. I'm sure
the gold-digging bitch was eager to oblige. So I
rented a canoe, rowed out to where the yacht was
at anchor, climbed aboard, tiptoed inside and...."

"And?"

"And I fainted." Petticord's eyes darted back and
forth between Blakeley and Nathan. "I fainted and
landed on poor Lulu. Well, wouldn't anyone with
an ounce of sensitivity? My God, I get sick just
thinking about him lying there."

Nathan, who had remained expressionless
throughout most of the interview, almost smiled.

"As a matter of fact, friend, so do I," he said.

Petticord's eyes flashed angrily. "Don't call me your friend or chum or buddy or palsey-walsey or anything of the kind! Not while you're trying to pin this horrible crime on me just because you find my sort repulsive." Starting to gag, he put his hand over his mouth and spoke through clenched teeth. "Now get out of here, both of you. I have to use my slop bucket!"

"Bones!" Nathan called out.

"Yeah?" Fatzinger came running from around the corner.

"Open it up," Nathan said. "We have to leave in a hurry."

"Oh shidt, und I chust cleaned oudt hiss cell."

Petticord's skin turned pale. With sweat pouring over his makeup, his face looked like a finger painting done by a blind man. Fatzinger fumbled with his keys and found the right one. In another second or two, Blakeley and Nathan were out of the cell, leaving Petticord to retch in private.

Chapter Two

When Nathan and Blakeley stepped outside the station house, Hudson was leaning against the faded brick wall, hoping to catch a rare breeze. The temperature seemed to have risen ten degrees in the brief time the two men had been inside. Blakeley and Nathan fanned themselves with their hats, both pleased to be out of Petticord's stifling cell.

"Well, what do you think of him?" Hudson asked. "Or should I say her."

"He isn't much of a suspect," Blakeley acknowledged, "but we'll do our best with him."

"I'm not sure I agree with you," Hudson said. "The judge must think he's a pretty good suspect, considering the size of the bail he set for him."

"That tends to happen when a chap like Hazleton is murdered, doesn't it?"

"Yes, it does," Hudson said and smiled. "Did you get him to open up? All I got was pouting and weeping. For a while there, I thought I was back on my

31

honeymoon with Gladys."

"Well, he told us what he was doing on the yacht," Blakeley said. "Trying to patch up his romance with the deceased."

"There's your motive, Dr. Blakeley," Hudson said, still smiling. "Hell hath no fury."

"That, and a will in which Petticord may or may not have been included," Nathan said. He was checking his shoes and the cuffs of his trousers for dust and other debris that he might easily have picked up in the jail cell. "I'll look into his story anyway. Unfortunately, most of what Petticord told us we already knew. Everyone agrees that Hazleton was a jerk and a bully who treated people like bedbugs."

The men fell silent as a pair of young ladies from Miss Fudderman's Latin School came within hearing distance. Almost in unison, they ceased fanning, donned their hats, and tipped them as the girls passed by. When the girls were gone, they resumed their feeble efforts at creating a breeze.

The girls from Miss Fudderman's were easy to identify by their spring and summer uniforms: plaid trailing skirts, high-collared and heavily starched white blouses with tiny black bows, another black bow in their hair, and small straw hats with plaid bands that matched their skirts. Blakeley knew the uniform well; his daughter Rosie had been a student at Miss Fudderman's for a time.

When the girls were a few yards up the street, one of them, a dark-eyed beauty with a subtly flirtatious walk, turned to look back. Nathan wondered for a moment if she intended to drop a perfumed handkerchief where he was bound to see it. She blushed when Nathan winked at her, then she turned with a well-rehearsed huff of indignation. The girls giggled as they went on their way.

Blakeley recognized the ritual. Rosie was of the

same age. It was a harmless celebration of self-discovery, which he found a great deal more charming in someone else's children.

"It's also possible Mr. Petticord is protecting someone," Blakeley said, getting back to the matter of the suspect. "He and some of his chums could have gotten together, discussed a common insult, and decided to get even with Mr. Hazleton. The condition of the corpse doesn't rule out a group murder."

"Well, whatever the case, Petticord will probably be with us for some time," Hudson said. "He doesn't seem to have a lawyer or any friends; so I doubt he'll be able to raise the bail."

Blakeley thought the matter over and nodded his head. "That's very true, Lieutenant," he said. "But considering the strain on your facilities at the moment I don't envy your position. With Mr. Petticord in custody, however, we will have a good chance to investigate him without any interference. Of course, should someone come forward to bail him out, I'd like to know who it is. I do hope that isn't the case—it will be difficult to learn more about him and to keep an eye on him if he's freed on bail."

"I'll leave all that to you," Hudson said and bowed grandly. "It'll be enough for me to keep him here."

"One more thing," Blakeley said before he and Nathan departed. "Please be certain there are no sharp objects in Mr. Petticord's cell. Nothing he might use to slit his throat."

When they returned to the carriage, Blakeley and Nathan found that the youngsters left in charge of Hecuba had taken good care of her, though the urchins had tripled in number when Blakeley arrived with his pennies. Little Napoleon apparently knew how to instill loyalty.

The mare whinnied when she saw Blakeley and

Nathan, but it was an unenthusiastic greeting. Hecuba was wise enough to realize she had more work to do in the sweltering heat.

As Nathan drove the carriage along River Drive, he and Blakeley could see the Hazleton yacht anchored 200 feet from the shore. It looked quite peaceful in the temporarily lazy water. Only the red flags on the four buoys surrounding the yacht gave any hint of the terrible violence that had taken place on board just a short time earlier.

The banks were filled with curious onlookers, some of them peering through field glasses. They had taken their lunch hour to see what they could see. But all that was visible from the shore were the bored men of the Eleventh Precinct, who were pacing the deck and keeping the public at a distance.

"Would you like to wait until after lunch to have a look, Nathan?" Blakeley asked, without removing his gaze from the river.

"I think I'll pass on lunch and just have a glass of lemonade," Nathan said.

"No breakfast, no lunch," Blakeley admonished. "That's an unhealthy practice, my boy."

Despite Blakeley's well-intentioned advice, Nathan could see no point in eating a lunch that he would no doubt lose the moment he stepped aboard the Hazleton yacht. So he feebly excused himself. "That's true, but I want to start investigating Petticord's story right away."

"I should like very much to meet that woman who left with Louis Paul Hazleton," Blakeley said. "If in fact it was a woman."

"If in fact she exists at all," Nathan said, guiding Hecuba around a portly old woman who strolled into their path and scowled as they passed. "The club steward might have been teasing Petticord, just as he claims Hazleton and his friends used to."

"That's entirely possible."

"I'll see what I can find out," Nathan said.

"Very good."

"Well, it's a beginning."

They passed an old building whose facade was undergoing some renovations. Like so many others in the neighborhood, it belonged to Irwin Heester, arguably the most hated man on the east side of the Schuylkill. He was carping at some laborers as Blakeley and Nathan went by. Judging by the workers' inscrutable smiles and their just-off-the-boat clothing, Nathan doubted they had any idea what was bothering their employer.

"I believe I've a task that Ralphie will enjoy," Blakeley said, his spirits revived by a moment of inspiration. "Someone will have to dive into the water around the yacht to see if a murder weapon can be found. And I can't think of anyone better suited for the job. Of course, I shall take your suggestion and tell him to be especially alert for a grappling hook. In any event, it will keep him out of trouble for a while—and out of Sophia's way. She's been very distressed by his behavior since he came home."

Nathan nodded sympathetically, but he had to bite his lip hard to prevent himself from smiling. For his friend Ralphie had caused his mother grave concern more often than Nathan could remember.

Ralphie Blakeley, known to his friends as Beef, was home from yet another institute of higher education with few alternatives left to him. He had begun his studies at Princeton, chiefly because Blakeley had friends in high places there. But his stay had lasted only until the end of the first football season. Ralphie had almost made it through one whole term at the state university, and he had actually come close to completing a full year at a small state normal school up in the Pocono Mountains. Then had come the army and a brief stint in Tampa, where it had been his dubious fortune to catch the eye of his commanding officer's nymphomaniacal wife. When a jealous rival brought their flirtation to the colonel's attention, only a clerical error had saved Ralphie from a long assignment in the heart of the Everglades.

Blakeley had had hope recently when an agricultural college in a remote corner of North Dakota expressed an interest in his son, but when Ralphie's grades from his previous schools had finally made their way out west, the dean of the college suddenly changed his mind.

Now, with his luggage again unpacked and little hope of any academic future at all, Ralphie was making his mother increasingly nervous. It was not that Ralphie was ever anything less than a gentleman; he was never rude or thoughtless, rarely rowdy, and always well-meaning and eager to help. It was just that Ralphie was, as Blakeley so often told his wife, Ralphie, and they could do little to change him. But immersed as she was in planning the charity ball, Sophia had little sense of humor, and she had made it very clear that she regretted her husband's insistence on sparing the rod while they had raised their children. Although he knew Sophia and Ralphie really loved each other deeply, Blakeley was only too happy to help his son keep away from his mother at present.

"What do you think of that idea?" Blakeley asked.

Despite his best efforts, Nathan smiled. He was Ralphie's best friend, and he had no doubt that his friend would have legions of female admirers along the riverbank by late afternoon. Ralphie would be in his true element.

"It sounds like a lot more fun than interviewing the people in Richard Petticord's circle," he said.

Blakeley weighed his decision for the next quarter mile or so while Nathan concentrated on guiding Hecuba. Traffic along the drive was heavy in the late morning, mostly private carriages and an occasional wagon on its way to supply the neighborhood businesses. Blakeley and Nathan passed one of Harry Hackett's horse-drawn hearses on its melancholy way to the embalmer's lab. A little farther along the way, a beer wagon crossed before them and a burly driver named Manus Finnegan waved at Nathan, who waved back. A horseless carriage, dark blue with gold trim, driven by a goggled, white-coated gentlman passed by. When the machine coughed out puffs of thick, acrid smoke, Hecuba snorted her disapproval.

Across the street, Nathan noticed a very pretty young lady, her strawberry-blond hair visible when she shifted her parasol to protect her from the sun. He couldn't tell for sure, but he thought her eyes were green. She had a familiar look, with her graceful, confident, almost too proud walk and the elegant cut of her lavender dress. She seemed to take everything in without appearing at all interested in her surroundings. Nathan could almost smell the scent of gardenias wafting off her.

But, of course, she wasn't who he wanted her to be. It was somebody else—some other bright-eyed and beautiful woman who might break his heart if he gave her the chance.

"Nathan," Blakeley said, as if he could read his friend's thoughts, "Sophia and I have a surprise for you. I was going to leave you in the dark until we got to the house, but on second thought I believe it's best to warn you."

"When did she get in?" Nathan asked, knowing what was coming.

"Last night. It seems a Spanish gunboat was rumored to be in the area her ship was to pass through; so her ship had to turn around," Blakeley said. "She looks splendid."

"Allison never looks less than splendid."

Blakeley could not help noticing the irony in Nathan's voice. "She'll be very pleased to see you."

Nathan started to speak, but instead held his silence. He concentrated on Hecuba's tail as the mare shooed away a persistent horsefly.

"Won't you be pleased to see Allison?" Blakeley asked after a full minute of silence had elapsed.

"I'd just as soon get my buggy and be on my way," Nathan said, guiding the carriage off the main road.

"Now, see here, Nathan—"

"I have to check the waterfront for strange people who use grappling hooks on other people. Then I have to look into Hazleton's will. And then I have to trace his itinerary," Nathan said, "not to mention getting a profile on Richard Petticord. I don't have time for lunch. Sorry."

"Now see here, Nathan," Blakeley said, as they drove along the elm-shaded drove that led up to the Blakeley estate, "you're elated that she's back safe and sound."

"I never wished her otherwise," Nathan said. He glanced away toward the Schuylkill, hoping Blakeley would drop the subject.

"Then why all of this juvenile petulance?"

Nathan glared momentarily. He did not like Blakeley's choice of words, but he let it pass.

"Dr. Blakeley," he said, "trust me. It isn't easy being in love with Allison Meredith."

"There is nothing wrong with ambition in a woman, Nathan."

"I didn't say there was."

"Well, what exactly did you say?"

"When did I say what?" Nathan asked.

"Whatever you said to Miss Meredith the last time you spoke."

"Oh, that."

"Yes. That."

"You mean, before she took off on another long trip in search of the greatest article ever written?" Nathan said dryly.

"If you must put it that way," Blakeley said.

"I said—are you sure you really want to hear this?"

"Confound it, Nathan. Miss Meredith and you mean a great deal to me," Blakeley said, "and to Sophia and all the other Blakeleys, for that matter. Of course, I want to hear it."

They made their way carefully around a dip in the roadway that Blakeley had been meaning to have mended for the past year, but never had. For a moment, Nathan listened to the humming, chattering, and chirping that filled the woods, and as he listened, he summoned up the memory of his last conversation with Allison Meredith.

"All right," Nathan began, "I said—well, no, I asked—'Will you marry me, Allison?' And she just sat there on the bench in the moonlight, smelling like gardenias and looking like a goddess. She was wearing that rose-pink dress with the white lace that made me trip over my feet when I first saw her wearing it. I could see those big green eyes of hers flashing in the moonlight. I could even see her beautiful strawberry-blond hair as clearly as in the day time. Dr. Blakeley—it was so wonderful. And then she said, in her damn voice that's so soft and sweet, 'Just as soon as I get back.' 'Back? Back from where?' I asked. 'Cuba' she said. '*Cuba!*' I said. 'Women aren't supposed to go to Cuba. There's a war going on down there, with people shooting Gatling guns and throwing bombs and catching yellow fever and—' 'I know, I know,' she said. 'That's why I'm going, Nathan.' She told me it took all the charm she could muster to get some people in

39

Washington to grant her permission. And so I said, 'Fine, go to Cuba. Go to China for all I care. Only I want you to know I'm not good at waiting around, playing the clown back home.' 'If that's the way you want it,' she said, 'that's the way you'll get it. Good-bye!' And that's what we said the last time we spoke. End of story.''

"I see," Blakeley said, somewhat embarrassed that he had forced his friend to dredge up such a painful memory.

Nathan simmered in silence for the rest of the drive.

"It happened less than a mile from here?" Sophia Blakeley gasped. "How horrible!"

Sophia stood with her husband and Nathan in the foyer of her home. She had greeted them there, refusing to allow either another step into the house until they told her what business had required Blakeley to depart before she could kiss him good morning. In her arms, she held Thomas Aquinas, a big, fluffy black-and-white cat Nathan had rescued from a snowbank one Christmas season and immediately presented to Sophia. Her husband's story had upset her so greatly that, had the cat not yowled crossly, she would have dropped it on its head.

"Horrible, to be sure," Blakeley said, taking Thomas Aquinas from his wife and setting the cat gently on the floor. "It will not, however, affect our private lives. I insist on it. Nothing will disrupt the lunch hour." He bent down to peck his wife on the cheek. She had to stand on tiptoe to receive the kiss. "And what is that tantalizing aroma?" he asked, sniffing heartily.

"Mrs. Snopkowski has prepared a turtle soup for lunch. She must have poured a whole bottle of sherry into it," Sophia said and turned to Nathan. "Forgive my rudeness, dear. This business is so ghastly. I must say, though, I was beginning to wonder if we'd ever see you again."

His irritation over his lost love forgotten for the time being, Nathan bowed to Sophia. There was something about her that always made him feel better, no matter how downcast he had been only a moment earlier.

Sophia Blakeley was a classic beauty reminiscent of the days of Byron and Shelley, although she would no doubt protest even a remote association with such notorious libertines. Sophia was, as Blakeley had once described her, an outspoken proponent of moderation—within healthy limits, of course. Despite her insistence on propriety, however, Sophia had an adventurous side of which few would accuse her. She read Balzac, Beaudelaire, Flaubert, and other thinkers considered risqué by more staid women, but the only way anyone ever learned about her secret pursuits was through unconscious hints she tossed off in conversation.

Nathan had never told Sophia that he was aware that her literary tastes were somewhat avant-garde. Nor had he told her what her daughter Rosie had once whispered to him in a moment of adolescent sophistication. It seemed that Sophia owned, amid the many prim paintings in her collection, a very earthy nude by a Frenchman named Caillebotte. Blakeley had also told Nathan about a time when Sophia had dragged him to New York to see a play by a man she called, "that terrible Ibsen fellow who writes about social diseases." After their trip, she had worried for weeks that she had been seen at the theater by someone from Philadelphia who would all too willingly ruin her reputation.

For her refusal to be totally restrained by her society's mores, Nathan found Sophia irresistible. And although he knew she would protest any compliments to her person, insisting her work on the

41

ball had put her into an unattractive dither, Nathan could not help waxing romantic.

"Mrs. Blakeley," he said, kissing her hand, "you have the priceless beauty of a great work of art. And I must say, I don't know how I could have stayed away so long."

"Egad," she said, brushing back a few stray strands of her deep brown hair, "not in front of my husband, sir! But do tell me where you've been keeping yourself."

Hoping to avoid the subject he knew she had in mind, he pressed her hand gently and said, "All you had to do was come up with a really good homicide and, poof, instant Nathan McBride."

"Well, I wish it weren't quite so hard to do. But now that we have you here, can we tempt you with some turtle soup?"

"Thank you, no, Mrs. Blakeley. There's something about a turtle—especially with a whole jug of wine in it—that reminds me of my landlady."

Sophia laughed girlishly and leaned closer. "You will come back though, won't you? Sometime?"

"Certainly. Sometime." Please apologize to ... Mrs. Snopkowski for me."

He was out the door and down the stone steps before either Blakeley or Sophia could say another word.

"That was rather awkward, Ian," Sophia said.

"I fear I broke the news clumsily."

"But you were right to tell him," Sophia said. "Obviously, he's in no mood for surprises."

"You don't know the half of it, dearest. Has the post arrived?"

"You've a cable from Harrisburg that looks quite important."

"Harrisburg? From the governor?"

"I don't know. I haven't read it, darling. I left it in your study." She kissed the tip of her index finger

42

and touched his nose. "I must assist Mrs. Snop-kowski immediately."

As Sophia headed for the kitchen, Blakeley went to his study. There on his desk lay the cable. He ripped it open and read it.

DEAR BLAKELEY STOP YOU WILL RECALL WITH WHAT RELUCTANCE THIS OFFICE AGREED TO COMMUTE THE DEATH SEN-TENCE GIVEN CHRISTOPHER BEECHAM FOR THE MURDER OF HIS MOTHER STOP IF EVER ANYONE DESERVED THE GAL-LOWS IT WAS THAT FIEND STOP BUT IN LIGHT OF YOUR ESTIMABLE REPUTATION AND EXCEPTIONAL SERVICE TO THE COM-MONWEALTH I YIELDED STOP IT IS NOW MY UNHAPPY TASK TO INFORM YOU THAT BEECHAM HAS ESCAPED GRATERFORD PRISON STOP GIVEN HIS FEELINGS TO-WARD YOU I SUGGEST YOU GET PROTEC-TION STOP YOURS GOVERNOR WILLIAM A STONE

"Christ blast it!" Blakeley cursed. He folded the cable and shoved it in his pocket, glancing around to see if anyone had heard his growl.

Only Thomas Aquinas had. The cat had followed him and had been about to purr and rub against Blakeley's leg. But his exclamation startled the cat, and it ran a few feet away with its fur up and ears back.

Blakeley knelt and whispered an apology. The cat walked gingerly back to him. He rubbed it under the chin and picked it up.

"Well, Thomas," Blakeley said, standing up, "you're a wise and renowned philosopher. Just what the devil do I do now?"

* * *

It was cool on the veranda because of the shade provided by an awning and the gentle breezes that blew off the river. But Mrs. Snopkowski, the cook, was screeching in her native tongue and waving her large meaty hands, warning two of the scullery maids not to spill a drop of soup out of the tureen they were carrying from the kitchen to the table. Since she never screeched in English, it was never clear what was bothering the cook at such times. So the maids merely nodded and went on chatting as if she were not there. Victor, the butler, as was his way, was trying to hide behind a huge fern lest the cook should put him to work.

At the table, Sophia watched as Ralphie gulped down his second sandwich and Rosie studied her smile in a tiny mirror. Over and over again, she started to count to ten, trying not to let her children unsettle her composure. Before she could finish, however, her resolve would break down, and she would silently censure herself for allowing her husband to raise their offspring so liberally. But she had promised Blakeley a peaceful lunch, and a peaceful lunch it would be. Besides, there was no need to let the world know her nerves were frayed, much as they were.

The charity ball was getting out of control. The moment it was over, Sophia swore she was resigning from the Tuesday Ladies. Never again would she allow anyone to take advantage of her good nature.

For a moment she let her mind wander, picturing all the Tuesday Ladies floating in the steaming tureen with the rest of the turtle meat. The image pleased her immensely.

Sophia wanted nothing more than to get back to her painting, to the safe never-never world of her studio, where things took shape as she wished them to be. That afternoon, for example, she wanted to put the finishing touches on Rosie's portrait, the one she'd started a month earlier after she and her husband had noticed their daughter's inexorable transition into young womanhood. Gone was the girlish awkwardness, slowly replaced by the fresh beauty of a blooming flower. Sophia wanted to capture the metamorphosis for Rosie, for Blakeley, for herself.

Instead she would spend hours haggling like some fishwife over the price of clams and oysters. Later she would try to find some musicians capable of playing seventeenth-century instruments who would not want to charge her a price equal to McKinley's war debt.

Her revery was shattered by another screech from Mrs. Snopkowski; and despite herself, Sophia scowled when she noticed Victor hiding behind the fern.

Although Sophia disliked the uproar the cook kept her house in, she knew quite well why she and her husband indulged the cook. Bozena Rzimski Snopkowski was considered the culinary genius of epicurean Philadelphia. Victor Primrose, however, was another matter. An actor who had played butlers almost exclusively—save for one stint in Buffalo as a butterfly in a springtime pageant and another as a corpse in a melodrama in Wilmington—he was generally considered the worst butler in three states.

But what Victor lacked in industry he more than made up for in shrewdness. And much to her dismay, Sophia fell victim to his underhanded tactics time after time. For each year at the height of the Christmas season, when all men and women of good will did their best to tolerate even the worst of fools, Victor's survival instincts would lead him to Sophia. He always approached Sophia after she had already humored Mrs. Snopkowski by drinking some of the cook's homemade dandelion wine, which was rumored to be capable of stripping paint off a battlewagon. When he was sure Sophia was at her weakest, Victor would appear, looking like an orphaned puppy. He would weep until she promised to keep him on for another year or until the right producer discovered him—whichever came first, he would stipulate.

Hours later, free of the effects of the wine, Sophia would remember with horror what she had done. Then, close to tears herself, she would tell her poor dear husband what she had promised. Full of love and understanding, and possibly a little resignation, Blakeley would soothe Sophia by convincing her that perhaps in the upcoming year they could reform Victor of his devious ways. For whatever agreement Sophia made, he would honor as if it were a treaty binding two nations.

Despite the eternal disorder of her household, Sophia could never doubt her husband's love. And so thinking, she bestowed a doting look on him as he stepped onto the veranda.

"Good afternoon, Victor," Blakeley said to the butler. At the sound of his employer's voice, Victor flinched and dashed away.

Doing his best to keep a stiff upper lip after the news of Beecham's escape, Blakeley chose to let his servant's ineptitude pass without comment. Rather, as he took his seat at the table, he glanced around at his family and exulted halfheartedly, "Ah, the aroma of turtle soup."

"Yes, it is delicious," Sophia said. "Was it good news from the governor, Ian?"

Blakeley hesitated, fully realizing the danger his entire family faced as a result of Beecham's once again being on the loose. But he didn't want to frighten them unnecessarily; so he decided not to mention anything until he had more details. "Nothing that can't be taken care of," he said.

"That's good," Sophia said. "Now, would you care for a cream cheese and olive sandwich, or would you prefer one of Ralphie's creations?"

Cream cheese and olive, like watercress on white bread, was the kind of dainty finger food Blakeley usually ate out of politeness to his wife. But the events of the day had dulled his appetite, and it would take more than weeds and paper to get it back.

"What is that, Ralph?" he asked.

Ralphie started to speak but his answer was muffled. He gulped and started again. "Ham, hot mustard, Swiss cheese, onion, pickles, Polish sausage, and olives on rye, Dad. Oh, yeah, and cream cheese and anchovies."

"That's it, the anchovies," Rosie said, gagging. "I knew there was something even more disgusting than usual."

She licked her little finger, ran it across an eyebrow, and smiled again into the tiny mirror.

"Please do not groom yourself at the table, Rose," Sophia said.

"Yeah," Ralphie agreed. "Just like a chimp."

"I think I'll just have a small bowl of soup," Blakeley said. "And where are our guests?"

At the mention of her houseguests, Sophia frowned, but not about Allison Meredith, whom she greatly admired. It was her other guest—the Spanish diplomat Don Orlando Malachea y Guzman—who caused her consternation. "I don't believe Don Orlando is up yet. I really don't think he's been sleeping too well."

"I hardly think it's a wonder that he might have some restless nights under his present circumstances. And what of Miss Meredith?"

"She'll be along presently, Ian. I'm sure she's just working on an article and lost track of the time."

"I suppose I'll have to tell her about Nathan," Blakeley mused.

"Poor, dear Nathan," Rosie said dreamily. "I think men are especially attractive when they're going through a period of angst."

"A period of what?" Ralphie asked, but instead of waiting for an answer he turned his attention from the conversation to his meal.

Rosie smiled haughtily. It was an excellent word she had only recently learned from a friend who was attending Bryn Mawr. She had asked for terms to drop in conversation with serious students of philosophy, like Nathan McBride, and the friend had mentioned angst and weltschmerz and several other words too difficult to pronounce. Rosie was quite pleased with the words, for she was certain they would catch Nathan's attention.

But her mother was appalled. "You will leave his angst alone," Sophia commanded and looked to her husband for support.

He shrugged as if to say he saw no harm in the word, but troubled by his wife's agitation, he did his best to change the subject. "You know, dear, he can be very stubborn. I can't blame him much in a way, though."

"Who, Dad?" Ralphie asked, taking a respite from eating.

"I'll tell her, Ian," Sophia said before Blakeley could answer Ralphie. "It will be easier coming from another woman."

"Tell who, Dad?" Ralphie asked.

"Whom," Rosie said.

"Thank you very much, dear," Blakeley said. He started to answer Ralphie, but stopped when Sophia rolled her eyes at her children. He took her action as a hint to drop the topic of Nathan and Allison before Ralphie and, more importantly, Rosie got involved in it.

Conversation fell into a momentary lull as the family continued their lunch, and Blakeley's mind returned to Christopher Beecham. As he chewed a slice of bread absently, he thought, "Damn me! Of all the ridiculous complications. I shall have to track down that minister and make him speak up. Damn me."

"You're terribly pale, Ian," Sophia said. "Is there something troubling you?"

"No, dear," Blakeley said. He tried to put up a good front by eating a few more mouthfuls of his soup. But he could tell from Sophia's worried glances that she was obviously unconvinced. So Blakeley sought a logical reply and tried to deliver it in an even voice.

"Well, actually, dearest, I was just thinking about the charity ball and how unfair it is that you should have to shoulder the burden."

"Yes," she said, seemingly satisfied. "It is."

"He wasn't thinking about that at all, Mother," Ralphie said, laughing.

"Eh?" Blakeley asked with a start.

"He probably heard about Rosie's new beau, Weird Willy Weber," Ralphie said, catching tiny morsels that flew out of his mouth as he laughed.

"At least Wilberforce doesn't have to wear a feed bag at the dinner table," Rosie huffed.

Ralphie laughed again. "Wilberforce!"

"May I remind you to be civil while we are eating?" Sophia snapped.

Before Blakeley could intervene, the cook and the two maids came in to remove empty plates from the table. Mrs. Snopkowski, her arms folded imperiously, looked on as the two maids, sweating from the heat in the kitchen, went about their duties. These maids were new to the Blakeley staff. Servants tended to stay for brief periods after meeting the Blakeley's cook and butler. And Sophia could never get any experienced servants from the area, because stories of Mrs. Snopkowski and Victor were known throughout the servants' quarters of Philadelphia. As a result, the Blakeley's domestic employees were usually new immigrants. The two maids clearing the table were just off the boat from Wales.

Ralphie winked at one of them—a blue-eyed, apple-cheeked wench named Dumpling, who might have stepped right out of a Hogarth sketch. She winked back, curtsied, and left. At the doorway, she turned and smiled, which caused Mrs. Snopkowski to screech again.

"A little dalliance this afternoon, brother dear?" Rosie said.

"Huh?"

"Where will you meet her this time? The hayloft? The gazebo? Or will any old flowering bush suffice?"

"Rosie, please," Sophia said, her face flushing red. "This is not France!"

"Make no plans for this afternoon, Ralph," Blakeley said, casting a warning glance at his daughter. "I shall require your assistance in an investigation."

"This must be real important," Rosie said sarcastically.

"Don't interrupt Dad, Rosie." Ralphie put his sandwich down. "What can I do for you, Dad?"

"I need someone to search for evidence around the Hazleton yacht," Blakeley said. "That is, unless there's a danger of your sinking after all the food you've eaten."

Ralphie whooped, gulped down the rest of his sandwich, grabbed a handful of hard-boiled eggs, and ran off. At the doorway, he almost collided with Allison Meredith and Don Orlando Malachea y Guzman, but they had the good fortune to step aside at the last second.

Right on their heels, Thomas Aquinas stuck his head out on the veranda and sniffed curiously. Suddenly he growled and dashed away, apparently in search of a safe haven.

"Ralphie has never been known for his restraint, Don Orlando," Blakeley said, wondering if the cat was still spooked from his earlier outburst.

"Yes," Sophia said. "Please excuse his rudeness, Don Orlando."

The Spaniard smiled. "Indeed."

He and Allison seated themselves amid greetings and desultory comments from the remaining Blakeleys. But when offered the savory delicacies spread out on the table before them, neither showed much interest. Each had a very good reason for his indifference.

Don Orlando had been the Blakeley's houseguest for the past month, ever since Blakeley had discovered that several government officials in Washington were thinking of jailing him for conspiracy to subvert the national war effort. Actually, Don Orlando had done more than conspire: he had been discovered passing information on troop strength through the supposedly neutral German embassy. But the State Department had kept the charge reduced to avoid involving the German government, and the Germans were relieved to get Don Orlando off their hands.

The old Spaniard was no stranger to Blakeley, nor were his activities much of a surprise. Don Orlando and Blakeley had met the previous February at a symposium on tropical diseases sponsored by the British embassy in Washington. Blakeley had gone there to hear a talk by Sir Trevor J. A. McCulloch, an old classmate at the Royal College of Surgeons who was just home from India and lecturing at large. Instead, Blakeley had found himself listening intently to the old fellow with patrician mannerisms and very troubled eyes who kept interrupting Sir Trevor with contradictory observations of things he'd seen in the Central American jungles. The man would apologize with each interruption, then proceed to point out that what Sir Trevor believed could have other causes, other treatments, and he did not hesitate to give his four or five logical reasons. He concluded his interruptions by repeating his apology and stating that he was not a physician, merely a statesman who had been thrust into many difficult but fascinating situations. Sir Trevor had taken exception to the interruptions and to the old fellow's popularity. The interloper was, after all, untrained and, to make matters worse, a Spaniard. Fortunately, matters of politics were never primary at such conferences, and Don Orlando's knowledge of everything in the under-investigated region of Central America was encyclopedic.

Later on, Blakeley and Don Orlando had dined together and shared a bottle of Napoleon brandy in a Washington club. The hours had been filled with laughter until someone interrupted all conversations and shattered the general conviviality with a message that someone, Spaniards presumably, had blown up the *USS Maine*.

From the day he had learned of his friend's difficulties, Blakeley had not taken the charges against him lightly; nothing about war could be taken lightly. And there was no doubt that the government could, if it wished, stand Don Orlando up before a firing squad. Indeed, the threat of a mere jail sentence was charitable in itself, and there were angry demands in some congressional quarters that the Spaniard be made an example. But when Blakeley saw Don Orlando on a visit to a military post in northern Virginia, where he was being detained in relative comfort while awaiting trial, Blakeley was so moved by the old man's deterioration that his charitable instincts were awakened. In the few months since the outbreak of hostilities Don Orlando had lost 20 pounds, his troubled eyes had become embedded in dark circles, and his once well-groomed silvery hair had turned a drab gray. Above all, he looked defeated, dispirited, and depressed.

So Blakeley had taken a dangerous step, risking the enmity of many powerful figures in Washington and closer to home who were not especially enamoured of him in the first place. He had protested the jail threat. It was unthinkable to put a statesman in irons, he'd overstated for dramatic effect. Don Orlando was, after all, the Spanish consul. And had he not made some effort, Don Orlando would not have been much of a Spaniard. "We are not barbarians!" Blakeley had insisted in a hastily arranged meeting with a friend at the British embassy. The friend had taken the issue all the way up to the Foreign Minister, Lord Salisbury. At length, the foreign minister had taken up Don Orlando's case with Secretary of State William R. Day, who had agreed with Blakeley.

And so, Don Orlando Malachea y Guzman had been placed in Blakeley's care for the duration of the war. In his own turn, Blakeley had appointed Ralphie Don Orlando's nominal jailer. For despite the occasional intrusion of military authorities, the government had washed its collective hands of the matter. No doubt, Blakeley surmised, they had intelligence officers lurking about his estate hoping to catch him being remiss in his duties. Such a failure could only work in the government's favor, because it would allow them to rid themselves of two troublesome foreigners.

So far, however, Blakeley had no reason to fear imminent deportation. Keeping Don Orlando under house arrest was a simple task that even Ralphie could manage. All he had to do was make certain the Spaniard was in his room by nine o'clock and that he didn't stray from the estate. Don Orlando never balked at his restrictions or tried to circumvent them in any way. He kept his depression to himself as much as he could, but he consumed great amounts of wine that brought on periods of gloom so intense he could not disguise them. He seldom made reference to the war coverage in the newspapers and magazines, though Blakeley knew that he read it and that it ate at every fiber of his being. Don Orlando was acutely aware that Spain's poorly trained, poorly disciplined forces would be no match for the huge war machine the Americans had assembled in Florida. The proud empire he had served so well for so long was close to its death throes.

With each successive day, Don Orlando exhibited less appetite and even less energy. Now and then he'd stroll the grounds and spend long periods gazing out at the river, evidently pondering his world after the war. It was apparent to the Blakeleys, who had grown fond of him, that despite their best efforts he had actually deteriorated in the month since arriving at their home. Only when the Madeira had taken hold of him and he indulged in memories did he ever seem to come to life. But these periods of liveliness were infrequent; and that afternoon, he was moving quite feebly.

Next to him, Allison Meredith stood in vivid contrast. She had risen early to ride Gladstone, Sophia's favorite gelding, over the trails that coiled around the far reaches of the property. After her exercise, she had bathed in preparation for lunch. Freshly scrubbed and smelling of gardenias, she wore a green dress that matched her eyes. Her strawberry-blond hair was pulled back and decorated with a green bow. None of her actions were accidental. Gardenia was Nathan's favorite scent, green his favorite color—especially on Allison.

Obviously unhappy that Nathan was not at the table, she suffered through the lunch until she could politely excuse herself. Then she bade everyone good afternoon and hurried into the house.

"I believe I'll have a word with Allison," Sophia said as she rose and left the table. Sophia knew all too well about the romantic poker game Allison and Nathan played, and she was sure the young woman needed a friend to console her after the disappointment of missing her former beau.

Allison's hasty retreat did not go unnoticed by Rosie either. And she mumbled an excuse as she followed her mother, her curiosity over the handsome police officer aroused.

Not wishing to leave his other guest alone, Blakeley remained at the table. "Quite a lovely day, eh, Don Orlando?" he said, feigning heartiness.

"*Mi padrón*," Don Orlando answered, "it is always a pleasant day here. I must apologize for being so late for this fine meal, but I thought I would be quite unpleasant company in my bad humor. If Miss Meredith had not convinced me to come, I would have stayed in my quarters."

"There's no need to apologize, Don Orlando. I know how trying the present times are for you. But tell me, Sophia mentioned that you aren't sleeping well. Did you sleep well last night?"

"Yes."

"Better than the night before, I trust?"

"Much better," Don Orlando said and patted Blakeley on the shoulder. "My dear friend, I know you are a physician, but please do not be concerned about my health. I have been in much worse condition."

Hoping to avoid becoming entangled in one of Don Orlando's long and gruesome stories, most of which dealt with the old fellow's time as a captive of Central American savages, Blakeley quickly changed the subject.

"Well, with the little you eat, I can hardly imagine how you keep your strength up. "You haven't had more than a sandwich Don Orlando, and Ralphie tells me you hardly eat anything off your dinner trays.

"Your son, I'm afraid, believes one starves himself if he does not eat like ten men."

Blakeley smiled to himself. Whatever headaches he seemed to find a way of giving his mother, the Brobdingnagian Ralphie was a source of great pride to his father. Very small at birth and given to mysterious fevers, his parents had often feared for his survival. But at the age of three, he had begun a special diet-and-exercise regimen Blakeley had designed specifically for him. The program succeeded far beyond its inventor's expectations, and Ralphie, like a plant under the influence of a remarkable new fertilizer, had sprouted into a muscular mountain.

"I'm afraid you're right," Blakeley said. "Won't you have another sandwich? They're quite small."

"Thank you, no."

"Some turtle soup?" Blakeley suggested. "It's superb."

"If you do not mind, Dr. Blakeley, I shall just have a glass of Madeira."

It was not what Blakeley wanted to hear, but he saw no point in arguing. "Why, pray, would I mind, Don Orlando? As they say in your language, *mi casa es su casa*."

Don Orlando nodded in appreciation of Blakeley's use of the age-old Spanish rule for hospitality.

"But no one likes a tiresome guest," he said, "as I am sometimes wont to become after too much wine."

Blakeley could hardly disagree. In one painfully honest moment recently, Sophia had expressed the hope that the war would end before all the Madeira in Philadelphia was gone. Ah, well, Blakeley mused, the war could not last much longer now that Havana had fallen. But, as he poured his guest a glass of wine, he said, "Nonsense."

"In particular a guest who would otherwise be in police custody or worse."

Don Orlando raised his glass to Blakeley's magnanimity and took a sip. Blakeley sipped his lemonade.

"The heat in your Philadelphia is more oppressive than one expects," Don Orlando said, and Blakeley started to get the feeling he knew where the old man's words were leading. "It is truly *la hora del burro*, as the peasants in our former colonies call it; only I have long ago fallen out of the habit of taking a siesta. My years in the service of dear Isabella and young King Alfonso were much too demanding to permit it. Ah, but this heat is not half as oppressive as that which I suffered through when I was taken prisoner by those devils in Copán. My friend, it was as close to hell as one would ever wish to go. I never expected to see a civilized face again...."

It was truly uncanny, Blakeley thought, how Don Orlando could always find a way to introduce one of his shopworn tales. But then, in a moment of guilt, he remembered how trying the times must be for the old man. He listened politely, nodding his head and muttering agreement whenever he perceived a cue, though his thoughts were once again on Christopher Beecham.

"Wretched ingrate," Blakeley thought. "Disgusting matricide. How dare he threaten me."

"In that climate," Don Orlando said, "in the dense jungle foliage, one learns to perspire in parts of the body where one has never perspired before, such as inside one's ears and beneath one's fingernails. Perhaps it is the harshness of the place that makes the natives so insensitive to pain. Those people have rituals, Dr. Blakeley, in which they actually walk through flames!"

"Astounding," Blakeley replied, as he thought, "Governor Stone must be fit to be tied now. Taking a political risk like commuting Beecham's sentence just to indulge my scientific whim. If people call me a fool, so be it, but . . . damn me!"

"There are many such mysteries there," Don Orlando went on. "Heathen things which I saw and still have difficulty explaining. Thank God, the Heavenly Protector, that I escaped those savages before I lost my mind."

"Heaven tests our spirits in many ways," Blakeley said.

"Well put, Dr. Blakeley, well put. In your heart you are a Spaniard," Don Orlando said, toasting his host and sipping again.

"Thank you," Blakeley said and laughed silently, thinking, "If Don Orlando believes he met some human devils in Central America, I wonder what he'd make of Beecham."

"It was especially painful," the Spaniard said, "when you consider that my purpose in going there was a charitable one. I was hoping to establish, with the assistance of the Dominican friars, a mission hospital for lepers to be staffed by doctors and nurses from Spain."

Blakeley hid another smile. He knew very well what Don Orlando had been up to in Central America. He'd been sent there to stir up a revolution or two, to get the natives restless. Spain wanted her old colonies back. Blakeley had learned all about Don Orlando's activities from a thick dossier that the State Department had sent him shortly before the Spaniard's arrival.

Blakeley lifted his glass of lemonade. "Let us drink a toast to your deliverance, Don Orlando," he said.

"And to your undying patience, Dr. Blakeley."

They drank. Then Don Orlando refilled his glass of Madeira before his host could do it for him.

"Sir!"

Blakeley and Don Orlando looked up at the sudden interruption. Victor, the butler, was standing in the doorway, chest out, shoulders back, face rigid. He did that part of the job well, having rehearsed it often for the stage.

"What is it, Victor?" Blakeley asked.

"Lt. Hudson is on the phone, sir. He says it's urgent."

The butler spoke with mocking disdain, the cause of which Blakeley was fully aware. Hudson was one of Victor's least favorite people. Several months earlier, the Blakeleys had discovered a number of their possessions missing: first some china and silverware, then a locket passed down from Sophia's great-grandmother in Lancashire, then, worst of all, a Joshua Reynolds original that Sophia had found in a London gallery, where it was believed to be a mere copy. It had taken Hudson only a few days to locate the items in a pawnshop owned by Stanley Boblinka, brother-in-law of Evalina Baccamatta, proprietress of Victor's favorite saloon. Victor had initially protested his innocence, then failing in that had wept and pleaded until Hudson agreed to return the goods to the Blakeleys without pressing charges. And he convinced Blakeley that in order to avoid embarrassment it would be better not to pursue the matter. For his part, Blakeley decided to keep Victor's guilt from his wife, because he feared the butler might not survive Sophia's retribution.

For a while, Victor was profoundly grateful. He tiptoed around like a chastened schoolboy. He showed so much deference to Hudson and Blakeley that it made them uncomfortable. And the courtesy, eagerness, and promptness were so unlike Victor that Sophia grew suspicious. But with time, the crisis passed, and so did Victor's fragile, fleeting gratitude. Still, the thought of what Hudson knew and what he might have done to him was more than enough to set Victor's nerves on edge.

As he stood before Blakeley, Victor fidgeted slightly, and Blakeley couldn't help wondering if his servant feared his day of reckoning had come. Enjoying Victor's uneasiness, Blakeley excused himself and followed the butler through the hallway to the telephone, where Victor, with unusual thoroughness, handed him the receiver.

"Thank you," Blakeley said. "I shan't require you anymore."

Victor remained by the telephone, smiling nervously.

"Victor?"

"Sir, whatever the nature of your conversation, would you please try to be brief?" Victor said. "I have need of the instrument. I was just about to use it when Lt. Hudson called."

"What is it, Victor?" Blakeley asked. "Out of gin?"

Victor huffed and marched away.

"Hello, Lieutenant," Blakeley said into the speaker. "I do hope this isn't serious."

"It is," Hudson replied. "Beecham's out."

Although the voice on the other end was unclear, Blakeley had no trouble recognizing Hudson's strident tone. People seemed to squawk through the damned gadget. Blakeley had hated to have to purchase it in the first place. He considered the telephone a means of invading his privacy, another of those things that would plague mankind in the coming century. But in his line of work, it was becoming a necessary evil.

"I've heard," he said. "A cable from Harrisburg."

"Do you want some protection?" Hudson asked.

"You're trying to get rid of Officer Fatzinger again, aren't you, Lieutenant?"

Hudson didn't respond immediately, as if he were unprepared for Blakeley's nonchalance. "What do you plan to do?" he asked a moment later.

"Well, I have Sgt. McBride of course, and Ralphie is badly in need of a purpose in life," Blakeley said.

"Just thought I'd check. They say Beecham swore he'd come after you."

"He did just about every time we met—especially the last time."

"When was that, Dr. Blakeley?"

"About a fortnight ago," Blakeley said.

"Two weeks?"

"Yes."

Hudson was silent. Blakeley thought the telephone had gone dead, as it often did without warning.

"Lt. Hudson, are you there?"

"Yes, yes, I'm here."

"Have I missed something, Lieutenant?"

"I guess the governor didn't mention this. Probably embarrassed," Hudson said. "Beecham's been out for almost a week, y'know. Only it was hushed up by the warden. Beecham had a really clever plan and the little minister was in on it. You see, the preacher smuggled in a file. He carried it in his Bible. Who looks in a Bible, right? Then he'd read from the Bible real loud while Beecham filed away at the bars. The guards used to walk away because they couldn't stand the preacher's voice. Later on, Beecham would fill in the cuts with beeswax, which was also supplied by the little preacher. When enough of the bars were ready, Beecham yanked them open. You know how strong he is. Crazy strong. He got the guard to come closer to his cell by complaining about a bad stomachache, opened the bars, and almost killed the guard on his way out."

"A week ago?" Blakeley said. "Good Lord."

"The warden was embarrassed, and he should be. So he kept it quiet as long as he could. Then when nobody could find Beecham, he called the governor. Great system we have here."

Blakeley was silent, stunned by the unexpected news.

"You there, Dr. Blakeley?" Hudson yelled into the speaker.

"Yes. Thank you, Lieutenant."

"If you need anything, just holler."

"I shall. Good day." Blakeley replaced the receiver and tugged at his Vandyke.

Victor stood in a shadowy hiding place around the corner and tapped his foot impatiently until Blakeley, deep in thought, walked away. When his employer had gone, Victor seized the telephone.

"Damned inconsiderate of him," Victor thought. "It's almost time for the first race."

Chapter Three

After departing the Blakeley estate, Nathan set about investigating Richard Petticord's story. A phone call from the precinct house to Hazleton's attorney only improved the suspect's case. For he was not mentioned anywhere in the dead man's will. So, his first lead having proved worthless, Nathan turned to the hidden circles in which Petticord and Hazleton socialized.

Before that afternoon, he had had no idea how many private clubs there were around Philadelphia that catered to Louis Paul Hazleton and those of his ilk. But he learned that most of them were a little off the beaten path. He tried to harbor no particular animosity toward their patrons, though no one seem especially happy to speak to him. When Nathan entered The Wilde West on Merion Road, a group that had gathered around a piano to sing *chansons innocentes* had ceased abruptly and stared at him, as if he were an alien creature unknown to them. At The Mummers in Haverford, the members had spoken to him only in pig Latin. "Such an ity-pay about Ulu-lay," several of the members had said.

For the most part, however, he'd been received civilly, though with all the warmth of a Russian winter. But for all his legwork, there had been no encouraging results—it seemed as though no one had noticed the mysterious woman with Hazleton.

Nathan had had better days. The grappling hook theory was only something he'd mentioned while he and Blakeley were grasping at straws. If worse came to worse, he would have a friend from the Sixth Precinct who knew the waterfront well look into it anyway, though he didn't expect the hunch to bear fruit.

Despite his lack of success, Nathan was glad for the work, because it filled his mind with thoughts about something other than Allison Meredith—for a time, at least.

It was late afternoon by the time he reached The Rod and Gun. The former sportsmen's club was in the Radnor Valley, west of the city. It had somehow fallen into the hands of a group of gentlemen from New York who liked its isolation.

The lounge of The Rod and Gun was a large room, cooled by shade trees that covered one side of the building. The lounge was bedecked with deer heads, stuffed fish, bearskin rugs, and other signs of its former self that the new management must have found quaint. In one corner, near a tall artificial plant, stood a more vivid reminder of the club's current orientation—a large statue of David in all his naked glory, except for a hunting cap, that was cocked at a rakish tilt. Nathan was not amused by what the club members must have considered an inspired caprice.

Oscar the steward was dressed in a white silk

shirt with a frilly front, a red flowing tie, and matching silk vest. His trousers were black velveteen, his slippers black patent leather. He was tall and good-looking in a delicate way, and when he spoke, Nathan detected a slight foreign accent, which may or may not have been authentic. Oscar also had Richard Petticord's effete disdain.

"Cheap!" he said in response to Nathan's query about the woman he had seen with Louis Paul Hazleton.

"Could you be more specific?"

"Really, Officer, cheap is cheap."

"Well, was it because she wore cheap perfume?" Nathan asked. He had noticed that Oscar's own cologne was less than subtle. The steward would have stood out in a flower garden.

"No." Oscar put his index finger over his mouth and thought. His nails had been filed into mean little points and carefully waxed. "I don't believe I noticed a perfume at all."

"Then what was it?"

"It was simply everything." Oscar let out a long, elaborate sigh and finished pouring a round of syrupy-looking drinks. "Excuse me, Officer Mc—?"

"McBride."

"The rest of the help doesn't come on until six, and *he's* utterly useless." Oscar darted an angry glance at a waiter who was lazily picking up dinnerware from a table just vacated. "Work, work, work."

Oscar picked up a tray and scurried off to a far table, where a group of well-dressed young gentlemen were exchanging gossip. The waiter, a beardless young man with hair slicked back and held in place with a jar of pomade, curled a lip as he passed.

Nathan glanced around and noticed how discreetly the tables had been arranged in shadowy places, where no one need be seen unless he wished to. The wines and liqueurs were foreign and expensive. The club had no apparent protection from outside intruders, but the protection was somewhere, probably upstairs behind the balcony in the form of a large ex-prizefighter. The other clubs Nathan had visited had been much the same.

The young waiter came over and placed several glasses on the bar. "Are you looking into that strange woman who gave Petticord fits?"

"Yes, I am," Nathan answered. "Do you know Petticord?"

"I certainly do," the young man said and snickered. "A fly on a piece of dung. Any piece of dung. Lulu Hazleton just happened to be the turd of the moment."

Oscar returned with a tray of empty brandy snifters in time to hear the waiter's comment. He gave the young man a look of grave disapproval for having clearly overstepped his bounds. The look must have made its point, because the waiter took his trayful of dishes and silverware and hurried off to the kitchen.

"Petticord was never one to leave a gratuity," Oscar said. Pinky finger extended, he picked up the snifters one by one and placed them in a sink filled with soapy water. "Nobody liked him. To me he was a—how do you say it?—a parasite."

Not giving a damn how cheap or generous Petticord was, Nathan turned his inquiry back to the matter at hand.

"You were saying the woman was cheap," he reminded the steward.

Oscar gave Nathan an exasperated look, as if to say he really had better things to do than answer tiresome questions, but he continued anyway.

"It begins with her choice of colors," he said. "Now, you must picture this dress in gawd-awful green and bilious yellow. And as if that were not

enough, there were daubs of red here and there."
He made a cursory gesture toward his chest. "Like
little pipings on the neckline. Can you picture it,
McBride?"

"All right, I can imagine the dress," he told the
steward, becoming more and more fed up with the
other man's condescension as the interview pro-
gressed. "Now, what about the woman herself?"

Oscar reflected. "Darkish."

"How darkish?"

"The late, unlamented Lulu fancied himself cul-
tured. He liked to quote Shakespeare, misquote
more often than not. That night he was mangling
the sonnets. 'Therefore my mistress' eyes are raven
black, Her eyes so suited, and they mourners seem,
et cetera, et cetera.'"

"Were her eyes really black?" Nathan asked.

"Dark brown," Oscar said.

"Would you say there was anything especially
mournful about them?"

For a change, the steward lost his glibness. "Not
in the sense of the sad, but there was something
indeed strange about them. That much I'd swear
to."

Nathan jotted a note about the woman's eyes, the
first encouraging note he'd written all day.

"And did Hazleton also quote, 'If snow be white,
why then her breasts are dun; if hairs be wires,
black wires grow on her head?'" he asked the steward.

"Where did you learn that?" Oscar demanded.

"I don't know," Nathan replied. "I think I just
made it up. Does it fit?"

"Somewhat. Her hair was very dark and her skin
was olive, I'd say. Her breasts were quite vulgar."

"Hmmmm, she sounds exotic," Nathan said.

"Exotic?" Oscar gasped. "Exotic? She looked like
an absolute piss pot, if you ask me."

"You're pretty sure about the dress?" Nathan asked, hoping to stem the steward's ire.

Oscar frowned. "Five years at the *École des Beaux Arts* in Paris studying design and you ask me that? I wasn't born to be a barkeep, you know."

"Sorry." Nathan put his note pad away. "Only one more question," he said, somewhat apologetically. "It's a touchy one, so please bear with me. Are you absolutely sure—"

"That she was a woman? *Mais certainement*, Officer McBride."

Nathan blushed and started to ask another question when Oscar raised his hand to indicate that he'd answer it without it being asked.

"The bulge," Oscar said knowingly. "It wasn't there. Unless one is pitifully underdeveloped, it's virtually impossible to hide a you-know-what under a tight-fitting dress. And it was a very tight-fitting dress." Oscar rolled his eyes in aesthetic disapproval.

Nathan nodded that he understood. "You're sure she had no name?" Nathan asked.

"The people in Lulu's entourage seldom had names, Officer. Louis Paul Hazleton was like a swath of blue serge. He picked people up like lint. Now if you don't mind, I have silver to polish."

Nathan closed his note pad and beat a hasty retreat, glad to have finished his investigation of Louis Paul Hazleton's favorite haunts.

It was nearly five o'clock, and the summer heat was still unforgiving as Nathan rowed a small boat out to the Hazleton yacht. The sun's rays reflected like golden needles on the Schuylkill's surface and dazzled Nathan's vision momentarily. He squinted against the glare of the sun as a large figure in a red swimming suit moved across the yacht. Although he couldn't see the man's face, Nathan guessed it was Ralphie because of the way he had rolled up the legs of his bathing suit and cut the sleeves to show off his muscles.

It wasn't long before Nathan knew he was right about the man's identity. For no sooner had the man dived off the yacht in a flash of red swimming suit and bare feet than a gaggle of girls on the riverbank cried out in dismay. When their hero broke the water's surface, the girls, some of whom wore the familiar uniforms of Miss Fudderman's Latin School, shouted out hearty cheers of admiration.

"You look exhausted, Beef," Nathan said when he drew his boat abreast Ralphie in the water.

"I sure am," Ralphie said, blowing out a mouthful of water as two of the teenagers pretended to swoon. "I think Dad really wants to drown me."

"Why would he want to do that?" Nathan asked and chuckled.

"Because Mother wants him to."

Deciding that the present subject was better left unexplored, Nathan asked, "Find anything down there?"

"Yeah. A pair of shoes that don't match, a couple of dead rats, six or seven whiskey bottles, a lady's corset that's twenty years old, and a fishing pole with a hook that got caught in my rear. And did Dad care? No! He just said, 'Keep swimming, dear boy, and the sting will go away.' Jeez crumps."

Ralphie imitated his father rather well, and Nathan had a hard time keeping a straight face. To prevent himself from bursting out in laughter, he quickly asked, "Is your father still aboard the yacht?"

"Yeah, but I warn you," Ralphie said, before he dived again, "he's in a very bad mood."

"Well," Nathan said to himself, as he resumed rowing, "maybe my news will put him in a better mood."

Two minutes later he was helped aboard the Hazleton yacht by a pair of guards from the Eleventh who were yawning and sharing a hand-rolled cigarette. Although he was sympathetic to the guards' ill fortune at drawing such a tedious assignment, Nathan casually rebuked them for smoking while on duty, then went below to the stateroom. There Blakeley was on his hands and knees, inching over the floor with a magnifying glass in one hand. The detective looked up when he noticed Nathan.

"This is the third time I've been over this cabin," he said, shaking his head, "without finding one shred of useful evidence. I've been into, around, above, and beneath every corner, compartment, nook, and cranny, and I've found nothing but jewels and spare change. Well, at least we can be sure robbery was not the killer's true motive."

"I have something that might cheer you up," Nathan said.

"The woman?"

"A good description. She's someone we can trace."

Blakeley rose to his feet, pocketed the magnifying glass, and leaned against the captain's liquor cabinet. Like the clubs where Hazleton had been a member, the cabinet was stocked with only the best.

Blakeley rubbed his eyes wearily. "Well, tell me what you've learned."

"The steward at The Rod and Gun club, where Hazleton was last seen alive, described her as dark haired and dark eyed, and he said that she wore a green dress with some red and yellow designs. Something tells me she's a real stunner."

"And a prostitute?" Blakeley asked.

"Presumably."

"Nathan, there are approximately ten thousand prostitutes working in and around Philadelphia even as we speak," Blakeley said. "And at last count, there were at least a thousand brothels scattered all over the city. Just how long do you plan to spend in search of our lady of the evening?"

"I think we can eliminate the brothels," Nathan said, undaunted by Blakeley's pessimism, "because Hazleton didn't have to solicit prostitutes. Whoever this woman is I think she goes out on her own and preys on wealthy men. Maybe only on wealthy young men, which would narrow it down. Maybe on wealthy young men of Hazleton's sort, which would narrow our search even more. You know, she might go after the spoiled, jaded types who require special treatment? Could be she knows some weird parlor games, and if so, that will help because word gets around in those circles. Look, maybe she's a lady Jack the Ripper!"

Blakeley was unmoved. "What if she isn't a Philadelphian at all, Nathan? What if she simply dropped in from New York or Boston or somewhere else?"

Nathan paused for a moment and wondered at his friend's strange behavior. He'd never seen Blakeley so negative.

"We have friends, Dr. Blakeley," he said, hoping to counter Blakeley's unexpected gloominess. "The police help each other. What if we got in touch with New York and found out somebody from the Four Hundred turned up recently in the same shape as Hazleton? Don't you think the guys on the New York force would be happy to compare notes?"

"Dark haired and dark eyed," Blakeley said, his pessimism unabated. "There must be a legion with similar features."

"Who is beautiful enough to tempt men to unimaginably gruesome deaths?" Nathan asked vehemently, his temper getting the better of him. When Blakeley eyed him sharply, Nathan composed himself and said gently, "What's bothering you, Dr. Blakeley?"

Blakeley sighed. "Let's get some air."

They went out on deck. Blakeley leaned against the railing and watched Ralphie's continuing efforts, he even smiled a bit at his son's persistent young admirers on the riverbank. Nathan took off his jacket, swabbed his brow, and pretended to watch a pair of sea gulls in the distance. But he was really glancing at Blakeley out of the corner of his eye. Blakeley's smile, small and passing as it was, encouraged him.

"Beecham's escaped," Blakeley said finally. "He's been loose for a week, but I was informed of it only a few hours ago. So here I am, trying to solve a homicide while looking over my shoulder, hoping to prevent my own."

Nathan shook his head and made a sarcastic noise, half laugh, half grunt, keeping his thoughts about the state's prison system to himself. But the annoyance was quickly overcome by alarm as he considered the imminent danger to Blakeley and his family.

"Well," Nathan said, hoping to reassure Blakeley, "if I were Beecham, I'd make a point to get as far from here as possible. Upstate, then off to New York or someplace where I could get lost in a crowd."

"But you aren't Beecham, Nathan. You're not mad as a hatter."

"Would you like me to post a few men around your house?"

"Thank you, no," Blakeley said. "Lt. Hudson already offered me the use of some of his more expendable officers. But I believe between Ralphie, you, and myself we should be able to withstand anything Beecham contrives."

"I'm sure of it," Nathan said, pleased at his friend's show of confidence.

For a moment, the two men stood without speaking, each considering the full impact of Beecham once again disrupting their lives. In the distance, the two sea gulls were squabbling over a piece of carrion. On the bank, a number of teenage girls had left. It was approaching dinnertime, and only a dedicated few remained.

Blakeley tamped some tobacco into his pipe and lit it. "Nathan, do you think there's a connection?"

"You mean between Beecham and the Hazleton murder?"

"Yes."

Nathan weighed the possibility. Blakeley's theories always had merit, but the connection seemed remote.

"Consider this," Blakeley went on, his spirits seeming to pick up. "Someone who is capable of murdering his own mother is no doubt capable of any number of atrocities. If ever I've met someone who borders on the satanic, it is Beecham. If you'd seen his eyes at our last meeting, when it took three of us to restrain him, you'd believe me. I found myself wishing I'd let the commonwealth hang him for the vicious animal he is. But he's a remarkably intelligent beast. If anyone could contrive a way of committing such a heinous crime and leaving no evidence, it is he. And consider this, Nathan: what better way to get at me than by committing a crime he knew I'd be asked to investigate?"

"Which was a foregone conclusion," Nathan said. "I see."

"Precisely, dear boy. The murder could be a means, if you will, of baiting the hook, of enticing me into his web."

"So the victim may be only incidental," Nathan said. "Chosen because Beecham knew Hazleton was important enough to cause the commissioner to enlist you."

"That could be the answer," Blakeley agreed. "I don't know if you ever heard, but it was well known around town that Beecham hated Hazleton. He had blackballed Beecham from joining those esoteric clubs you've been visiting. It seems he thought Beecham was insane—can you imagine that?"

One of the sea gulls had retreated, leaving the other to feast on the carrion. Below Blakeley and Nathan, Ralphie's head popped to the surface of the river. He blew out some foamy water and spied his father on the deck.

"But what about the woman in green?" Nathan asked. "Should we dismiss her entirely?"

"Hey, Dad!" Ralphie shouted. "How's about it? I'm starting to feel like a sponge!"

"By no means, Nathan," Blakeley said, ignoring his son's plea. "A female accomplice is perfectly predictable. Christopher Beecham is downright devilish with the ladies, you know. No pun intended."

"Hey, Dad!" Ralphie called again. Some of the teenagers squealed for fear that Ralphie might drown.

"He had plenty of time to map out his strategy," Nathan said, casting a quizzical glance from Blakeley to Ralphie.

"Yes, thanks to me," Blakeley said. "If ever I get another impulse to save a monster, please kick me, Nathan."

"Hey, Dad!" Ralphie called another time.

"Yes, in a moment, Ralph?" Blakeley said, then turned to Nathan. "Good heavens, I almost forgot Sophia's instructions. Nathan, will you please come to dinner this evening?"

Nathan winced. Dinner at the Blakeley estate—with Allison attending—was the last thing he wanted.

"I would regard it as a personal favor," Blakeley

said. "I do understand how you must feel about Miss Meredith these days, but dash it all, you're both very special to us. Couldn't we declare my home neutral ground? Somewhere that warring parties may live in harmony, if not affection?"

"Dad!" Ralphie started to splash about and pretend he was going under for good. The girls on the riverbank squealed again.

"All right," Nathan agreed. His gaze was full on Ralphie, and he half wondered if his friend was in real danger. "Seven-thirty?"

"Seven-fifteen. We'll have a sherry before dinner," Blakeley said. Then he signalled for his son to come out of the water. "I do hope the exercise has tired Ralphie out. It would be pleasant to have one evening when he doesn't drive his mother to distraction."

At the sign from his father, Ralphie climbed aboard the yacht, and much to his delight, the girls still on the bank swooned theatrically when he flexed his muscles with his customary lack of subtlety.

Nathan smiled at Ralphie's antics, and after a brief good-bye to Blakeley, he rowed back to shore and hurried off to the precinct house. He still had to complete some reports he'd promised Hudson he would take care of before the end of the day. He urged his horse along because he hoped to squeeze in a hot bath in the little time he would have left between his work and his dinner appointment. Since the main streets were busy with people heading home from work, he took a shortcut along a few back streets.

He eased his horse and buggy through a narrow, dusty stretch by the Reading Railroad plug line, where thieves and narcotics peddlers often did business by night and where the bodies of forgotten, nameless men and women were ofttimes found in the morning.

By day, the road was usually abandoned. Bummy Rummel, the neighborhood vagrant, was snoring under a blackberry bush, an empty bottle of muscatel still resting in his grimy, skeletal fingers. The drunk cursed and rolled over as Nathan passed.

Nathan forded Kirby's Creek at a shallow bend a few yards upstream of some youngsters who were splashing in the water. He paused for a moment to let the horse have a drink. The water was clean there. Downstream about a half mile, it was befouled by sulfur from Irwin Heester's ironworks, then dyed a deeper red by the bloody run-off from his rendering plant. A quarter mile beyond that the creek emptied into a sewer. Some of the youngsters in the water waved. Nathan waved back. On sweltering days 20 years earlier, he had splashed around in the same spot.

His horse sated, he continued on and went through Mary's Park, where lovers often strolled hand in hand on lazy Sundays or perfumed springtime evenings. There, he and Allison had spent a few flirtatious hours of their own. Memories to dismiss. Memories impossible to dismiss.

At the far end of Mary's Park, there was a shady trail that was just wide enough for the horse and buggy to pass through. It led to another, wider trail, which in turn led to a road a few blocks from the station.

As Nathan drove along the narrow trail, the horse was startled by a figure moving through a nearby clump of dogwood. Nathan drew the horse to a quiet halt. He calmed the horse with a softly spoken plea and watched as the figure plowed angrily through a pile of dead leaves collected over many autumns and blown there by swirling winter winds.

At first, Nathan thought it was another victim of

the Lordly Lilywaver, shaken and sputtering with outrage, hurrying off to find a beat cop or perhaps a confessor to report what she'd just been forced to look at. Nathan urged the horse to remain still and waited for the regal old man to step out of the brush, giggling and rebuttoning his fly. The bothersome exhibitionist had long since ceased to be a source of amusement. This time, Nathan swore, he was going to lock the Waver up until the the war was over.

But when the maiden tore her skirt on a bramble bush and uttered a four-letter expletive, the picture in Nathan's mind changed radically.

"Hold it, you!" he shouted.

The maiden was startled, but only briefly. "Oh, it's you, McSomething-or-other," Richard Petticord said. "What now? Do you beat me up?"

"Don't tempt me," Nathan said, directing his horse into Petticord's path. "What are you doing out of jail?"

A feline smile crossed Petticord's face. "Ever hear of bail, McSomething? It pays to have friends."

"Anybody I'd know?"

Petticord sniffed. "Gawd, I certainly doubt it. Now I must be on my way."

"I was under the impression the judge set a very high bail," Nathan said.

"Celebrity has its rewards," Petticord informed him.

"You still haven't answered my question, Petticord. Who bailed you out?"

"You wouldn't know the name," Petticord said with a patronizing air, "but it's Darling. Destiny's Darling."

"Really?"

"Really."

"Sounds like a racehorse," Nathan observed.

Petticord sighed and tugged his skirt out of the

bramble bush. "May I go now, McSomething?"

Nathan held his palms out and shrugged helplessly. "I guess I can't stop you now."

Petticord headed down the hillside over a narrow trail, taking the least-travelled route homeward to avoid any unwelcome encounters.

The horse shivered again and Nathan saw another figure cutting through the same clump of dogwood, stepping through the pile of leaves with a familiar manure-dodging stride, easing past the bramble bush and following Petticord down the hillside. He recognized the man at once and laughed despite his irritation at seeing Petticord out of jail. For Lt. Hudson had finally found the perfect assignment for Lt. Bones Fatzinger.

Chapter Four

Later that evening, Blakeley could not help cursing to himself as he looked around at his family and their dinner guests. The unpleasant situation that had arisen was not his fault; he didn't think that Sophia had told him about the additional guest, and so he had not warned Nathan. Then again, upon reflection, Blakeley decided that his wife might have mentioned the unexpected visitor earlier that afternoon. But the news about Beecham had him so preoccupied that it was small wonder he had not remembered. Sitting at the table, he felt terrible about what was happening anyway.

Of course, his wife should have given the matter some thought in the first place. Just because G. Lindsey Pratt, the famed war correspondent, had volunteered to help with the charity ball, she had completely overlooked both Don Orlando and Nathan's feelings. Her oversight was most out of character—the result, no doubt, of overwork. From the strained grimace on her face, Blakeley could tell that she too was mortified by the uncomfortable scene she had created.

For the past hour, Blakeley had tried with little success to make amends. And the longer he sat at the table, the more confirmed he became in his suspicions that Pratt had not offered his aid to Sophia out of altruism. Rather, Blakeley believed the reporter was digging around for information on the Hazleton murder. Failing in his efforts, however, Pratt had turned to boring his captive audience with stories of his adventures in the war against Spain.

"Strange bedfellows," Blakeley thought as he spied Don Orlando and Nathan rolling their eyes furtively while Pratt went on and on about his time in Cuba. His face flushed from too much wine, Don Orlando seemed almost incapable of containing himself as Pratt's tales of Yankee Doodle Derring-do and so-called unspeakable Spanish atrocities piled up in what Blakeley regarded as a great verbal compost heap. Despite the popularity of his dispatches from Cap Haitien and Key West among newspaper readers, Pratt was not gaining any new fans at the moment.

It was not that he was a complete charlatan. Pratt, like his colleagues, merely embellished the truth without conscience. But he was such a windbag—a George Bernard Shaw without wit or wisdom—that his already overbearing personality became insufferable. Blakeley was certain that only proper etiquette and Allison and his wife's presence kept Nathan from silencing the reporter with a solid punch to his face.

When he caught his wife, exquisite in silvery gray with tiny pink fleur-de-lis, fidgeting with her pressed duckling *marseillais* and watching the Spaniard nervously, Blakeley tried to move the conversation away from Pratt's war stories. Even though he realized it was an indelicate subject, and that he was opening himself up to Pratt's journalistic scrutiny, he mentioned the case he and Nathan were investigating. But Pratt would not cede his place in the limelight.

Rather, it was Don Orlando who unexpectedly commented on the grisly murders. With angry eyes fixed on Pratt, he said, "Who is to care about the passing of one hateful young man when so many heroes are being slaughtered in the war?"

Blakeley started to protest that murder was murder after all, and that the victim was not entirely hateful. To her credit, Sophia corroborated the last point because of the help Hazleton had given her with the charity ball in years past.

"Sure," Pratt said, refusing to be interrupted, "nobody is going to miss him, except maybe a few other deviates."

Then without missing a beat, he picked up with a war story that dealt with a group of drunken soldiers who had deflowered all the novices in a Carmelite convent in Matanzas. Ralphie and Rosie giggled at the word deflowered, Sophia gave each of them a murderous glance, and Blakeley was suddenly grateful that a cool breeze was wafting through the dining room.

Had it not been for Pratt's presence, Blakeley realized, the evening would have been perfect. The dinner was excellent. As usual, Mrs. Snopkowski, her beefy arms folded, stood some distance away, casting an intimidating eye on the servants and waiting for the customary compliments. Victor sulked and did his best to appear deathly ill as he served the wine, an appropriate white Bordeaux.

In contrast to Don Orlando, Nathan seemed much more in control of his emotions, aloof in fact. Blakeley had seen Nathan act in that manner before when he had to choose between keeping his composure or pommeling everyone around him.

As Pratt droned on with his war story, Blakeley gave up any hope of saving the evening. Although it had started off well, the dinner party had been doomed since the journalist's arrival—even the news that Petticord was free on bail, curious as it was, had not dampened Blakeley's mood. At a quarter past seven, Blakeley and Nathan had been chuckling about Fatzinger's new assignment over glasses of sherry when Victor entered the drawing room to announce G. Lindsey Pratt. Victor was almost as enamored of newspapermen as he was disdainful of policemen; he was fully aware that a favorable word in one column or another might get him back into the theater. So he had been especially stentorian when he introduced the new guest. "Sir!" he had said with more enthusiasm than Blakeley thought good for him. "Mr. G. Lindsey Pratt to see you!"

Pratt was ushered into the room with what might have been ruffles and flourishes had Victor had time to stage them properly. Tan, trim, and ostensibly suave in a suit he soon let slip he had had specially tailored at the city's finest shop on South Street, the reporter limped in supported by a pearl-handled cane. Blakeley knew all about Pratt's exploits in the war, and he had read several accounts of his celebrated wound. According to the official story in the papers, Pratt had stepped on the sword of a fallen cavalry officer, been taken prisoner, threatened with a ghastly end, and only by pure luck saved by Cuban partisans.

As he walked slowly across the drawing room, Pratt extended his hand to both men. "Pleased to meet you," he said to Nathan when Blakeley introduced them.

"I'm pleased to meet you too, Mr. Pratt," Nathan said.

"No, no, no," Pratt insisted, "my friends call me G."

"G?" Nathan asked. "You mean as in golly?"

And from that moment, Blakeley had watched the relations between the two men cool to a state of mutual dismissal. Sitting at the dinner table, Blakeley hoped that the discord between the two men would not become any more pronounced.

For his part, Nathan was determined to keep his calm in an attempt to salvage as much of the evening with Allison as possible. After encountering Petticord in the park and completing his paperwork at the precinct house, he had had just enough time to take a hot bath, shave off his five-o'clock shadow, and change into a new summer suit, which he was glad to have the chance to wear. Although his suit was a far cry from G. Lindsey Pratt's foppish ensemble, it served Nathan admirably—he had never needed expensive clothing to impress others. He had decided not to splash on some cologne when the cloying smell of Oscar the steward's came to mind. Now, seated across from Allison, he was glad he hadn't used any because his only bottle of cologne was a birthday present from her, and its scent would certainly have exacerbated an already uncomfortable evening.

Despite his general resolve to remain aloof, Nathan could not help being annoyed by the attention Allison was paying to Pratt. No doubt, he rationalized, it was natural for Allison to show interest in Pratt's career. Overbearing or not, he was a war correspondent, which was what Allison wanted very much to be. But Nathan couldn't help thinking that her fawning attitude might contain something more than just professional interest.

And Nathan couldn't help groaning to himself

when Pratt finished another of his long-winded tales and Allison asked, "Where did you say you were wounded, Mr. Pratt?"

"G," he corrected.

"G," Allison said with a shy giggle that set Nathan's jaw on edge.

"That's better. But to answer your question, I was wounded in the foot, obviously," Pratt said, holding up his pearl-handled cane and laughing much too loudly at his own pale humor.

Everyone at the table except Don Orlando either laughed or smiled politely. Even though he smiled, Nathan sensed his control slipping away from him. It was bad enough that he couldn't serve in the war, but he didn't need his face rubbed in his personal failing by someone like Pratt.

His restraint gone, Nathan was about to make a total ass of himself when Don Orlando leaned over to him and said, "My sources inform me that, had it not been for a broken rum bottle in a particularly foul *casa de putas*, our new friend would be nobody's hero."

Upon hearing Don Orlando's caustic remark, Nathan laughed loudly and drew several perplexed glances from the others at the table. But he let them pass and relaxed. He grinned appreciatively at Don Orlando, who seemed to know that he had just defused a potentially embarrassing scene.

Not to be outdone, Pratt continued talking about his wound. "I'm sorry, Miss Meredith, did you mean where on the map was I wounded? It was in Artemisa in the province of Pinar del Rio," he said and turned to Don Orlando. "You know the place I'm sure. The notorious Cabañas Prison is situated there."

The Spaniard blinked recognition, but showed no emotion. For a moment, an embarrassed silence filled the room.

A few seats away from Don Orlando, in a dress of white lace with off-white prints, Rosie was looking mature beyond her 15 years. She had planned her evening well to take advantage of the rift between Nathan and Allison. She had even slipped past the usually hawk-eyed Sophia wearing a padded bodice, which she hoped gave her the notorious Lillian Russell look. It was too late for Sophia to correct the problem gracefully, but punishment was sure to follow the dinner. When her mother's disapproval had caught her eye earlier, Rosie simply whispered, "Mater, you really must embrace the coming century." Her mother's withering glance assured her that a serious talk would follow.

But no matter what punishment she risked, Rosie was determined to make a play for Nathan. Her eyes had been fixed on him all evening. Alas, her carefully laid plans were to no avail, for the handsome policeman hardly seemed to notice her. So after Don Orlando said nothing to Pratt's comment about the Spanish prison, she decided she had better become more bold in her attempts to claim Nathan's attention. "Were you held captive in the Cabañas Prison, G?"

"No, Miss Blakeley," Pratt replied, "the Cubans took me to Morro Castle in Havana."

"That's nice," Rosie cooed absently, smiling past Allison and directly at Nathan. Then she snapped a piece of celery and smiled a worldly smile.

Nathan shifted uncomfortably in his seat and momentarily forgot his rival. A quick glance at his hostess told him he wasn't the only one to notice Rosie's actions. Vexed by her daughter's behavior, but too polite to scold her with guests present, Sophia drank her glass of Bordeaux with a most ungraceful gulp and signaled for Victor to pour her another.

"Must have been pretty scary," Ralphie said, gobbling up his second helping of everything and winking at the pert Welsh maid, Dumpling, who as always winked back.

"With Remington, Norris, and Crane?" Don Orlando said acidly.

Pratt had been dropping such household names all evening, chiefly and obviously for Allison's ears, and Nathan noticed she had never failed to make an appreciative response to each of them. Thrall, Scovel, Decker, Creelman, Bryson—all the stars, and G. Lindsey Pratt had worked with every one of them, shared food and drink with them, slept in muddy trenches and steaming jungles with them. But as far as Nathan was concerned, Pratt was full of verbal fertilizer.

"No, Don Orlando," Pratt said. "Just me and a bunch of nobodies."

"Were you all in the same cell?" Don Orlando inquired.

"For a while, until I was put in solitary confinement."

"And why did your captors do that, Mr. Pratt?"

"Because I refused to eat the swill they were feeding us, Don Orlando, I'm sure you've read about that in the papers."

"I've read what you reported, yes," Don Orlando said.

Pratt stared, and no one said a word.

While Rosie smiled flirtatiously at Nathan and Ralphie traded lustful eye contact with Dumpling, and Victor stood by looking as if he could barely lift the bottle of wine with which he again refilled Sophia's glass, Nathan couldn't keep himself from imagining that the conversation between Don Orlando and Pratt was turning into a Grand Inquisition.

"Was it worse in isolation, Mr. Pratt?" the Spaniard asked at last.

"It wasn't exactly a picnic," Pratt said vehemently.

"Oh? Can you recall it for us, Mr. Pratt?"

"At the dinner table?" He turned incredulous eyes on his hosts, as if imploring them to save him from a madman.

But before Blakeley or his wife could interrupt, Don Orlando said, "Yes, yes. We are all of us finished eating, Mr. Pratt, but for my young friend Ralphie, of course, and nothing disturbs his appetite. So do please tell us what you saw there."

"Don Orlando, if you don't mind, I'd rather—"

"Shall I begin it for you, Mr. Pratt?" Don Orlando asked in a tone he might have used with a slow child. "It was a narrow cell with a floor of rotting boards. You know it now, Mr. Pratt, do you not? After all, you invented it."

At her end of the table, Sophia turned pale. Her worst fears were being realized.

Pratt flushed angrily. "I never invented anything!"

Blakeley tried to speak up. "Don Orlando, please—"

"Let us get to the better part," Don Orlando said, ignoring Blakeley, as if unaware he had spoken. "Tell us about the rats and the cockroaches and the brutal guards who would not let you sleep for weeks at a time."

"This is inappropriate, Don Orlando," Pratt insisted.

"Is it, Mr. Pratt?" Don Orlando fired back. "Is it? How much did your newspapers pay you for that tall tale?"

"I beg your pardon!"

"They must have paid you a bonus for that one," Don Orlando said, his lips twisted in a wicked snarl. "Especially when you concocted the beautiful Cuban resistance fighter who seduced the stupid, drunken Spanish guard, then cut his throat and smuggled you out of Morro. After all, if they could pay you a bonus of five hundred dollars for the story about the cowardly Spaniard who went mad at the sight of all those gallant Americans and shot his *commandante*, surely the one about the prison and your daring escape was worth a thousand."

Don Orlando's voice had risen and he was out of his chair. The room was silent save for his voice and the sounds of Blakeley's futile attempts to intercede. Although he had nothing but sympathy for the extraordinarily awkward spot his hosts were in, Nathan gloated a little over the humiliation Pratt was suffering, especially since Allison was present.

Nonplussed, Pratt tried to save face. "If my employers are willing to pay me for risking my neck—"

"They pay you to make up lies," Don Orlando shouted as he started around the table toward Pratt. "That is what they pay you for! Lies like the one about marauding bands of Spanish soldiers raping women and burning the countryside. Lies like the one about the Cuban priest whose tongue was cut out for preaching a sermon against the King. Lies which grow in your head like voices that come in the night to a lunatic!"

Don Orlando was standing scant inches from the journalist and shouting into his face when he suddenly realized where he was and what he was doing. He stopped and looked at the stunned faces around him. In the doorway stood Mrs. Snopkowski holding a meat cleaver at the ready.

Noting the old man's trembling hands, the tic in his eye, and the perspiration running down his beet-red face, Blakeley feared that Don Orlando might suffer a stroke. He rose instinctively and went to his aid, as did Ralphie.

Don Orlando waved them off. "I am fine, *mi padrón*. Just a little too much wine, I think," he said, his voice quivering. "You must try to forgive me, Dr. Blakeley."

His eyes welling up, he could barely speak to the crestfallen Sophia. "*Señora* Blakeley, my behavior is unforgivable before you and your family and Sgt. McBride, whom I have learned to respect in my days as your guest. And before the beautiful Miss Meredith.... This is a horrible breach of etiquette. I deserve to be shot."

His eyes took on a feral cast when he looked again at Pratt. "But I cannot suffer this fool politely any longer," he said, his voice clearing. "Good night. Once again, please forgive me."

As he started to leave, Blakeley nodded at Ralphie, who hastened to assist the old man upstairs to his quarters.

After the Spaniard's abrupt departure, the dining room was silent until Victor spoke. "Well, so much for gratitude," he said and marched off, carrying a bottle that was still half full of Bordeaux.

Sophia turned to Blakeley. "Ian."

"I shall look in on him presently, dearest," he said. "Just as soon as he's settled."

Sophia tried to apologize to Pratt, but her words came uncertainly because, like Blakeley and Nathan, she privately believed he deserved the tirade. Despite Pratt's efforts to help her with the ball, she detested his hypocrisy. But of course, bad manners were bad manners.

"Don Orlando is under a terrible strain, Mr. Pratt," Sophia said feebly.

"G," he corrected, his good mood returning.

"Sorry," she said. "G."

"Mother, I think I'm about to be sick," Rosie said, her face suddenly ashen.

"Oh dear," Sophia said.

Rosie's queasiness would be blamed on Don Orlando's outburst, but the truth was Rosie had been skillfully sneaking Bordeaux when she was supposed to have only mineral water in her glass. Unaware of her daughter's chicanery, Sophia welcomed the opportunity to leave the table, and she led Rosie out of the room.

"Please try to forget this, Mr. Pratt," she said on her way out.

Pratt, who stood with the other men until the Blakeley women were gone, was unfazed by the scene. He sat down and sipped his wine.

"Still want to be a war correspondent, Miss Meredith?" he asked, smirking.

"Yes, G, I do," she said.

She looked into Pratt's eyes as she answered, and Nathan quietly seethed. He wanted to ignore her, but Allison had made it very hard for him to do so in her white dress with the blue trim. It was the same dress she'd worn on the night when they had found themselves alone in her apartment, a circumstance each had often blamed on the other, but neither had ever regretted. They'd seldom spoken about it either—that night when neither had noticed that it was almost dawn and he was still there, and they were sharing the warmth of their bodies, oblivious to the morning chill. Thinking about their night together as he sat at the table, the memory seemed more like an exaggerated fantasy. It had all been so perfect. But the thought of that night threatened to drive him crazy, especially since the smell of gardenias flowed off her as the breeze came through the dining room. If Nathan didn't do something, he was sure he'd end up as loony as Beecham.

"Look," Nathan said, the words popping out of his mouth without warning, "Don Orlando was only saying what he believes in his heart. I don't understand why everyone's so appalled."

For the first time that evening, Allison turned her attention away from Pratt. But when her big, beautiful green eyes flashed a reproving glance, Nathan heard himself meekly saying, "Of course, Don Orlando doesn't have to be right."

As he finished his wine, Nathan was certain that Allison had more than a professional interest in Pratt. And he hoped that no one—least of all Pratt—would notice the agitated shake of his hand that almost made him drop his glass.

"Things like this happen when you do the job right, Miss Meredith," Pratt said, not seeming to notice Nathan in the least.

"Allison," she said, returning her attention to him. "Please call me Allison, G."

"Allison." Pratt studied her eyes for a moment and smiled. "Did I ever tell you, Allison, about the time Norris, Crane, and I were almost drowned when our press boat overturned off Key West?"

"No," she said, absorbed. "I don't believe you did."

Nathan had had more of Allison's fawning interest than he could take. But he sat fingering his wine glass rather than making a scene and risking further censure from that pair of green eyes.

"Well," Pratt said, "we were setting out for Bahía Honda when a sudden swell came up and hit the little *Vamoose* on the port side. She wasn't much of a craft, mostly wooden and older than Methuselah, and she went belly up without any warning."

"How frightening!" Allison said.

"True. Particularly frightening for Crane. Poor Steve didn't know how to swim. We must have squeezed a gallon of salt water out of him. He was lucky Frank and I didn't lose him in the sea."

In his seat, Nathan still glowered. "That pompous piece of..." he thought, but his anger prevented him from finishing the metaphor.

Blakeley excused himself. "I suppose I should look in on Don Orlando." He smiled lamely at Nathan and left. Allison wished him good night. Pratt merely nodded and went on with his story.

"Fred Remington thought it was the funniest thing he'd seen since Hearst sent him there." Suddenly Pratt turned to Nathan and informed him, "That's William Randolph Hearst of *The New York Journal*, old boy."

"I know," Nathan said, his teeth firmly clenched to prevent a stream of obscenities from gushing forth.

Pratt went back to Allison. "You have to see the cartoon Fred drew. He has us splashing around like a school of hysterical porpoises."

"Porpoise poop," Nathan thought with a sudden flash of inspiration, and he knew the wine was getting to him. *"Pompous piece of porpoise poop. Perfect."*

"May I see that cartoon sometime?" Allison asked, her green eyes sparkling.

"Sure. I'll write to Steve," Pratt said. "I'm sure he'll send it along if I tell him what a lovely creature wants to see it."

"I can't wait," she said.

Somewhere in the kitchen, a pile of dishes fell to the floor.

In the hallway, Mrs. Snopkowski was screeching in Polish as the maid Dumpling yelled back in Welsh.

The cool breeze no longer wafted through the dining room, and a stagnant, airless pall fell over the room.

But in the midst of all this chaos, the only thing that Nathan noticed was Pratt's hand covering Allison's where it lay on the table.

Chapter Five

Nathan passed three long days after the abysmal dinner party. He and Blakeley did not succeed in making any headway in their investigation; nor, for that matter, could they or Lt. Hudson discover the mysterious benefactor who had posted Petticord's bail. To make matters worse, Bones Fatzinger had taken so well to his assignment to follow Petticord that when Petticord vanished without a trace Fatzinger followed suit. And no matter how deeply he tried to immerse himself in the investigation of the Hazleton murder, Nathan had no way to prevent memories of Allison and Pratt from creeping into his mind. As a result, the person he saw in the mirror each morning became increasingly more frayed and threadbare.

The fourth morning, however, Nathan had at last a real reason to smile. Just as he was reporting in to Blakeley, a call came from Lt. Hudson—there was a break in the case; they were needed at the city morgue immediately. The medical examiner had reported the discovery of the body of a strange woman, and Hudson thought it might be the woman they were searching for. He was heading over to the morgue that minute.

Barely able to contain his excitement at the news, Nathan rushed from the house without once looking about for Allison. But Blakeley would not be hurried again at eight o'clock in the morning. Only when he had straightened his vest, donned his suit coat, and bid Sophia farewell did he walk to Nathan's buggy. By the time Blakeley seated himself beside his friend, Nathan had calmed down a bit, but an anxious thrill made his hands tremble as he held the reins. He knew his perspiration that morning was due to more than wearing a suit in the late spring heat.

With thoughts of cracking the case racing through his mind, Nathan was barely able to respond to Blakeley's desultory remarks as he urged the horse along their usual route to the morgue. More than once Blakeley asked him to slow down, since the woman was evidently dead and, thus, not likely to disappear. But his pleas were not heeded.

Despite the speed at which they traveled, the two met delay after delay, and Nathan became firmly convinced that fate was working against them. An overnight fire in a warehouse on Falls Road had closed the street they were driving on; so they had to backtrack, then head north to City Line Avenue, where they hoped to catch a train into the city at the Bala station. But the train was leaving as they arrived at the station, and they were forced to drive through morning traffic in Overbrook as they headed south to Fifty-second and Hestonville. With each new delay, Nathan spouted a stream of oaths that gave Blakeley a hearty chuckle. Still, Nathan kept on. He would have run barefoot across streets of fire, like the Indians in Don Orlando's ramblings, to find out if the so-called strange woman in the morgue would move them closer to solving the Hazleton murder.

They didn't reach the morgue until most of the morning was wasted. The long detour had done nothing to assuage Nathan's anxiety. It took all his control to keep the horse from running down pedestrians in the busy neighborhood. More than once he drew dangerously close to a street vendor's stand and received a dark look. None of the people who filled the street dared do more. For the neighborhood was home to a recent wave of Southern Europeans, and they knew enough to fear a law officer's uniform in their new homeland.

Finally out of the carriage, Nathan and Blakeley were greeted at the morgue's entrance by Lt. Hudson. And either because of Nathan's frantic driving, or because his own excitement had increased as he drew closer to the mysterious woman, Blakeley was not in any mood to exchange pleasantries with Hudson.

"I thought you'd never get here," Hudson said, shaking hands with Blakeley.

"Yes, yes, we did have the devil's own time this morning. Now, I believe you have a strange woman for us to see, Lt. Hudson," he said.

"Yeah, I know I said strange. It's the right word, Dr. Blakeley, but—"

"Bless you, Lt. Hudson. Let's have a look." Blakeley flew by the policeman and was inside the building before Hudson could say another word.

"It's all the medical examiner told me: a strange woman," Hudson said to Nathan as they stood on the steps. He eyed Nathan closely. "Well, McBride, Blakeley must be working you pretty hard. You look a little drawn."

"Psychic tension, sir," Nathan said and managed

a smile, which he hadn't been able to do too frequently in the past few days. "Perhaps we should join Dr. Blakeley," he said, not wanting to put off any longer what he had waited the whole morning to see.

"Honest," Hudson said, as they walked into the morgue, "that was all the medical examiner told me: 'We have somebody for you to look at—a strange woman.' I wish he would have told me what he meant before I called you and Blakeley. I tried to call you back, but you'd already gone."

From Hudson's tone, Nathan could tell that all his nervous energy had been spent for naught, and he felt a great letdown. Nevertheless, what he found in the examining room did surprise him, although not for the reason he had expected. On the slab lay the body of a woman he recognized; neatly folded and laid on a table next to her were a minister's black vestments.

Staring dolefully at the corpse, Blakeley said, "I cannot deny that she's strange."

"Strangest preacher I've ever seen," Hudson said.

"Do you remember her, Nathan?"

"Cybel Ashbaugh, Christopher Beecham's art patroness and always passionate admirer."

"And, from what we can see now," Blakeley said, "the little minister who helped him escape from Graterford Prison."

Blakeley and Nathan had come to know Cybel Ashbaugh during the trial of Christopher Beecham. Each day she had sat in the gallery, casting lethal glances at them and adoring smiles at Beecham. She had brought him taffy and Turkish cigarettes, and stayed as close to the defense table as she could. The guilty verdict against Beecham had made her faint, when Blakeley had succeeded in having Beecham's death sentence commuted, she had gone to Blakeley's home to kiss his hand.

"She was so great an admirer," said Blakeley, "that she was not permitted to visit him in prison. She had to invent a way to be near him."

"Nice payoff she got for springing him," Hudson said.

Cybel Ashbaugh's body was swollen and decomposed after more than a week in the water. Overcome by the stench of rotting flesh, the three men held handkerchiefs to their faces and breathed cautiously.

"You can't tell now," Blakeley said, "but the minister was much thinner when I saw her at the prison. Miss Ashbaugh must have virtually starved herself."

"She darkened her hair too," Nathan said. "I remember a chubby blond at the trial."

"Look at the bruises on her neck, Nathan," Blakeley said, pointing. "Do you see anything unusual?"

From a distance, Nathan studied the corpse's neck just above the white linen cloth that hid the rest of the body. He had no desire to get any closer.

"Well," he said after studying the neck for a time, "she was obviously strangled."

"By a person whose middle finger is missing," Blakeley said. "See there?"

Against his will, Nathan moved a step nearer the body in order to inspect the wound more closely. "Right, I remember now," Nathan said when he saw what Blakeley's trained eye had spotted at once, "the telltale missing finger. It's a dead giveaway." He regretted his choice of phrasing immediately.

Hudson laughed at Nathan's embarrassment and waved his hand before his face. "I don't know how you get used to that. I was at Gettysburg and a lot of other lousy places, but the smell of death still makes me gag."

"It's good you still have a sense of smell, Lieutenant," Blakeley said.

"Well, if I don't get out of here soon I may lose mine," Nathan said. "Do you think we could get some fresh air now?"

"Eh? Oh, yes, of course."

"Thank you, McBride," Hudson said. "I was about to say the same thing."

Blakeley pulled the linen over the corpse's head and pushed the slab back into its niche in the wall. Without a moment's hesitation, Hudson led the way back to the entranceway. There, they took deep gulps of the fresh air that was heavily laden with the exotic scents of the local vendors.

Across the street from the morgue, a man from an Aegean island was selling black olives and fresh fruits. A grocer's board advertised spinach pie and shish kebabs. And in the window of a restaurant, a Greek chef stood preparing dolmathes and kakavia for the evening's menu. In front of the morgue, an Italian vendor was arranging fresh fish and vegetables in neat rows. A man with a pushcart selling fresh fruit chanted, "Konn-ta-lo-pay! Watta-mel-lo!"

Blakeley sniffed heartily, fully enjoying the wonderful odors of the ethnic neighborhood. But Nathan and Hudson were busy fanning their faces, still trying to clear away the smells of the morgue.

Shaking his head, Hudson said, "I'll never understand lunatics like Beecham. It's bad enough he runs around killing people. But where does he get his crazy ideas? I mean, what idiot would bite off his own finger?"

"It's really very simple, Lieutenant," Blakeley said. "You see, Beecham fancies himself a scholar. He's especially enamored of the ancients. There was a chap in Greek mythology named Orestes who murdered his mother, then in a moment of grief bit off his middle finger. Beecham, of course, is anything but a tragic hero. He's a scoundrel incapable of grief, but he's addled enough to think what he did was noble. All he had was a sick obsession with his mother and what he perceived as her infidelities."

"I see," Hudson said and continued to shake his head in disbelief.

"Where did they find Beecham's latest victim, Lieutenant?" Nathan asked.

Hudson fumbled in his pocket and pulled out a piece of paper. "In the shallows of a creek about a mile and a half from the prison," he said, referring to the paper. "She was stuck on a jagged rock and hidden under a lot of green scum in the shadow of a big willow tree. I guess they couldn't find her until she bloated up and rose to the surface. The county sheriff's people brought her in. Here's the report they delivered with her."

Blakeley perused the report, folded it, then put it in his vest pocket. "I see they found his prison garb in a tree trunk not far from where they found her body. She must have been waiting there for him with a change of clothes."

"Yeah, the sheriff has an interesting theory about that," Hudson said. "He thinks she was waiting with a prison guard's uniform. Beecham put it on, infiltrated the search party, and led it astray until he was in a position to slip off unnoticed. Clever."

"Diabolically so. Well, thank you for your help, Lieutenant," Blakeley said, mustering a smile.

"Don't mention it, Dr. Blakeley," Hudson said. "Hell, it took you two so long to get here that I had all morning to check her out. I really am sorry for misleading you. I knew the minute I got here that she wasn't your mysterious woman in green. But I guess you needed to see this anyway."

"Poor, deluded Cybel Ashbaugh," Blakeley said, almost to himself. Then he thought, "I caused her death. How many more deaths will I be responsible for before we stop this madman?"

Chapter Six

As Cybel Ashbaugh lay dead in the Philadelphia morgue—yet another victim of having loved Christopher Beecham too well, but certainly not too wisely—the fiend who had taken both her love and life was on the prowl, hoping once again to turn his charms to ill ends. Since he'd stolen back into the city, Beecham had set about implementing his devious plot to avenge himself on his nemesis, Dr. Ian Blakeley. He didn't intend to be as disappointed with Blakeley's demise as he had been with his escape from Graterford.

The whole episode had gone off too easily; it lacked all the drama he so craved in life. He'd thought disguising himself as one of the men out to capture him would be exciting, but the dullards had never suspected that he was working against them. Even killing Cybel, after all those months of careful planning, had been a letdown.

Still, she had had the last laugh. For she had not

brought the funds for his flight from the prison. The few dollars Beecham had found on her corpse were just enough to buy some food and to rent a room in one of the city's poorer neighborhoods. Desperate as he was for money, he'd tried to blackmail one of the high-society sodomites who had often propositioned him in the past. But the bastard had laughed at Beecham's threat of exposure, threatening in turn to report Beecham's presence to the police. Beecham had taken care of that score, however, and anyone else who thought he could get the best of Christopher Beecham would get the same treatment.

Now, as he stalked the shop-lined streets in the afternoon heat, Beecham cursed the dead woman for his damnable poverty. He muttered to himself and shoved shoppers out of his way as he headed down busy Lancaster Avenue. The sight of a blind beggar stopped Beecham dead for a moment, and he pondered the immense pleasure he'd derive from cold-bloodedly destroying the man, as he'd done to so many unfortunate vagrants in his last murderous spree. A flurry of skirts and blond hair in the mailing shop behind the mendicant distracted Beecham from his reverie, and Beecham's black mood lightened immediately, as if his prayers had been answered by some dark god. And indeed, they had.

Straightening his collar, Beecham walked over to the mailing shop, again damning his erstwhile benefactor. If Cybel had brought the money with her to the prison, he wouldn't be forced to wear the same suit of clothes day after day. He was surprised the suit had held up in the current heat wave and knew that it wouldn't do so indefinitely. But, on reconsidering the matter, Beecham saw a role that he could play that would use his shabby clothes to good effect.

A bell above the door announced Beecham's entrance into the shop, which was fortuitously empty of other customers. A young clerk stood behind a counter clicking a wad of gum in her open mouth. She raised her head listlessly to examine the new patron, then lowered it again, seemingly uninterested.

Beecham took a step inside the doorway and stopped, fixing his eyes on the woman. Yes, he decided after he'd seen that familiar damp, hungry-bloomers expression on her face, she was just what he wanted: an idiot. He wondered how far he'd have to go to get all he needed out of her. Silly women like the clerk always wanted small talk and maybe a quick visit to the storeroom that they could remember when they were with their simpleton beaux. Whatever it took, Beecham would gladly do, as long as he finished before the clerk's boss returned and ruined his plans.

"Excuse me," Beecham said with his best smile. "I'm sorry to interrupt you."

"Yes, what is it?" the clerk said. She worked her jaws fiercely on her gum.

"I had to be sure."

"About what?" The clerk drummed her fingers slowly on the countertop.

"You are, aren't you?" Beecham asked as he gazed longingly into her baby-blue eyes. "I mean, I'm not mistaken, am I?"

Embarrassed by his scrutiny, the woman blushed. "Of course, I'm the clerk. What is it you want?"

"That's not it at all," Beecham said. He took a deep breath, as if what he was about to say demanded a great expenditure of energy. "I saw you through the window, and I didn't think I was mistaken."

"Oh, don't be so tiresome. What is it you want?"

"Well, it's just that I didn't know that the living,

breathing model for the Gibson Girl lived in Philadelphia," Beecham said.

"Me? You thought I was the Gibson Girl?" the clerk said, and in that moment she was unwittingly snared by Beecham's trap. Still chewing her gum, but more daintily, she raised a hand and absently twisted her locks. "Don't get me wrong—you're not the first to think I was her. You're not disappointed, are you?"

"Most assuredly not," he swore. "The Gibson Girl is, of course, the epitome of womanly beauty. But I find her so cold. Her face lacks something. Character—that's what it is. Character. Your face has so much more that could never be captured in a drawing. I see it especially in your eyes. Such remarkably expressive eyes."

"Who? The Gibson Girl?"

"No, no. I mean you. Your eyes," Beecham said. When the clerk giggled at his compliment, he could hardly refrain from crying out that she was a simpering moron. "What is your name?"

"Juliet." She winked her eyes coyly as Beecham crossed the room, seemingly lost in admiration of her beauty.

"Juliet? Why, surely if the Bard had ever seen your face, he would have spared his Juliet."

"What's a bard?" She leered across the counter, resting on her elbows, her face mere inches from Beecham's.

"The bard—Shakespeare," he said, flinching slightly at the woman's stupidity, which plumbed to depths that even he had not expected. He abandoned any idea of impressing her by reciting Romeo's lines from the balcony scene, certain they would soar beyond her dull peasant intelligence. "I know all of Shakespeare. I'm a poet."

"A poet," she said, her expression as awed as if she had just looked upon the face of a god. "I love poetry. And I like ice cream, too. And player pianos 'cause you can pretend. And funny papers on Sunday—I like them best."

Beecham gripped the edge of the counter with both hands to keep himself from throttling Juliet to death. If he didn't think he'd be spotted from the street, he would have ended the half-wit's miserable existence before she could draw another breath through her slack mouth. But he surprised himself when he held his face locked with a fool's grin and said, "But you do like poetry?"

"Oh, yes. What kind do you write? Is it love poems?"

Beecham frowned and turned away. "Well, the truth is I'm a bit down on my luck right now. I had to sell my typewriter, and with the war and prices as high as they are, I can hardly afford paper much less a new typewriter."

Juliet reached out her hand and gripped his arm. "You poor dear."

"No, no, a poet should be down on his luck. At least, that's what everyone seems to think. Suffering, struggling, alienation—they're all important to my development as an artist."

"That's terrible. All that suffering, struggling, and—" Her face went blank for a second, as if alienation were too deep a word for her to utter, let alone comprehend its meaning. But then she brightened. "Well, if it's only paper you need, we've got lots of paper. Here take some." She reached to a shelf behind her and offered Beecham a ream.

Playing his role to the hilt, Beecham accepted the paper with a trembling hand. "You are the kindest person I have met since I came to Philadelphia. I don't care what anyone says about brotherly love—this is such a cold city."

Juliet mumbled something inane about giving the city a little more time, but Beecham ignored her. He needed just one more item to set his plan in motion. "If only I had a typewriter, I could sit down this minute and compose a sonnet to your beauty. Alas...."

"You could write a poem right now?" Juliet said. "Just like that?"

"With you for my inspiration, how could I not? And typewriters make my words flow so smoothly."

"Well," she said, "we've got one in the back room that I suppose I could lend you. But you'd have to bring it right back. If it's gone more than a day or two my boss will find out, and he'd take it out of my pay. And typewriters are expensive, you know."

"How can I ever thank you?" Beecham said. He seized one of her hands to kiss, but she drew it back quickly.

"Goodness, where's your middle finger?" Juliet said, pointing at his raised hand.

"Oh, the devil," Beecham thought, fearing he'd lost his chance, but his cunning didn't desert him in his moment of need. Holding his hand before him mournfully, he said, "I lost it for the love of a beautiful woman."

"Really?" Juliet asked, her voice lost in a romantic fog. "Does she look like the Gibson Girl too?"

"No, she doesn't," Beecham said, and he sniffled sadly. "Or I should say she didn't. She's awoken to another dawn than our own."

"How sad," Juliet cried, taking hold of his maimed hand. "How very sad."

Two hours later, just as the afternoon heat started to subside, Beecham sat at the desk in his sparsely furnished rooms. His hands rested on the keys of the typewriter that dim-witted Juliet would never again see. Thinking back on the scene with the simpleminded clerk, he could barely control his mirth as he tapped out the words of his poem. Once again his genius had succeeded.

"No doubt by now you've found poor Cybel," he typed, then stopped.

"Damn," he said, as he read over the line, "the little twit might have told me that the d and the p were off."

His hands shook above the keys as he studied the line over and over again. The unaligned characters so disturbed his aesthetic sense that he considered abandoning the letter to Blakeley until he could find a better machine. But he couldn't wait any longer, he decided; his burning urge for vengeance needed to be slaked soon.

Beecham sipped from a glass of brandy, then set it on the desk, next to his prized volume of Homer, and proceeded.

"No doubt by now you've found poor Cybel,
Looking worse than she has in years.
The fish, I'm sure, on her nose did nibble
And on the old cow's eyes and ears.
She's meat for worms now. So shall you be,
You in whose mind I'm a fiend from hell.
A gadfly, a demon I promise to be,
'Til I've driven you into a padded cell
Or else the grave, I haven't decided.
It's all the same to a proud man though.
When your world your character has derided,
It's a hell on earth hotter than below.
Take heed, my dear Blakeley, for I'm all around
you,
Awaiting the day when my Furies have found
you."

A lupine smile covered his face when he completed the poem. He read it and reread it, committing it to memory, assuring himself that Blakeley could not help but be terrified. At last, he folded the page carefully and sealed it in an envelope. His one regret was that he would not see Blakeley quaking when he received the letter. But he would meet with Blakeley soon enough, and then he would revel in Blakeley's final moment of fear.

Chapter Seven

Despite the generally accepted notion that Alexander Graham Bell had performed a great service to mankind, Blakeley was starting to believe the Scotsman had really cursed man with his invention. For the third time in six days, a phone call had ruined any hope Blakeley had of a restful morning out of the still broiling summer heat. Hardly had Blakeley sat down to his breakfast than Nathan called with ominous news—another murder had been committed involving a wealthy man-about-town.

And so it was that Nathan, Allison, and he sat in his landau, its roof closed against the morning glare, while Ralphie drove them along precarious roads at breakneck speed. Outside the carriage flashed the tidy, manicured Main Line countryside, where the estates resembled small duchies and the roadways were lined with rows of hedges that might have been trimmed by God. Inside the carriage, Blakeley couldn't help watching with some amusement as Allison and Nathan nervously ignored each other. Although he knew Nathan would rather have just about anyone else in the world accompany them to the crime scene, Blakeley had assented to Allison's request to accompany so she could report the story for her newspaper, *The Philadelphia Bulletin*. Indeed, Nathan had vehemently protested against her joining them, but he had not tried to argue when Allison claimed he would let her go if she were a man. From that moment, he had fallen silent, expressing his displeasure with scowls. Since they would have to shout to be heard above the din of the wooden wheels clacking along the brick road, however, Allison and Nathan had a good reason to avoid conversation. But Blakeley could not miss the clandestine looks of longing they gave one another when sure the other wasn't paying attention.

Aside from the noise, Blakeley could think of only one other reason for their reticence—Pratt. Nathan feared, no doubt, saying some unnecessarily harsh words about the correspondent that, no matter how true, would be ungentlemanly and certain to harm his already tenuous relationship with Allison. For she had been Pratt's almost constant companion since meeting him.

As they headed for the suburban village Radnor over a yellow-brick roadway cracked and puckered after a score of changing seasons, the coach now and then struck a particularly rough spot. Outside in the driver's seat, Ralphie would whoop like a cowboy, then quickly apologize with a thinly muffled laugh. Each bump caused Allison to wince and bite her lip. Blakeley thought her reaction peculiar until he remembered that Sophia was greatly annoyed with Allison for having spent the whole of the previous afternoon riding a tandem bicycle with

Pratt. When he realized the cause of her agony, Blakeley mutely commiserated with Allison. But on the seat next to her, Nathan would fight back a smile with each lurch of the coach. Finally, he opted for a sarcastic expression that could mean nothing less than whatever pain Allison suffered served her right for making such a fool of herself over Pratt.

The carriage sped, meanwhile, through the heart of suburban affluence that was supported by the city's working class. Stately mansions and sprawling estates bordered the roads Blakeley and his friends traveled. In some way or another, each of the splendid homes reminded Blakeley of the country estates he had left behind him in England years earlier.

The silence in the carriage was broken when a tall, severe-looking building with rows of beady little windows came into view, and Ralphie shouted, "Hey, Dad, isn't that Miss Prickett's, where Rosie was kicked out?"

Blakeley cleared his throat. "I don't believe so, Ralphie," he said in much too low a voice to be heard by his son.

"Hey, Dad!" Ralphie repeated.

"I heard you!" Blakeley answered with obvious annoyance, then said philosophically, "Yes, Ralphie, I guess you're right."

"I thought so," Ralphie said, laughing so hard he could be heard above all the noise.

Blakeley grimaced as he studied Miss Prickett's School for Young Ladies. Rosie had indeed attended the school for a short time, but she had readily earned her dismissal for dressing a mannequin to look like the headmistress, Odilia Prickett, and sitting it on a chamber pot in the chapel. Sophia had been outraged, of course, and blamed her husband for raising their children too leniently. As for Blakeley, he had never liked the hatchet-faced Odi-

111

lia Prickett, and he still found the whole situation quite humorous. Despite his amusement, he realized that his daughter's school days had been only slightly more successful than her brother's. Miss Fudderman's Latin School, Miss Manley's Select, Miss Prickett's School for Young Ladies—the list seemed endless.

Blakeley's lugubrious meditation was suddenly interrupted when Ralphie shouted a warning he could not understand and the carriage came to a sharp halt. Blakeley tilted momentarily, then fell back into his seat, catching his monocle, which had popped out abruptly. Allison flew out of her seat with a yelp and landed against Nathan, whose arms just happened to be open and ready. Instinctively, he closed his arms around her. Face to face, Allison and Nathan blushed as they gazed into each other's eyes. She started to mumble an apology when a man's voice outside the carriage threatened them.

"Are yiz from a newspaper?" the man said. "Cuz if yiz are, I'd jist as soon blow yer heads off as leave yiz step another foot onto Aimwell Acres!"

Blakeley stuck his head out the open window at the mention of Aimwell Acres, for that was the scene of the latest murder. He spied immediately, amidst a copse of blue spruce, a short, unkempt man waving a shotgun back and forth from Ralphie to the cab and back to Ralphie. The grizzled man wore a moth-eaten plaid hunter's cap and a flannel shirt stained at the armpits. The corners of his mouth were heavily eroded from years of exposure to nicotine.

Allison, acutely aware that there were many lunatics around who detested journalists, eased herself off Nathan's lap and slid back onto her seat, gesturing with her finger to her lips that she did not wish to be identified. When Nathan grinned and shrugged his shoulders, she made a face and said, "I mean it."

Blakeley replaced his monocle and shouted, "I say, put that weapon down, or I shall have my son throttle you to within an inch of your filthy life!"

The man smiled through broken brown teeth. "You sure as shit ain't too smart, mister, talkin' like that while I'm holdin' this here shotgun."

"Now see here," Blakeley said, but he was interrupted by Ralphie.

"I'll handle this, Dad," Ralphie said, then jerked Hecuba's reins.

The mare swung her long, noble head into the grizzled little man's shoulder. The shotgun went off and the blast echoed through the valley as the man fell off balance. Hecuba lurched in brief panic, but held her ground.

As Allison was thrown into Nathan's lap, she let out a horrified yelp, but once again she did not extricate herself from his grasp immediately.

Ralphie was down from the driver's seat in no more than a second, landing practically on top of the grizzled man, cuffing him once, and wresting the shotgun out of his hands. "Sonbitch!" the man swore as Ralphie cuffed him again and knocked him to the ground. Ralphie could have treated the man worse, but he wasn't angry enough to use excessive force. The important thing was that the grizzled little man didn't know that.

"And I don't like your language either," Ralphie said as the man lay stupefied on the ground. "There's a lady present."

To ensure the man would no longer threaten them, Ralphie carried his shotgun over to a nearby spruce and broke it against the tree's trunk. Then he kicked away the barrel and the stock. They flew over the tree and into a trout stream in a manner reminiscent of a ball Ralphie had once kicked to beat Columbia.

"I got more guns, mister," the strange man said as he watched the wooden stock land with a splash. "Lots of 'em."

Ralphie picked the man up by his collar. "Yeah? Well, maybe I'll just stick one of them—"

"That will be enough, Ralph," his father said sharply. "Whoever you are, sir, we are most assuredly not newspapermen. Show him your badge, Sgt. McBride."

Nathan smiled and winked at Allison, who reluctantly slid out of his lap and onto her seat. While she rearranged her bonnet and straightened out her skirt, she decided the moment at hand would not be the proper time to quibble over the gender difference between herself and a newsparman.

"Too bad G isn't with us today," Nathan said with a syrupy smile.

Allison readjusted a strand of hair behind her ear. "I'll be sure to tell him all about it," she said, smiling back.

"Excuse me," Nathan said. He climbed out of the coach door and waved his badge in front of the grizzled man's face. The man studied it with suspicion. "You can read what it says, can't you? Sergeant, Philadelphia Police Department."

"I recognize it," the man said and spat some tobacco juice onto the drive.

"Good," Nathan said. "Now my friend is going to let you go, and then you're going to tell us who you are and what you're doing here."

Ralphie released the little man, who had been standing on tiptoes in his grip. When he was loose, the man massaged his neck and looked longingly off in the direction of his broken shotgun.

"I got another shotgun can turn you into Swiss cheese," the man said. "Cop or no cop."

"And I'll bet my friend Beef here can kick you just as high and just as far as he did your other gun," Nathan answered. "Once again, who are you?"

"I got a better right here than you do," the man said. "I'm the caretaker. Me 'n the missus look after the place while the Aimwells are away. And we're sick of people disturbin' us while we're grievin'."

Blakeley spoke from within the cab. "Your grief is what has brought us here. What is your name, sir?"

Some brown spittle remained in the corner of the man's mouth. He licked it off, then said, "Nemo Hooper."

"Well, Mr. Hooper," Blakeley said, "we're going to grant you the rare privilege of showing us to the main house and the scene of the crime. Lead on, please."

Ralphie climbed back into the driver's seat, and Nathan joined him. Blakeley had entertained the idea of asking Nemo to ride along in the coach, but the brown spittle lathering the caretaker's face changed his mind. Instead, Nemo started off on foot, muttering oaths as he led the way across the Aimwell estate.

Sprawling across parts of the small villages of Rosemont and Villanova, Aimwell Acres touched Radnor, another nascent Philadelphia suburb, on its western border. There, a row of blue spruce similar to the one the carriage had just passed separated the estate from a thoroughbred farm. Designed in the manner of an eighteenth-century country estate, Aimwell Acres was filled with an impressive array of neoclassical statues, flower gardens, and maze-like hedge arrangements.

As he led the others, Nemo continued to talk to himself, and Nathan and Ralphie were both glad that Allison could not hear him, because the grizzled little man had a creative genius for vulgarity. Nathan thought he could place the accent somewhere in the middle of the New Jersey pine barrens.

It took ten minutes to get to the imposing Aimwell mansion, which, as Blakeley had expected, was a perfect example of stately and symmetrical Georgian architecture with white stone cornices and Ionic pillars. There was even a fountain in the middle of the drive.

In front of the mansion, her arms akimbo and foot tapping impatiently, waited Nemo's wife. She was slightly taller and considerably wider than her husband, and when she spoke she showed even fewer teeth in front.

"Where ya bin, Nemo?" she demanded, scowling fiercely. "And who the hell're they?"

"Shut up 'n get me my shotgun, Theophilia."

"Don't get bossy with me, you old sore," the crone said. She pointed at a pile of leaves about 50 yards away. "I bin askin' you to burn that heap since last fall. If it ain't burnt by suppertime, you'll be sleepin' on it rest a the summer."

Nemo went off, still muttering to himself. Blakeley got out of the cab and helped Allison down.

"Yiz'll have to excuse Mr. Hooper," said the crone. "He's touchier than usual today. All that commotion last night has his old nerves on edge. And who're you?"

"I'm Dr. Ian Blakeley."

"Kinda late fer a doctor," Theophilia said with her toothless, sarcastic grin.

"Yes," Blakeley said. "I know. These are my associates. We're investigating Mr. Aimwell's murder."

"Ain't everybody? Ain't seen so many cops since the last time the mister drug me to an Irish wake."

"Did you see it happen?" Blakeley asked.

"Nope," Theophilia said, shaking her head deliberately. "Jist him comin' home last night 'n that terrible mess this mornin'."

"What time did he come home?" Blakeley asked.

"Oh, late. Midnight or so, musta bin. Me 'n Nemo was sleepin' when young mister Aimwell's carriage come past the window 'n woke me up. The window's open cuz a the heat,'n the carriage sounds like a goddamn locomotive on that brick road. Ol' Nemo can sleep through anything, but not me."

Blakeley jotted a note in his pad and said, "Was it unusual for Mr. Aimwell to come home at that hour?"

"Master Aimwell?" she cackled. "Hell, no. He had the run a the place since his folks went off to Provincetown for the summer 'n that wild sister a his decided to stay in town with her artist friends. He'd come 'n go as he pleased." She frowned suddenly. "Well, what the hell am I tellin' you all that for? That goofy lookin' cop who's bin hangin' around can tell you the same thing. I got work to do."

After she walked away, Blakeley and the others followed the walk that led from the cherubim-laden fountain in the circle up to the handsome edifice. A local constable stood at the door and he recognized Blakeley whose face had been in the newspapers more often of late than the good doctor thought seemly. The constable directed them up the stairs and told them to take the hallway to the left. The bedroom was around the corner. When he saw Allison going along, the constable said, "You sure you want to go in there, miss?"

"I have a strong stomach," she said.

"I sure hope so, miss."

On the way to the crime scene, the foursome came across what seemed to be scores of constables and sheriff's deputies at every turn—an obvious testimony to the social prominence of the victim. Before they entered the bedroom, Blakeley took Allison aside and repeated the constable's warning. "This will probably exceed your worst nightmares, Miss Meredith."

"Dr. Blakeley," she replied, unfazed, "my worst nightmares deal with some other writer getting to a good story before I do. And this looks very good."

He traded helpless looks with Nathan and Ralphie and said, "As you wish, Miss Meredith.

The sheriff of Delaware County, under whose jurisdiction the crime had been committed, greeted them at the bedroom door, beyond which lay the victim. He closed the door in haste when he saw Allison. A burly, graying, fatherly looking man with a drooping mustache and big hands, he was obviously very unhappy to see Allison there. "You don't really want to—"

"Yes, Sheriff, I do," she said rather testily.

"I don't know," he said, then dropped his eyes to the floor.

Blakeley noticed at once the strange coppery scent of blood that seeped through a tiny crack under the bedroom door.

"Please," Allison said, her voice less forceful, "do not patronize me, Sheriff. I'm not a feeble woman who has to carry smelling salts."

Suddenly the door swung open and a man from the county coroner's office stepped out. "All yours," he said to the sheriff and left without ceremony. It had been his job simply to pronounce the victim dead.

Allison looked into the bedroom and said, "Good Lord!" She covered her mouth with her hand.

Blakeley was the first to enter the room. Like Nathan, he held a handkerchief over his mouth and nose. Ralphie started to enter, but stopped when he noticed Allison turning white and going limp. Without a second thought, he helped her to a nearby stool.

"I gather nobody exaggerated," Nathan said, coughing.

"I'm afraid not," Blakeley agreed.

They glanced around the room. It was spacious and relatively uncluttered, in vivid contrast to the cramped, busy fashion of the day. Reginald Aimwell's family had excellent taste. Neither he nor they would have approved of the mess left behind by his murderer. As Blakeley approached the four-poster bed and studied the body, he could not help wondering how one person could have possibly caused so much destruction. It seemed that any object that had not been anchored down had been strewn about as if caught in a whirlwind.

To Blakeley and Nathan's regret, there was no wind at that moment—not even a zephyr—nothing to weaken the pervasive odor of death as they examined the room.

Blood was everywhere. From the wall, a figure in a Gainsborough original peered down at the carnage, its canvas and gilded frame stippled with blood. Blood soaked the feathers that spilled out of the gaping hole in the mattress under the stiffening body of Reginald Aimwell. It soaked the Persian rug and caked the shiny maple floor.

The newcomers could sense the violence still contained within the four walls. If they hadn't known differently, they might have thought they had stumbled upon the site of a desperate battle fought between two great armies, only all the pain and horror had been inflicted on the loser and the winner had departed without a hint of human regret.

"Look at these gashes on the floor," Nathan said. He squatted carefully at the bedside, hoping to avoid getting blood on his clothing.

Blakeley stepped gingerly around a big, damp maroon spot and studied the long deep marks gouged out of the floor near the bed. Then Nathan and he examined Reginald Aimwell.

The dead man's hair was parted neatly in the middle and slicked back with pomade. His black handlebar mustaches were carefully trimmed, his teeth clean, his eyes pale blue. But his skin was white as chalk, and dried blood made ugly little cobwebs on both sides of his mouth. Although Aimwell's face might have been attractive and agreeable when he was living, it was marred in death by a look of paralyzed terror that was quickly becoming all too familiar to Blakeley and Nathan. Aimwell had only been clothed in a dark blue velveteen robe when somebody had savaged his torso and lower body. The robe was black where it had soaked up pints of blood.

When he could no longer stomach examining the corpse, Nathan readily conceded that bodies were Blakeley's province and returned his attention to the gashes on the floor. He ran his index finger across one of the marks and estimated its depth at about a half inch.

"Somebody could have done this with a metallic instrument," he said. "A rake perhaps. If the attacker was in an uncontrollable rage."

"See if you can find some chips or shavings amid the papers and other things," Blakeley said.

"Hey, Dad!" Ralphie said from the hallway. "I have a theory about all this. Do you want to hear it?"

"In a minute, Ralph." Blakeley took a comb from his vest pocket and knelt beside Nathan to run it through a dried stain he'd noticed on the Persian rug. "You know, Nathan," he said, his voice muffled under the handkerchief he held over his mouth, "with all the papers and such strewn about, just as they were on the Hazleton yacht, one is tempted to think the murderer was looking for something."

"You mean something that would link somebody

to Reginald Aimwell's way of life?"

Blakeley asked, "Are you sure he had that in common with Louis Paul Hazleton?"

"Well, everything else looks the same, doesn't it? The mess, the method. Guess I'll have to pay another visit to Oscar at The Rod and Gun Club," Nathan said and groaned.

"If you do happen to find anyone who looks like an especially promising suspect, please do not try to bring him in yourself, Nathan. From the looks of things, he has the strength of a tiger or a bear."

"Or a werewolf," Ralphie said as he stepped cautiously into the room. He too held a handkerchief over his mouth and nose.

"You're a big help, Beef," Nathan said, looking up.

"Jeez crumps, Nathan. You don't know everything."

"Be careful where you step, Ralph," Blakeley directed. He was running a comb through the nap of the rug where it had been shredded by the attacker. "How is Miss Meredith faring?"

"Woozy, Dad, but she'll be all right. Mostly she'll be mad as heck when she finds out she fainted."

In the hallway, the sheriff was kneeling beside the stool and waving a small vial of smelling salts under Allison's nose. The vial looked ridiculously small in his hands. He had found it on a dresser in the master bedroom and sniffed it when the sights and smells had threatened to get to him. Allison was grimacing through her fog and trying to wave it all away. When she muttered, "Please don't tell Nathan," the sheriff assured her that he wouldn't even though he had no idea who Nathan was. He ceased his ministration only when Blakeley called to him from within the bedroom.

"Who discovered the murder, Sheriff?" Blakeley asked as he studied rug fibers under a magnifying glass that he carried in his coat pocket.

"A cop's been hanging around here for some time," the sheriff said from the doorway. "Says he heard some noises and went in to investigate."

"Was he Mr. Aimwell's bodyguard, Sheriff?"

"Beats me, Dr. Blakeley. He said he wouldn't say nothin' until you or officer McBride got here."

"What's his name?" Blakeley asked.

"Wouldn't give us that either. He's down in the kitchen eating his second breakfast. Or his first lunch."

Blakeley looked at Ralphie. "Please bring him to me."

"Right away, Dad," Ralphie said, leaving. "You'll remember what I said about a werewolf, all right?"

"I certainly shall, Ralph."

Ralphie paused along the way to check on Allison, who was now sitting up and shaking her head. "Must be the prettiest punch-drunk fighter you ever saw, huh, Sheriff?" he said, then blushed when he realized Allison had heard him.

Trying to conceal his embarrassment, Ralphie asked a constable stationed at the head of the stairs where the mysterious policeman could be found. He directed Ralphie downstairs to the kitchen, and Ralphie hurried away.

Back in the blood-strewn bedroom, Blakeley and Nathan both shook their heads at Ralphie's theory as to the killer's identity.

"I think he really means it," Nathan said.

"It must be poor Don Orlando's fault. Nowadays he keeps to himself and speaks mostly to Ralphie. He's fired up the boy's imagination. The more outlandish the stories, the more Ralph seems to like them. It was one thing when he simply told of what he'd actually seen in his travels, but now he's going on about mythological beasts and other drivel. He's even inspired Ralphie to read a book. Some nonsense a Frenchman wrote about a thing called the *loup garou* that terrorized Paris twenty years ago. I tried to explain that such things are the manifestations of psychotic disorders, but naturally Ralphie would have none of that. It's not as much fun as goblins and ghouls, I suppose. Would to heaven he'd read his university assignments with the same intensity."

At the sound of Blakeley and Nathan's voices, Allison blinked away her cobwebs and said to the sheriff, "I'd like to get up now. Would you mind helping me? My legs are a little wobbly."

"Sure," the sheriff said, "but you aren't thinking of going in there again, are you, miss?"

"I never quite got in there the first time," she said with a nervous smile.

"I wouldn't advise it, miss. We're out of smelling salts."

"When the horse throws you, you get right back on the horse. Am I correct, Sheriff? Besides, I was taken by surprise last time."

The sheriff got up and helped her off the stool. When she was up she felt much better.

"Are you coming with me?" she asked.

The sheriff shook his head. "I think I'll pass, miss."

Allison approached the doorway resolutely, took a handkerchief from her sleeve, and covered her nose and mouth.

Blakeley held his magnifying glass up to Nathan. "It isn't exactly a *loup garou*," he said as Nathan peered through the lens, "but the family does own a Tibetan mastiff. See the hairs, Nathan?"

"You're not going to blame this on a big fluffy dog, are you?" Allison asked, her bravest face mostly hidden under the handkerchief.

The two men looked up when she spoke, both clearly pleased to see her on her feet and alert. Blakeley lowered his magnifying glass and his handkerchief long enough to let her know he was smiling appreciatively. He had always admired Allison's spirit.

Allison Meredith wasn't her real name. Her real name was Margaret Mary McInally, Maggie to family and friends when she was growing up in Fishtown on the Back Channel. The more genteel Anglicized Allison Meredith came years later when she was trying to get the editors at *Harper's* and *The Atlantic Monthly* to take her seriously. In those days she had even tried using men's names to get in the door.

Nathan would have liked her best as Maggie, had he known her in the early days, but they had grown up in different, if equally rough, parts of town. She'd been Allison since he met her. Allison, who transcended the world's vulgarity. Allison, an ode, a symphony, a Mona Lisa. Allison, who lived on a pedestal of his making.

He thought he detected the sweet smell of gardenias as she came into the room. It floated temporarily over the pungent stench of death. She must have laced her handkerchief with the scent.

"I can't say you didn't warn me, Dr. Blakeley," she said. "Next time I'll pay closer attention."

"I was just showing these fibers to Nathan," Blakeley said. "You see, there was a Tibetan mastiff in the family during my childhood. It belonged to my cousin Nigel and it was called Confucius. It was Confucius's fur that I first studied under the microscope that my Uncle Derek gave me as a Christmas present. That and some fibers from my cousin Antonia's cat Terpsichore."

As Blakeley discoursed on his childhood, Nathan looked into Allison's eyes. When he saw them floating up so that he could see little but the whites, he rushed to her rescue. "Do you think we've seen all we have to see here?" he asked.

As he drew Allison from the room, he again caught the sweet smell of gardenias that wafted off her handkerchief, and hundreds of memories flooded his mind. He was pleasantly surprised when, rather than protesting his assistance, Allison gave him a shy, but grateful, glance.

"I believe we have seen enough," Blakeley said, taking a final, cursory glance around the room. "This is not the best place to discuss cats and dogs anyway."

Hardly had they stepped into the hall than Ralphie came running up the stairs, two at a time. He was out of breath and laughing.

"Hey, Dad, you'll never guess who I found in the kitchen!" he said as he halted before the others. "Now I know what Mrs. Hooper meant when she mentioned a goofy looking cop!"

"Ralph," Blakeley said, "you seem to have forgotten that this is a murder scene, not a place of jollity."

Ralphie ignored the complaint and pointed toward a gangly figure that plodded down the hallway with an unmistakable manure-dodging gait while chewing on a leg of mutton.

"Officer Fatzinger?" Blakeley asked. "Is that you?"

Dressed for plainclothes duty, Fatzinger wore his best Sunday suit: a big bow tie, a candy-striped jacket, and plaid trousers that rose high up his leg. When he saw Fatzinger, Nathan remembered that Lt. Hudson had often said Fatzinger looked like the end man in a minstrel show.

"Bones," Nathan said, "what're you doing here? And why haven't you reported in to the precinct house?"

"Line a der duty, Sarge," Fatzinger replied, picking some meat out of his teeth. "Hello, Dr. Blakeley," he said and burped; then when he saw Allison, he added, "Sorry, miss."

"You know him?" the sheriff asked.

Nathan nodded. "You were supposed to be following Richard Petticord, weren't you?"

"Und dott's chust vott I did, Sarge," Fatzinger said proudly. "You wanna see him? Down in der roodt cellar mit da rest of der sausages I locked him up."

"Petticord?" Blakeley said. "He's here?"

"Who's Petticord?" the sheriff asked.

"Under the circumstances," Blakeley said, "I'd say he's a suspect."

"A suspect?" The sheriff scowled at Fatzinger. "And you kept him hidden?"

"Vell, I tink so," Fatzinger said. "I caught dott sow's tail myself. I vussn't gonna let nobody else take him in und get der name in der papers. You tink I'm dumb I'm shidt." He chewed the rest of the mutton off the bone, put the bone on a convenient Chippendale table, and rubbed his hands on his pants. "Vell, maybe we oughta go let him oudt before he freezes off hiss leedle bratwurst."

Noticing Allison again, he blushed briefly and gestured for everyone to follow.

He led them down the hallway and stairs, across the front room, through another hallway that led to the kitchen at the back of the house. There, a door opened to reveal a flight of wooden steps that descended into blackness.

"Does anyone have a light?" Blakeley asked.

The sheriff produced a blue-tipped match and lit it with a flick of his thumbnail. In the sudden flare, he spied a coal-oil lamp on a shelf at the top of the steps. He took it down and set the wick ablaze.

"All night oudt in der bushes keepin' an eye on der haus I vuss," Fatzinger said. "Und denn der wagon comes in after midnight mit der lady und der dead guy. He vuss laughin' und havin a good time, drinkin' schnapps probably."

"A lady?" Blakeley asked.

"Yeah," Fatzinger giggled. "Some lady."

With the aid of the lamp, he led the way through the dank storeroom, past crates of canned goods, shelves of dusty utensils, and racks of wine, until they reached a locked wooden door on the ground in a far corner.

"No wonder my men couldn't find him," the sheriff said when they stopped in front of the door.

Fatzinger laughed as he unlocked the door and lifted it up. "Der first ting youze find oudt vennever youze watch a haus iss how to find der kitchen und der roodt cellar."

The sheriff waved the coal-oil lamp into the opening of the root cellar and barked, "All right, you, c'mon outa there!"

As if returning from the dead, a figure slowly climbed out of the frigid root cellar. At first, all that appeared was a head that groped at the ladder's top rung. Then came the top of a tossled head and two frightened eyes that blinked fiercely in the dim, but stark, lamplight. Finally, as the rest of Petticord's face withdrew from the sepulchral gloom, the chattering of the teeth broke the silence that had fallen in the cellar.

"Diss here's yer lady," Fatzinger announced, taking Petticord by the scruff of the neck and forcing him to come out.

With a cry, Petticord slapped away Fatzinger's hand and slowly crawled out of the cellar, shaking with cold and fear. When he was out he fell and rolled onto the dirt floor, where he lay whimpering softly.

"My God," Allison Meredith gasped. "He's naked."

Chapter Eight

A short while later, all those who had been present in the root cellar adjourned to a lavishly furnished drawing room. Nemo and Theophilia Hooper had been summoned by Blakeley, and the moment they appeared, he launched a volley of questions at them concerning Richard Petticord.

"Not only did you not tell us about the woman," Blakeley said as he finished berating the caretaker and his wife, "but you neglected to say anything about Mr. Petticord. I'm terribly disappointed in you both."

"I'm no secret here," Petticord said, his teeth clenched. He was still naked, but seated in a Hepplewhite chair, he hid his nudity beneath a blanket that Nathan had brought from one of the mansion's many bedrooms. "I was Reginald Aimwell's personal chef."

"Oh?"

"Yes, Dr. Blakeley," Petticord said, his dark eyes

flashing defiantly. "I'm an excellent Cajun chef and Mr. Aimwell liked Cajun food. Ask anyone."

"I shall," Blakeley said, and he started to pace the room in obvious agitation.

Petticord ran nervous fingers through his dark, formerly well-groomed hair and glanced away. He then pulled the blanket closely around himself and shuddered as if he had felt a sudden chill. Since everyone had come to the drawing room, Petticord had explained, and no one had reason to disagree, that he had been totally unaware of Allison's presence in the room when he came up from the root cellar. He swore that if he had not been blinded by the harsh light of the coal-oil lamp he would not have revealed his nudity. All the same, he resented being cast naked into the cellar by Fatzinger, and when he found the door open he hadn't wanted to lose what might be his only opportunity to escape his frigid prison. He offered Allison an apology and she accepted it graciously.

Allison was seated across the room at a respectful distance from Petticord, sketching the scene and all its participants and jotting occasional notes of lines she did not want to forget. Sketching the scene of a potential story was a trick she'd taught herself in the course of her career; it had a mnemonic effect that enabled her to recreate the atmosphere rather than merely recording what had been said and done. Even though her sketches helped her write news stories with a distinctive flavor, she still relied on her notes for the main points of her articles because, naturally, there were lines she wished to quote accurately. She regretted that the inane restrictions imposed by her editors would make some of the more piquant quotations lose their edge. Without a doubt, if she were to use Nemo's description of Petticord, it would read: "[a] d—m male w—-e."

Across from Allison, by the fireplace, stood the burly sheriff, Calvin Burns. As Blakeley paced about the room, Burns smoked a pipe and rested his elbow on the mantel. He moved as little as possible so as to avoid knocking over any of the delicate figurines that filled the room. Next to him, his arms folded and face wearing a grave expression, slumped Officer Fatzinger, and a few feet away from them, Ralphie leaned against the baroque wainscoting of the archway, eating a large ham sandwich.

In another Hepplewhite chair adjacent to Petticord's, Nathan sat silently. As was his wont, he was content to let Blakeley ask the questions, but stepped in when he wanted something clarified. He looked as if he had no sentiments whatsoever concerning the present situation, but Allison knew by several barely recognizable gestures that he was amused by much of the spectacle before him.

Despite the gruesomeness of the crime committed, Allison shared some of Nathan's amusement. Once or twice she had felt a smile playing on her lips, and she had to concentrate even more as she sketched the grizzled, foul-smelling caretaker and his mean, pig-eyed old wife, who sat next to him on a Louis Quinze sofa gumming a piece of saltwater taffy.

At last, Blakeley stopped in front of the sofa and, waving an accusatory finger, said, "Explain yourself, Mrs. Hooper. Why didn't you tell us about Mr. Petticord?"

"I didn't mention the sissy boy," Theophilia said, "'cuz I fergot all about him."

Petticord huffed and crossed his legs, rearranging himself in his chair.

"Mrs. Hooper," Blakeley said curtly, "how could anyone forget him? You told us everyone was gone except—"

"I know what I told yiz," Theophilia snarled and

pointed at Petticord. "If I didn't bring him up it's on accounta poor Master Aimwell's reputation. No sense showin' that sodomite to the whole world fer God 'n everybody to laugh at, and have them all thinkin' young Aimwell was a sodomite too."

There was a pause while everyone except Allison, who was absorbed in her task, looked at Petticord as if to ask, "Well, was he?" But the suspect merely shrugged his shoulders.

Nathan groaned to himself. He had visions of making another visit to Oscar the steward at The Rod and Gun.

"Is that why you also forgot to mention the woman who came home with Mr. Aimwell?" Blakeley asked.

Theophilia reached into the back of her mouth, where some taffy had stuck to one of her few teeth. When she had dislodged the candy with her little finger, she said, "Coulda bin somebody's wife, couldn't it?"

Again Nathan glanced at Petticord, and again Petticord shrugged.

"Usta be all kinds a women comin' 'n goin'," Nemo said. "Good lookin' ones, too."

Allison looked up, then quickly returned to her sketch. She was uncomfortably aware of Nemo's eyes undressing her.

"Can you describe the woman who came home with Mr. Aimwell last night?" Blakeley asked. When a minute passed and neither the caretaker nor his wife responded, he turned directly to Nemo. "Was she also good looking, Mr. Hooper?"

"Sure as shit good lookin'."

"But weren't you asleep? Mrs. Hooper said you never woke up."

Theophilia swallowed her taffy, sucked her gums once, and said grumpily, "He was awake."

"I see."

"Wakes up every time he hears a horse 'n carriage in the middle of the night and looks out to see what kinda tart Master Aimwell—rest his soul—drug home. Old Nemo usta wake up at the sound a wagon wheels like a hog hearin' slop in the trough. He'd slaver some, then grumble out loud that fellas like Aimwell get all the berries, and here he was stuck with a damn tree fungus."

Several heads turned as laughter was stifled. Blakeley succeeded in keeping his face free of expression.

"Then you can describe the woman for us, I presume?" he asked.

"Dark hair, green dress," Theophilia said.

"Big tits," Nemo added.

"Shut up," his wife said. "Old fool."

Blakeley glanced at Petticord, who squirmed when the detective asked, "Did she have dark eyes?"

"Couldn't tell," Nemo said and cast a venal, toothless grin at Allison. "I ain't much fer eyes anyways."

"Can you tell us anything about the dress, Mrs. Hooper?" Nathan asked.

"Green, I told yiz," the crone said.

"I know, but did you notice anything on the dress, like a decoration around the top? You know, near the...."

"Bodice," Allison said, without looking up so as not to break her concentration. Her sketch of the caretaker and his wife was nearly complete.

Theophilia shook her head. "It was too dark 'n she was too far away for me to tell. These eyes ain't so young."

"Woman sees good enough when she wants to," Nemo grumbled.

"But you're sure at least that the dress was green?" Nathan asked.

132

The crone scowled. "Are you deef?"

"Green dress, sure as shit. Just like them," Nemo said and pointed a gnarled finger at three green dresses draped over the back of an unoccupied chair.

When all those gathered in the room shifted their attention to the dresses, Petticord blanched, and Allison threw off a quick sketch of his terrified face, while wondering if she could incorporate Nemo's recurrent quote in her article. Maybe her editors would accept, "Sure as s—t," if she used it only once.

When no one asked another question for a while, Theophilia stood up and said to Blakeley, "If yiz're done askin' questions, old Nemo here's got leaves to burn, and I gotta go use the privy."

"Sheriff?" Blakeley asked.

Burns started and almost dropped his pipe when Blakeley addressed him. Then he shook his head. "Nope."

As was evident from his discomfort, Sheriff Burns was out of place in the midst of all the opulence. By their mere presence, his huge uncouth hands seemed to imperil the fragile Wedgwood and delicate china figurines that were in no short supply throughout the room.

"Very well, you may go, but don't leave the premises," Blakeley said. "We may need you again."

"Where the hell're we gonna go?" Nemo asked. On his way out, he winked at Allison as she glanced up from her work. Behind him, his wife scowled at Allison, causing her to flush and drop her eyes to her pad.

When the Hoopers were gone, Petticord waved at the air and shuddered. "Dear Gawd, where do they find them?"

The sheriff carefully tapped his pipe tobacco into the fireplace and said, "I've been lookin' at you and wonderin' the same thing, Petticord."

"I told you," Petticord insisted, "I was Mr. Aimwell's personal chef!"

"I heard you, Petticord, but you also look like a darn good suspect to me. Why don't you tell us how you wound up here in the first place?"

Petticord sighed and answered the sheriff in a weary tone, as if he were speaking to a slow learner. "Mr. Aimwell became smitten by the kind of food one finds in New Orleans."

"Did you meet him there?" Blakeley asked.

"What?" Petticord snapped, annoyed by the interruption. "No, no."

"Then he wasn't there when Mr. Hazleton was?"

Petticord rolled his eyes. "I really couldn't say. All I know is he liked the food; so he must have visited New Orleans at some time, wouldn't you say? Now, may I go on, Dr. Blakeley?"

"Do."

"Thank you." Petticord sat up in the chair and tucked his legs under him. "As I've said, I am an excellent Cajun chef. I needed a job. A friend of a friend told Mr. Aimwell about me and, *voilà*, I'm hired. Does anyone want my recipe for jambalaya?" He looked around defiantly and stopped at Nathan. "How about you, McSomething?"

Nathan raised his head slowly. He had been focused on Allison, who sat cross-legged, her foot keeping time to some melody in her head. The vision before him had a mildly hypnotic effect that he found rather pleasant; so he was not pleased to be disturbed by Petticord's unwarranted jibe.

"Did Aimwell like you in green, Petticord?" Nathan asked. "Is it a popular color this year?"

"You're disgusting, McSomething," Petticord hissed.

"Can you explain the three green dresses we

found in your closet then?'' Nathan asked, ignoring Petticord's protest.

"I like green, McSomething. I look good in green.''

Allison smiled to herself. It hadn't been so long ago that Nathan, in a moment of ardor, had admitted he always liked her best in green. Memories of time spent with Nathan rushed through her mind and made her sigh wistfully.

Despite the present discord in their relationship, she was fond of Nathan. But his hesitation to commit himself to her had gone on long enough. If he wouldn't pledge his love on his own, Allison had decided upon returning from Cuba, she would have to help him along. And her flirtation with Pratt seemed to be making Nathan jealous enough to act. If his behavior in the coach, when she had not quite accidentally landed in his grasp, didn't prove his increasing boldness, his actions down in the dark cellar had. For, several times when the lambent light was failing, Nathan had grasped her familiarly, under the guise of aiding her through the darkness. But the gentleness of his touch told Allison otherwise. Still smiling, but now at the apparent success of her strategy, Allison placed her sketch in a folder and rested her pad on her knee.

"Dis here's yer lady in green,'' Fatzinger declared. "A lady in green mit der chin whiskers.''

"Stop trying to crucify me!'' Petticord shouted. His face turned quickly from its drab off-white to a deep maroon, and his body was seized by convulsive sobs.

Uncomfortable looks were exchanged around the room. Despite Petticord's behavior, Allison felt sorry for him. She knew that Nathan and Blakeley felt the same way, but in their official capacity, they couldn't show their sympathy—not while the suspect might be on the verge of blurting out something they had to know.

"Mr. Petticord," Blakeley said, placing a comforting hand on the other man's shoulder. "Please dismiss from your mind the notion that we're here to pass judgment on your way of life. Frankly, I've no time to ponder its negatives or positives, nor do I especially care to. And if I may speak for Sgt. McBride, neither does he."

That much having been said, Blakeley's tone became forceful and deliberate. "It happens, however, Mr. Petticord, that you keep finding your way into our investigation of these two very ugly murders. Make no mistake about it, Mr. Petticord, you are a suspect. What else can we make of a man who was once found passed out on the gutted corpse of his erstwhile lover, and who has now been discovered, by an officer of the law, naked and hysterical in the bedroom of another victim?"

"Dott's how I found der chicken's pizzle," Fatzinger said. "Yellin' at der dead guy mitoudt der clothes on."

"Can you explain that, Mr. Petticord?" Blakeley asked. "You'll agree, I presume, that it's rather peculiar behavior."

Petticord stared ahead for a long time. Finally, when he was composed enough to speak, he nodded his head.

"I was asleep in my quarters," he said. "Sound asleep. My accommodations are on the same floor as Mr. Aimwell's bedroom, as you know. But it wasn't for the reasons you might have suspected. He used to rap on my door as he passed to let me know he had company, and so I should prepare his breakfast for two. He was slick about it, just a tap-ta-tap like that. I doubt if his companions ever even realized he'd done it. I'd awaken for a second or two then fall off to sleep again. I was used to it because more often than not he'd have company. He was quite the lothario. He used to enjoy a hearty breakfast precisely at nine, no matter how late he'd caroused. Worked up an appetite in bed, I presume."

Petticord gave a faint smile. "Mr. Aimwell was fond of grilled trout and fruit compote with pecan rolls—especially the rolls. So I'd get up early, sometimes before dawn, to bake them. I'd serve him and his companion breakfast in bed. I suppose you might say he regarded me as his eunuch, someone who could get close to his women with impunity."

Petticord cleared his throat. Then with another faint smile, he said, "I learned that there were only two kinds of women in Mr. Aimwell's life: those who hid their identities under the covers and those who didn't give a fig who saw them." His expression abruptly became haughty and smug, as if he were about to offer information that would prove, beyond a shadow of a doubt, that he was falsely suspected. "You'd be surprised whom I'd find. The *stories* I could tell. But if I named names now, none of you would believe me. Actresses, of course, and similar trollops, but heiresses and debutantes also, several of them well-known in the neighborhood. I even saw the wife of a prominent senator. I don't want to give anything away, but she's blond with brown eyes and favors—"

"Mr. Petticord, please get to the point," Blakeley said. "None of us is even remotely interested in your gossip."

But there was a silence brought on by perverse curiosity, and Petticord noted with triumph that Blakeley was speaking only for himself. Even Sheriff Burns had set aside his pipe in anticipation of the salacious gossip to come.

"You can all read about it when I write my book," Petticord said and unfurled his legs, careful to keep himself appropriately wrapped.

"Mr. Petticord, about last night, if you please."

Petticord looked at Fatzinger, who blushed when Petticord announced, "I sleep in the buff. *Au naturel.* It's not uncommon in the New Orleans heat, especially on sultry summer evenings, no matter what the old biddies may tell you. I had a hard time falling asleep last night, but when I did, I was dead to the world. I vaguely recall hearing the horse and carriage on the road and remember the tap-ta-tap sometime thereafter. So I knew Mr. Aimwell had a friend, but I couldn't tell you if she wore green or red or whether she was also *au naturel.* All I know is that I went back to sleep, but was awakened later by a terrible gust of wind. I thought I was in a hurricane for a moment."

"I heard dott too," Fatzinger said, looking bewildered, "und I thought it vuss gonna rain."

Nathan and Blakeley shared Fatzinger's perplexity. They remembered the pervious night as being stagnant, as still as death.

"I didn't hear no wind," the sheriff said. "It was so hot and sticky I didn't sleep a wink all night. I was awake when they came to tell me about the Aimwell boy's death."

"May I continue, Dr. Blakeley?" Petticord asked. "It isn't easy to talk about last night. I have to keep going, or I may become sick before I finish."

"Please."

"When I heard the wind, I got under the covers," Petticord said, as engrossed in telling his story as the others were in listening to it. "I expected a sudden chill, but I felt nothing. It was just as hot and stuffy and oppessive as before. There wasn't a hint of a breeze, just the sound of wind and then . . . then a terrible, piercing cry. It was so long and so shrill that at first I didn't even think it could come from a man. But it was a man. It was Mr. Aimwell."

"I heard dott too," Fatzinger said.

"You've no idea how frightened I was. The

screams were ungodly. I thought perhaps Mr. Aimwell's bed had caught fire, because he had a terrible
habit of falling asleep with his cigar burning. I
didn't waste a minute. I got out of bed and rushed
to the door. I snatched my robe from the bed-post
as I went. I threw it on, but the pocket of the damn
thing got caught on the doorknob. Instead of pausing to extricate it, I simply tore it off and ran to
poor Mr. Aimwell's bedchamber. And...."

Petticord was in a cold sweat. His body cast off
a sour odor as he struggled to finish the tale. "And
when I entered his room, I saw him." Petticord's
voice started to trail off, and what he said next
seemed more like a question he was asking himself
than a statement of horrible fact. "I think he was
still alive for a second or two. He'd long since ceased
to cry out but...he seemed to recognize me. His
mouth moved once before he expired."

Petticord turned to Blakeley, his pupils distended
like those of an opium fiend. "No wonder I
screamed. No wonder I was hysterical when that
cop found me. My God! Who wouldn't have been?"

He gripped himself like a child with a stomachache and rocked back and forth in his chair.

"Mr. Petticord," Blakeley said softly, but ur-
gently, "what do you think he was saying?"

When Petticord made no response, Blakeley persisted. "Mr. Petticord."

"What?" Petticord snapped. He suddenly remembered the question. "I don't know."

"Try, Mr. Petticord," Blakeley said. "It could be
vitally important. Was it your name?"

Petticord was annoyed by the intrusion. He
wanted to retreat into another state of mind in
which he would be free from the police and questions and memories of gutted bodies and the terrible stench of death.

"Reginald Aimwell III didn't even know my

name," he said. "I was Cook to him. That's all."

"What then could he have said?"

"I don't know!" Petticord covered his ears and folded up, hugging himself, rocking more deliberately. "Stop torturing me."

Sheriff Burns had had enough. "Let's go, Petticord. We have a nice clean cell and some brand new jailhouse clothes waiting for you."

Blakeley signaled for the sheriff to give him another minute. It was possible that Petticord was merely playacting. It was also possible, indeed very likely, that Petticord was answering their questions to the fullest extent of his knowledge. But because of the ghastly crimes Petticord had recently witnessed, it was possible that the symptoms Blakeley was observing were those of a man whose credibility would soon be forever destroyed as his mind slipped into irreversible madness. He had to get what he could out of Petticord while he had the chance.

"Mr. Petticord," he said gently, "if you will answer just this one question for me. I promise I shan't ask another thing of you until you've had a chance to rest."

Petticord stopped rocking and slowly met Blakeley's gaze. When Blakeley saw Petticord's eyes, he became convinced that the suspect was on the verge of insanity, perhaps only for a while, perhaps forever.

Blakeley repeated his question. "Mr. Petticord, what do you think Reginald Aimwell was saying just before he died?"

Petticord blinked his eyes and thought. "He might have trying to say, 'Why? Why is this happening?' I think that's what it was. His mouth was forming a w. Yes, that's what I believe he was saying. 'Why?'"

Petticord's voice trailed off. He fixed his eyes on

something no one else in the room could see and resumed his rocking.

The room fell silent again. Ralphie, who had been so fascinated by the story that his ham sandwich was still unfinished, spoke up for the first time. "Werewolf," he said.

"Eh?" Blakeley asked, surprised by his son's voice.

"Oh, c'mon, Beef," Nathan said wearily.

The sheriff looked at Ralphie. "What the hell's a werewolf?"

Blakeley closed his eyes until the temptation to roar an ungentlemanly curse in Allison's presence had passed.

Ralphie knew what was going through his father's mind, and he quickly assuaged Blakeley's rising ire. "Look, Dad, Aimwell's last word could've been why, but it also could have been werewolf. Jeez crumps, they both start with a w, don't they?"

The sheriff crossed to Petticord. "I gotta lock you up, Mr. Petticord. You're just too good a suspect to let loose," he said, taking the distraught man by the arm and helping him out of the chair. Burns turned to Fatzinger, who was hovering anxiously before him. "Don't worry, I'll make sure Lt. Hudson knows you made the collar."

Fatzinger beamed at the sheriff's assurance.

"We'll be in touch, Mr. Petticord," Blakeley said as the sheriff led the suspect out of the room. "Chin up. We may find evidence to release you."

The sheriff nodded to everyone as he left. Petticord floated past the others and under the baroque archway like a zombie. His mind was already heading toward a place where the morning sun was a candy apple and the clouds were made of cotton candy.

"What do you think, Dr. Blakeley?" Nathan asked.

"Frankly, I don't know what to think. Petticord's story is quite bizarre, but so is everything else about these murders."

"Vell," Fatzinger said, threatened by the sudden idea that he would lose all the glory for capturing a savage murderer, "name fer me a better suspect."

When neither Blakeley nor Nathan answered, Fatzinger straightened his big bow tie and practiced the heroic look he would assume when the newspaper photographers took his picture. He already envisioned the front-page picture and article about Officer Wilmer P. Fatzinger, the scourge of criminals everywhere. People would read about him from Philadelphia to Ebenezersville, and his girlfriend Strawberry Knockleknorr would have to be extra nice to him because a hero could have any girl he chose. His fantasy so overwhelmed him that Fatzinger actually forgot it was lunchtime.

Chapter Nine

Blakeley, Allison, and Ralphie departed Aimwell Acres gratefully, pausing only to sniff some red and white roses in a garden. Behind them, on the rise where Nemo was burning leaves, a puff of blue smoke obscured the horizon and gave the stately mansion an appropriately sinister look. Instead of making one of their number, Nathan elected to accompany Fatzinger back to the precinct house. He had no doubt Fatzinger would have a hard time convincing the other policemen that he had succeeded in capturing a suspected murderer.

It was early afternoon by the time Blakeley and the others approached the entrance to his estate. The sun was hot, even though it was hidden by a yellowish-gray sky, but the breeze drifting across the open cab of the landau helped to elevate Blakeley's formerly downcast spirits somewhat. Gone was the rank odor of blood that had lingered in his nostrils and clung to his clothing, but he shared a desire voiced by Allison to soak in a tub of hot soapy water. And he dearly wished Ralphie would stop yelling like a cockney hansom driver and slow down to a speed more suited to the country roads along which they traveled. Every time he tried to reprimand his son, however, his words were lost in the clatter of the wooden wheels.

"So what do we have so far, Miss Meredith?" he asked as Ralphie steered their carriage up the drive with his customary disregard for the comfort of his passengers. "A woman in green who has dark hair and dark eyes and looks to many observers like someone of easy virtue. Rather a paltry set of data for hours of investigation."

"I gather you don't believe that she and Richard Petticord are one and the same," Allison said.

"No," he said, "I don't."

"Neither do I."

"But I've been authorized to see to this matter only within the confines of Philadelphia," Blakeley said ruefully. "Neither the commissioner nor I can extend our jurisdiction beyond the county lines. Besides, I can readily understand Sheriff Burns's reasons for locking Petticord up. The evidence may be circumstantial, but it's better than some that I've seen put men on the gallows."

Allison thought about the situation a moment. For most of the ride, she'd been quietly sucking in air, risking sunburn and freckles to rid herself of all queasiness. Long forgotten was the discomfort she had suffered going to Aimwell Acres. Now, bursting with story ideas, her mind hurtled along at a speed far faster than Ralphie would ever drive.

"May I go over this briefly, Dr. Blakeley?" she asked. "Just in case I missed something? I was foggy for a while there, and I want to have accurate details for my story."

"Of course, Miss Meredith. It might be useful to me, too."

She opened her note pad and thumbed through it. "There were no witnesses to either murder?"

"No. Unless of course you mean the woman in green."

"Same manner of death?"

Blakeley nodded. "Identical."

"The cause of death was shock?"

Blakeley grimaced. A pathologist's conclusion that a victim had died of shock was often a matter of wishful thinking, as when he would tell the survivors of some poor soul who had died in a fire that their lost loved one had died from inhaling too much smoke, not roasting to death. Certainly it was reasonable to presume that Hazleton and Aimwell had suffered a quick and massive physiological response to the attacks. Death could have come from a loss of blood pressure. It could have—but did it?

"Is the precise cause of death of great importance to your story, Miss Meredith?" he asked.

"I don't think so, but may I bring it up later?"

"If necessary."

She went on. "Both victims were found lying on their backs, their bodies torn by some very sharp instrument."

"Yes."

"But no weapon has been found?"

"That is correct," Blakeley said. "Nathan and I considered a grappling hook. However, Nathan has informed me that the only local chap who made a habit of using it on enemies was a merchant sailor named Nino Spagnol, and he died a year ago in a dockside brawl in Liverpool. My friends at Scotland Yard confirmed his death by cable yesterday."

"That doesn't mean that there couldn't be another mean-tempered sailor on the loose," Allison suggested.

"True," Blakeley agreed. "But Nathan's friends in the waterfront precinct have been all over the dives and flophouses. They've questioned at least a hundred dangerous characters down there, and they've found no connection whatsoever to Hazleton at least. Of course, we shall have to do the same for Aimwell, but frankly, I've pretty much dismissed the thought of a grappling hook."

"And you haven't considered any other weapons?"

"None seriously, Miss Meredith. There are not many weapons one can carry that could do so much damage in so little time. Remember, Mr. Petticord and Officer Fatzinger found Mr. Aimwell's body only minutes after hearing the disturbance." Blakeley grunted and shook his head. "What I find most aggravating is not the absence of a weapon. It's the absence of any evidence to speak of."

Allison checked off several items in her note pad. "No witnesses, no weapon, no evidence. What about motive?"

Blakeley considered her question. It was too soon to bring up Christopher Beecham, though Allison, like every other literate person in Philadelphia, was well aware of his escape. Ever since the local press had learned of Beecham's escape, the newspapers, especially the yellower ones, had announced it with screaming headlines, reveling in the opportunity to rehash the sordidness of Beecham's crime as well as taunting Blakeley and Governor Stone. The cartoonists were having a grand time with Blakeley's monocle, Vandyke, and more than ample girth. But the news had brought no joy to his wife and daughter, both of whom were convinced Beecham was at that very moment awaiting an opportunity to kill his enemy. Sooner or later Blakeley would tell Allison about his suspicions, but for now Beecham's possible connection to the Hazleton and Aimwell murders was flimsy, and the less the madman was mentioned the happier Sophia and Rosie would be.

So he smiled and said, "Motive? You tell me, Miss Meredith."

"I've thought about a few things," Allison said and referred to her notes. "Both victims led rather hazardous romantic lives. Wouldn't you agree?"

"Most certainly."

"In both cases the scene of the crime was a mess, as if someone had ransacked them in search of something."

"Something incriminating," he said.

"Yes."

"We thought of that. Billets-doux or the like."

"Yes," Allison said, encouraged. "If what Richard Petticord says is the truth, there must be quite a few people around Philadelphia with something to hide."

"But Miss Meredith," Blakeley said, searching for an adequate term that would not seem condescending, "if Mr. Petticord is telling the truth, Mr. Hazleton and Mr. Aimwell practiced different romantic styles."

Allison blushed slightly. "Dr. Blakeley," she said, trying not to appear to belittle her friend's overly delicate choice of words, "we are both no doubt aware that these are sophisticated times. Witness the eclectic romantic styles of the decadent poets."

"Eclectic," Blakeley thought. "That's a nice word for it. Decadent indeed."

"Which leads us back to poor Petticord, doesn't it?" he said, smiling because he appreciated Allison's blushing regard for propriety. "And to the mysterious woman in green."

Allison returned her note pad to her purse. "It's all so frustrating,"

"It certainly is."

In the driver's seat, Ralphie whooped and urged

the beleaguered Hecuba to hurry, as if they were not merely on a carriage driving up to his home, but were in reality on a stagecoach racing into Tombstone with a band of warring Apache close behind. Not slowing a bit, Ralphie circled the fountain in front of Blakeley's house.

The fountain was by no means as ornate as the fountain that adorned the front of Aimwell Acres. No vomiting gargoyles or urinating cherubim were in evidence, just a large stone flowerpot from which water gushed with a gentle, calming babble. The water spilled out of the stone pot into a circular pool, where Rosie had been caught swimming recently on a hot night. The spectacle had created quite the tempest in a teapot. Rosie was by no means improperly dressed; it seemed to Blakeley wondrous in fact that someone could remain afloat in such a silly, cumbersome costume. All the swimsuit allowed was a glimpse of calves and forearms, which Mrs. Snopkowski had thought far too much. And so, instead of attracting Nathan's attention with her splashing about, Rosie had only received a loud, angry, puritanical tirade from Mrs. Snopkowski and had once again given her mother quiet fits.

When he drew abreast the house, Ralphie yanked on Hecuba's reins and shouted, "Whoa thar, yuh cussed varmint!" Hecuba skidded slightly on the stone pavement, and the carriage halted abruptly.

Blakeley gritted his teeth as he was thrown violently back in his seat. He helped Allison back to her seat, because she had once again been thrown askew by Ralphie's driving, then he turned to vent his anger. But Allison stopped him.

"What about the wind?" she asked.

"Eh?"

"The wind that Petticord and Officer Fatzinger

both mentioned," she said. "I'd forgotten all about that."

"Yes," he thought. "What about the wind?"

"Do you think it was in their minds, Dr. Blakeley?"

"Good point, Miss Meredith. Surely, Petticord could have dreamt it," Blakeley mused, "but Officer Fatzinger too?"

"Officer Fatzinger could have been sleeping, too," Allison said, "awakened only by the screams. He, too, could have dreamt of a wind."

Blakeley nodded, as he rose. There was the incredible mess of papers and other lightweight items strewn about both murder scenes. A strong, sudden gust of wind could explain that. But it had been such a stagnant night that a strong breeze seemed as improbable as Petticord and Fatzinger sharing a *folie à deux*.

"Officer Fatzinger will undoubtedly protest our insinuations," he said, opening the door of the cab. "Nevertheless, I shall question him about it."

Allison thanked him and went off to her quarters to write a rough draft about what she'd seen and heard that morning. Then she intended to soak in a tub of gardenia-scented water for at least a half hour before dressing for a Wagner concert she was attending that evening with Nathan and the Blakeleys.

Ralphie drove the carriage around to the stables, where he let the grooms take care of the horse. Then he bounded off for another large sandwich, a session with his barbells, and a rendezvous with Dumpling, the agreeable maid.

Inside the house, the strains of Brahms came from the drawing room, where Sophia was relaxing after an arduous morning in her studio. Although it was one of her greatest joys, painting exhausted her. But playing the piano, which she did with remarkable ease, had the same effect on Sophia that golf or fishing had on a pressured businessman. Painting was a passion; the piano—despite the fact that some had called Sophia an accomplished pianist—remained a therapy.

If the truth were told, the current uproar in her daily routine kept Sophia in constant need of therapeutic diversions. Don Orlando's whims and moods and ill health had set her on edge since the first day he had arrived in Philadelphia. And the longer he stayed under her husband's aegis, the more Sophia felt responsible for his well-being. Despite her efforts to make her guest comfortable, his ever-diminishing health was, in Sophia's eyes, an indictment of her abilities as a hostess.

Aside from her guest, her own daughter concerned Sophia greatly. She had always been leery of her husband's overly liberal ideas on raising children, and their abysmal academic performances proved beyond a shadow of a doubt that discipline was wanting. Nevertheless, Rosie had always held a special place in her mother's heart. So when Sophia spied the first bloom of Rosie's youth, she was determined to capture her daughter's beauty on canvas. After discovering Rosie's sleight of hand with the wine on the evening Don Orlando lost his composure, her passion to record her daughter's departure from childhood cooled. At present, she was firmly convinced that Rosie was a changeling, and no child of her own.

But what upset Sophia the most—in fact, terrified her—was the news of Christopher Beecham's escape. The newspaper accounts had shocked her, and her anger with her husband and Nathan for withholding their knowledge precipitated a scene far more vitriolic than Don Orlando's attack on Pratt. None of their soothing or cajoling could assuage her ire or her fear of what heinous crime the madman might perpetrate against her loved ones. Blakeley's assurances that Beecham meant harm to no one save himself did little to allay Sophia's fears. Rather, every time he went anywhere, she was afraid she would never see him again. But she forbore to maintain a calm facade for the sake of her children, who were also understandably upset upon learning that Beecham was at large.

And so, that hot late spring day, Sophia had abandoned her paints, distracted as she was by all her cares, and retreated to the drawing room. Without removing her well-stained smock, she hastened to the grand piano, paying no attention to the daily skirmishes between Victor and Mrs. Snopkowski and the household staff. Seated in the sun-drenched room, she ignored everything around her—the sheer curtains suspended on a slight breeze; Thomas Aquinas as he padded across the plush divan and armchairs, shedding a trail of hair; the little Welsh maid who had earlier dusted the tables and overloaded bookcases; even Victor when he stumbled in carrying a letter on a silver salver—and she concentrated on her music.

When Blakeley entered the drawing room, Sophia was still immersed in her music. She smiled as he pecked her on the check, but he couldn't help noticing her smile was more from relief that he had returned unharmed than from good cheer. He lingered with his hands on his wife's shoulders, enjoying the last few bars of a pleasant *Liebeslied*; only as she finished did he remember where he'd been and step back.

"I fear I smell like the proverbial polecat, my love," he said. "We've been wallowing in the mud again. You may wish I keep my distance."

"Nonsense, Ian. If that had truly concerned me, I'd never have married a forensic scientist. I recall a flower arranger, a fellow named Chumley from

151

Crewe, who absolutely adored me. Besides, I've no sense of smell just now; I spent the morning amid paint fumes."

"The rhododendron bush?" Blakeley asked, referring to the project Sophia had begun after dropping work on her portrait of Rosie.

"No." She smiled impishly. "It's a secret."

"Something avant-garde, as it were?"

"You'll see." She played another few bars. "Where's Nathan?"

"He went back to the precinct house with Officer Fatzinger," Blakeley said. "After which he has to try to get more information on a fellow named Petticord who has the unfortunate habit of popping up at the scenes of homicides."

"Is that why you dashed off so suddenly?" she asked.

"Yes," he said. Blakeley knew how nervous his wife was about his present situation, and he wanted to spare her any undue anxiety. So he quickly changed the course of their conversation. "That's a lovely piece you're playing, dearest."

"It has a long German name, *Ach, Elslein, liebes elslein mein*."

"It sounds much prettier when you play it," he said and turned his nose in the direction of the kitchen. "Is that what I think it is?"

"It is," Sophia said. "It should be ready soon."

"*Magnifique*," Blakeley said. "Mrs. Snopkowski hasn't prepared sautéed kidneys in weeks. I suppose it's a good thing Nathan didn't come along for lunch. His palate is too American to enjoy such delicacies."

Sophia stopped playing. "Nathan is going to the concert this evening, isn't he?" she asked apprehensively.

"Yes, yes."

"He understands he'll be escorting Allison?"

152

"He does, and he is acting most gracious about it."

Sophia eyed her husband suspiciously. "Are you sure about that, Ian?"

"Well," he pondered. "He did ask, and I quote, 'Are you sure G won't mind?'"

"Oh, pshaw. It sounds like another evening of icy civility," Sophia said. "But I'm quite happy he'll be with us. I'll feel a good deal safer. You know, I really don't understand why you insist on refusing police protection."

Blakeley stepped over to the window and drew back the curtain. "Dearest, I've told you that I don't need police protection because I'm constantly in the presence of police."

"But what about now?" Sophia asked. "Anyone could try to kill you now."

Not turning to his wife, Blakeley squared his shoulders and held his breath a few seconds. He bunched the curtain in his clenched fist, then dropped it. Outside, an unfamiliar buggy headed up the drive toward the house, but Blakeley didn't give it a second thought.

At last he faced his wife. "I will consider the matter further. But I don't wish to be held captive by that maniac."

"Thank you, Ian. Now, I'm afraid I must ask you to perform another unpleasant task. Would you mind looking in on Don Orlando? I fear his health is getting worse."

"That would hardly be surprising, my dear," Blakeley said. He crossed the room and stood at the opposite end of the piano, still loath to approach too near his wife in his noisome condition. "The old fellow imbibes enough Madeira to float a battleship."

"Ian, really!" Sophia said. "How much wine Don Orlando drinks is not the point. He hasn't left his room all morning, and he never touched his breakfast. If he dies while he's my guest, I'll never forgive myself. Please promise me you will look in on him."

"I'm certain it's the Madeira, and I'm sure he's still embarrassed about that scene with Pratt. But I'll speak to him. Perhaps I can talk him into a period of temperance." He pulled his watch from its fob and glanced at it. "I suppose I have time before lunch."

"I would appreciate anything you can do, Ian," Sophia said. As Blakeley turned to the door, she resumed her playing, then paused. "I almost forgot, Ian. I believe Victor brought a letter in for you earlier. It's over there on the table."

To the strains of a Brahms's melody, Blakeley opened the envelope. Postmarked Philadelphia, it was apparently an unremarkable correspondence. But when he unfolded the letter, Blakeley saw he was mistaken. For there, 14 lines exploded in his face. His expression impassive, Blakeley read and reread the poem. The meter was uncertain, the rhyme forced. But the message was unsettlingly clear, and it burned its way into Blakeley's consciousness. Although Beecham had not bothered to sign it, he had not needed to.

"My God," Blakeley thought, as he stared at the letter, "he thinks I've murdered him. How the devil can I battle a man who thinks he's dead?"

Sophia looked up from her playing and said, "Is something the matter, dear?"

Blakeley stuffed the letter back in the envelope. "No, no, dearest. Just a letter from an old friend."

Sophia started to ask another question when Victor entered the drawing room without knocking, as was his wont, and startled her. She struck a sour chord.

"A gentleman to see you, sir," Victor announced.

"Who is it, Victor?" Blakeley asked impatiently.

"I've no idea, I assure you," Victor said huffily.

Sophia rose, her eyes wide with fear. "Ian, it's Beecham. I know it is."

Blakeley shook his head. He had to snuff the embers of distress before they consumed Sophia entirely. "Christopher Beecham wouldn't dare come here now. He's too much of a coward, I assure you. Despite Victor's incompetence, I am certain my guest means me no harm."

When Victor blushed, Blakeley detected a telltale rheuminess in the butler's eyes. "Victor?"

"Sir?"

"Have you been at the liquor cabinet again, Victor?"

"Sir!" the butler said and stamped off, no doubt to sulk in his room for the rest of the day.

"Damn me!" Blakeley said as Victor retreated.

"Ian, how unlike you," Sophia said.

"Forgive me, dearest," he said, silently cursing his loss of equanimity caused by Beecham's letter. "It's been rather a hectic and unsettling day. The last thing I need is to put up with Victor's antics."

Without a word, Sophia sat down at the piano again. Although her husband had not meant his comment as a rebuke, she felt it as one because of her annual failure to see through Victor's trickery.

Blakeley tucked the letter in his suit pocket. "I suppose I shall have to see who my mysterious visitor is."

"Do please remember to look in on Don Orlando, won't you?" Sophia said.

"The moment my visitor leaves."

Blakeley withdrew from the room, forgot about the delectable smell floating through the house, and failed to notice the guilty blush on the face of the maid Dumpling as she curtsied when he passed her.

In his study, there was a man seated at his desk.

He wore a smile that was much too broad, much too toothy. "Hiya, Doc."

Blakeley scowled. "What the devil are you doing here?"

"You remember me, don't you? Spector, from the *Morning Star*?"

"I certainly do, you slandering wretch."

"Now, now, Doc—"

"Don't call me Doc!"

Spector put his hands up, palms open, and grinned as he said, "Sorry! I forgot you English guys are sticklers for formality."

"And get out of my chair!" Blakeley demanded.

Of all the yellow journals, the *Morning Star* was the yellowest, and ever since Bernard Spector had discovered him, Blakeley had become its most reluctant celebrity. The detective had shared the dubious honor of having been taunted on its pages with as much regularity as the knaves and charlatans who actually enjoyed the publicity. Lately, his coverage had been merciless.

"All right!" Spector said and rose, but instead of leaving he merely perched on the corner of the desk.

"I asked you what you're doing here," Blakeley repeated.

"I come in peace, Doc. Honest."

"How the devil did you get in here, you microbe?"

Spector chuckled. "Your butler comes real cheap—a fifth of gin is all he wanted to let me in." He chuckled a little more when he saw the ire in Blakeley's face. "But anyway, like I said, I've come in peace. I wondered if you've heard the latest about Beecham—"

"I have nothing to say about Beecham!"

"Wait a minute, all right? This is for your own good, Doc. We wouldn't want to see you wind up like Magwood."

"Magwood?" Blakeley asked. "You mean, Judge Magwood?"

"Yeah, that's the guy," Spector answered. "I'm glad you recognize the name."

Certainly Blakeley recognized the name. Blakeley could still see the Honorable Algernon Magwood's long, lugubrious face as he listened to Blakeley's argument for Christopher Beecham's guilt—the argument the jury had found so ironclad. It had been Magwood's pleasure to sentence Beecham to the gallows; he had not taken kindly to Governor Stone's decision to commute the sentence.

"What about Judge Magwood?" Blakeley asked.

"Oh? You didn't hear about it then."

"Explain yourself, Spector, then get out of here before I do irreparable harm to your body."

"It seems the good judge's throat was cut from ear to ear, Doc." Spector ran a thumb across his throat, gagged, and laughed. He had the forced laugh of a spiteful child. "Bled like a pair of cheap socks."

Blakeley stared at him in outraged silence. Spector smirked and said, "Looks like young Beecham's closing in, huh?"

Blakeley started to speak but the lines of Beecham's threatening sonnet played through his mind as if on a scratched record and stopped him. The news was appalling in itself, but to hear it through such an odious messenger was enough to cause an upset stomach. When Blakeley moved his mouth again, he could only say, "Wh...uh...?"

Spector jumped up. "That's it, Doc!" he said. "Hold that pose!"

Spector yanked at a drape that hung in front of a large open window, exposing a thin little man who crouched under a black cloth behind a camera.

There was a flash and a puff of acrid smoke, and before Blakeley could regain his sight, the thin little man had eased both himself and his camera through the open window. Then he ran frantically across the lawn toward the horse and buggy Blakeley had seen earlier from the drawing room.

"Hey, thanks a lot, Doc!" Spector said with a guffaw. "You shoulda seen you face, fer Chrissake!"

Blakeley lunged at him, but Spector dodged.

"I can see it now, Doc," Spector said. "Definitely front page stuff. 'Blakeley Goes Berserk!'"

Blakeley lunged again. He roared as he tripped over a typewriter stand and lost his monocle as he fell. "Christ blast it!"

"Then right under the headline," Spector taunted as he went out the window, "the subhead reads, 'Famed Detective Scared Stiff by Momma's Boy.' See ya, Doc. Got a deadline to meet!"

Spector was racing off to join his photographer by the time Blakeley was on his feet. The two men whooped as they drove away.

Blakeley was pounding his desk in anger when the door flew open. "Dad, what's going on!" Ralphie asked. "It sounds like Yale's playing Harvard in here!"

Dressed in a bathing suit for a session with his barbells, Ralphie was eating one of his favorite corned beef, cream cheese, salami, and pickles on rye doubledecker sandwiches. Blakeley took heart when he saw his son.

"I cannot recall ever being happier to see you, Ralph," he said.

"Huh?"

"Ralph, do you remember the lane that leads across the field and ends a few yards from the entrance gate? It takes you approximately four-and-one-half minutes to make your way across it."

"Four minutes maximum, Dad," Ralphie corrected him. "Even on a full stomach."

"That's even better," Blakeley said. "Listen,

158

Ralph, if you leave immediately, in exactly five minutes you will find a horse and buggy at the gate, and in it you will find that Spector fellow and a man with a camera. I would appreciate greatly your appropriating the second gentleman's plates."

Ralphie grinned. "Here, Dad. You can finish my sandwich."

Before Blakeley could thank him, Ralphie was dashing down the lane toward the gate. Blakeley smiled, took a bite of the sandwich, and put it down.

"Very well, Mr. Spector," he said, as he straightened his tie and dusted himself off. "We shall play by your rules."

Chapter Ten

Later that afternoon, as Blakeley watched Ralphie picking the lock on an apartment door, he realized that he had never appreciated his son more than on that day. For, despite his shortcomings, Ralphie's true talents had shone with the unabated brilliance of the sun outside. Albeit, Blakeley chided himself silently for encouraging all of Ralphie's skills—some of which were decidedly less than legal.

Ralphie's worth had begun to increase in his father's eyes when he had intercepted Spector's buggy as it left their estate's grounds. Although Ralphie's account of the incident had been replete with glowing praise for himself, Blakeley fully believed that the photographer whom Spector had duped into doing his dirty work was frightened close to incontinence the moment Ralphie stopped them and demanded the plates.

Blakeley's estimation of Ralphie rose higher still

for his invaluable help in tracking down Cassie Aimwell, sister of the maniacal enchantress's latest victim. With Nathan off inspecting the clubs the murder victims had once frequented, and Sophia adamant that he should not be unprotected from Christopher Beecham's menace, Blakeley had to rely on his son. To his surprise, however, not only had Ralphie been able to sweet-talk Cassie Aimwell's address from the Hooper crone, he had also been able to intimidate the self-important doorman at the Fogwell Arms without uttering one verbal threat. He had merely leveled his impressive girth before the doorman, who was much slighter of build, and hinted ever so gently that Miss Aimwell would be more than disappointed should he not be admitted. When the doorman relented, Blakeley had the distinct impression that Cassie Aimwell was as uninhibited as her dead brother had once been.

As they had walked up the stairs to Cassie Aimwell's quarters, which were on the building's top two floors, Blakeley shook his head. No prude himself, he could only wonder what had become of propriety. From the outside, the Fogwell Arms hardly looked the lair of dissolute libertines. It was proudly Victorian and fit in well with the European flavor of the park that dominated the center-city neighborhood that Blakeley knew well. More than once, he had found himself paraphrasing Henry James's description of Rittenhouse Square as the closest an American could come to strolling along a city park on the continent without hopping the pond. And often were the times Blakeley had marveled at the architectural delights around the park, not the least of which was the Fogwell Arms. From its facade, he ventured a guess that it was the work of either Hunt or Garrison—and hardly the proper realm for the idle rich to indulge their more prurient appetites.

At the heavy oak door of the apartment they sought, both father and son paused. They had come expecting to find Cassie Aimwell; instead they exchanged puzzled glances upon reading the legend inscribed upon the door. For well-wrought, gilded letters announced the chambers to be the residence of Destiny's Darling. With a start, Blakeley recognized the name of Richard Petticord's unknown benefactor, and he understood with a flash how Petticord had been placed as a cook so easily.

"Boy," Ralphie said, his voice low, "I'll bet she's a strange one."

"Strange?" Blakeley thought. "I think we'll have to find a better word for a woman who would aid the man who might well have become her own brother's murderer."

Without speaking a word, Blakeley rapped the brass knocker against the door. No one answered, but both men could hear muffled sounds inside.

Ralphie reached forward and twisted the doorknob, only to find the door locked. He turned to his father, with a mixture of bravado and sheepishness on his face, and asked, "How bad do you want to see Miss Aimwell?"

"I think it quite worth our while to break down a door if it will help us prevent another murder."

"That's not quite what I had in mind, Dad," Ralphie said as he pulled a file from his wallet. "I learned this in the army."

Embarrassed by his assumption that his son was nothing more than a means of brute force, Blakeley didn't question what possible use picking locks might have been in fighting the Spanish. Still, he couldn't help admiring his son's heretofore unknown skill. If Ralphie weren't such a bother to his mother—and could refrain from dwelling on such childish notions as his werewolf fixation—Blakeley would have actually felt proud of the lad.

Less than a minute elapsed before the lock clicked to and they entered the apartment. Contrary to what the name on the door had led them to expect, the rooms were somewhat modest in their adornment. Beyond a small foyer, a hall led down to an open window; various rooms lay to the right of the hall. Blakeley looked into a small study in which books lined several shelves. Throughout the room, there were vases filled with violets and yellow roses, some on small tables with lace-edged cloths on top. Large ferns loomed like sentries at both ends of the room.

Next, Blakeley passed a stairway carpeted in deep green that led up to the next floor where, he presumed, bedrooms looked out on the park. The walls of the hall and stairway were a tastefully muted green decorated with tiny oval mirrors. A very prominent portrait of a nude that stopped Ralphie in his tracks hung opposite the stairwell.

Blakeley left his son to ogle the naked figure—a strikingly beautiful blond, tall and elegant, with a lascivious leer that belied the demure air of the painting's soft shades—and he tiptoed to a closed door farther down the hall. Standing on a large needlework rug, he put his ear to the door, listened for a moment, then began to sniff the air.

As Blakeley inhaled an odor that he knew well, having encountered it quite frequently in his days with Scotland Yard, Ralphie tore himself away from the nude and, eyeing his father suspiciously, breathed deeply. "Yep. It's ether, Dad."

Blakeley was amazed by his son's casual worldliness. It appalled him that the Cassie Aimwells of the world would indulge in so wasteful a practice; but to think his son partook too was yet another indictment of his own shortcomings as a father. "I didn't know you were so familiar with the substance."

"Ah, jeez crumps, Dad," Ralphie whined. "The next thing you know you'll think I'm an opium fiend. I only know what it is because I smelled it all the time when I went to those goofy college parties."

"Oh, so that's what you did at college," Blakeley said severely, though he was somewhat mollified by his son's denial.

"Not all the time—only when I wasn't playing football or baseball."

"And who, pray tell, would ever use ether?"

Ralphie shrugged his shoulders, then assumed a very stiff posture and spoke in the affected accents that Victor thought made him sound like a proper butler. "The artistic crowd, of course."

Blakeley couldn't speak for a moment because Ralphie's imitation of Victor threatened to make him burst out with laughter. "Good heavens," he said when he could speak without chuckling, "don't they fall asleep?"

"Sometimes," Ralphie said, amused by his father's naivete. "But it's what they do before they fall asleep that makes it fun."

Blakeley frowned his disapproval and returned his ear to the door. "I think I hear something. It's faint, rather like a humming sound. Listen."

Ralphie concentrated. He had just started to hear the humming when suddenly a loud clanging noise caused his father and him to recoil. "What the heck was that, Dad? It sounded like a gong."

"I believe it was," Blakeley replied, rubbing his ear.

"Jeez, a guy could go deaf."

"Quiet, please."

After his ears had stopped ringing, Ralphie whispered, "So, what do we do now?"

A finger to his lips, Blakeley turned his attention
back to the humming sound beyond the door. As
the droning grew more distinct, he realized it was
not so much a hum as a chant, as if someone were
praying aloud in a monotone. At once, he was reminded of the Gregorian chants he had heard in
the dark, foreboding monasteries of Europe. But
just as he decided that he should be hearing Latin,
the speaker's voice rose slightly, and he recognized
his own language. But it was the flat, uninspired
English of an automaton or somnambulist.

Blakeley tried the knob on the closed door, found
it unlocked, and gestured for Ralphie to follow him.
Ether fumes cloaked them like a noxious fog as they
entered a large, luxuriously furnished room. The
velvet drapes were drawn, but just enough light
seeped through to let him see the mahogany furniture, the embossed vermillion wallpaper, the delicate lace curtains, and the beaten-copper fireplace
with pewter accessories. The suite did not disappoint Blakeley; it was what he expected of an Aimwell. But the company—and the general disarray—
did disappoint him. Not to mention the fact that
he didn't think anyone, no matter how rich and
careless, could indulge in an orgy so soon after a
sibling had been brutally murdered.

"These pampered philistines," Blakeley mur-
mured to himself.

Bohemian types dressed in exotic clothing
lounged about on ottomans and Oriental rugs in
various stages of consciousness while a man wearing a turban and a velveteen suit read aloud from
a newspaper. Whenever he finished a section he
would nod to a girl in a skimpy harem costume,
and she would lift her mallet and strike the gong.
The loud, ringing crash would snap someone out of
his or her stupor, then he or she would get up, sniff
one of the rags lying near the ether bottle on a

165

nearby table, and slobber over the nearest body.

"What a sad state our culture is in," Blakeley whispered.

"Aren't you inspired, Dad?" Ralphie joked and covered his mouth.

"Shhhh."

Several of the guests had joined behind a sofa into what appeared to be a sweating, groping, grunting, heavily breathing octopus-like creature. Now and then a foot or part of a head would become visible, then disappear into the living lump.

"Welcome to ancient Rome, Dad," Ralphie whispered, and Blakeley put a finger up to shush him again.

"What's that guy reading, Dad?" Ralphie asked. "It sounds like something out of that rag Spector writes for."

"I believe it is, Ralph," Blakeley said, suddenly amused.

The man in the turban took another whiff of ether and continued chanting. "Dabriola's Fish Market. Twenty-six twenty-five Dock Street. Fresh mackerel, two cents a pound. Halibut, three cents. Two pounds minimum. First come, first served!"

Someone from the writhing mass paused to applaud. The harem girl hit the gong.

"I know that fellow in the turban, Ralph," Blakeley said. "He's a convicted sneak thief."

When Blakeley spoke, Ralphie nudged his arm and shushed him. For he was far more interested in what was going on behind the couch than in what his father was saying.

"Benny's Eatery," the man hummed on. "Five thirty-one South Street. Blue-plate special. Liver and onions, ear of corn, pie, and coffee. Eighteen cents."

The reader nodded at the harem girl. As she was about to strike the gong, she spied the two intruders and gasped. The man in the turban got up.

"You are not welcome here!" he said, pointing to the door. "Get out!"

"Hello, Mr. Clarke," Blakeley said, unfazed by the threat.

"I beg your pardon, sir," the man said. "I am called *L'étoile*."

"Yeah," the harem girl said as she readjusted her spangled brassiere, which had slipped lower with each swing of the mallet. "He's called *L'étolie*. He's our maestro. Who the hell are you?"

"His name is Edward P. Clarke, but the police know him as Fast Eddie Clarke," Blakeley replied. "And I know you too Miss Schwartz."

"I don't believe you've had the pleasure of making my acquaintance, mister," she said.

"Gosh, Dad," Ralphie said as he stepped over a snoring guest, "you know everybody."

"Out, out, I say!" Fast Eddie demanded.

Two young men took a step forward but quickly retreated from Ralphie's well-practiced glower.

Most of the crowd had come out of its stupor. Suddenly, the room seemed a great deal neater as the guests retrieved their discarded clothing and hastily dressed. Some had already left, and Blakeley presumed without scrutinizing the crowd that few among them were notable for their social prominence in the city.

"Sorry, Mr. Clarke," he said, "or if you prefer, *M. L'étoile*, but I'm not going anywhere until I've spoken with Miss Aimwell."

"And don't even dream of throwing us out," Ralphie said, just in case the two young men had gathered their courage. A quick glance apprised him that those two toughs were among the first to leave.

Some of the female guests were more stout-hearted. "Philistine," one said. "Ignoramus," said another.

"If you're so tough," a girl with long red hair said to Ralphie, "why aren't you off killing Spaniards?" Ready with a sharp reply, Ralphie turned to see her buttoning up the front of her dress and forgot his retort in a boyish blush.

Another woman said, "Why don't you take a whiff of the rag and join us?" She was making no effort to rebutton anything. Ralphie blushed even deeper, but his gaze lingered all the same.

A woman emerged from behind the couch and swaddled herself in a silk bed sheet, which had been draped over the sofa. She looked Roman in the makeshift garment. Blakeley presumed that was not by accident. Her hair, now in disarray, had been curled and arranged to look like someone out of *Ben Hur*—someone who might have granted special favors to doomed gladiators. Her eyelids looked drowsy under strange white makeup.

Ralphie's jaw dropped. "You're the girl in the painting," he stammered.

"How crude of you to notice," she said, taking a black cigarette from a silver case and lighting it with a black candle in a sterling-silver holder.

"Miss Aimwell?" Blakeley asked.

"That is my pedestrian name, sir. Cassandra Aimwell. Cassie on the decadent society pages. But here I am Destiny's Darling. And you, sir, are trespassing."

"I'm terribly sorry to interrupt, Miss Aimwell," Blakeley said, fumbling a bit for the proper words under such indecent—if not downright disgusting, considering her brother's death—circumstances. "But we failed in every other effort to contact you."

She yawned deliberately. "Might it have dawned on you then, gentlemen, that I did not wish to be inconvenienced?"

"Well, yes it did," Blakeley said, "under the present circumstances, but—"

"I cannot tolerate the telephone," Cassie said, ignoring Blakeley's apology. "I very rarely answer it. And I let my mail accumulate into a six-inch stack before I open it. And sometimes I do not open it. I burn it. Does that tell you anything, Mister . . . ?"

"Forgive me, Miss Aimwell," Blakeley said, amused that such a libertine would share his opinion of the telephone. "I am Dr. Ian Blakeley, and this is my son, Ralphie."

"I've heard the name," she said indifferently.

"We're both terribly sorry to have to disturb you at such a traumatic moment," Blakeley said.

"I didn't think it was so traumatic," she said and leered at the seedy young man near the sofa, the one she'd been grappling with a few minutes earlier. "How about you, Billy?"

"It's Willy," he said, stepping into his trousers.

Cassie nodded without interest at his correction.

"It wasn't traumatic at all," the redheaded girl said, buttoning her shoe. "It was the best fun ever till you two busted in!"

"Yeah," said her friend, who still lay atop the ottoman, sniffing an ether rag.

"What does traumatic mean?" the harem girl asked, scratching an armpit dense with tangled hair.

"It means a terrible shock," Cassie said, suddenly reading something in Blakeley's face and manner. "What don't I know?"

"It's about your brother, Miss Aimwell," Blakeley said evenly. "I gather you really don't know."

He took the newspaper out of Fast Eddie Clarke's hands. "That's my script!" Fast Eddie objected.

"The story will be rather explicit, Miss Aimwell," Blakeley said, turning to the front page and handing her the newspaper. "This particular paper isn't noted for its journalistic subtlety."

For papers like Spector's *Morning Star*, the murder of Reginald Aimwell had come at an opportune time. With victory after victory for the American forces, the war with Spain had taken on a predictable monotony. The headlines on that day's special late morning edition blurted out:

"BLOODY MURDER AT
MAIN LINE MANSION."

Cassie turned pale and gasped for air.

"Aw, shit," Belinda, the harem girl, exclaimed. "There goes our party."

"There goes more than that," Fast Eddie groaned.

"You know what they're talkin' about, Eddie?" Belinda asked. "What's that she's readin'?"

"Shut up," he said.

Cassie read a little farther, then let the newspaper fall to the floor. She looked very frail. When she started to tilt, Ralphie caught her and eased her into a chair. "First Miss Meredith, now Destiny's Darling," he thought. "I'm getting good at this."

Blakeley looked around at the few remaining people in the room, all of whom stared in confusion, not sure what to do. Except for the unbuttoned girl lying on the ottoman and the man still snoring on the floor, they all milled about as if waiting to be paid for services rendered.

"Under the circumstances, I think it best you leave," Blakeley said, hoping to get Cassie alone to question her properly.

But Willy, who was irked at being withdrawn from the mass of bodies, took exception. "Look, mister, me 'n the lady was jist gettin' acquainted," he said.

"Get out of here," Cassie demanded, as if speaking to a servant.

"Listen to her all of a sudden," Willy said. "The rest of us can go to hell now that the swells are here.

As if she wasn't doin' what the rest of us trash were doin'. As if it wasn't her idea in the first place! As if—"

That was as far as Willy got before Ralphie picked up a well-saturated ether rag and pressed it into his face. There were a few muffled four-letter words; then Willy went limp.

Dragging the seedy dandy by the collar, Ralphie ushered the rest of the crowd out the door. But it wasn't an easy task. For the motley crowd complained that they had nowhere to go. The redheaded girl protested that she burned easily and shouldn't go out in the sunshine. And Belinda, the harem girl, called Blakeley and Ralphie a couple of pus boils and other such niceties. Their whining might have gone on indefinitely had Ralphie not donned a fierce grimace and, herding them to the door, suggested they all go to the sewers with the other rats.

Blakeley picked up the snoring man, roused the unbuttoned girl on the ottoman, and shoved them gently but unequivocally toward his son at the door.

At last, all the undesirables save Fast Eddie had departed. Blakeley studied the sneak thief for a moment, then told Ralphie, "Check Mr. Clarke's pockets before throwing him out."

"Got him, Dad," Ralphie said, picking up Fast Eddie and carrying him out of the room.

"I'm gonna get sick!" Fast Eddie yelled.

On a couch, where she slumped still wrapped in the sheet, Cassie was staring straight ahead, biting her lip, and sniffling. Blakeley sat beside her on a footstool.

"I'm terribly sorry, Miss Aimwell," he said softly. "Believe me, I presumed you knew."

"Did it have to be such a horrible death?"

"If it helps at all," Blakeley said, trying to lie with credibility, "we believe it was over quickly."

"Are you sure?"

"Entirely."

"Did you see him after . . . ?"

"Yes, Miss Aimwell. The sheriff's department summoned me at once. I'm a forensic pathologist by training and a detective by default. It's my case now."

"I'm grateful," she said. "You must be very good, if being in the newspapers a lot means anything. I do read the newspapers, you know."

"Do you think you can answer some questions for us, Miss Aimwell?"

"Hard questions, Dr. Blakeley?"

"Some of them."

Cassie did not answer. She took a deep drag on her perfumed black cigarette, exhaled, and snuffed it out.

The shock had sobered and chastened her. She gathered up the silk bed sheet so that it almost covered her entire body. Her sudden modesty made Blakeley feel strangely intrusive. After all, he had walked in unannounced. As she tucked her feet under her on the large chair, in much the same manner as her friend Richard Petticord had hidden his nakedness earlier that day, Blakeley observed that her toenails were trimmed and polished, but her ankles were dusky and the soles of her feet were stained, as if she had been wading through mud puddles.

"Ah, *la vie bohême*," he thought. "How naive it makes people."

And with that thought, he decided to put her at ease with some lighter conversation, so as not to upset her fragile state of mind, as had happened earlier with Petticord. "I noticed at your parents' home that your family owns a Tibetan mastiff."

"Owned," Cassie said, her red-rimmed eyes showing surprise. "He went to the Great Soupbone in the Sky, as Daddy says, about two weeks ago. How did you know?"

"Dogs and I communicate on a special psychic cable, Miss Aimwell."

"Nancy was Reg's dog. Nancy." She thought for a moment and shook her head. "That says something about Reg, too. Nancy was a male, you see. I'm sure he hated wearing that big pink bow every year in the Easter Parade. I wanted to call him Genghis Khan or something more appropriate than Nancy. But it was Reginald Aimwell's dog and Reginald Aimwell was a joker. He wanted to name the silly dog after a bearded lady he'd once seen in a side show. Hence, Nancy it was. No wonder the poor dog became an alcoholic. Reg used to give him a bowl of the Glenlivet a day. Nancy probably died of cirrhosis."

Ralphie returned and started placing silverware beside the ether bottle that rested atop the small table next to Cassie.

"He had these in his coat," Ralphie said, setting down various utensils. "These were in his pants pockets, and I found this gravy boat under his turban."

"The police have good reason to call that scoundrel Fast Eddie," Blakeley said.

Ralphie winced and produced a silver spoon wrapped in a handkerchief. He handled it with special care. "This fell from the harem girl. You wouldn't believe me if I told you where she had it. Better wash it thoroughly, Miss Aimwell."

"Thank you," Cassie said, smiling at Ralphie for the first time. She turned back to Blakeley and, with a glimmer of challenge in her voice, said, "Nice company I keep, right?"

Blakeley took a deep breath and said, "Miss Aimwell, we are not here to study the liberal customs of your class. As the three wise men put it: *Noli audire, noli videre, noli dicere malum.*"

173

Ralphie looked up and said, "Jeez, Dad, can't you ever speak in English."

"It means," Cassie said, "that your father regards me as a spoiled, inconsequential brat."

"Oh," Ralphie said and shifted his eyes away from her.

Even Blakeley was sorry he'd been so blunt. The tears she'd been trying to fight back came on. When Cassie started to sob, Blakeley touched her shoulder.

"I don't know where I find them," she said feebly. "That one, the one you called Fast Eddie, told me he wanted to find an art patron. He said he was unappreciated because his art is so avant-garde. He must have thought up *L'étoile* on the way here. The cow with him said she was an artist's model."

"Hah!" Ralphie roared.

"That was fine with me," Cassie said, ignoring Ralphie's outburst. "I've done that, too, as you've noticed. The flesh is here to be on display, immortalized. As for the others, I've no idea where the hell they came from. The usual hangers-on, I suppose. Any port in the storm suits their needs, and I was only too willing to give them shelter."

"Miss Aimwell," Blakeley said, "that is not important now."

"What is important?"

"Miss Aimwell—"

"God, I need a bath," Cassie said, cutting Blakeley off. "I feel as if I've been wallowing in garbage."

"Miss Aimwell," Blakeley persisted.

"Poor Reggie. Poor, poor Reggie. How awful. To think he was being torn to shreds when I was—"

She was out of control, weeping, rocking back and forth on the couch just as Petticord had. Blakeley couldn't help wondering if she had come to Petticord's aid because she thought she'd found a kindred lost spirit who might fill the void in her

174

life. But now, as her face twisted with pain, she appeared beyond help.

They let her weep into a large pillow for a while. Ralphie went off to find the kitchen and make some tea. Blakeley got up and killed some time by admiring the pewterware atop the mantel over the elegant fireplace. When she was finished, she wiped her eyes and nose with the hem of the silk bed sheet.

Weeping becomes some women; their tears fall delicately, like petals on a pond after a springtime shower. Cassie's did not. Her tears left ruddy blotches on her cheeks. Her nose was red and her eyes had aged considerably under the ghastly white makeup.

She lit another black cigarette and blew out a puff of blue smoke. Blakeley gave her another moment to rearrange the bed sheet and wipe her hair away from her forehead.

"I'll answer your questions now," she said. "Even the hard ones."

"Very good, Miss Aimwell," Blakeley said. "I suppose I should begin by asking you why you bailed out Richard Petticord."

She looked surprised. "How did you know that?"

"I didn't until I happened upon your adopted name."

"My adopted name," she said with a faraway smile. "That, too, is a fraud. Destiny's Darling: peacemaker, love teacher, earth goddess, champion of an enlightened new order."

"About Mr. Petticord—"

"I'm getting there, Dr. Blakeley. Be patient."

"Sorry," he said formally. "Do continue, please."

She chuckled bitterly. "Well, as you can see, Dr. Blakeley, Destiny's Darling is a collector of misfits. It's a hobby of sorts. And when someone told me— please do not ask who, because it was no doubt in the middle of an ether-induced haze—that Lulu Hazleton had been murdered and that the police were trying to send some poor wretch to the gallows for it because of his sexual orientation, I simply knew I had to act."

"But that wasn't the truth, Miss Aimwell. I can attest to it personally."

"It doesn't matter whether it was or was not," she said. "When I discovered that the poor wretch was none other than Richard Petticord I would have bailed him out anyway. It was I, you see, who had hired him as Reginald's personal chef. I was the one who had heard about a fellow from New Orleans who needed a job. And knowing my brother's affinity for New Orleans cuisine, I made the arrangements." She inhaled another deep drag off her cigarette. When she expelled another puff of blue smoke, it circled her head momentarily, like a halo, before dissolving. "Richard Petticord wouldn't harm a fly."

"You knew, of course, about Petticord's sexual orientation when you hired him?" Blakeley asked.

"I certainly did," she said, somewhat annoyed by the question.

"Did you also know the late Mr. Hazleton?"

"Everyone knew Lulu Hazleton."

"Did you know about his sexual orientation also?"

She nodded that she did, again with some annoyance. "Is this a prelude to a sermon about Sodom and Gomorrah?"

"Do you travel in those circles, Miss Aimwell?"

"What circles do you mean, Dr. Blakeley?"

"Perhaps I should rephrase the question," he said. "Does Destiny's Darling travel in those circles?"

Cassie stretched her mouth into a patronizing smile. "If you mean the dissipated, ne'er-do-well crowd that Lulu kept about him, she did—when the lunar tides suited her."

"Was your brother a fellow traveler?"

She snickered at the suggestion. "My brother Reg was a rake. His friends will tell you he could charm the drawers off a Carmelite. I am personally acquainted with at least a dozen bluenosed beauties in and around Philadelphia whom he deflowered as a mere pup. One can only guess how many he bedded in his maturity. Frankly, and at the risk of offending your sensibilities any farther, Dr. Blakeley, I've always envied my brother his excesses." After one last deep drag, followed by a final puff of blue smoke, she snuffed out the cigarette. "But not one of his adventures was of the sodomite variety. I collect the misfits, Dr. Blakeley. They weren't Reginald's sort of thing."

Blakeley jotted a note. "I told you I had to ask some hard questions."

"I understand," she said with a stiff smile.

"So I gather your brother knew about and tolerated Petticord's private life."

"I'm quite sure he didn't give a damn about it. Petticord is a fine chef. Had he burned the roast, it would have been another thing."

"Well, since you didn't know about your brother's death," Blakeley said, "I'm sure you don't know that Petticord is in jail again, charged this time with your brother's murder?" As Cassie's eyes grew wider, Blakeley softened his voice. "His arrest happened too late to make the newspapers. He is at present the leading suspect."

Cassie gasped. "You mean, the man I got out of jail may have murdered my brother? I may have allowed it to happen? Oh my God."

She started to weep again. This time Blakeley walked over and let her collapse in his arms. "We don't know yet if Petticord did it," he told her.

"There are many unanswered questions. What you've just told me about your brother may help quite a bit. We're not very comfortable about Petticord as a suspect, no matter how badly it looks for him."

Cassie was sobbing into Blakeley's vest, and he was trying to comfort her by patting her on the back gently when Ralphie came back to ask where the tea was stored. Ralphie did a stagy imitation of someone quite shocked, then quickly disappeared when he saw the lack of amusement on his father's face.

"Poor Daddy," Cassie said eventually, her face still buried in Blakeley's vest. "He'll have to look elsewhere now."

"Daddy?" Blakeley asked.

"Yes." She sat up, wiped away her tears again with the hem of the bed sheet, sniffled, and collected her thoughts. "Despite his philandering ways, Reginald had a lot of those things a man looks for in an heir to the throne. You realize, I'm sure, that Aimwell Industries is vast. Our holdings in this country alone would stagger the imagination: coal, natural gas, cotton, a railroad or two, cattle out west, ammunition for the glorious war effort. Now Daddy has big plans to get into foreign markets, and poor Reg had all the ruthlessness you'd want in someone chosen to expand your empire. The way he collected women and disposed of them should tell you something. I loved him dearly, but Reg had no conscience. Poor Daddy. This will not sit well with him."

"I suppose you know then," Blakeley said, "that I have to ask who is your father's second choice."

"I am," she said, smiling slightly. "I guess Aimwell Industries is in for some troubled times." She stared for a moment, then said, "Is there anything else, Dr. Blakeley? I have a massive headache."

"Ether will do that, Miss Aimwell."

"I shall try to remember that."

"There is one more thing, if you'll indulge me for another few minutes. It's rather remote, I'm afraid, but did your brother ever mention a woman who prefers to wear green? We believe she has dark hair and an olive complection. Dark eyes."

"Dr. Blakeley," she said and smiled through her hurt. "Really."

"I've a good reason for asking, Miss Aimwell. Your brother was seen with a woman of that description shortly before he was murdered."

Cassie shifted and ran her hand through her hair, considering the question put to her. "Dark hair and eyes, olive coloring. Well, Reg did have an appetite for Mediterranean women. He must have liked the smell of garlic. I can't recall any of his conquests in green though."

"Was he particularly fond of any one of them?"

She grinned. "I can think of a few who weren't too fond of him. There was the Sicilian woman who threatened to throw acid in his face, all because of a few sweaty minutes they'd spent behind a bandstand in the park. Daddy had to pay her off to get him out of his hair."

"Do you know her name?"

"Oh, something eeny or oney. There was another one who showed up at Daddy's office keening and tearing her hair out, threatening to cut her wrists on the spot if Reg wouldn't marry her. God knows how much Daddy had to pay her to get rid of her." Cassie picked up the newspaper, glanced again at it, and tossed it across the room. "Well, at least Daddy won't have to worry about that kind of thing anymore." Her eyes filled with tears. She bit her lip and fought them off. "You may find your woman in green if you're lucky, Dr. Blakeley, but I doubt it. Reg was like any other man. Now and then he .

wanted a primitive, exotic-looking woman who liked to screech and claw his flesh."

Ralphie returned with tea. The tray with the tiny cups and delicate little pot was awkward in his hands, but the sight of him seemed to sooth Cassie's spirits.

"How about you, Ralphie," she said. "What kind do you prefer?"

"I like mine with a little lemon," he said, handing her a cup of tea. "But I couldn't find it. I couldn't find the milk or sugar either. I sure hope it isn't weak."

"A very strange girl, indeed," Blakeley thought, not altogether certain how sorry he felt for her. But he was certain she would love another drop of ether to help her escape reality for a while.

Cassie seemed to read his thoughts. Suddenly composed, she said, "Well, thank you for your interest in my brother's death. If you don't mind, I guess I have to find something appropriately funereal to wear for the next few days. Will you excuse me?"

Deciding not to challenge the brave front Cassie was putting up, Blakeley thanked her for her cooperation. When the door was closed behind Ralphie and him, he could hear the young woman weeping hysterically.

The sky was dark as they left the Fogwell Arms. Thunder crackled in the distance, and a stiff breeze was making dusty swirls along the street. Men lowered their heads and held the brims of their straw summer hats. Women protected their skirts and their dignity against sudden updrafts. Across the street, tree limbs swayed furiously. Blakeley and Ralphie climbed into their cabriolet and hurried home, hoping to beat the imminent storm.

"Of course, I knew what she meant, Dad," Ralphie said, as if in response to a query from his father. "I know a free spirit when I see one."

"A free spirit, to be sure, Ralphie."

As they raced along the city streets, the clouds overhead became even more dark and menacing. Suddenly a peal of thunder exploded, and they hit a rut, jarring Blakeley from his seat.

"Please look where you're going, Ralph. I would like to be in one piece for the concert your mother and I are attending this evening."

"Sorry, Dad," Ralphie said. "You know, I think Miss Aimwell wanted me to stay behind and comfort her in her time of need. I wasn't born yesterday."

"Good," Blakeley said as he cast an anxious eye skyward. The storm clouds were in the northeast; they would have ample time to drive home—barring any unexpected accidents.

"But she isn't my type" Ralphie said, steering their horse away from another rut. "She reminds me of Amelia Tutwyler, the girl Mother wants me to court because she coughs a lot like Elizabeth Barrett Browning."

Blakeley chuckled. "You prefer your damsels in distress more robust, I presume."

"Listen, Dad, that business about me and Dumpling is all in Rosie's head. Sometimes I think she tries ether, too."

"Ralphie, don't speak of your sister as if she were a common strumpet."

"Jeez, I'm only joking." He pointed toward the sidewalk. "Hey, Dad, look over there."

They passed Fast Eddie Clarke and his ratty entourage, who shouted four-letter epithets and made obscene gestures at them. Ralphie gestured back, but Blakeley paid little attention to their actions. He was preoccupied with thoughts of a case in which he had two corpses, no clues, and, at the moment, no hope of solving.

Chapter Eleven

Several hours later, the thundershowers had passed through the Philadelphia area, leaving behind them cool breezes and scattered puddles on the unusually quiet city streets. Those abroad that evening were enveloped by a fog so thick it wrapped around them like loving, maternal arms, or so Christopher Beecham thought. From his perch atop a building on Broad Street, Beecham felt strangely soothed by the fog's embrace. Had it been any other night, he might have been lulled to sleep by it. At that moment, however, he was much too excited to think of sleep.

The day so far had given him great success. While murdering that half-wit Magwood, he had felt the energy of an avenging fury pulse through his body. Never had Beecham imagined it would be so easy to kill the man who had condemned him to a living death. He'd simply slipped into Magwood's house, found a hunting knife, and sliced the judge's throat as he slept. A wallet bursting with money lay on the judge's bureau, much to Beecham's delight; for he'd have to make no more trips to those bloated swells who'd once feared him, but now threatened to expose him. And to add a touch of poetic justice, Beecham stole one of Magwood's rifles—the one he held in his twitching hands in his hidden aerie—to end forever the life of that gadfly Blakeley.

Beecham laughed softly as he craned his neck over the parapet. A few blocks north, a stone-faced William Penn hovered, just visible, over the city, his back to the madman, as if he couldn't bear to witness the scene to come. But Beecham paid no heed to the founding father. It was the fog he reveled in, the fog that protected him. Ever since childhood, he'd thought the fog a warm, nurturing, loving woman, because when the mists rose about his family's mansion, harboring unspeakable phantoms that haunted his troubled mind, his mother had always come to comfort him. But unlike his mother, the fog had never betrayed him, and there on the rooftop, it would conceal him until he had completed his dastardly deed.

As the hour drew upon eight, traffic on the city's main thoroughfare, both pedestrian and carriage, began to increase. For no amount of unpleasant weather could keep the local elite and those who aspired to its lofty, and by no means impecunious, milieu from attending the concerts at the prestigious Academy of Music. Outside of the Tuesday Ladies' Restoration Ball, these concerts were the height of fashionable society's evening life. If one was noticed by the chosen people who, by some grace, made up the monied class, happiness was ensured; if one was missed—or worse, snubbed— only misery could ensue.

Beecham had always hated these concerts, and watching the carriages arriving steadily at the

Academy building, he relished the thought of raining havoc on the event. Below him, the carriages stopped before a canopy erected in front of the block-long stone building, and their passengers, dressed in their finest evening attire, walked along a red carpet that climbed the center of the wide staircase that led inside. As Beecham spied on the concertgoers he kept himself low. For the Academy building rose a few floors higher than the one he was atop, and he didn't want some bungling idiot to ruin his revenge.

From the corner south of the canopy, a figure walking along a dimly lit section of the fog-shrouded street caught his eye—a figure he knew all too well, could never, in fact, hope to forget. Tall and portly, the man escorted a woman, whom Beecham believed to be a shade too thin for his enemy's beloved wife, but he conceded readily he might have been mistaken because of the darkness and fog.

"Leave it to that devil to sneak in from the side," Beecham muttered. "But he won't escape so easily." Beecham raised the rifle and, kneeling, took his aim. He would wait until the couple was in full light, then fire.

"Blakeley the triumphant," Beecham chanted, ignoring the unpleasant sensation of cold, brackish water that seeped through his trousers and soaked his knee. "Blakeley the smug. Like Agamemnon returning from Troy with his spoils, stepping onto the Tyrian purple carpet, marching with the grace of a demigod into the forbidden Temple of Apollo."

His target was precisely where he wanted him, lined up with no place to hide. As the two people moved onward, they became distinct in the murkiness. After they had taken a few more strides, Beecham could see the telltale Vandyke, but no monocle reflected the light from the gas lamps. His finger twitched on the trigger. A few steps more were all that he required. As a slight string of spittle eased itself down his chin, Beecham felt himself close to rapture.

One step, and another, then the man and the woman stopped as if surprised, the woman pointing at something nearby. Beecham's gaze flickered a second to see what was holding off the moment for which he had so long waited, and then, in utter despair, he cursed aloud.

"Miserable fog!" he said. For, indeed, in the evening's gloom, he had almost murdered the wrong man. Needlessly ending another's life gave Beecham no pause, of course; but that night, he would have only one chance to kill, and he had to kill the right man.

And there, descending from a landau, was the right man, resplendent in formal wear, stiff in his proper bearing. Beecham cried out again and leveled his rifle at Blakeley's head. But at that very second, the horse leading the carriage bucked under the apparently unexperienced hand of the driver, causing it to lurch forward and screen the detested pathologist from Beecham's view.

"That goddamned horse!" Beecham ranted, barely able to keep himself from jumping off the roof to plummet, like some latter-day Icarus, onto his foe. But he struggled to master his emotions by clamping down on his remaining middle finger. Breathing heavily as he gnawed on broken skin and neared the knuckle bone, he slowly calmed down. Blakeley had to leave the theater sometime, and he wouldn't be so lucky again.

Meanwhile, across the street, blissfully ignorant of any danger, Nathan watched as Blakeley heartily reprimanded Victor for his incompetent handling of the carriage, which had almost sent Sophia sailing out onto the street with Allison behind her.

"Victor, are you capable of doing anything without causing harm to everyone in your vicinity?" Blakeley demanded of his butler. "Mrs. Blakeley almost fell to her death on the cobblestones."

Doing his best to maintain what little dignity he had while cowering under his employer's ire, Victor could only say, "I told you I had little experience managing these beasts."

As if she could understand him, Hecuba snorted and took a quick step forward, pulling the carriage ahead. When the carriage lurched anew, Sophia couldn't catch herself, and she fell into her husband's arms, the hem of her gown rising indecorously above her calves.

Attracted by the commotion, people gathered about the foursome, one of whom was sure to suffer a mishap before getting to his seat inside the concert hall. But Allison stepped safely to the street, and the lone injury sustained was to Victor's fragile ego, which was bruised severely by Blakeley's public censure. Only after he'd sent Victor on his way, with strict instructions to return no later than eleven o'clock, did Blakeley notice the already dispersing crowd. Drawing himself up, he turned to his wife, who was slowly regaining her composure with Allison's help.

"I'm sorry, dearest," he said. "Victor really does bring out the worst in me."

And it was true. No sooner had he returned home from his visit to Cassie Aimwell, than he had launched into an hour-long tirade that had almost sent the butler into paroxysms of terror. So virulent had been Blakeley's excoriation that even Don Orlando had left his room to uncover the source of the horrified wailing. The sounds reminded him, Don Orlando told Nathan upon his arrival, of cries he had heard quite often while in Central America—

even the cries he himself had made when Indians had kidnapped and tortured him.

But in the end, Victor had vowed fealty to Blakeley and sworn on several dead relatives' souls that he would never permit anyone like Bernard Spector in the house. Not at all appeased, Blakeley was forced to accept Victor's pleas for supplication. As it turned out, the groomsman had left the estate for the day, and Ralphie had disappeared. Although no one knew for certain where Ralphie had gone, Rosie had dropped several far-from-subtle hints he was off on a tryst with Dumpling. With no other alternative, Blakeley commanded his simpering servant to hitch the mare to the landau, and so had begun a very uncomfortable and unnecessarily eventful ride.

As the foursome stood on the pavement, the object of some mirth for what was left of the crowd around them, Nathan did his best to ease his friend's troubled mien. Dusting off Blakeley's shoulders, he said, "Well, now that's all settled, I'm sure we'll enjoy the concert."

"I most certainly will not," Sophia said, her composure still ruffled, "not with that madman still loose."

"Really, dearest," Blakeley said, "even Beecham is not mad enough to try to kill me in public."

"Dr. Blakeley's right," Allison said, while she straightened Sophia's shawl. "Christopher Beecham has only killed when his victims were alone and helpless. He's an absolute coward."

"Do you really think you can predict the actions of a madman?" Sophia asked, and turning around, she caught a brief glance of the last two people who still gawked at them. The couple were unremarkable in themselves. The woman was pale and underfed, her gown faded and two seasons behind the latest style; the man tall and stoutish in his tight suit. More than anything, it was his Vandyke beard that gave Sophia a start. "Ian, darling, look at that man! He looks exactly like you."

"Who? That man there?" Nathan asked, then laughed. The man was indeed similar to his friend in general form, but as he well knew the differences between the two men went far beyond the physical.

Checking his mirth when Sophia blushed and Allison frowned at him, Nathan said, "I'm sorry, Mrs. Blakeley, but this fog must be playing tricks on your eyes. Besides, I don't think you'd want anyone to tell you that Dr. Blakeley resembles Simeon Dorsett. He's the most notorious slumlord in West Philadelphia. His tenants call him Mr. Eviction, because he sends goons in the middle of the night to toss everything they have out the window."

"I quite agree with Nathan," Blakeley said. But he couldn't help studying the form retreating into the hall. "And now, I must demand we all forget Christopher Beecham, Victor, and women dressed in green. We're here to enjoy this concert. Besides, my love, should Beecham wish to kill me, he'll be befuddled by our friend Mr. Dorsett. What better way for me to hide than to have a double nearby? I can't think of a disguise that would more confuse someone with a brain as addled as Beecham's."

His decree spoken, not without a few attempts by Sophia to interrupt him, he led his wife up the stairs into the building. Hesitating for only a second, Nathan offered his arm to Allison, and she accepted it as naturally as she had been refusing all his overtures of late.

His breath uneven, his heart aflutter, Nathan proudly escorted Allison to the Blakeleys' box. Lovely on an ordinary day, the woman he adored above all others was quite astonishing that evening. Her strawberry-blond hair glittered like a beacon in the fog-shrouded night, signaling a message of love to Nathan, promising him splendor. Her lavender gown was trimmed with white lace and cut daringly low. And a white silk swath girded her delicate midriff and accentuated her bosom. As if under a spell, Nathan even forgot to be embarrassed by his own evening clothes, which he'd noticed earlier were a bit more frayed than he'd remembered. But how could anyone notice him beside that enchanting temptress?

His reverie continued for several moments, until finally they stopped before the box and Allison said, "You don't think Mrs. Blakeley has anything to worry about, do you? I'm positive that Beecham is too much of a coward to dare strike at Dr. Blakeley in public."

Before Nathan could answer, a voice behind them hailed Blakeley, and Nathan muttered, "Speaking of cowards."

It was Pratt, the renowned journalist and bane of Nathan McBride's existence. "Hello," he said in greeting. "I must say I'm surprised to see you all here tonight."

Nathan presented a stony face to Pratt, but his features softened when Allison kept her arm in his and made no move to slip away, even when Pratt raised her hand and kissed it. In fact, if he wasn't mistaken, Nathan swore to himself that Allison tried to pull her hand away from the officious journalist.

With his arm firmly about his wife's waist, Blakeley began to usher her into their box. "Good to see you, Pratt," he said, a bit too merrily. "Perhaps we can talk during the *entr'acte*."

"Ian, don't be rude," Sophia said, refusing to allow him to lead her forward. "Good evening, Mr. Pratt."

"G," he said, stopping amid the friends. As could only be expected of a famed war correspondent after his well-reported brushes with death, Pratt dressed better than most men in the theater that evening, better than most men on the eastern seaboard for that matter. For with fame came money, though not the wisdom with which to spend it wisely.

"Of course," Sophia said in response to Pratt's reminder, "G. But whatever do you mean you're surprised to see us? As sponsors of the orchestra, we would not miss tonight's performance."

As Blakeley raised his hand to make a point, Pratt said, his tone half coy, half surprised, "Surely, you don't mean to tell me you don't know what Beecham did this morning. Killing Judge Magwood, I mean."

When Sophia gasped, Nathan and Allison stepped in to intervene between her and Pratt. Their actions, although unheeded, were not necessary, however, because the lights dimmed signaling the beginning of the performance, and Pratt bid the two couples farewell.

At once furious and appalled, Sophia yanked her arm from her husband and stormed to her seat. "I should demand we leave immediately," she said when the others had taken their places. "And I would if I didn't know that Victor won't be back for hours."

"Now, dearest—"

"Don't talk to me like that. How dare you not tell me that Judge Magwood was murdered. For all we know, Beecham could be waiting here to kill you. You may like to tempt fate, but I haven't any desire to be a widow. And think of the children."

No one escaped Sophia's wrath. She had no doubt that Nathan and Allison were complicitous with her husband's attempt to foster her ignorance of the danger lurking about them. It was well into the first part of the evening's program before she could relax without intermittent outbursts that drew general condemnation from the boxes near them.

Nathan sympathized with his friend as he sat silently suffering his wife's rage. But even before the overture from *Rienzi* had concluded, Nathan relaxed into the half-light of the hall, and he had eyes for no one but the beauty leaning toward him, her shoulder touching his ever so slightly. Pieces from *Lohengrin*, *Tannhauser*, and *Parsifal* passed unnoticed. And only during the *Tristan and Isolde* selection did he stir, when Allison dropped her program and he bent to retrieve it. Never had Nathan known such perfect rapture as that evening, sitting there with that beautiful creature for all to see. But the lights rose too soon, and too soon the intermission arrived, ending his bliss.

Sophia had, by that time, almost forgiven her husband and the others their duplicity. And though she would have liked to stay by Blakeley's side until they were safely home, she did have to speak with more than a few members of the Tuesday Ladies who were shirking their duties relating to the upcoming ball, now only two weeks away. She secured her husband's promise that he would not give Beecham the opportunity to sneak up on him; then, Allison accompanying her, she took a turn about the hall, where any number of groups of white- and silver-haired women had gathered to chat. As she left her box, Sophia confided to Allison that, by merely making a few phone calls to secure services of various caterers and other hired help, Pratt had provided her more invaluable service than the collective body of indolent wealth that paraded before them.

Blakeley and Nathan beat a hasty retreat outside, meanwhile, to escape the stuffy enclosure of the concerthall. Atop the steps leading up to the building, they took up positions in the shadows of a marble sphinx. Blakeley struck a match that flickered a moment, illuminating his beard and nose in the murky gloom, then lit his pipe. "Damn that Pratt," he said between puffs. "If not for him, this should have been a splendid evening."

"I don't know," Nathan said. "It still seems to be going off pretty well."

Blakeley nodded his agreement and smiled, happy that his friend and Allison had at last begun to cease their romantic sparring. Neither of them spoke for a few minutes, as they enjoyed the chill, fresh air. But when they heard Pratt shouting Blakeley's name, they groaned in chorus.

"Dr. Blakeley," Pratt shouted again, causing the pathologist to shrink into the shadows, as if to avoid being found.

When the correspondent dashed past their position on the portico, the men realized that Pratt was chasing someone else, whom he had mistaken for Blakeley in the fog.

"It's that Dorsett fellow he's running after, isn't it?" Blakeley asked.

"Yes, it is," Nathan answered, chuckling. "Poor devil, he has no idea what trouble he'll attract because he happens to vaguely resemble you at a distance."

No sooner had the words left Nathan's lips than a rifle shot exploded onto the gaslit street, creating an instant state of chaos among the erstwhile placid concert crowd. Without a thought, Nathan threw himself in front of his friend and hustled him behind the imperturbable sphinx. Screams and shouts of terror broke out as men and women dashed to and fro or fell to the ground, many of them fully convinced that the Spanish had invaded the city.

"Really, Nathan," Blakeley said, drawing himself up. "I think I'm intelligent enough to take my own cover."

"Sorry, Dr. Blakeley, I guess it was just a reflex."

The young sergeant waited a moment before he peered around the statue to the street. A second shot not yet in evidence, he felt it safe to leave Blakeley and to help the other policemen trying to restore peace to the area. And his help certainly was needed. The well-dressed members of the mob were still rushing about in unqualified horror. Their cries rang out unabated, the din they raised seeming to echo off the heavy fog. More of the concert audience poured out of the theater, as if they believed the building was about to be razed. Police officers hastened through the throngs attempting to quell further mayhem. But the sight that caught Nathan's attention was Pratt running about with a nimbleness surprising in a man with such a serious leg wound.

Leaning halfway around the younger man, Blakeley said, "Can you make out what Pratt is shouting?"

"I think he's calling for help," Nathan said and hurried down to be of what assistance he could. He was nearly upon Pratt when he saw a man's body lying in a puddle of blood. The dead man's puzzled face was raised to the sky, as if asking why this injustice had been visited on him.

"It's Dr. Blakeley," Pratt ranted at Nathan. "My God, they've killed Dr. Blakeley."

Vaguely wondering who the reporter thought the supposed assassin might be, Nathan knelt close to the body and examined the upturned face. Contrary to Pratt's assertion, the dead man was Simeon Dorsett. And whoever had killed him was a perfect shot. The single bullet had penetrated the dead man's brain, but left his face intact. As he studied the corpse, the words he had spoken to Blakeley a few moments earlier rang in his ears, and he had no doubt who had fired the bullet or why.

Standing directly behind Nathan, Pratt had discovered his error and sought to hide his ebbing panic by jotting notes on the murder in a little-used notebook. When Blakeley approached them, Pratt said, with the chummy air of a man just let in on an inside joke, "I feel like an ass, Dr. Blakeley. I thought this was you."

"Yes, yes," Blakeley said, brushing him aside. He stooped over the corpse and started sharply. "Oh, no."

"I'm afraid so, Dr. Blakeley," Nathan said. "Mr. Eviction himself. I know no one's going to miss him, but even he didn't deserve to die this way."

A uniformed policeman approached the crime scene and immediately recognized Nathan. Pulling the officer aside, Nathan explained the situation. Then the officer called over some other patrolmen and had them cordon off the area.

"We're in luck. That was Officer Malone," Nathan told Blakeley. "He said his men found the weapon on a building across the street, and they have a witness. He was on the other side of the building on Juniper Street."

"I hope I have as much luck keeping Sophia from learning that Mr. Dorsett was killed until we get home." Blakeley surveyed the stairs and the portico hastily, anxious to intercept his wife should she draw near. But the only person he recognized among the sea of shocked faces was Pratt, who hovered over the scene like a vulture, scribbling down every detail.

The uproar had greatly subsided by the time Malone returned, leading a tattered figure who reeled so violently he appeared in imminent danger of defying gravity and falling up. Another uniformed officer escorting them gingerly held a Winchester .73 rifle, as if expecting it to go off in his grasp.

"Hiya, McBride," the tattered little man said as

he capered to and fro. "Whassamatter?"

"Bummy? What are you doing here?"

"You know this mug?" Malone said.

"Sure, he's the biggest drunk in my precinct. What're you doing down here, Bummy?"

"Came over for supper at the mission," Bummy answered, his besotted mind not quite understanding what had caused all the commotion, even though the dead man lay at his feet.

Examining the rifle, Nathan shook his head slowly. "It smells like this rifle was recently fired. So at least we have the murder weapon. But I'm afraid Bummy isn't the best witness we could get."

"Nonsense, Nathan." Blakeley faced the drunk and, carefully enunciating every word, he said, "Mr. Rummel, what were you doing behind that building this evening?"

Bummy focused dull eyes on his interrogator, then smiled as if in recognition. "I was sleepin' and dreamin' of my sweetheart, Cap'n."

His response elicited more than a few suppressed chuckles and smiles. Even Blakeley paused a moment before continuing his line of questioning. "Did you see anyone in the alley? A young man running away as if he were being chased by someone?"

"Didn't see anybody, but some bugger stepped on my head. Woke me up just when I had my sweetie in my arms."

The mirth, although out of place, had become general among all those present, until a woman's voice rose over the scattered noises of the crowd and called, "Simeon! What are you doing over there?"

Nathan and Blakeley sobered and exchanged pained glances. "Mrs. Dorsett," Nathan said, recognizing the wan little woman, who stood with her arms akimbo and her face gravely set.

Hoping to spare the woman any undue pain,

they walked over to her. "Simeon, what are you—" Mrs. Dorsett broke off when she realized her mistake. She dropped her arms, as if taken aback. "You're not Simeon." She looked past them to the inert form sprawled on the ground. "Oh, my God! Simeon!"

Before anyone could stop her, she dashed to her husband, Blakeley and Nathan one step behind her. Trembling and weeping, she leaned over her husband, then collapsed into Nathan's waiting arms.

Blakeley checked the woman's pulse, then assured Nathan she was in no danger. But any relief he felt was tempered by the sight of Sophia standing 20 feet away, looking terrified by the scene being played out around her. His eyes upon her, he was mystified when she shouted out, "Ian! Look behind you."

Before Blakeley could move, a flash burst forth, sending ripples of shock through the distraught crowd. A hyena laugh echoed off the surrounding buildings as two men retreated south down Broad Street.

Blind momentarily, Nathan cursed aloud and almost dropped Mrs. Dorsett. "Spector!" he shouted after the fleeing men. "I'll get you."

Several policemen chased after the reporter and his photographer, but surprise was on their side, and they escaped with ease in a waiting carriage.

A short while later, the body of Simeon Dorsett was loaded into an ambulance, and his wife, having revived somewhat, departed with it. The crowd had dispersed, except for a few who hung on out of morbid curiosity. The police had concluded their investigation of the crime scene. But they had a long night ahead of them. For most of them were sent to track down the unknown sniper, and others to search through the damp, labyrinthine alleyways for Bummy Rummel, the lone witness, who had wandered off in the confusion caused by the photographer's flash.

The Blakeleys and their friends were awaiting Victor's imminent return, sorting out the evening's events. Despite all the turmoil, Nathan couldn't help secretly reveling in the scent of gardenias that wafted off Allison in the cool breeze. But his happiness was short-lived. For just as the coach came into sight, Pratt appeared at Allison's side.

"Miss Meredith," he said, "I have a proposition for you."

"Yes?" she asked, her body straightening.

"I have notes on everything that happened tonight. Why don't we go down to my paper's offices and write the story together? I'd share credit, of course, and you know that wouldn't hurt your career."

"Oh, that would be wonderful," she said, appearing to forget about Nathan. "Your office isn't far from here. Why don't we walk?"

With a quick good night, they went off into the fog, leaving Nathan behind, alone and miserable again. But as their figures began to disappear, he thought he caught Allison glancing back at him, as if daring him to fight for her. Taking up the challenge, he bade the Blakeleys good night as well and set off in pursuit.

When they were alone, Sophia said, "We have a lot to talk about, don't we, Ian?" Her anger, although attenuated by weariness, was evident.

"Yes, we do, dearest," he said.

With his customary ineptitude, Victor drove the landau along at a jerky pace, which Blakeley had no doubt was caused by a full fifth of gin. The ride home would not be easy.

"Dearest," he asked, as the carriage lurched to a stop before them and Hecuba reared up in protest of the sudden stop, "have you ever felt terribly homesick for England?"

Chapter Twelve

The following day dawned bright and sunny. But as he sat in his dining room, Blakeley could not tear his eyes away from the shrieking headline on page one of *The Morning Star*:

IF YOU SEE THIS MAN, STAY AWAY
Where He Goes, Death Follows.

Opposite his nominal jailer, Don Orlando chuckled and waved his eyeglasses in mock accusation. "I shall have to keep an eye on you, *mi padrón*," he said. "I had no idea you were such a dangerous fellow."

Blakeley chuckled with him. Though their laughter was disdainful, it cheered Blakeley. For that morning was the first time the Spaniard had shown any life and humor since the episode with G. Lindsay Pratt.

"We all have our little secrets, Don Orlando," he

said as he finished reading the article about the violent events of the evening just passed.

The drawings accompanying the article were surprisingly accurate renderings of their subjects, Blakeley thought, because Spector was determined that everyone would know precisely who he was. The artist had taken great pains to exaggerate his features so that no one would mistake him. One column's width away from Blakeley's portrait was the same artist's depiction of Simeon Dorsett. That drawing flattered its subject and would no doubt raise a hue and a cry among the general citizenry. They would decry the fate of a solid and respected businessman whose only fault had been a passing resemblance to a pompous overweight Englishman. Blakeley dreaded public reaction already.

"This is preposterous, Dr. Blakeley," Don Orlando said, gesturing at the paper. "Even with artistic license, any fool can see that Mr. Dorsett's features are not those of a gentleman. God forgive me for speaking ill of the dead, but he looks no more like you than I do Mr. William Randolph Hearst." He shuddered noticeably when he pronounced the name of the man who had single-handedly created the yellow journalism that fanned the flames of war against his beloved empire.

Blakeley smiled appreciatively. "Thank you, Don Orlando. I must say you're in better spirits today."

"It is perhaps because I am so agitated by these newspapers," Don Orlando said. "They make my heart race faster."

Blakeley nodded in agreement. To the extent that there were a number of burly gentlemen with Vandyke beards around Philadelphia, Blakeley knew he was well on his way to earning their complete and unabated hatred, which was obviously what Spector wanted. He surmised there would be many bar-

bers kept busy trimming away Vandykes in the
coming week.

Close to the front-page portraits was the picture
snapped the night before that showed Blakeley,
mouth agape, staring at the camera with Simeon
Dorsett's corpse in the background. Spector's editors had undoubtedly given him a sizable bonus for
it, because rags like *The Morning Star* only used
photographs when they knew that the photos would
help sell more copies than usual.

For a Sunday, *The Morning Star* was uncharac-
teristically serious. Ordinarily it was a collection
of cartoons and advertisements. Rarely did so many
lurid events occur in a single day that would fill the
few pages open for news and require the displace-
ment of the paper's normal contents. But the discovery of the murders of Reginald Aimwell and
Judge Algernon Magwood had been manna from
yellow journalists' heaven. And the muckrakers
must have felt especially blessed with the shooting
at the Academy of Music.

With an exclamation of disgust, Don Orlando
picked *The Morning Star* up from the table and
tossed it aside. "The cook can use these pages to
wrap up the garbage."

"A good idea, Don Orlando," Blakeley said, shaking a bottle of tonic he'd ordered for his patient. He
opened it then and poured out a spoonful. "Mrs.
Snopkowski will be grateful. Now, open your
mouth please. This tonic works so effectively you'll
be able to wrestle with Ralphie in no time."

Don Orlando swallowed the tonic, grimaced, and
took a deep breath. His eyes narrowed when he
spied a copy of *The News*, the paper that had long
sponsored Pratt's journalistic endeavors. "That
worthless scrap isn't even good enough for Mrs.
Snopkowski to use," he said. "I hope all this nonsense will not too greatly upset your dear wife."

Blakeley shook his head. "After last night, I don't think she could become much more upset," he said, his mind wandering back to the argument he and Sophia had had until he promised to keep her informed about all of Beecham's misdeeds and to accept any protection offered against the miscreant. That issue settled, Blakeley had administered a sleeping draft to prevent his wife from losing sleep; as a result, she had slept so well that she had almost risen too late to attend her weekly church service, which she rarely missed.

As Don Orlando clucked his sympathy for his hostess, Blakeley said, "It's very kind of you to be so worried about Sophia. You know, of course, she's been very concerned about your health of late. And I do think it would ease her mind if she saw you in better spirits. So, if you don't mind my asking, have you kept your promise, Don Orlando?"

"A Spaniard is nothing if he is not a man of his word, *mi padrón*. I drank only three glasses of wine yesterday. But you must excuse me if I drink a little more today. I am most profoundly disappointed to see the very beautiful and honorable Miss Meredith in the company of such a scoundrel," he said, pointing to an article on the front page of *The News*.

It was the byline to the news story, not its conservative headline, that raised Don Orlando's ire:

**SNIPER GUNS DOWN BUSINESSMAN
AT CONCERT
By G. Lindsey Pratt
with Allison Meredith**

Allison had shown Blakeley the piece when Nathan had dropped her off the night before. Despite her modesty, he was sure she had written the entire article. For all in all, it treated him fairly. And even Allison's sketch of his face was accurate, if not flattering, and he appreciated that she had included his monocle—a touch that added dignity to his features and made him appear less like a hapless victim.

If Pratt could be believed, the story would also run on the front pages of *The New York Times* and *The Washington Post*, and perhaps on the second page of *The Pittsburgh Post*, since there would be interest on the other side of the state, but less immediacy. Farther west, the article would be abbreviated in *The Chicago Record* and probably run on page three because Blakeley was not particularly well-known there. And in San Francisco, where Blakeley had no fame, but the name G. Lindsey Pratt was familiar to the legions of newspaper readers rabid for war news, *The Examiner* would most likely cut the story in half and title it something like "PHILADELPHIA SHOOTING." No matter how brief the space allowed the news item, however, Allison's name would appear for the first time from coast to coast.

Allison had been ecstatic about the article—until she saw the morning edition and discovered Pratt's treachery. After she and Nathan had left the offices of *The News*, Pratt had written another article that ran as a sidebar and read in part:

"...the callous observations of Det. Sgt. Nathan McBride demonstrate a terrible injustice to the people of Philadelphia. How are the citizens expected to respect a man who would stand next to a corpse and say, 'No one will miss [Mr. Dorsett]'...

"And the officer is so incompetent that he allowed the only witness to the crime—a besotted fellow nicknamed Bummy Rummel—to escape...."

Pratt had missed no tricks in sabotaging Nathan's career, going so far as to have the artist for the article portray Nathan with the menacing glare of a villain in a cheap melodrama. He even captioned the picture "Nobody's friend."

If Blakeley had not restrained Allison, she would have visited on Pratt a fate far worse than Dorsett, Magwood, or Aimwell had met. And even though the article would cause Nathan trouble, Blakeley had no doubt that his friend would face any charge since Allison was back in his arms.

Fully aware of Allison's anger over the article, Don Orlando tossed the copy of *The News* on the floor atop the other paper. "If I were Sgt. McBride, I would tell that fellow to choose his weapons and meet me at dawn."

"I'm sure something like that has crossed Nathan's mind, Don Orlando."

Blakeley opened a window to allow fresh air to flow through the dining room. It was a fine morning, cool, bright, and sunny. Thy Schuylkill, brown in its shallows after the previous day's heavy storms, ran calmly through the picturesque countryside. The sky was blue and cloudless for a change. On such a clear day, sailboats would crowd the river by noon, and carefree people would line the shores. How Blakeley wished he could be among them.

"Listen to the song, Dr. Blakeley," Don Orlando said.

"Eh?" Blakeley suddenly noticed a bird in a tree nearby. "Oh, yes, the cardinal."

"His song plays sweetly through the open window."

"It does indeed," Blakeley agreed. "It makes it easier to dismiss the likes of G. Lindsey Pratt from your mind. After all, it is Sunday, and I suppose one should dwell on the positive."

"I am afraid Sunday is no different from any other day," Don Orlando said ruefully.

"Don Orlando, if you would reconsider—"

The old Spaniard shook his head. "No, Dr. Blakeley, I must ask your indulgence in this matter. I do not wish to see a priest."

"I happen to know your religion means a great deal to you."

Don Orlando looked at him quizzically.

"You pray at night," Blakeley said. "Ralphie tells me he hears you when he comes to your door to see how you are before he goes to bed."

Suddenly flustered, Don Orlando said, "I did not know that I had an audience, Dr. Blakeley."

Noticing the other man's vexation, Blakeley moved quickly to assuage it. The old man had been spending much of his time in bed of late, another indication of an ebbing spirit, and his coming down to breakfast that morning was the first hint that he might be recovering. Blakeley didn't mean to be the cause of any relapse in his health.

"Nathan goes to Mass at the chapel of Villanova College," Blakeley said, changing the subject. "He knows one of the priests very well—a Father Gorman. He's fluent in Spanish and he told Nathan he would be pleased to come here on Sundays to say a Mass for you. He can even hear your confession and administer the Holy Sacrament, if you wish. Frankly, I'd feel better if you'd let him. I forgot all about your religious needs when I agreed to keep you here under house arrest. And as you know, all the government intends to send are those annoying military intelligence officers," Blakeley added, referring to the various officials who periodically appeared to bully the sick man.

Touched by his host's concern, Don Orlando chose his words carefully, so as not to offend him. "Once again, *mi padrón*, I do not know just how to tell you this without making you think ill of me, but I am quite bitter toward our Holy Mother the Church." He paused, then continued reluctantly, "The Church has stood by while Spain, her loyal servant, is being butchered like a fallen bull."

"Bitterness is a terrible burden, Don Orlando," Blakeley said, and Don Orlando nodded in agreement as Dumpling entered the room to clear the table.

"Good morning, Dumpling," Blakeley said, assuming a cheery tone.

"Good morning, sir," she said, curtsying. She set a tray on the table and stacked dishes atop it.

"Mrs. Snopkowski must be ecstatic that Victor is being punished, wouldn't you agree, Don Orlando." Blakeley said, pointing at the remains of their breakfast. "We haven't had such a wonderful breakfast in ages. And I can't remember the last time we had blinis."

When Dumpling raised the full tray and started to leave, Don Orlando raised his hand to stop her. "You're not going to forget to take away my toast and strawberry jam, are you?" he asked Dumpling.

Blushing and smiling, she nodded shyly.

"Take them with you then, my child," he said.

"Oh, thank you, sir," the young maid said, placing the toast and jam on her tray and hurrying off.

"The child has a very strong sweet tooth," Don Orlando said when Blakeley glanced at him curiously. "What you saw has become a ritual with us. Every morning she brings my breakfast to my room, and every morning I give her the toast and jam."

"I see," Blakeley said, while thinking, "No doubt, Ralphie has discovered Dumpling's weakness as well."

"I hope you do not think me indecorous, but I cannot see any harm in continuing our ritual just because I took my meal at the table today."

"That's quite all right," Blakeley said in response to the kindly smile and healthy glow on Don Orlando's countenance.

As Dumpling left, she nearly collided with Victor, who was rushing in the doorway. Victor frowned when the girl went by, as if she were at fault.

"Sir," he said, careful to keep a safe distance from his employer.

"Yes, Victor?"

"You have a visitor, sir," he said frigidly. "Lt. Hudson."

Blakeley smiled mysteriously. "I don't suppose you know why Lt. Hudson is here, Victor?"

"He does not confide in me, sir."

"I wonder why that is, Victor," Blakeley said, enjoying the butler's discomfort as he taunted him for his past transgressions.

"I'm sure I don't know," Victor said nervously.

"Well, then, show him into the laboratory, please."

"Very good, sir," Victor said and started to leave.

"One moment, Victor," Blakeley said. "Before you show Lt. Hudson in, I've a question for you."

"You have, sir?"

"Yes. Just how did Mr. Spector know to be at the Academy of Music last evening?"

Victor blanched at the question. He knew how precarious his situation was. "I'm quite sure I've no idea, sir. Did he find you?"

"Obviously."

Victor showed no emotion as Blakeley scrutinized his face, but merely said, "Shall I show the lieutenant in, sir?"

"Victor?"

"Sir?"

"Surely you read the newspaper this morning."

"Only the theater section, sir. The rest of it depresses me."

Blakeley stared harder, but Victor's face was as stolid as granite. "Show Lt. Hudson to the laboratory, Victor," he growled.

"At once, sir."

Turning to his houseguest, Blakeley said, "Please excuse me, Don Orlando. I've some business I must attend to."

"Of course. It's such a fine day I think I shall walk the grounds for a while."

"Splendid. Enjoy yourself, but don't exert yourself too much." Blakeley paused a second, then asked quietly, so as not to embarrass the Spaniard again, "You will remember your promise, won't you? No Madeira until this evening?"

Don Orlando nodded. "You are my protector. I shall honor your wishes."

"And please reconsider your rejection of the priest's visit."

"I shall, *mi padrón*. I shall."

But as he left Don Orlando behind, Blakeley knew from the weary look in the old man's eyes that there was little chance of his changing his mind. Despite the Spaniard's denials, Blakeley knew also that his lapse in faith weighed heavily on his mind.

Walking to his basement laboratory, it occurred to Blakeley that there was irony in his caring about Don Orlando's soul since he was rather nonchalant about his own. Sophia had asked him to go to church that morning. It would help to ease his anxieties, she had said, and to atone for all his recent offenses against their marriage vows. But Blakeley had begged off because most of the congregation had probably read an account of the previous evening's events on the front page of some paper or other. He had visions of old women turning apoplectic when they saw him passing their pews.

So, abandoning her husband at the breakfast table, from which he too would have retired had Don Orlando not suddenly appeared, Sophia had dragged Ralphie and Rosie off, but not before telling Blakeley that they would pray for the safety and salvation of his soul. Ralphie had nodded piously at her words, then grinned when his mother wasn't looking. And Rosie had almost sneaked out of the house wearing lip rouge, but Sunday mornings always made Sophia more vigilant. The rouge was washed off rather roughly and replaced by a pout that Rosie would certainly wear through the entire service.

"Good morning, Lieutenant," Blakeley said as he entered his laboratory.

Hudson was holding a small metal tube. "One of the men from the Tenth found this on the roof just where we expected. The gunman had a good clean shot down to the steps below."

Blakeley studied the empty cartridge through his monocle. It was marked "WRA Co. 44 WCF."

"It's a centerfire forty-four forty," Hudson said. "It ought to fit the Winchester."

On a nearby table rested the Winchester .73 the police had found after the shooting. When he had called to arrange their appointment earlier that morning, Blakeley had asked Hudson to bring the gun with him so that he might run a few tests on it before too many others went over it and destroyed all traces of evidence. Hudson had met with resistance from the officers of the Tenth Precinct, but had won possession of the weapon when he had threatened to call the commissioner.

Examining the rifle, Blakeley said, "Yes, this cartridge will fit. Good work, Lieutenant."

"For a change, everything fits, Dr. Blakeley. But

I'm afraid you're not going to like it."

"Beecham?" Blakeley sighed.

Hudson nodded. "We had men out checking all the gun stores. Turns out the gun and ammunition were purchased at Tryon's on Chestnut Street. The boys had to get the manager out of bed, and they tell me he raised hell. But they got the receipt anyway." He paused, then added, "It was sold to Judge Magwood two weeks ago."

Blakeley shook his head. "I'm sure Beecham thought in his own twisted way that it was a fitting instrument to use to kill me."

"Anyway," Hudson said, "I've put this much together. Beecham hit his target and, begging your pardon, thought it was you. Then he ran across the roof to the rear of the building and climbed down the fire escape. Only he misjudged the last few feet in the dark, and when he fell to the ground, he landed on one of the garbage cans, probably hurting himself. In the fall he dropped the rifle, and not knowing the guy cursing behind the pile of garbage was only Bummy Rummel, he forgot it and took off as best as he could before anyone else spotted him."

"That's the scenario exactly, I'm sure," Blakeley said. "But we must have proof positive that it was Beecham who fired the rifle."

"And how do we get that?"

"Fingerprints, of course," Blakeley said as he dusted powder on the rifle's stock, barrel, and trigger.

"So you think those prints will tell you for sure that it was your friend Beecham, do you?"

"My dear colleague," Blakeley answered smugly, "dactylography will soon become as common a part of police work as flat feet are today."

Hudson smiled incredulously. "Who says?"

"Sir Francis Galton, with whom I had the pleasure of working at Scotland Yard."

Hudson arched an eyebrow and pretended to be mystified. The recording of fingerprints was not something new to him. The department had been entertaining the idea of adopting the practice for the past year or so. But there were some doubts about its validity. Since the technique fascinated Blakeley, however, Hudson showed polite interest.

"Now," Blakeley said as he studied the gun under a magnifying glass, "Galton explained that the sweat ducts of the body exude a colorless, transparent secretion of water, salt, urea, and fatty matter, which makes it sometimes unpleasant to be in a crowd on a hot day. And since this secretion is both aggravated and intensified during periods of great stress, such an emission will leave oily prints of the palms, feet, fingertips, and so on. It follows that since the commission of a crime is, in most instances, a stressful experience, prints should be left here and there as evidence. Look at this, Lieutenant."

Under the magnifying glass in Blakeley's hand, Hudson studied a set of remarkably clear fingerprints that the powder had revealed on the barrel of the rifle.

"You see these tiny whirls and even this little scar?" Blakeley said, pointing them out with a blue-tip match. "They're identical to those on a set of Beecham's prints I made before starting to work with him in the prison. As it happens, however, we shan't require them. See here, Lieutenant?" He ran the magnifying glass over the part of the stock where a print was obviously missing. "Ladies and gentleman, presenting Christopher Beecham."

"You mean he could fire a shot that accurately without a middle finger?"

Blakeley grunted. "It is one small measure of how much Beecham hates me, Lieutenant. Actually, I'm probably lucky in a sense. Had Beecham not been so eager to do me in, he might have been less impetuous and would therefore have murdered the right man."

There was a brief tap on the door, and Victor entered looking quite annoyed.

"What is it now, Victor?" Blakeley asked.

"Sir, that sheriff is on the telephone. He wishes to speak to you."

"Sheriff Burns?"

"I presume so, sir," Victor said and looked away when, just to annoy him, Hudson wagged a finger at him, as if to warn the butler to be on his best behavior, or else. . . .

"Please excuse me, Lieutenant." Blakeley rushed off to the alcove where the telephone was located.

"I hate to disturb you on a Sunday morning, Dr. Blakeley," Burns said when Blakeley answered, "but I have some bad news I thought you'd want to hear."

"It's quite all right, Sheriff," Blakeley assured him. "What's on your mind?"

"It's about the suspect Petticord."

"Oh?"

"I had him put in a cell away from the other prisoners. I do that with people like him for their own good."

"Yes, go on," Blakeley said.

"Well, I left strict orders for the guards to keep an eye on him. He was acting funny, as you saw when we arrested him. Anyway, I guess the guards weren't listening, because, at some time between midnight and three o'clock this morning, he made a noose out of his prison shirt and hanged himself on the bars of his cell."

Blakeley couldn't respond. But as he stood numbly, the phone clinched in his hand, he felt his stomach fluttering violently.

"I'm sorry, Dr. Blakeley," Burns said. "The best I can do is discipline the guards and look for Petticord's next of kin."

Blakeley was silent a moment longer; then he sighed deeply. "Let me know if you need help, Sheriff," he said at last, "especially with the first task."

Chapter Thirteen

Sheriff Burns called again a few days later to take Blakeley up on his offer, not to punish the negligent guards, but to find someone—anyone—who might be interested in claiming Richard Petticord's body. It was as if word had gone out to all the members of his underground community that it was best not to have heard of him, the sheriff contended.

The search for a surviving relative had become not only frustrating, but too time-consuming for the already depleted resources of the local constabulary. Even leads that should have borne results proved fruitless. At Blakeley's request, Lt. Hudson had wired a friend on the New Orleans force and asked him to canvass the French Quarter and other of Petticord's haunts. Alas, all Lt. Hudson's friend could report was that the dead man's family had disowned him and thought it was best they were finally rid of him.

At last, on yet another bright, hot afternoon in a

late spring that had long since given way to the dog days of summer, Blakeley asked his wife, "What do you think, dearest? Can we help?"

The Blakeley family and Nathan, all casually arrayed in loose-fitting clothing meant to make the temperature more bearable, sat in the shade of the side porch, enjoying glasses of lemonade. Indolence hung in the air like an opium-drenched miasma, and the taint of Christopher Beecham was blessedly absent from their lives for a few restful moments. No one had said very much for some time before Blakeley put his question to Sophia. Ralphie, in fact, was dozing fitfully, and Rosie had kept unusually quiet, because she was either worn out by the heat or tongue-tied by her infatuation with Nathan.

Dabbing herself modestly with a handkerchief, Sophia said, "That's a splendid idea, Ian. I've no quarrel with it."

"It's settled then," Blakeley said. "Mr. Petticord shall rest under an apple tree near the river. Now, who shall we get to perform the interment ceremony?"

"That may be a problem," Sophia said.

"What? Won't the Reverend Mr. Debbenham be available?" Blakeley asked archly.

Sophia frowned at him, but did not say anything. She appreciated her minister because he was one of the most tireless workers in the city in his clerical duties. But her husband did have a point that he tended to lay on the fire and brimstone a bit much. For all his strong points, the good minister had no sympathy when it came to anyone who acted against the precepts of his church. He'd more than likely recommend that Petticord be buried at a crossroads with a stake through his heart, as the elders of his faith had punished suicides in less-enlightened times. And if he realized that Petticord had been accused of murder, he'd suggest even worse.

"I'm sure Father Gorman will perform the ceremony," Nathan said when Sophia remained silent. Rosie's eyes grew large at Nathan's words and her face lit up, but Nathan acted as if he didn't notice.

"Really, Nathan?" Blakeley asked. "Even if he knows the man died by his own hand?"

"I'm sure Father Gorman would do it even if Petticord was guilty of murdering Hazleton and Aimwell."

"Jeez crumps, Nathan," Ralphie said, waking from his nap, "Petticord wasn't a werewolf."

Condemnation of Ralphie's ludicrous theory was general on the porch, Rosie going so far as to punch her brother, much to her mother's dismay. But Ralphie was asleep again before their censure could take effect.

"Father Gorman isn't your run-of-the-mill priest," Nathan said as Ralphie began to snore heavily. "He used to be a missionary in Central America. He even spent some time as a captive in the jungle, just like Don Orlando. He's seen a lot of unbelievable things, and he's not as quick to condemn people's weaknesses as other clergymen."

"Will you ask him, Nathan?"

"Certainly, Dr. Blakeley," Nathan said. "It will give me a chance to feel important."

Indeed, outside of being back in Allison's good graces, Nathan had great need of finding something to bolster his self-esteem. For since the night of the concert, his life had turned upside down. Pratt's article had brought down a firestorm of antipathy from people all over the city. And it had necessitated an arduous search for Bummy Rummel, who despite the best efforts of the police was still at large. Nathan didn't suspect Bummy of complicity in Simeon Dorsett's murder, but knowing Beecham's hatred of the indigent, he feared for the man's safety should Beecham take it in mind to track him down. No sooner had Bummy been safely brought to the Eleventh's lockup, however, than Nathan was summoned to the commissioner's office.

Commissioner MacDonald had spent the night of the shooting at the wedding of Dolcinella, daughter of Nunzio Gazzo, who controlled the city's docks, to Vito, son of Attilio Baccamatta, who controlled South Philadelphia. MacDonald had awoken more hungover than usual to discover the citizenry up in arms owing to the acts of a madman—and what G. Lindsey Pratt, the famed correspondent, called, "the police's inept handling of a situation that our brave boys in Cuba would never have allowed to arise."

With the self-righteousness that only a career politician could muster without the slightest hint of shame, the commissioner suspended Nathan for two weeks without permitting him to utter a word in his defense. And when, in an outburst of contempt, Nathan had called his superior a hypocrite, he was rewarded with another week's suspension. Then, to make matters worse, he had tracked down Pratt at the offices of *The News* and, finding him hiding under a desk, blackened the reporter's eye with a solid right to the face. That action had earned another week without pay.

One month's suspension meant the loss of $100.00 in salary, give or take a few dollars for kickbacks to City Hall. More than ever before, Nathan wanted to join the army. Just as soon as the funeral service was over, and he'd returned Father Gorman to the monastery at Villanova, he intended to visit a recruiter and argue his case for enlistment.

And so it was that, the morning following the Blakeleys' decision to lay Petticord to rest on their peaceful estate, they gathered around a freshly dug grave, with Nathan, Allison, and Father Gorman rounding out their number. Their somber attire and the black parasols that protected Sophia, Rosie, and Allison contrasted starkly with the glorious weather, which was as hot and summery as on every morning of the past week. Only an occasional breeze off the river made its way up the hill and through the trees. Where the sun sneaked through the shade, steam rose from the dewy grass. But the azaleas were in brilliant bloom and the scent of lilacs wafted gently around them.

Having discovered that Don Orlando and Father Gorman had a common bond in their experiences in Central America, Blakeley had hoped to cajole the Spaniard into speaking with the priest. He was certain their meeting would ease the older man's troubled conscience. But, unexpectedly, Don Orlando had continued his recovery, appearing that morning for breakfast and actually eating a plateful of food. Jokingly, Blakeley had credited the tonic he had prescribed for the turnabout in Don Orlando's health, but in reality he was somewhat puzzled by it. And when Don Orlando refused his request to visit with Father Gorman, with more vehemence than his polite facade could hide, Blakeley had again not pushed the issue.

Shortly after the service began, the mourners were interrupted by the arrival of a visitor, who entered quietly after leaving her carriage on the drive.

"Do you know her, Ian?" Sophia asked in a respectful whisper.

"Yes, darling," he said in the same tone. "Her name is Cassie Aimwell."

Sophia gasped. "*That* Aimwell?"

"Yes."

"Oh, the poor dear."

Blakeley looked at Nathan, who returned his quizzical glance. Rosie was less reverent. She watched Cassie walk gingerly across the grassy knoll that separated the driveway from the grave and whispered to Ralphie, "Another *belle dame sans souci*, brother dear?"

"Huh?"

Sophia quickly shushed them. Father Gorman was praying over Richard Petticord's open grave, the coffin having been lowered a moment earlier. The priest was reciting a prayer he had used when a Central American Indian died and he was not certain if the deceased had been converted to Christianity.

"I'll bet you Mother likes her," Ralphie whispered to Rosie as Sophia turned her attention to Cassie, who stood beside the grave and pulled a fashionable Spanish veil over her face to pray.

"Why?" Rosie asked.

"You'll see."

Cassie looked mysterious behind the veil, like a figure out of Goya. She seemed fragile in the woods, almost spectral.

All eyes remained on her for a moment, then returned to the burial service.

Father Gorman was a dimunitive, white-haired gentleman in his fifties who went about his work in a crisp, undramatic manner. He appeared fatigued and paused several times, as if to catch his breath. At the end of the service, he scattered a handful of dirt over Petticord's coffin and, as the tiny clods hit the lid, said, "Remember, man, that thou art dust and to dust thou shalt return." There was a disunified smattering of amens, and the two gravediggers whom Blakeley had hired for the occasion started to shovel dirt into the grave.

Sophia had selected a simple white marker with a decorative cross painted at its center; above the cross was printed the name Petticord, and below it the date of his demise. It would serve to remind the world of the Petticord's life until they could have a proper gravestone carved.

"Good morning, Miss Aimwell," Blakeley said as the small group broke up and started back to the house. "I didn't expect to see you here."

Cassie lifted the veil and pinned it to the brim of her bonnet. "I'm sorry I interrupted the service," she said. "Today is my driver's day off, and I got lost along the way. You might say it's the story of my life, Dr. Blakeley."

"We're pleased to see you in any case, Miss Aimwell, or would you prefer...."

Cassie smiled and said, with more than a hint of self-deprecation, "Destiny's Darling went out the door with the rest of the fools you frightened away. Gone forever and good riddance. Thank you."

Blakeley smiled back. "You must join us for breakfast. Our cook has prepared enough for a regiment."

"My stomach is much too queasy these days, Dr. Blakeley."

"Tea then?"

She nodded. "Tea sounds fine." She paused, frowned, and said, "I'm terribly ashamed of myself, you know."

"Miss Aimwell, if you're referring to the day we barged in on you unannounced," Blakeley hastily fibbed, "I assure you it's forgotten."

"It isn't just that," she said, "not that that alone isn't cause for penitence. It's about poor Richard as well. I should have taken care of his burial instead of leaving it to you, but I was preoccupied with my brother's death. Do you understand, Dr. Blakeley? Please say you do."

"Of course I do," he said. As they strolled a few feet ahead of the rest of the group, Blakeley took her arm and turned to the others. "Permit me to introduce you to my friends and family. You've already met Ralphie."

"Hello, Ralphie," Cassie said nervously.

"Hello," Ralphie answered. He also spoke nervously because he knew he was being scrutinized by his sister.

After being introduced, Rosie said under her breath, "She looks a bit frail for you, brother dear."

The morning sun did seem especially cruel as it shone on Cassie's porcelain face. Blakeley introduced her to Father Gorman, then to Allison and Nathan.

As Blakeley was introducing her to Sophia, Ralphie turned to Rosie and replied out of the side of his mouth, "That's what I meant, sister dear. Mother thinks the more you look like a ghost, the more you look like a lady. I can read her mind."

"If Mother could read Cassie Aimwell's mind," Rosie whispered, "They'd hear her gasping from here to California."

"How do you know so much about Cassie Aimwell?"

"She's a legend in her own time, brother dear."

They noticed their mother looking in their direction and quickly donned looks of sobriety.

The party proceeded uphill toward the house, where Mrs. Snopkowski had been waiting impatiently for the service to end before the bacon turned too crisp and the waffles soggy. Until Cassie's arrival, breakfast had preoccupied Ralphie's mind. He was certain by the look on his mother's face that he would be seated next to the now prim-and-proper Miss Aimwell. Dumpling would definitely smell a rat, and if he ever hoped to enjoy the maid's company again, it would cost him at least three boxes of chocolates.

Victor met the party at the front door. He was

irked by a telephone call that had come just as he was about to call Bulgarian Charlie, his main supplier of gin.

"A message for you, sir," he announced to Blakeley. "Lt. Hudson again."

"Does it sound important, Victor, or can it wait?" Blakeley said. "As you can see, this is no ordinary moment."

"Well," Victor said, his voice loud enough for all to hear, "as you know, the good lieutenant is a man of few words, but from what I gather there's been another murder—a messy one like that Aimwell case."

"Good Lord," Blakeley said.

"How horrible," Sophia said. She noticed Cassie's mouth opening, then her color turning bilious green. "Catch her!" she shouted to Ralphie.

"Nice work, Victor," Rosie said. "You sure have a way with words."

"I beg your pardon?" Victor said huffily.

"Jeez crumps," Ralphie muttered, holding Cassie in his arms.

"Oh, the poor dear," Sophia said. "You must get her into the house and out of the sun right away."

"Jeez crumps," Ralphie repeated, sweeping Cassie up and carrying her into the house.

Father Gorman, who had been silent since the end of the ceremony, turned ashen for a moment and started to shiver, as though a sudden gust of cold air had just hit him. Allison saw him and signaled Nathan, who took the priest by the arm.

"Are you all right, Father?" Nathan asked, studying the man's eyes.

"Yes, I'm all right, Nathan."

Nathan had seen heart attacks before, and the clergyman showed all the outward signs of suffering one. "You look very pale. Are you having trouble breathing?"

"No," the priest said flatly. "It's nothing like that."

"Do you want Dr. Blakeley to examine you?"

Father Gorman shook his head. "I know what you're thinking, and it isn't that."

"I hope not," Nathan said.

The priest looked around, noted that most of the party was following Ralphie into the house, and lowered his voice. Allison understood his actions to mean he wished to speak to Nathan in private. So she joined Sophia.

"This is going to sound like something out of a gothic novel," Father Gorman said. "I dreamt of that murder last night."

Nathan stopped dead. "Are you sure?"

"Yes," Father Gorman said. "I could see it all vividly. And my screams certainly convinced everyone at the monastery that something awful had happened. I had to lie to the provincial and tell him that I'm subject to these spells because of the malaria I suffered in Central America. If I hadn't lied, the good Lord only knows what they would have done to me. They all think me quite mad."

"Why would you have to lie about a nightmare?" Nathan asked. "Everybody has them. I must average one a week on my job."

"I know, Nathan. That's what I've been telling myself. But last night wasn't the first time I woke up everyone in the monastery with my screams. You see, it happened six nights ago, and six nights before that too."

When Nathan opened his mouth incredulously, Father Gorman nodded his head. "Yes, Nathan, I dreamt about the murders of Reginald Aimwell and Louis Paul Hazleton before they happened too."

Chapter Fourteen

Nathan's head was reeling: everything Father Gorman had dreamed had become graphic, disturbing reality the moment Nathan entered the home of the latest victim. Jack Hawthorne—heir to an empire that included the nation's largest textile mills, ship-building interests throughout the world, and scores of specialized metal shops—was a well-known gadabout, an avid hunter, and a collector of rare furs. In fact, it was on a rug made from the hide of a Kodiak bear that the police had found Hawthorne's disemboweled corpse, the way Father Gorman had described it.

As he had ridden to Hawthorne's Main Line mansion with Blakeley, Allison, and Ralphie, Nathan said very little, perplexed by Father Gorman's claims. And upon learning the validity of the priest's dreams, his quandary deepened. Gorman had sworn his friend to secrecy until he could decide what course would be proper for a man of his station to take. Nathan had assented hesitantly. But seeing that the priest might be of use in solving the case, and perhaps might save some unfortunate men from the same fate Hawthorne had met, Nathan doubted the wisdom of his agreement.

Seated with the others in Hawthorne's well-furnished parlor, Nathan knew he shouldn't hesitate to investigate all avenues open to him, because catching the murderer would put him back on good terms with Commissioner MacDonald. And at present, getting back into MacDonald's good graces was no small feat. For with each new murder, popular opinion turned ever more against the police, and the increasingly lurid newspaper accounts of the mysterious woman and her crimes weren't helping matters. Papers of varying stripes had assigned reporters to seek out her identity, and newspaper artists had ceased lampooning Blakeley and the police to focus on the woman G. Lindsey Pratt had labeled The Green Lorelei, which even Nathan admitted was clever, although he did not share the thought with anyone.

Naturally, *The Morning Star*, under the direction of Bernard Spector—who knew that the public wanted to be entertained no matter what license he had to take with the truth—had depicted the woman as sultry and wanton, with her gown cut low, one eyebrow raised, and her mouth opened slightly, as if whispering a siren's message of death into some unwary man's ear. As time passed, the woman became even more lascivious, and so much had been made of the color green that it was the favorite shade for clothing that summer, which, of course, was an unwelcome development for Blakeley and others trying to find her. The murderer's notoriety so enraged the commissioner that he was working his limited forces overtime in order to catch her. With the heat and the strain already put upon the diminished police force, the required extra duty threatened to cause strife in the ranks if it continued too long.

All in all, June of 1898 promised to be a profitable month for the local newspapers, and the murder of Jack Hawthorne only added more grist for the mill. But it had, at last, provided a much-needed break for the police's investigative endeavors. It seemed that a chambermaid had seen the unknown woman in green as had no other person still alive.

And there she sat, Miss Betty Jane Stamm, as Blakeley paced before her, asking question after question. The chambermaid appeared torn between her own innately suspicious nature and the urge to enjoy all of this sudden attention. She bit her lower lip occasionally and fidgeted when she answered Blakeley's questions. Betty Jane seemed to be the sort who could blend in with the dishwater, a young woman dull of mind and expression, and Blakeley's confidence in her as a credible witness faded with each minute. But he was anxious to get everything she had to say down on paper before the gentlemen of the press got wind of the murder.

"Would you repeat that for me, Miss Stamm?" he asked, writing a line in a notebook.

"I said she was creepy, especially in the eyes." Betty Jane sighed impatiently and picked at a wart on her thumb.

"Creepy," Blakeley repeated. "I see. Can you define the word creepy for me, Miss Stamm?"

"Creepy means, y'know, like she could give you the bejeebers jist by lookin' at you. I know *I* was all goose pimply when I seen her."

"Where exactly did you see her?"

"In the garden with the Mister."

"Mr. Hawthorne, that is?"

"Yeah. He was the Mister when his father was

away. Then he thought he was the cock a the walk."

"Did you see Mr. Hawthorne and the woman up close?"

"Yeah."

Blakeley glanced around at Nathan, Allison, and Ralphie, and when none of them made a move to interject any questions, he continued. "How close were you, Miss Stamm?" he asked.

She nodded at the wall, a scant four feet away. "Like from here to there," she said.

"You must have been practically on top of them."

"I was behind the hedge."

"Which one?"

She pointed through a large window that faced the sprawling green lawn that lay before the mansion like a carpet. "That one by the duck pond. They were walkin' along arm in arm."

"Were you following them?"

"Of course not," she snapped. But when Blakeley stopped pacing, she added, "Well, not at first."

"Go on, Miss Stamm," he said, jotting another note.

"Well, y'know, we ain't supposed to smoke in the house," she said, "even though Mr. Hawthorne smokes—smoked—like a damn chimney hisself. So I snuck out to the bushes where I could smoke in peace. I usta put the cigarettes out in the duck pond 'til the old Mister found one and threatened to ax whoever was doin' it. So now I bury my butts under one a the rose bushes."

"That's why you were behind that hedge then?"

"Didn't I jist explain that?" she said, turning around angrily.

Blakeley stared into her face. She scowled, bit her lip, and picked again at the wart. What he had seen in her eyes was rather encouraging: anger, suspicion, defensiveness, and a lot of hostility that Miss Stamm herself did not understand, but no uncertainty. No matter how briefly acquainted Betty Jane Stamm and the truth had been the rest of her life, Blakeley was positive that, at least for the moment, they were bosom companions.

"What time was this, Miss Stamm. Approximately."

"Around eleven. I'd just turned down the Mister's bed, and I was gonna sleep after my smoke."

"Did you see them do anything else besides walk around the duck pond?"

"Whattaya wanna hear? That they done it on the grass?"

"If that is what you saw, Miss Stamm."

"Well, they didn't," Miss Stamm said, then added, "The lady in green woulda got her ass all wet on accounta the dampness if they did."

Allison blushed at the remark. Nathan and Ralphie hid their smiles. Blakeley dismissed the chambermaid's impertinence.

"What did you see, Miss Stamm?" he asked. "Please."

"They stopped walkin' fer a minute. He kissed her hand. Let's see," she said, thinking a moment before continuing. "The lady looked up at him and he kissed her on the mouth. She let him. Then they turned around and went up to the house."

"You hesitated for a moment, Miss Stamm. Was there a reason?"

"Listen," she said huffily, "when it comes to somebody's reputation, I'm damned careful what I say."

"What was the woman wearing?"

"Somethin' green."

"I know that, Miss Stamm, but—"

"It was kinda brazen, if you ask me. I know I'd never wear it."

"How could you tell it was brazen?" Blakeley asked. "The light can't be very good out by the duck

228

pond at that time of night."

"You callin' me a liar?"

"Not if you keep talking, Miss Stamm," he said. "Tell us whatever you can remember about the woman. Hair, eyes, anything."

Betty Jane looked down at the wart on her thumb. It was bleeding. She put her thumb in her mouth and licked it, but it bled again.

"She was dark haired and olive complected like the newspapers say," she said, studying the wart as she spoke. "I can't swear nothin' about the eyes. I followed them up to the house."

"Why?"

"Huh?"

"Why did you follow them? If Mr. Hawthorne had seen you, he'd probably have fired you."

"I know, I know." Betty Jane shrugged her shoulders. "You gotta take yer chances now and then, right? In my line a work, knowin' the dirt and lettin' the high and mighty find out sorta accidentally that you know the dirt can mean a nice surprise in yer Christmas stockin'. Know what I mean?"

She looked at Allison for confirmation, and Allison smiled.

"See?" Betty Jane said, pointing. "She knows what I mean."

"Go on, please," Blakeley said, careful to hide his exasperation.

"Besides," Betty Jane said, somewhat breezily, "I was curious. It ain't nice to joke about the dead, but me 'n the other girls usta always wonder what kinda woman would take up with the Mister. I don't care how much money he had, he was still a worm. Big ears, beady eyes, and he strutted around as if he was worth lookin' at. Ugh! So anyways, I followed them. And I can tell you this much, she mighta been creepy, but she was a helluva lot better than he deserved. I remember thinkin' at the time,

229

'Jeez, what some girls won't do fer money.'"

"You're being very helpful, Miss Stamm," Blakeley said. "We appreciate your assistance."

"Yeah?"

"Yes. Now, Miss Stamm, can you remember anything else about the woman besides her hair and the green dress?"

"What's it worth to you? That's what I'd like to know."

"Well, would you like your name in the newspaper, Miss Stamm? You could become a celebrity."

"Yeah?"

"And with a very nice description of you," he said earnestly. "Why, you'll feel like a famous actress."

She smiled, then looked puzzled. "Which one?" she asked.

When Blakeley looked around for help, Allison said, "Anna Held."

"Yeah," the chambermaid said, "Anna Held. I always thought I looked like her, only I'm built better."

Ralphie and Nathan tried to turn away, but Betty Jane saw their smiles and heard Ralphie snorting. She glared at them and fell silent.

Blakeley tried to save the moment. "There, there, Miss Stamm—"

"Yiz can all go to hell."

"My friends are merely allergic to the yellow roses in the garden. So am I." He touched a handkerchief to his nose. "I've been on the verge of sneezing since I arrived."

Betty Jane pouted for a moment, during which Blakeley darted an angry look at his son and associate. Ralphie and Nathan immediately regained their composure.

"Nobody got a better look at her than I did, y'know," the maid said finally. "So nobody better make fun a me no more." She looked up at Blakeley and said, "Listen, I got right up to that big stuffed bear across from the door to the Mister's study. And I got a real good look at her before the door closed. Nobody else can say that or they're liars."

"The woman in green," Blakeley said, "is she as beautiful as the newspapers say?"

"Looked like a Spanish *señorita*, if you wanna know."

"Did you hear her speak?"

"Some."

"Did she have a Spanish accent?"

"How the hell would I know a Spanish accent?"

"Did she speak with any kind of accent at all, Miss Stamm?"

"Well, she didn't sound like she was from Philadelphia." Betty Jane thought for a few seconds. "No, I can't say she talked funny. Actually, she sounded smart."

"That's good, Miss Stamm." Blakeley jotted notes in a hurry. "Can you describe her voice?"

"It was a nice voice, but they were whisperin' mostly, so I can't really describe it."

"Tell us what you saw through the keyhole, Miss Stamm."

She blushed and said, "He kissed her again, the Mister did, then she let him slobber all over her neck. I think some clothes come off."

"You think?"

"Well, yeah, some clothes come off," she replied and glanced at Allison somewhat apologetically. "But then they moved around to the far side a the room, and I couldn't see much after they got on the couch, or I guess it was on the floor cuz that's where they found him. On that rug with the teeth. I remember thinkin', 'Goddamn it, can't yiz do it where I can see yiz?'"

Obviously, the evening of her employer's tryst

231

with the Green Lorelei had not been the first time that Betty Jane Stamm sneaked up to a door and watched Jack Hawthorne through the keyhole. She seemed overheated by the memory.

"So, you saw nothing else after that?" Blakeley said, preparing to fold up his notes and end the interrogation.

"Oh, I seen a few things," she said, frowning at the interruption. "Only that wind or whatever it was hurt my eyes and I had to look away."

For the first time since they had met the chambermaid and listened to her prattle, Blakeley and his associates looked at each other with serious faces.

"Describe the wind, please," Blakeley said quickly.

"It was like a blizzard or somethin'. Everything was blowin' around in the room, papers 'n all everywhere. I got somethin' in my eye, a speck of dust or somethin', so like I says, I looked away. That's when the thing roared and—"

"What thing?"

"The *thing*," she said. "I dunno. I thought the goddamned bear was alive all of a sudden. I jist about messed my bloomers when I heard it."

Ralphie, who had been paying little attention to the maid's story, suddenly exclaimed loudly and beamed triumphantly. But before he could speak, his father cast him a warning glance to hold his silence.

When Betty Jane paused after Ralphie's outburst, Blakeley had to prod her to continue. "Then?"

"Then what the hell do you think? I took off like a rabbit and I didn't realize until I was halfway down the stairs that the Mister was screamin' like a soul in hell up there."

"You kept running?"

"All the way to the servants' privy," she said. "I

232

locked myself in." She looked around for anyone who would dare censure her action. "Well, wouldn't you?"

When no one disagreed, Blakeley asked, "Is there anything else, Miss Stamm?"

"What the hell more do you want?"

"Nothing, Miss Stamm. I believe you've covered everything. Would you mind sitting down with Miss Meredith here and describing the woman again so she can sketch her portrait? It's very important to us."

The chambermaid made a pinched, humorless smile. "Like I says, what's it worth to yiz?"

Blakeley looked into the dull eyes for a moment, then took out his wallet. "Very well, Miss Stamm," he said and handed her a five-dollar bill.

She snatched the money out of his hand, made sure of its denomination, and put it in her pocket. Her eyes grew brighter when she saw Blakeley removing a second five-dollar bill.

He held it out. But when she reached for it, he pulled it back.

She scowled suspiciously. "What're yiz up to?"

"This is to purchase your silence, Miss Stamm, when the other reporters interview you," he said. "Give us a few days before you say anything."

Her jaw dropped. "But what about becomin' a celebrity?"

"You can trust Miss Meredith to treat you well," he said and waited for her response. "Well?"

She nodded and he handed her the money. Betty Jane snatched the bill and put it in her pocket.

Allison rose and said, "Let's go out on the patio where we can make use of the sunlight."

When the women were gone, Ralphie finally had his chance to speak. "Did you hear what she said? Now what do you think about my werewolf theory?"

"I think, as I always have, that had you spent as much time studying as you had reading dime novels you'd be a genius," Blakeley replied. "As for the rest of Miss Stamm's story, it seems to be fairly reliable, although she is of questionable character. But she has corroborated Mr. Petticord's story about the wind."

"What do you make of the wind?" Nathan asked.

"I haven't the slightest idea, Nathan," Blakeley said, "but clearly it cannot be dismissed."

"Neither can my stomach, Dad," Ralphie said. "Mind if we eat now?"

"Yes, I do, Ralphie. I don't want you going up to the study and depositing your lunch on the floor. The investigation is difficult enough as it is."

"Aw, fiddlesticks," Ralphie muttered as they climbed the marble staircase, the same one Betty Jane Stamm had raced down with Jack Hawthorne's screams following her.

Much to Blakeley's chagrin, Bones Fatzinger was stationed at the door to the study. Hudson had used the excuse that, since Nathan was suspended from duty, Blakeley's task force needed more manpower, and he had duly assigned the eager, but incompetent, Fatzinger to fill the vacancy. Hudson and Blakeley would have words about that soon, Blakeley thought, as he watched Fatzinger peel a hard-boiled egg and drop the shells into his helmet.

"Look at Bones," Ralphie said, envious of the officer's food. "All of this hasn't disturbed his appetite, has it?"

But his father didn't relent, and the men continued to the study. Much of the house was decorated with stuffed wild animals. In the hallway, they passed a puma, a wild pig, and a rare leopard, and the thought occurred to Nathan, who quelled it immediately, that it was the height of irony that Jack Hawthorne had been gutted like his trophies.

"Oh, jeez," Ralphie gasped as Fatzinger opened the door to let them in the study.

"Dott's some vunderful big schtink, huh?" Fatzinger giggled, then swallowed the rest of his egg. "Chust like der shed around butcherin' time, by Chessus."

As the three men looked over the room, Ralphie wasn't the only one who had to struggle to catch his breath. Though the body had been taken to the morgue, the pungent stench of death clung yet to the carpet and assaulted their nostrils. Once again, the men were forced to shield their noses with handkerchiefs, lest they should be overcome by the noxious odor of death.

"Still interested in lunch, Beef?" Nathan said absently, for the room was exactly as Father Gorman had described it.

"What're we doing here, Dad?" Ralphie asked, his voice muffled by the handkerchief he held tightly over his mouth. "The police have been going over this darn place for hours."

"Well, Ralph," Blakeley said, "you heard Miss Stamm say Hawthorne and the woman removed some of their clothing. Perhaps we can find some of it."

"The police would have found it by now, Dad."

"Are you quite sure of that?"

Ralphie walked over to a window and said, "Maybe it blew out in the wind." He picked up a piece of paper, one of many strewn about the floor. "If you expect to find a little green fiber or something in here, Dad, you must believe in miracles."

"I find it curious, Ralph, that someone who disdains miracles would at the same time argue a case for goblins and ghoulies."

"I never said anything about goblins or ghoulies, Dad."

"Ralph," Blakeley said, effectively silencing his

son, "I am going to search the couch with a magnifying glass and hope to find, if not a green fiber, perhaps a hair follicle belonging to a dark-haired woman. You and Nathan are going to pick up these papers to see if anything on them can lead us to a rational conclusion."

Ralphie could not miss the irritation in his father's voice. He nodded wearily. "Yes, Dad."

Blakeley knelt beside the couch, carefully avoiding the blood staining the carpet around the area where the bearskin rug had been. The rug had been removed and taken to Blakeley's laboratory, where he would go through its blood-saturated fur hoping to find a trace of anything belonging to the woman in green. He believed the rug would be more fertile ground than the scene of the crime had so far proven.

Distracted by thoughts of Father Gorman's second sight, Nathan joined Ralphie in scooping up the papers that littered the room. Most of the papers were bills with payment stamps, and the larger portion of the bills related to Hawthorne's obsession with hunting. There were invoices for guns and ammunition and for clothing needed to aid survival in the wild. Nathan and Ralphie also found agreements made with taxidermists, a draft of an article Hawthorne had been writing on how best to bring down an elephant, and travel arrangements for past expeditions to the snowy peaks of the Himalayas, the wilds of Canada, and the jungles of Africa.

Ralphie picked up piece after piece of paper, read them, then tossed them into a waste can. He was annoyed by his father's smugness, miffed by Nathan's aloof behavior, and hungry beyond all bounds.

"All right, Dad," he said at last, his stomach getting the better of him. "How did the Green Lorelei get out of here? I'd like you to answer that rationally."

Blakeley looked up, noticing his son's irritation. "Ralphie, if you don't mind—"

"Do you see any female footprints?" Ralphie asked. "Something that might have been made by a small foot in a high heel? There aren't any. Right, Dad? Neither in here nor outside."

"We haven't finished looking outside, Ralph," Blakeley said and returned to his magnifying glass. "The chambermaid has just informed us of Mr. Hawthorne's movements when he was in the company of the woman. We shall attend to that presently."

Still in the hold of his ruminations, Nathan continued shuffling through the papers. Suddenly he plucked a document from the pile and perused it. "Do hunters visit Cuba for anything, Dr. Blakeley?"

"I suppose so," Blakeley mused. "For wild boar perhaps. Why do you ask?"

Nathan walked over to the couch and showed him a pair of documents, one of which was a bill for a voyage to Cuba on the *S.S. Hispañola*. The other was a schedule that detailed the ship's departure from Boston, a stop at Freeport in the Bahamas and a projected arrival time in Havana.

"Hawthorne was planning to go there as soon as the war was over," Nathan said, pointing to the date marked on the schedule. "People are so confident that the war will end before the summer is over that cruise lines are already scheduling passengers for early fall."

Blakeley was still studying the travel arrangements when Ralphie walked over to the open window.

"And how about this, Dad?" he asked, persisting in his peevish refutation of his father's investigation. "When we got here these windows weren't open wide enough for a pygmy to get through. And even if your Green Lorelei—"

Blakeley scowled. "She is not my Green Lorelei, Ralph."

"All right, Dad. But even if she had the power to shrink herself and squeeze through, these windows she'd have to sprout wings too, because it's a long way down."

"I noticed that, Ralph." Blakeley said, frowning. The more his son questioned him, the more he felt his failure to discover answers that might even approach the rational. But they existed, he was certain. All he required was perseverance—and perhaps a little luck—to come up with them.

"It's as if the lady just disappeared into the night," Ralphie concluded.

"No one simply disappears, Ralph," Blakeley said evenly.

"Well," Ralphie said, dropping the handkerchief he held before his nose and spreading out his palms for emphasis, "have you found any fibers? Any hairs?"

"It could be," Nathan intervened, always the peacemaker, "that the fibers and hairs were so scattered by the wind that we'll never find them."

But his supposition only encouraged Ralphie. "And what about that wind, Dad?"

Blakeley got up, put his glass in his pocket, removed his monocle, and pinched the bridge of his nose. "Very well, what about it, Ralphie?" he said.

"There was no breeze last night, remember? It was stagnant, just like the night Reginald Aimwell was murdered and Petticord heard the wind. Or don't you believe the chambermaid?"

Blakeley took part of the curtain near the window and examined it for a moment. It was a section that had been caught in a latch when the wind caused the cloth to billow through the opening in the window. There was a small tear.

"Presuming, Ralph, that I do not doubt either Mr. Petticord or Miss Stamm when their statements include mention of a terrible wind," he said, "just what would you make of it?"

Ralphie started to speak, but changed his mind. "I guess I don't know, Dad," he said, putting the handkerchief back over his nose. "I guess that's why you're the detective, not me."

Blakeley shook his head. "I believe we've seen all that we'll ever see here," he said. "Have you looked at all the papers?"

"All accounted for," Nathan answered.

Fatzinger giggled like a child when the three men left the room; then he bit into a handful of scallions. But his mirth was lost on Blakeley and the others as they headed out to the patio.

Before they joined Allison and Miss Stamm, Nathan took Blakeley by the arm and let Ralphie walk on alone. He could tell how disappointed the detective was that his efforts to find even the smallest piece of evidence had once more proven futile. He felt discouraged, too. A case with no clues could frustrate a man to the point of madness. Nathan couldn't withhold information that might save them all a great deal of grief, and so he had made a decision.

"You have something on your mind?" Blakeley said.

"Yes, I do."

"I thought you seemed rather reserved, Nathan. What's troubling you?"

"It's Father Gorman," Nathan said slowly, not sure how his friend was going to react to the story he had to tell.

"Oh?"

"This is going to sound very strange," Nathan said, "but even before we got here I could have

239

described for you what we saw. The colors in the room, the size and shape of the open window, the position of the sofa, the trophies, and above all, the body on the bearskin rug."

Blakeley blinked. "Really?"

"Really."

"What does this have to do with Father Gorman?"

Sparing no details, Nathan told Blakeley about the priest's nightmares. Although skeptical of such instances of foresight, Blakeley was convinced of its veracity by the minutiae that the priest had detailed to Nathan earlier that day.

"I hope this doesn't make Father Gorman a suspect," Nathan said as he concluded the bizarre tale.

"No, of course not," Blakeley said, then added, with not a little irony, "but it would be nice to have at least one suspect at hand."

For the first time that afternoon, a hint of a smile flickered across Nathan's careworn face. "What do you make of these dreams?"

Blakeley chortled nervously. "I haven't the foggiest notion, dear boy. But I'd like to speak with Father Gorman as soon as possible. Do you think you can arrange it?"

"Let me call him," Nathan said hesitantly. "I'm sure he'll be very anxious to talk to you."

Their conversation concluded, the two men joined the others on the patio. There they found Ralphie taking large breaths of the fresh air, in an effort to cleanse his nostrils of the stench of the crime scene. Allison and the chambermaid sat on a stone bench, and it was immediately apparent from her loud braying that Betty Jane was in a foul mood.

"Looka this pitcher," she said, snatching a pad from Allison and holding it up for the men to see.

"I ask yiz, does this look at all like Anna Held? Huh?"

Allison winked and made a helpless gesture. She was carefully peeling off a glove and putting her artist's tools away.

"Of course not, Miss Stamm," Ralphie said.

"I toldja," the chambermaid said, turning to scowl at Allison.

"It looks just like you," Ralphie said, causing Betty Jane to turn her scowl full upon him.

"Where the hell are your eyeglasses, mister?" she said. "Since when do I have a mole on my nose?"

"It doesn't look like a mole," Ralphie said, studying the sketch. "It's more like a pimple."

Miss Stamm stiffened, her face reddened, and she tore the picture into small pieces.

"Yiz better not put my pitcher in the paper, lady," she warned Allison, "not if yiz know what's good fer yiz." Then, before storming off, she turned to Blakeley and said, "Don't think I'm keepin' my mouth shut when the other reporters get here. Not after yiz let her insult me."

"But, madam," Blakeley said, starting to remind her that he'd paid for her silence, but she proceeded into the house before he had the chance.

Nathan smiled at Allison. "Warm day, Miss Rembrandt," he said.

"I think I'll stick to writing," she said. "Actually, I was doing my best to flatter her. I have no idea where the mole or pimple came from. It must have been a fly speck on the paper. Anyway, we were getting along well enough until she asked me to do her portrait."

Blakeley, who had been staring in the direction of the chambermaid's exit, looking as if he could have calmly flayed her alive, turned and asked, "Did she help you at all with the woman in green, Miss Meredith?"

"I think so," Allison said, unfolding her sketch pad to display the drawing she had made from the maid's description.

"Look at those eyes," Ralphie said.

"Creepy, huh?" Allison said, mimicking Betty Jane's voice.

"They'd give me the bejeebers if I saw them for real," Ralphie said.

"Do you think it's an accurate rendering, Miss Meredith?" Blakeley asked.

"If Betty Jane can be believed, it is," Allison said. "She told me to put madness into the eyes, and I had to try it a few times before she said it was right."

Birds fluttered and chirruped in the fountain behind them as they studied the woman in the drawing. She was beautiful by any standards. Her features were fine, almost patrician, but cruelty marred her smile. If madness could be captured, Allison had succeeded. As for the eyes, they were otherworldly, hypnotic. Pure, unadulterated malice poured out of them.

"Do those eyes remind you of anyone?" Blakeley asked.

"They're Christopher Beecham's eyes," Allison said without hesitation. "I remembered his eyes from the sketches I did during his trial. When Betty Jane said to put madness in the woman's eyes, Beecham came right into my mind."

"They're a perfect match, I should think," Blakeley said.

Noticing the detective's weariness at the mention of his bloodthirsty adversary, Allison changed the subject. "I can paint the dress when I get back to Mrs. Blakeley's studio," she said as she gestured across most of the gown. "This is all green, of course, a very lush shade of green—so lush, in fact, that Betty Jane said it glowed."

"Satin, perhaps?" Blakeley said.

"I asked the same question," Allison said, "but all I got back was that it glowed. I gather it was just a very bright color."

"The steward from The Rod and Gun Club did say it was vulgar," Nathan said, then smiled as he recalled Oscar's actual words. "I'll check on the lighting in the hallway to see if it makes any difference."

Allison pointed to some ornamental designs on the gown. "This piping along the neckline is red and yellow, and it's also very bright, like cardinal and gold."

"Hello," Blakeley mused aloud as he studied the designs. "Is this something new, Nathan?"

The ornamentation was quite different from anything currently in fashion. It was far more exotic than the prevailing taste of the era. Arranged in odd patterns, the piping resembled glyphs of unknown origin.

"Oscar mentioned some daubs of red and yellow, but he never said anything much about the designs," Nathan said. "But then, the dress wasn't to his taste."

"Will you . . . ?"

"Yes," Nathan answered Blakeley's unfinished question. "I'll go back to The Rod and Gun Club and ask him. But I hope he doesn't think I want a membership."

"That's a good chap," Blakeley said, happy to see Nathan's spirits so much improved since revealing his knowledge of Father Gorman's dream. "Miss Meredith, are you reasonably certain Miss Stamm is correct about these designs?"

"I asked her twice about them, and she got huffy about it," Allison said. Assuming the chambermaid's bray, she added, "I was close enough to pin a tail on the Mister like as if he was a donkey, and my eyes are perfect, and who are you to suggest that I don't know fancy clothes when I see 'em?"

When in the mood, Allison had a fine flair for mimicry. Her imitation of Betty Jane Stamm amused everyone, especially Ralphie, who guffawed noisily. Blakeley glanced at his son, and the laughter faded.

"I'm sure Miss Meredith appreciates your applause, Ralph, but please remember there was a murder committed here a few hours ago."

Embarrassed by yet another reproof, Ralphie rolled his eyes and grumbled, "Jeez crumps, Dad."

"Those patterns adorning the neckline of the gown could be very important, Miss Meredith," Blakeley said. "I've a strong suspicion that they may lead us to the identity of our murderer."

"If Betty Jane hadn't seen that woman with Jack Hawthorne, I'd say that only Christopher Beecham was capable of such brutality," she said.

"Perhaps you're right, Miss Meredith. Perhaps this mysterious woman in green is Beecham's accomplice. It's possible Beecham was waiting for the woman to lure Hawthorne to him. Betty Jane couldn't see everything through that keyhole. I'm not ruling out any possible suspects until we catch the murderer. We can only pray to stop the culprit before he or she strikes again."

"You're right, Dr. Blakeley," Allison said. "But right now, I want to file my story so that I can get full credit."

"I have to go visit Oscar again," Nathan said, not completely feigning distaste, "but I can drop you downtown first since I'm in no hurry. Would you like a ride?"

Allison smiled coyly. "I thought you'd never offer."

Ralphie gagged and made smooching noises at

his friends. But for Blakeley's part, he was happy that circumstances were working out well for someone. Perhaps, he reflected, it was a good portent for all concerned.

Chapter Fifteen

Sophia Blakeley had known happier times—days when her children had been respectful, when her husband wasn't pursued by a pathological killer, when her responsibilities to the Tuesday Ladies didn't hang over her like the sword of Damocles. Those times seemed long past and, despite their inevitable flaws, halcyon. At present, not even her treasured piano playing could relieve her of her incessant worries. And that particular day, Sophia was in dire need of relaxation. Richard Petticord's funeral had been bad enough with the unexpected arrival of Cassie Aimwell. But when her husband and the others had rushed off to the scene of yet another murder, her fears were reinforced.

Hoping to soothe herself, Sophia retreated to the drawing room and the piano, only to be interrupted by Don Orlando, who was upset by yet another Spanish defeat. For a solid hour, Sophia commiserated with him over his dying empire. By the time

Don Orlando left to take a walk of the grounds, his spirits much improved, Sophia was completely overwrought. For, as a direct result of her generous nature, she had the unfortunate habit of sympathizing with people in pain to such an extent that, much to her great distress, she would feel their problems as her own.

The drawing room having become the scene of more distress, Sophia abandoned the piano and, in the late morning, took to her paints. The rigors of her art would assuredly carry her mind to a plane free from quotidian horrors. In the shade of a young evergreen and a flowering plum bush, she set to work recording the fine day on her canvas. Honeysuckle hung in the air, a reminder of a pleasant past. And Thomas Aquinas, having spent the morning and all his energy in luckless pursuit of squirrels, slept peacefully on a bench nearby.

Calm pervaded the woods surrounding the house, and Sophia had just eased into a gentle rhythm, blocking out all but her canvas, when a hand touched her shoulder and startled her. Her brush flew over the canvas, ruining the landscape.

"Ian!" she said, catching sight of her husband's face. "You scared me half to death."

"I'm terribly sorry, dearest," Blakeley said. He kissed his wife on the cheek and noticed she trembled slightly. "Damn me! Look what that fiend is doing to us."

Sophia cringed at his harsh remark. "Ian, don't be vulgar."

Chastened, Blakeley fell silent. Neither spoke for a moment, choosing rather to revel in the comfort their presences brought to one another. Blakeley reached out and clasped his wife's hand, and she gladly returned his grip.

"Will Nathan be staying for lunch?" Sophia asked after a while.

"I'd think you'd rather send Nathan to the devil than have him to lunch," Blakeley said, hoping to lighten their somber mood.

Despite herself, Sophia laughed briefly. The truth of the matter was that she should have been furious with Nathan. Ever since he had blackened Pratt's eye, the correspondent had disappeared from the Blakeley's lives—and with him had gone the only help Sophia had in finalizing the fast-approaching Restoration Ball. But the ball would go off with or without Pratt by her side, and Sophia secretly celebrated the loss.

Relieved his joke had elicited a happy response, Blakeley said, "I'm afraid that Nathan has driven Miss Meredith to her newspaper's offices. She wanted to write her story with all the details fresh in her mind. We made some interesting discoveries this morning, and they may be the exact clues we need to set us on the path to finding that murderous siren."

That bit of news sobered Sophia. "This latest murder—was it as ghastly as the others?"

"I'm afraid so."

"If everyone wasn't saying the murderer is a woman," Sophia said with a pronounced shudder, "I'd swear Christopher Beecham is responsible."

Blakeley smiled broadly upon hearing his wife echo Allison's belief. "And what makes you think I haven't begun to think exactly the same thing?"

"Really, Ian? But what about the woman in green?"

"As I was telling Miss Meredith not an hour ago, Beecham is a devil with women. I'd bet he could convince a woman to help him with a murder as easily as snapping his fingers. After all, he convinced meek little Cybel Ashbaugh to help him escape from prison, and you know he'd use all his cunning to avenge himself on me."

"That is true," Sophia said, shuddering again. "But why would he want to murder those other men?"

"Consider who they were, dearest. All three victims were wealthy men-about-town. Their paths more than likely crossed Beecham's in the past, and the Lord only knows what they thought of him. Maybe I'm not the only person in this city with whom Beecham feels he has unfinished business. Perhaps he plans to kill all his enemies with the help of this woman before he escapes forever."

"Ian, that's got to be it!"

"We shall see," he said. "Now, it's almost time for lunch. So, let's drop this business for the time being."

"Certainly," Sophia said.

"Lunch will be especially relaxing today," Blakeley said, his eyes gleaming mischievously, "because Ralphie won't be joining us." Then in answer to a questioning glance from his wife, Blakeley added, "He went into town. He said he had some business to attend to."

"Monkey business, no doubt," Sophia said and laughed at her remark.

"That's better, dear." Blakeley hugged his wife. "All this mess will be behind us soon, and we'll all be right as rain."

"We will, and thank goodness, but I'm afraid Don Orlando will never be the same again."

Blakeley considered his wife with wonder. It was a true mark of her generosity that amid the current turmoil she could worry about another's problems. "I'd rather thought he was improving of late."

"His physical health has been," Sophia said, "but I'm afraid his spirits are as bad as ever. I was with him in the drawing room earlier. He's absolutely devastated about the bombardment of Santiago. I wish the newspapers weren't so awful about this war. You'd think that the Spaniards were devils incarnate."

"Dearest, we can't stop the press from doing what they have to in order to sell papers. And no matter how one-sided the stories are, you know as well as I do that it is the truth about the war that is really making Don Orlando so depressed."

"Yes, Ian, but I wish sometimes that we could shield him from it. He gets such a look in his eye when he's talking about the war. It makes me think he wants to do something absolutely desperate."

The newspapers the previous evening and that morning had been especially exultant over the way the war was going. Santiago was being pounded to dust, and Teddy Roosevelt's Rough Riders were performing amazing feats of derring-do at La Quasina. Don Orlando's proud Spanish empire was fading quickly and irrevocably, being ground into pieces by the intractable thrust of the ambitious Americans. Blakeley and his wife could see that the old man's plight was bitter and lonely, but they could decide on no course of action that would help him in his sorrow.

"When I spoke to him earlier, he went on and on about his years in the King's service," Sophia said. "I heard the tale of his being taken captive by the jungle Indians again, and how every six days they tortured him and forced him to drink their strange potions. Of course, I listened politely, but the story does upset me so."

"I shall look in on him," Blakeley said, "immediately after a steaming hot bath."

"Good," Sophia said, as her husband started to leave. "Incidentally, someone's been trying to call you on the telephone. Victor said he sounded quite upset when you weren't here."

"Lt. Hudson?"

"I don't believe so."

"I'll find Victor and ask him," Blakeley said, entering the house. Once inside, he inhaled deeply, for the wonderful aroma of Mrs. Snopkowski's seafood chowder emanated from the kitchen. Blakeley wanted nothing to interfere with the approaching meal, but his hopes waned quickly when he spied Victor stumbling down the hall toward him. To Blakeley's distress, his butler's penitent behavior had lasted only a little longer than the time between his fortifying nips of gin or brandy or whatever other kind of alcohol was at hand. If he hadn't been bound by his wife's promise, Blakeley would gladly have sacked his tippling servant and kicked him off the grounds personally. That recourse not open to him, Blakeley forbore to practice patience in his intercourse with Victor.

"Sir, there is someone on the telephone who wishes to speak with you," the butler said with more animation than was his custom. It was almost as if he were reciting a text, he exaggerated his words so.

Although Blakeley usually kept a few paces from his servant, because of the usual reek of alcohol, he didn't have to move away despite the fact that Victor was practically on top of him, and he was surprised to smell bay rum where formerly there was gin. Studying his servant closely, Blakeley was further astonished that, for the first time since he had employed Victor, the man even seemed to have dressed correctly, with all his buttons hooked through their proper holes. And then there was his face.

"Victor, is that theatrical makeup I see?"

"Sir, my cheeks are naturally rosy," Victor bristled. "Now, we mustn't keep the gentleman waiting. This is the fourth time he's called this morning."

"Did you think to ask who he is?"

251

"Well, frankly no, sir," Victor said. "He's quite rude. He sounds like a filthy fellow, a drunkard perhaps; so I refused to commune with him. In the words of the poet Shelley, 'I do not suffer the rank breath of the herd.'"

"That was Byron, not Shelley, and furthermore, I've asked you repeatedly to—"

"Yes, yes," Victor said, dismissing Blakeley with a curt nod. "I must be off now. I've an appointment with Mr. Hermie Hinsky this afternoon."

"Who, pray, is Hermie Hinsky?"

Victor twisted his mouth into an astonished grimace that only the worst actor could possibly have believed would have passed for horror at another's ignorance, and not a severe attack of dyspepsia. "Why he's a producer, sir. A New York producer."

"Forgive me. I should have known," Blakeley said, his expression deadpan.

"He's come to town to cast some of the peripheral roles for a new a play. And, sir," Victor said, his voice dropping into a conspiratorial stage whisper, "one of them is the role of a butler."

Blakeley took heart. "Does that mean—"

"Yes!" Victor beamed. "I shall once again don the greasepaint and tread the boards. But I must not be late. Cheerio, sir."

And he was off to the city, impeccable in his tie and tails and bowler hat. Blakeley noticed a package under Victor's arm, wondered for a moment what it could be, then started toward the alcove outside his study, where the phone hung on the wall. He was so amused by his butler's absurdity—and buoyant at the possibility of at last being freed from his abuses—that he couldn't be angry with him, and it wasn't even Victor's afternoon off.

Having worked up a sweat, Blakeley loosened his tie, and before he answered the call, he removed his coat and hung it over a chair in his study. He hoped the caller would not interfere with his plans for a steaming hot bath and relaxing lunch.

"Blakeley here," he said, when he picked up the receiver. "What can I do for you?"

The voice on the other end was rude and the speech slurred. "Blakeley, where you been? I don't like to be kept waitin'."

"I beg your pardon?"

"I been tryin' to get yiz all mornin'."

"Are we acquainted, sir?" Blakeley demanded.

"Sorta."

"Well?"

"My name's Rose. Alvin Rose," the caller said. "Yiz chased me off yer property a coupla weeks ago. I was with Spector from the *Mornin' Star*. Dat big ape of a kid a yours took some a my equipment, like as if it was his."

Blakeley recalled the incident and chuckled. "Yes, of course I remember you. How could I forget? You were the photographer. I've never seen a man run so fast. My son the ape said he thought your trousers were afire. We had a jolly good laugh over the incident, the ape and I."

"Glad you thought it was funny," Rose griped. "Yiz cost me my job, and it was the first steady one I had in a year. Now I'm back on the skids."

"Very well, Mr. Rose," Blakeley said, anxious as always to get off the telephone, "you'll have your equipment back by this evening. I shall order the big ape to deliver it."

"Good," Rose said, "but that ain't what I called about."

"I'm afraid it has to be," Blakeley said, starting to hang up. "It's all I have time for."

"Wait, Blakeley, I got somethin' for you."

"Whatever it is, Mr. Rose, I don't want it. Good—"

The receiver was virtually on the hook when Blakeley heard Rose shout, "Blakeley! I got yer lady!"

Blakeley paused, then slowly raised the receiver to his ear. His day was improving. First, the chambermaid had provided a description; next, Nathan's news about Father Gorman was nothing short of a godsend. It would be too much to ask for a possible third lead in one day. Too stunned to believe his good fortune, Blakeley proceeded cautiously. "What lady?"

"The green lady. Who the hell else would I call about?"

"Mr. Rose, if this is a jest—"

"You heard me right."

"Go on, Mr. Rose," Blakeley said, not as yet unsure that Rose wasn't harassing him with false information.

"You ain't gonna hang up till I tell you, are you?"

"Not if you get on with it immediately. I've no time for charlatans."

"I ain't no fake, Blakeley."

"You'd better not be," Blakeley warned the photographer. "Because if you are, I'll send the ape to visit you on another matter."

"All right, all right," Rose said quickly, and Blakeley could envision him gulping air as the thought sank in. "I took her pitcher last evenin'. Her 'n Jack Hawthrone come by my studio last night around seven," Rose said. "Hawthorne was kinda lickered up, in a silly mood. I figgered he musta bin slummin' when he found her, but she was real good-lookin'. She probably wanted the pitcher so's she could prove she got along with the swells. Some a dem tramps like to do dat. Advertisin', ya know That sonofabitch Hawthorne said he'd pay me when I delivered it. Now I'm stuck fer—"

"Where are you now, Mr. Rose?" Blakeley asked impatiently.

"At a friend's place. I had to borry a telephone on accounta I can't afford—

"Do you have the photograph now?"

"It ain't developed yet," Rose said. "You interested?"

"Where can we meet, Mr. Rose?"

"At my studio," Rose said, and Blakeley thought he could detect a slimy grin in the other man's voice. "It's on the corner a Third 'n George, third floor. I'll have the pitcher developed by the time ya get there. Oh yeah, and Blakeley, this is gonna cost you plenty. I figger you owe me one, bein' that yiz cost me my job 'n all. . . ."

Blakeley didn't hear the rest of the message. He had already hung up the receiver and was halfway out the door. But he soon found that getting to Rose's studio was going to be an ordeal in itself. For Ralphie had taken one of their carriages, and Nathan and Allison had gone to her office in his buggy. And when he went to the stables, he discovered there were no fresh horses to pull the other carriage. So, unless he planned to run to Rose's studio, only one form of transportation was left to him—his dreaded automobile.

"Damn me!" Blakeley said, dashing behind the stables to where the Winton had stood idle for longer than he could remember. Ever since he'd purchased the horseless carriage, after months of incessant prodding from his children, he had hated the machine. He especially hated to drive it into the crowded city. And more than once, he'd sworn that someday he would tear the telephone off the wall, put it in the passenger's seat, and push the Winton off a cliff.

That thought occurred to Blakeley again as he cranked up the engine, and he couldn't help smiling. But his smile subsided when the machine coughed to life. His eagerness to see the photograph Rose claimed to have was greater than his trepidation, however, and he jumped into the cab with only slight hesitation. As he headed down the drive past Sophia, the engine backfired and caused her to mar her canvas with yet another unsightly splash of paint. And Thomas Aquinas jumped up and scurried away like a black-and-white cannonball bounding across the lawn.

"Ian!" Sophia shouted as her husband drove away. "What about poor Don Orlando?"

"I shall see him this afternoon, my pet!" Blakeley said, almost colliding with a tree when he turned to answer his wife.

He raced through the archway at the front of their property, the Winton building up horsepower as he sped along. Concentrating heavily on his driving, Blakeley didn't realize he was smiling again for several minutes. But why shouldn't he be? He might at last be closing in on the Green Lorelei herself.

But what about that fellow, Alvin Rose? Certainly, he was far from an exemplary character. Might he be so unsavory a character and so hard up for money that he would hire some dockside strumpet to pose with some other no-account who happened to resemble the late Jack Hawthorne?

Blakeley reached for his pocket to be sure he had a photograph of Jack Hawthorne he'd taken from the dead man's home. At least he could be certain it was the victim in Rose's photograph should the man try to deceive him. But there was no photograph and, for that matter, no jacket either. In his excitement, he'd left his jacket draped over the chair in his study. Although he realized it was very ungentlemanly to be out in public in just his shirt-sleeves, Blakeley was much too anxious to return home for propriety's sake.

Blakeley followed the river drive to Nicetown Lane, going southward in fairly light traffic. It was cool along the river and through the park, and he was pleased with the progress of the Winton over the rough roadway. The pedestrian traffic grew heavier as he approached Girard Avenue, and he had to move cautiously to avoid the children, newly released for their summer vacation, as they darted across the road without warning. Then at Girard, he had to stop completely because city employees were installing a sewer.

"Damn!" he muttered, making a note to himself that he must try to control his tongue. Shirtsleeves were bad enough—an unmannerly vocabulary was inexcusable.

When it became apparent that he would not make speedy progress along Girard, Blakeley decided to follow Thirty-fourth toward Market Street. But along his new route, the number of carriages seemed to multiply tenfold. Blakeley was momentarily confused by the hordes of pedestrians crowding the street, then remembered he had chosen the busiest part of the afternoon to drive through the center of the city. And to make matters worse, traffic was even heavier when he turned eastward on Market. Despite his earlier self-remonstration, he cursed his ill luck again, having no other outlet for his exasperation.

Blakeley passed several department stores and, out of the corners of his eyes, spied an amorphous blob of shoppers that covered the street and sidewalks. But he went blind with rage when the traffic on the bridge over the Schuylkill slowed almost to a standstill. Passers-by gawked at the Winton coughing out blue puffs of smoke as Blakeley sat idle. Many of them recognized the detective from the news stories concerning the Green Lorelei murders, and they taunted him from the sidewalks. To make matters worse, just as traffic began to move again, the Winton suddenly stalled. While Blakeley recranked the engine, he was the target of much blasphemy from the drivers of carriages he was holding up. Despite it all, Blakeley was too preoccupied with what lay ahead to pay much attention.

Finally, he was across the bridge and traveling eastward at a reasonable pace. At Seventeenth Street, the traffic slowed again, and he sat still outside the busy railway station, simmering, biting his tongue, once more conscious of people staring at the Winton, which was shivering and threatening to stall again, and its indecorous driver.

Then Blakeley caught sight of a stiff-looking man in a bowler hat who had just left the railway station and was working his way through the crowd. "It's the strange bird himself," Blakeley thought upon recognizing his butler. He wondered again what was in the package Victor was carrying under his arm.

"Victor!" he shouted. "I say, Victor."

His servant noticed him and started to wave back. Then he stopped, as the Winton suddenly shot a blast of exhaust at him. His face blackened like that of a ruffian or a common laborer, Victor quickly marched off with grim determination.

"Hrmp!" Blakeley said and drove on.

At Twelfth Street, he turned north toward George. In that neighborhood, the streets grew more and more shabby. The traffic was lighter, but Blakeley had to concern himself with dodging roving drunks and easing through narrow lanes on which wagons had stopped in the middle of the road, some of them forever. Abandoned or burned-out buildings lined both sides of the street, and rubbish was piled everywhere along the roadway.

Alvin Rose's studio was in a three-story wooden structure that jutted into the street at the corner. Its outside walls had been defaced with posters and fading messages at eye level or at a level as high as those posting them had dared to stretch while standing on the broken pavement. One window of

Alvin Rose's building was boarded up, another shattered.

Since the human population on the street was sparse, it was not surprising that there was space to park the Winton in front of the building. Blakeley checked his pocket watch as he eased out of the Winton and discovered that the trip had taken twice as long as he'd hoped. He wondered if the wretch was still there, or whether the long delay had made him turn to the newspapers to sell his discovery.

Suddenly he paused and chastised himself. Might the supposed picture of the Green Lorelei be another of Christopher Beecham's plots to destroy him? The devil was certainly capable of disguising his voice, speaking like a gutter whelp, and luring him into an ambush. Even if the caller were truly Alvin Rose, the photographer certainly had motive enough to conspire with the devil to murder him.

Blakeley studied the building, his suspicions mounting quickly after they had been unleashed. The building had the appearance of an old hotel, the kind where sailors from merchant ships at anchor on the Delaware would stay because of its proximity to the docks and the speakeasies. Inside, where the lobby used to be, Blakeley found no one; only a counter and a row of tiny pigeonholes suggested a desk clerk still worked there.

Blakeley paused at the foot of the stairs, thinking, "Wonderful place for an ambush...." But he had come too far to stop. He took a breath and climbed the stairs. A noise ahead of him stopped him dead. His back pressed against the wall, he broke into a heavy sweat, and his heart throbbed wildly until he discerned that all he heard was a woman's drunken cackling. The laughter was followed by a man's angry voice. In another room, a baby started to cry.

Relaxing and continuing his ascent, Blakeley wondered what sort of depravity had brought Jack

Hawthorne to such a place. On the third floor, the smell of chemicals told him he had found the photographer's studio. When Blakeley tapped on the door, there was a momentary shuffling of feet before Rose said, "Izzat you, Blakeley?"

"Yes, Mr. Rose."

"What took you so long?"

"Traffic, Mr. Rose. Now, do open the door like a good chap."

"You alone?"

"Yes," Blakeley replied wearily. For all he knew Beecham was inside, preparing for the kill. "Are you?"

Rose ignored the question and said, "You sure?"

"Why don't you open the door and see?"

"I ast you a civil question, Blakeley."

Their conversation traveled quickly through the thin walls. A man with a stubbly beard and a potbelly that squeezed through a greasy undershirt appeared at the top of the stairs. "You're disturbin' the peace, bud," he said, and Blakeley recognized his voice as the one he'd just heard in the domestic spat downstairs.

In no mood for another idiotic encounter, Blakeley approached the man calmly. Wearing a smile most often seen on the faces of charity seekers, he said, "I'm terribly sorry. You see, I'm here collecting for the Philadelphia Ballet and Horticulture Society. Do you wish to give something? Or do you want to stand there smelling like a dead camel and annoying me because I have to look at you?"

It was a line he'd once heard Ralphie use, and he had no idea that it would work as well for him. But he said it with such a strange smile that the man instantly retreated down the stairs.

"Who's out dere with you?" Rose shouted.

"A frightful collection of bogeymen," Blakeley growled. Rose's nonsense had gone on long enough,

but at least it had convinced him that Beecham was
nowhere nearby. The madman could never have
waited so long to cut his enemy down. Convinced
that he faced no danger, Blakeley moved to end
Rose's stalling. "Open the door before I kick it in."

"You got my equipment, Blakeley?"

"Let me in and you'll see," he said, silently cursing himself for not thinking to bring the camera
and other equipment confiscated by Ralphie.

Rose didn't say a word, as if he sensed Blakeley's
deception, and the door remained closed. His self-
possession almost totally gone from being so close
to evidence that might solve the case, but not able
to attain it, Blakeley was preparing to take desperate measures. But as he stepped back and prepared
to kick in the door, Rose said, "I ain't showin' you
nothin' till I see some green. So yiz can jist put
somethin' under the door right now, if yiz wanna
do business."

"Very well, Mr. Rose," Blakeley said and slid a
dollar bill under the door.

"This is an insult, Blakeley! It'll cost yiz at least
a fin."

Blakeley glowered as he slid another dollar bill
under the door, but that time he moved to action.
Knowing that Rose was at the door, waiting to grab
the money, Blakeley took one quick step back and
kicked the door with full force. Flying open, it hit
Rose's head with a thud and sent him flying backward. Once in the apartment, Blakeley discovered
his instincts about Beecham were right. No one else
lurked inside.

Looking at Rose as he sat on the floor whining
and rubbing his head, Blakeley remembered him
clearly. He was wearing the same wrinkled white
suit he'd worn on the day he was with Spector. His
collar was open and he wore no tie. Even with the
heavy smell of chemicals in the air, Blakeley could

easily detect the alcohol on his breath and in his pores as he helped him up.

The studio resembled an indoor junkyard. Pieces of photographic equipment fought with clothing, wine bottles, and dirty dishes for space on an all-purpose table and the floor. All that suggested the studio's true purpose was a high-backed chair facing a camera on a tripod, and those tools of the trade were practically hidden in a fairly neat niche against the wall.

Rose noticed Blakeley assessing the room and sneered. "It's all I can afford on accounta you got me fired."

"Well, perhaps this is the day when your luck takes a better turn, Mr. Rose. Where is the photograph?"

"It ain't done yet."

"Mr. Rose!"

"Hey, I had to go all the way up to Twentieth and Ferry to borry the telephone. I put the pitcher in the chemicals as soon as I got back."

"Not a penny more until I see it, Mr. Rose," Blakeley said, taking the photographer by the lapels. "And if this is a cheat of some sort, I shall cart you off to Fairmont Prison and put you in irons personally."

"All right, have it your way," Rose gasped as Blakeley released him. "I'll get the pitcher and you get out yer money."

The photographer stepped over toward a black curtain, saying, "Only if it gets all frigged up cuz it ain't in the chemicals long enough, it's your fault."

He disappeared into his darkroom. Much too agitated to sit, Blakeley paced the room in silence, chill fingers of dread racing down his spine as he imagined what would have happened if the moment he had broken down the door he had discovered a pistol at his heart. Or if Beecham had flown through the black curtain like some evil spirit ready to seize him by the throat. "Beecham be damned," he said and immediately chastised himself again for his language. He promised himself it would not happen another time.

On the all-purpose table, some photographs that lay partially beneath a plate of beans and a soiled napkin caught his attention. Featuring a fat, unattractive nude, they were just the sort of picture that a denizen of the realm of flotsam and jetsam such as Rose would claim were artistic.

Rose had been gone for several minutes when Blakeley heard a pained cry from behind the black curtain. He ducked instinctively and pressed himself against the wall by the curtain. "Are you all right, Mr. Rose?"

A moment later, Rose came out, his face quite pale and his jaw trembling as he tried to speak. But no words escaped his previously loquacious mouth as he stared blankly at the photograph he held.

Blakeley seized the photograph. He too turned pale upon first examining it. Then he turned red.

"Mr. Rose," he said, advancing with more than a hint of menace in his posture, "if this is some kind of ploy—"

"It ain't! Honest, Blakeley, it ain't."

Blakeley was silent, his eyes darting from Rose to the photograph then back to Rose.

"I ain't nuts either," the photographer said, "if that's what you're thinkin'. And I ain't no con man." He backed up, keeping his distance from Blakeley, and pointed a palsied finger at the wall. "Jack Hawthorne was sittin' on that chair, see? You gotta admit that's him, ain't it?"

Unless the man was a perfect double, the picture showed Jack Hawthorne seated in the chair, wearing a silly, drunken, lascivious grin and what looked like the clothing he'd had on when Blakeley had seen his shredded corpse that morning.

"And she was sittin' right beside him," Rose went on. "Her ass was on the arm a the chair and her arm was around his neck. She was playin' with his hair and ticklin' his ear, makin' it hard fer me to take the pitcher cuz they wouldn't sit still. Looka the goddamn grin on his face."

Blakeley looked again at the photograph, at the perfectly tailored summer suit and Italian shoes and the look on Hawthorne's face that said something was indeed going on as he posed. Hawthorne's eyes were even staring up and slightly away from the camera, as if at some friendly intruder.

"Very well, Mr. Rose," Blakeley said. "It's Jack Hawthorne. But where the devil is the Green Lorelei?"

He could hear his own voice trailing off uncertainly as he asked his question. From the looks of him, Rose needed a drink very badly. Spotting a half-empty bottle of rye on the table, Blakeley passed it to him.

"That's what I'd like to know," Rose said, his hands too shaky to open the bottle and take a drink.

Chapter Sixteen

Even as Blakeley was meeting with defeat and disappointment, his inimitable manservant was confronted by a woman who was more than his match in unabashed surliness. Hermie Hinsky's private secretary, Emma Shmeckman, was quite the intimidating woman. Behind a wooden railing that split Hinsky's rented office in two, she sat vigilant and grim, as if her life would be forfeit should she open the gate to the wrong person. Over six feet tall and weighing just a little more than John L. Sullivan, she was, Victor ventured to guess, even more threatening than Mrs. Snopkowski. So when she ordered him to take a seat in the back of the room, he did not protest, as he would have with a meeker woman; he merely gave a customary huff. But that huff was sufficient to annoy Emma. In full view of the horrified thespian, she moved his name to the end of the list of actors to be auditioned for the role of Smithers the butler, then pointed to an empty seat at the rear of the room.

"The nerve," she said as Victor walked sullenly through the rows of would-be bit players and took his seat, the mysterious box still firmly in his grasp.

Hermie Hinksy, producer of such dubious benchmarks as *The Sultan's Slave* and *Dames of Ancient Rome*, had taken a top-floor office on the Schuylkill's east bank, no doubt since the rents on the unfashionable, and at times unquestionably dangerous, LaRoche Street were far lower than those in the city's theater district. To Victor's dismay, the elevator in the dilapidated building did not work. So by the time he had climbed the hot stairs, he resembled the sweet-smelling servant who had left the Blakeleys' home an hour earlier only in his unbounded optimism, which not even the sight of a score of other actors milling about the waiting room could abate.

For another man, not blessed with the absolute, albeit deluded, faith in his acting abilities that blinded Victor, it would have been disconcerting to sit among 20 other gentlemen, all dressed in tie and tails, stiffly upright, and seldom looking to either side—rather like fun-house reflections of himself. But it was one of the trials that P. Waldo Smyrl, now Victor Primrose, had become inured to over the years in countless waiting rooms, all of them at least as drab as Hermie Hinsky's, but in faraway ends of the circuit like Pocatello, Tombstone, Peoria, and Iowa City, even a border town called Outhouse, Texas. Victor was prepared, however, to go through the tedium and humiliation all over again, because it was only a short step from those backwaters to New York, London, Paris, and all those places were far, far away from the Blakeleys and their ceaseless demands.

He smiled at the box in his hands. If Dr. Blakeley only knew the role he was playing in starting Victor's new life. Surely, the cigars the box held were a sign from heaven that Victor Primrose was destined to make his long-overdue return to the theater. Why else would that rude limping deliveryman have brought them on the very day of his audition—and at a time when no one was about to realize the cigars had even been delivered?

Although Victor drifted in and out of sleep, he sat perfectly upright as the afternoon traffic rumbled along the street outside. Now and then, he would jump slightly when a passing trolley clanged its alarm. Finally, three hours later, when he had come close to working up courage to approach the harridan masquerading as a secretary, Emma said, "Mr. Hinsky will see you now, Primrose. Get a move on. He's waitin'."

"Wouldn't do to keep old Herm waiting," Victor said with forced joviality.

"It's *Mr.* Hinsky," Emma corrected him coldly. "And what's that thing you're carrying?"

"My, uh, lunch, madam."

"Better not cause no bugs, because I hate 'em. I'd rather blow a place up than have bugs."

"Oh, it won't, madam."

Not assured by Victor's denial, but weary of his presence, Emma nodded toward the office where Hermie Hinsky granted his audiences. Victor scurried through the gate in the wooden railing, acting as if a moment's hesitation would lose him forever the glorious future he envisioned.

Inside the office, he found a small, sallow bald man with the head of an overgrown ant counting dollar bills bound in a thick roll. It was Hinsky's well-known custom to accept monetary tribute in return for granting players a chance to work for a while. Only when he stuffed the roll of bills into his pocket did he acknowledge Victor's presence.

"Primrose," he said in a voice that was at once

nasal and gravelly. "Jeez, you're still alive?"

"Last time I checked," Victor said, pinching himself and smiling inanely.

He started to sit in a chair across the desk from where Hinsky was seated, but quickly jumped up when the producer said, "I didn't say you could sit, Primrose. I don't like it when people take things for granted."

"Sorry, sorry," Victor babbled, then remembered the package. "Goodness, I almost forgot your present, Mr. Hinsky. A box of your favorite cigars."

"How the hell do you know what kind of cigars I like?" Hinsky said, as he pushed his glasses back on his nose. Sliding glasses were another of his trademarks.

"*Hoyo de Monterrey José Gener Excalibur*," Victor said proudly. "Did I pronounce the name correctly, Mr. Hinsky?"

"Close enough."

"You see, I once played a—"

"Put 'em on the desk," Hinsky ordered. "Now you may sit."

"Thankyew."

"And don't gimme none a that English crap, Primrose, cuz I happen to know where you come from."

Victor blushed. "That, sir, is a filthy lie about Secaucus. I assure—"

"Look, it's gettin' late and I got a train to catch back to New York. So speak."

"Speak?" Victor said, giggling nervously. "What is there to say except that I've come here for the role of Smithers in your next production, *Randy Dandy*.

"*Randy Mandy*, Primrose." Hinsky snickered. "Dandy, jeez."

"Oh, yes, of course. *Randy Man*—"

"And I ain't so sure I really need a butla now.

All's he is is window dressin', y'know."

Victor shuddered, the golden dream of his glorious future fading quickly before the grim reality of his mundane life. "Oh, sir, I—"

"I might just have Smiddas written out," he said, snapping his fingers. "Maybe give his lines to the French maid instead. What the hell, they don't come to look at no snooty butla."

Victor winced. "Oh, please don't, sir. It would be a big mistake."

Hinsky leaned forward and frowned. "I don't make mistakes, Primrose."

A servile grimace was the best response Victor could muster under the circumstances. "Yes, yes. Terribly sorry."

Hinsky was silent for ten seconds that added excruciatingly painful years to Victor's life. Finally, he said, "Open the box a cigars. Let's see if they're really my brand."

"Oh, they are," Victor said, perking up enough to speak in a mincing tone. "They are."

"Oh, they are, they *are*," Hinsky said in a prissy voice as Victor tried to open the box gracefully, and almost collapsed into tears when he couldn't. "Pretty shaky, Primrose. Are you still on the sauce."

"I'm afraid I don't know what you mean."

"The sauce, Primrose. The booze, the barleycorn. You know, the main reason why nobody wanted to hire you no more."

Victor blanched. "I've not had a drop—"

"In an hour!"

Victor laughed uneasily and pretended to concentrate on the cigar box.

"What a bunch of bums," Hinsky said. "I haven't seen one acta since I got here. No kiddin'. A bunch a drunks and sissy boys all afternoon. What a waste a time."

Victor ignored the producer's complaints. They

were among the many annoyances he'd prepared himself for. Besides, there was a modicum of encouragement in the last insult: Victor would gladly settle for being the best of a bad lot.

At last, he opened the box and held it out to Hinsky, who sucked an imaginary piece of food from his teeth and selected a cigar.

"Thankyew," Hinsky said in the same prissy voice with which he had mocked Victor earlier. He sniffed the cigar noncommittally, bit the tip off, and spat it out. The tiny piece of tobacco sailed past Victor's face and over his shoulder. Then, with the cigar firmly between his teeth, Hinsky said, "Well?"

Not having actually mastered the role of a butler, Victor was frightfully befuddled by Hinsky's question. Straining for another clue as to what the producer meant, he asked, "Sir?"

"Well?" Hinsky repeated, staring angrily.

"Well, what?" Victor asked, then quickly added, "Sir."

"Well, what the hell do you think I want? C'mon, I got a train to catch."

"Yes, of course. Terribly sorry, Mr. Hinsky," Victor said hastily and reached for the matchbox on Hinsky's desk. Victor was so intent on shedding his present position of drudgery for the boards that he never imagined Hinsky would expect him to perform the menial tasks of a domestic servant.

"Teddibly sorry, Mista Hinsky," the producer sneered as Victor struck the match. "Careful with that. You'll boin my nose."

Victor held the match in a hand so tremulous that the flame nearly went out as he lit the long cigar. Hinsky puffed a few times, then blew smoke across his desk, straight into the other man's chest and face.

Ignoring the insult, Victor steeled himself to all abuse. He was determined that he would make his triumphant return no matter what. He was ready for the big time, and the world was ready for him. Petty offenses from a petty man like Hermie Hinsky were trivial impediments to be endured at the moment and remembered later when Hinsky, wearing the same clothing, only threadbare and dirty, would come to him, hat in hand, and beg for a few seconds of his time.

As Victor awaited his decision, Hinsky puffed once more and blew out more smoke, evidently approving of the cigar's quality.

"What the hell," the producer said finally, sucking some more imagined food out of his teeth, "I guess I'll keep the butla in."

"Bless you, sir!"

"Yeah," Hinsky said, considering the matter, "maybe I can have him double as the drunken dogcatcher. Can you talk in an Irish brogue, Primrose?"

Victor was elated. He'd always thought his brogue was one of the best outside of South Boston. "The divil, ye say," he blurted out. "Faith 'n begorra."

Hinsky shook his head. "Jeez, that's terrible."

"Oh?" Victor blanched but refused to panic yet. "Well, er, then py yiminy, maybe vee can make him a Swede!"

Hinsky looked as if he'd just stepped in something foul. He continued to shake his head. "Naaaa."

"Ach!" Victor said desperately. "Vell denn, vott iff—"

"Save yer breath, Primrose," Hinsky said, waving him off. "I'm goin' back to New York for my butla. You Philly guys don't show me nothin'."

"But, sir!" Victor cried.

Hinsky ignored Victor's protest. "Now, if you'll excuse me...."

"But—"

The producer stopped him with a wave of the hand in front of his face. "I can understand your disappointment, Primrose. It's never easy findin' out you ain't got what it takes." He reached into his pocket and pulled out a coin. "Here, take it. It's only a half a buck, but maybe you can buy some gin or somethin'. Who knows? Find some cheap floozie in the back alley. It'll make you feel betta. Now go."

Victor refused to leave. He stared Hinsky in the eye. The producer turned red and said, "Whattaya want, a whole dolla? Hit the road, Primrose. And, oh yeah, thanks for the cigars."

Victor's face was ashen. Never had anyone made him so angry. Hinsky looked uncertain for a moment when Victor, in an uncharacteristic show of manliness, seized the box of cigars and slammed the door as he left.

"Disgusting Philistine," Victor said and marched across the room toward the door, muttering oaths and gritting his teeth.

Emma stood and stared imperiously as Victor passed her desk. "What was that you said under your breath?" she demanded, but Victor ignored her and reached for the door handle.

"How dare you ignore me," Emma said. She was about to grab Victor by the ear and drag him back to Hinsky's office for a severe reprimand when an explosion lifted her off her feet, sending her cursing and tumbling over the wooden railing.

The blast echoed across the entire area of the city east of the Schuylkill and could even be heard aboard the ships sailing up and down the Delaware. Its force sent Victor crashing through the door and halfway down the stairs. Outside, on the crowded sidewalks of LaRoche Street seven stories below, horses balked and pedestrians scattered to avoid the debris flying out of the walls and windows of the office Hermie Hinsky had rented, but which no one else would have the dubious honor of renting ever again.

Chapter Seventeen

Hecuba took her time plodding westward along Lancaster Avenue, passing only the oldest, weariest draft horses, but neither Blakeley nor Nathan urged her to pick up her pace. Already having made two trips into the city hitched to the ponderous landau, the mare had done a full day's work. Even though she was now pulling Blakeley's cabriolet, she trotted slowly, for she was tired.

Seated in the carriage, with its top protecting them from the direct rays of the merciless sun, Blakeley and Nathan were also weary. After his excursion to Rose's studio, Blakeley had driven home, and he had barely reached his property before the Winton overheated and stopped. Dispirited and disgusted by the failure of the technological marvel, Blakeley left the automobile and walked up the drive. His body soaked in sweat, he thought of nothing but escaping his cares for a short while. A relaxing bath, perhaps a short nap, and maybe a bite to eat since he had missed lunch—that was all he required. But Sophia had set into him for rushing off alone despite the fact that Christopher Beecham might be skulking about, awaiting his next opportunity for revenge. And then Nathan returned from his travels.

Ostensibly, Nathan had come to take his mentor to interview Father Gorman. But from his curt and snappish conversation, Blakeley suspected his friend had turned to duty out of a desire to escape whatever was bothering him. The object he wished to escape could only be a certain beautiful blond-haired reporter, who, whether he liked it or not, played young Nathan McBride like a harp, plucking at his jealousy like strings that could only play out of tune.

Blakeley was only too aware that if he had questioned Nathan's sullen behavior the police officer would have been hard put to deny his assumption, because it most certainly was the root of his evil temper. But if truth were known, Nathan's disposition, although far from its usual sober equanimity, had improved markedly upon hearing Blakeley's tale of woe; the deeply felt sympathy and regard he held for those closest to him wouldn't allow him to wallow in self-pity.

As they drove along, however, a throbbing in his brain reminded Nathan of what had passed earlier, but it abated as he told Blakeley about his day, deleting only the events irrelevant to the case at hand. His drive with Allison had been pleasant, if uneventful, until Allison had mentioned that she hoped to convince Pratt that her story about Jack Hawthorne's murder should be picked up by the wire services. His influence and connections would ensure its acceptance, she said with more enthusiasm than Nathan cared for. And he had fallen silent then, only grunting the most basic replies to her excited conversation.

After dropping Allison at her newspaper's offices, Nathan brooded on G. Lindsey Pratt, putative war hero, his mood souring with each passing second. If it took going to Cuba to win Allison Meredith's heart and soul, then he would go to Cuba, tapioca knee and all. He had no job holding him back, he wasn't so sure he even wanted to return to the force after being treated so shabbily. He'd march into the first recruiting office he could find and sign up ... and the officer in charge would make him do some deep-knee bends. When the officer heard the sickening swoosh in Nathan's damaged joint, he would ask Nathan to raise his trouser leg, and he would see the knee with the angry red semicircular scar. The officer would shake his head and send Nathan on his way, as his counterpart had done before. After suffering yet another humiliation, Nathan would still be unemployed, not to mention bereft of hope of besting his rival for Allison's affection.

It was in a very black temper that Nathan entered The Rod and Gun Club for his second interview with the steward Oscar. Had any of the clientele been of the mind to approach Nathan, on whatever pretext, that unfortunate man would have come away having learned some curses that even he, who lived his life with the insouciant world-weariness that marked the members of the club, had never known existed. But Nathan's furrowed brow and rigid bearing warned off any chance encounters. So it was Oscar, that amiable fellow, who became the target of his anger.

"Gutted another one, did she?" Oscar said when Nathan approached him, unaware that the chipper indifference he exhibited toward the horror of the murderous spree endangered his own life.

"Afraid so," Nathan answered. "A man named Hawthorne."

"She certainly is a busy person, and so am I, McBride. Besides, I've never heard of anyone named Hawthorne being a member here, though Lord knows he may have paid us a clandestine visit or two."

"What do you mean?"

"Now and then, one of our members may bring a guest who is a nonmember," Oscar said, winking playfully. "That's all. Of course, these guests usually use aliases or claim to come here on some other mission. You know, McBride, this is your third visit here."

Nathan gritted his teeth and said, "It's my second visit."

"Who counts?"

"I want you to take a look at this drawing. We believe it may be a good rendering of the woman we're after."

"I have work to do."

"It won't take more than a minute. And it's police business," Nathan said, relying on the fact that Oscar had no knowledge of his suspension to make the statement threatening.

Oscar rolled his eyes, emitted a deep, irritated sigh, and glanced at the drawing "Oh dear Gawd."

"Is this the woman you saw with Mr. Hazleton on the night of his death?"

Oscar snickered a few times as he studied the glyph-like patterns on the dress. "I can't remember."

"What the hell do you mean, you can't remember?"

"I have an erratic memory. It comes from having had to forget so many things I see around here."

Nathan knew what was coming next, but asked, "What are you getting at, Oscar?"

"It's like this, McBride," Nathan answered. "Not only am I forgetful, I'm very, very poor. I wouldn't be surprised if a club steward isn't paid almost as wretchedly as a cop. So if you want to jog my memory, maybe you should offer me something in the way of—oh, how should I say it—a gratuity. Or else I might just save my story for one of those newspaper reporters. Maybe I'll just call that Pratt fellow. I'm sure he pays well."

And with that comment, poor Oscar discovered, too late, that Nathan McBride could only be pushed so far. Of course, as he finished relating the story of his interview with the steward, Nathan didn't think it necessary to mention the fat lip with which he had rewarded the steward for his troubles.

"Forget Oscar," Blakeley said, hoping to alleviate his friend's foul mood as quickly as possible. "The mere fact that he wished to sell us the information tells us he recognized the woman in Miss Meredith's drawing."

The two men then fell silent as they continued their journey. At Gray's Road, they paused to let a large beer wagon cross before them, then turned onto Montgomery. The avenue was wide enough for traffic to flow eastward and westward freely, and there was a lane in the middle to allow for passing. Rows of prosperous, well-kept shops, grassy plots, elm trees, Tudor-style homes, and gingerbread houses lined the street at civilized distances from each other. But the suburban charm was lost on Nathan, who had lapsed back into his fantasies of enlisting for service. Suddenly, it occurred to him that, as a medical doctor, Blakeley might be able to help his cause. He had to approach the subject delicately, however, not wanting to betray his true motivation.

"Dr. Blakeley," he said as they passed a flower shop in the village of Rosemont.

Blakeley was deep in thought as well, seemingly concentrating on the monotonous flicking of Hecuba's tail as she chased away horseflies. Among other weighty matters, his mind was preoccupied with what he should make of the photograph Alvin Rose had taken. He roused himself at once when Nathan spoke. "Yes, what is it?"

"I don't know how to tell you this, but—"

"Oh, I know. You intend to join the army."

"How did you know?"

"It dawned on me when we passed that recruiting station back on Haverford Road," Blakeley said.

"I must have missed it."

"Only barely, dear boy. I thought you were going to drive into it. It's best to pay attention to your driving."

"Well, no matter, I still intend to sign up."

"And the army will promptly reject you."

"Not if you said I'm physically capable of—"

"I'll do no such thing!" Blakeley said, and he proceeded with a long list of reasons why he refused to help. Chief among them was his wish not to see a healthy young man made a cripple.

Defeated, Nathan said, "Then there's only one other thing I can do."

"You'll wait out your suspension and return to work."

Nathan had been carrying a stale Sweet Caporal in his shirt pocket for just such a moment—a moment when his life would take a sudden turn and he would have cause to celebrate. Lighting it, he said, "No, Dr. Blakeley, I'm going to look for another job. Damn the Philadelphia Police Force." The cigarette tasted as bitter as his words, but he kept his face free of emotion.

Blakeley could not pretend such disinterest. Ever since Nathan's unfair suspension from the force, he had been considering making an offer of temporary aid, but he hadn't come out with it because he knew Nathan too well. The desperation in Nathan's voice at that moment spurred him to action.

"Nathan," Blakeley said cautiously, "you really should reconsider your actions. Don't be rash. I will gladly pay you for your invaluable assistance for the duration of the month. Maybe by then you'll think better of quitting."

"That's kind of you," Nathan said, choking on the Caporal's smoke, "but no thank you."

"Pride goeth before the fall."

"So does the summer," Nathan said, smiling appreciatively. "Thank you, but I can't accept your charity."

"Charity be dashed, Nathan. You deserve to be paid for your work, whether by me or by the city."

Their conversation was momentarily interrupted as they paused at Roberts Avenue to allow a group of suffragettes in their primly starched uniforms to cross before them. The women marched determinedly, carrying a banner into a church for a rally.

"Besides," Blakeley said as Hecuba started moving again, "what would you do?"

"You forget that I was once Lillian Russell's bodyguard. There must be another famous body somewhere in need of protection."

"You hated that job."

"I was less than excited by it," Nathan said, "but it paid well. Maybe some blue blood who doesn't want to be the next Green Lorelei victim will hire me."

"I shall contact Governor Stone," Blakeley promised, "and ask him to speak to Commissioner MacDonald. Such petty creatures as MacDonald are easily intimidated."

But Nathan no longer entertained the same confidence in public officials that Blakeley did, and his doubts extended to Governor Stone and beyond.

"Thank you," he said without enthusiasm. "That's very kind of you."

They passed some more shops and then a small wooded area in Rosemont. Hecuba took her time climbing the hill leading up to Villanova. At Ithan they turned left and onto a lane leading to the college.

Suddenly, Nathan felt uneasy. For not only had he betrayed Father Gorman's trust by telling his story to Blakeley, he had also failed to call the priest to tell him that Blakeley wished to discuss his dreams. Unsure how Father Gorman would react to their visit, he flicked the stale cigarette onto the roadway, but it's acrid taste lingered in his mouth.

Next to him, Blakeley was also uneasy. How could he ask a man of the cloth, a scholar at that, about such inane matters as flesh-and-blood creatures whose images could not be recorded on a photograph?

"Does Father Gorman have a sense of humor?" he asked.

"Hmmm, well, yes," Nathan said. "I think so."

They crossed under a railroad trestle and followed the lane to the center of the campus. There, they stopped under a tree in a field across from the Augustinian monastery and tethered Hecuba loosely to its trunk. As they walked into the monastery, Nathan spied a familiar robed figure and hailed him.

"Dr. Blakeley," Nathan said, "this is Father Capone, the provincial of the order."

Father Capone was a man with a ready smile and a girth that matched Blakeley's. He was pleased to meet the detective. "I've been reading about you," he said. "You and Nathan lead interesting lives."

"We certainly do," Blakeley said, shaking the provincial's hand. "And in fact, it's one of the events in our interesting lives that brings us here today."

"We were hoping to corner Father Gorman," Nathan said. "Is he on the campus?"

The provincial gave Nathan a look that suggested he understood the purpose of the visit. It was a split-second glance, cloaked in a smile, but Blakeley caught it.

"You see, I have a houseguest named Don Orlando Malachea y Guzman," Blakeley said. "I'd like to arrange some spiritual guidance for him, and Father Gorman seems a likely candidate."

Father Capone was far from convinced by Blakeley's explanation, but he knew Blakeley by reputation, and certainly Nathan McBride wouldn't involve the college in a scandal. "I suspect you'll find him somewhere around here," he said. "He takes long walks."

"A healthy practice," Blakeley observed.

"Yes, I suppose so," Father Capone said and smiled as he went on his way. "Father Gorman misses his missionary days. A college can be very confining. If he's back from his walk, you may find him in the chapel."

Blakeley and Nathan walked around the monastery toward the chapel. There were rosebushes in bloom, and white blossoms fell from the apple trees lining the walk.

"He didn't believe me, did he?" Blakeley asked.

"No. I'm quite sure he didn't."

"See what I mean, Nathan?" Blakeley said. "I couldn't function without you."

"Thank you," Nathan said. "At times like this, I need a boost of the spirit."

"So you see," Blakeley said, "it wouldn't be charity if I paid you."

Nathan did not answer, for Father Gorman stood on the chapel steps. His expression was wary, and Nathan immediately regretted having revealed his secret without first asking his permission.

But Nathan's fears were for naught, and as he greeted the priest, Father Gorman said, "I must say I expected you a good deal sooner."

"You expected me to tell Dr. Blakeley?" Although Nathan was relieved, Father Gorman's remark hurt him.

"I think that's why I told you. If I'd had the courage, I would have told him myself. But since you seem to have taken my dreams seriously, I know that you don't think me insane."

Nathan and Blakeley started to protest, but Father Gorman stopped them with a wave of his hand. "I've been thinking a lot about my dreams. In fact, that's what I was thinking about on my walk today. I was out on Spring Mill Road, and before I knew it, I was all the way out by the Aimwell property. You must know how far that is. In the old days, I used to cover a hundred miles from Puerto Barrios to Copán on foot in order to tend to my people."

"Copán?" Blakeley said. "I believe that was where Don Orlando was held captive."

"I told you they had a great deal in common," Nathan said. "But Father Gorman, whatever possessed you to go to the Aimwell estate?"

"To tell you the truth, Nathan, I don't know. Morbid curiosity, perhaps."

Overheated by his long walk, the priest swabbed his forehead with a handkerchief he carried in the sleeve of his heavy black robe. In the wilds of Central America, he had no doubt been at liberty to dress more reasonably in the heat.

"I have an office across the way," Father Gorman said. "We can talk there."

The three men followed a winding path that cut through a cemetery, where generations of Augustinian monks had been laid to rest. At last, they came to an old building with a silvery dome. Father

Gorman's first-floor office was small but comfortable, and a flowering laurel bush kept out the sun's brilliant rays. Through an open window, a sloping field of wild flowers was visible.

Father Gorman tapped the side of a teapot and shook his head. "I realize it's teatime, Dr. Blakeley," he said, "but I let the stove go out hours ago. All I can offer you is colored water, I'm afraid."

"It's much too warm for tea anyway," Blakeley said.

"Where should I begin?" the priest asked, settling into a chair.

"With the nightmares, if you please," Blakeley said.

"They're terrible."

"Have you had any on nights when murders were not committed?"

"No." Father Gorman pointed to a calendar. "I can tell you when I've had them. On the night of the sixth when Louis Hazleton died, then on the twelfth when Reginald Aimwell was murdered, and finally last night. I've circled the dates on this calendar because I've been trying to figure out a pattern. But I haven't any idea if one exists. All I know is that each time I have another nightmare it's worse than the last."

Blakeley proceeded apologetically. "I hate to have to ask you this, Father, but would you mind—"

"Describing my dreams?" Father Gorman's weary eyes showed resignation. "I fall into a light sleep, and my body gets very warm. That's why I was tempted to think my first dream was only a recurrence of malaria. I came down with that, you see, after I escaped my captors in the jungle. I almost went mad at the time, and don't think that hasn't preyed on my mind lately." He considered what he'd just told them and added, "But I'm sure my dreams aren't caused by malaria."

"What then?" Blakeley asked.

Father Gorman smiled nervously. "I'm a theologian, Dr. Blakeley, not a physician. I was hoping you could tell me."

Blakeley got up and paced the room, stopping before a tall bookcase. "Nathan tells me you gave him a very vivid description of Hawthorne's murder."

"I did."

"Again, I hate to ask you this, because I can see the strain this whole business is putting on you, but would you please describe your last dream for me?"

"Certainly." Father Gorman paused to collect his thoughts. "For a moment, I thought I was in the woods, the jungle perhaps. I saw wild animals everywhere—a puma, a leopard. Then I realized the animals were not alive. They were stuffed, and I was in a well-furnished room. It was a den or a study with deep leather chairs and a large mahogany desk. Hanging on the wall was the head of a jungle cat—a jaguar, to be exact. I saw many of them in the old days. The jaguar was immediately behind the desk, just above a tall-backed leather chair. The draperies were of a dark color, maroon. They were billowing."

Blakeley took a step forward. "Was there a strange wind in the room, Father Gorman?"

"Yes," the priest said, staring off as he recalled the scene. A thin line of perspiration lay on his trembling upper lip. "Papers were flying in all directions, but I can't recall hearing anything like a wind. I think it was as silent as a tomb in there."

"Where was Hawthorne?"

"On the sofa," Father Gorman sputtered. "He was partially undressed. I saw the sudden terror in his eyes, as though something of indescribable evil had just appeared before him. He seemed almost frozen with fear. I was as close to him as I am to you at

285

this moment. His screams awakened me. His screams. Oh, God...."

Blakeley and Nathan exchanged worried looks. They hadn't thought their questioning would so disturb the clergyman.

"I'm sorry you had to relive that, Father," Nathan said, "but Dr. Blakeley had to hear it from you. You do understand?"

"I do," Father Gorman said. He massaged his temples, trying to chase off a sudden headache.

"Are you all right?" Blakeley asked.

Father Gorman nodded. "Just very tired."

"Is there anything else?" Blakeley asked.

"Yes, there is," the priest said. "It's what's been troubling me the most from the beginning. I saw each of those murders very clearly, and I know I should feel horrified during my dreams, but it's only when I wake up in a cold sweat that I feel any pity for the victims."

"You mean," Blakeley said, "you see the murders all from the murderer's point of view? And you're concerned because you seem to share the murderer's feeling?"

"Yes, I do," Father Gorman said, fully aware of all the question implied.

"I wouldn't worry about that," Blakeley said, trading a concerned glance with Nathan. Quickly changing the subject, he pulled a folded sheet of paper from his breast pocket. "Show Father Gorman this drawing, Nathan."

Nathan unfolded Allison's sketch of the woman in green, and handing it to Father Gorman, he asked, "Do you recognize this woman from your dreams?"

"I don't recognize the woman," Father Gorman said, studying the sketch closely, "but are these little designs around the neckline supposed to be bright red?"

"Yes, the dress is green with red and yellow ornamentation."

"These designs are called death's eyes," the priest said. "They resemble tiny red bells that jingle on the headdress of the Mayan god of death."

"Are you sure?" Blakeley asked.

"I have a rare book here somewhere that explains their significance," Father Gorman said, searching through a bookcase behind his desk. "It was written by a Spanish monk named Lorenzo Del Vaille in 1791. According to legend, he was under a spell of some kind."

Suddenly, Father Gorman put his hand to his chest, breathing in sharp, shallow gasps.

"This can wait," Nathan said, stepping over to help the priest when he saw his knees buckling.

"A spell of some kind," the priest repeated, "but...."

"Catch him, Nathan," Blakeley said as the priest collapsed, but Nathan was already too late to stop his descent.

Chapter Eighteen

The lockup at the rear of the Eleventh Precinct was busy the next morning. Outside, the hot weather made throats thirstier and tempers shorter; inside, the conditions were even worse. And the weathermen predicted the day would get even hotter as it wore on.

Nathan had been rather quiet all morning, and judging from his listlessness and lack of attention, Blakeley assumed he had spent a sleepless night. Sitting in the young policeman's buggy, Blakeley wondered if, somewhere deep in his subconscious, Nathan was harboring a bit of guilt. He had, after all, betrayed Father Gorman's trust, and despite the priest's reassurances, Nathan might not have forgiven himself for causing his friend the undue stress that resulted in his collapse.

Fortunately, the clergyman was not so bad as he had seemed at first. When Father Gorman collapsed, Blakeley had made him comfortable on the floor, and Nathan rushed off to seek help. Feeling the priest's pulse and checking under his eyelids, Blakeley had cursed the absence of his medical bag until Nathan returned with the carriage. They only had to drive a mile to the village of Wayne, where a chap named Van Arsdale had an office; after running some quick tests, he ruled out a stroke or a heart attack. Father Gorman, Van Arsdale diagnosed, was suffering from extreme exhaustion. So he sent the priest to bed for a time, sedated him to be sure he slept, and ordered him to refrain from taking long walks until the weather turned cooler.

"He had to take the long walks," Nathan told Blakeley the next morning as he reined in his horse before the precinct house. "Just before he fell off to sleep, he told me it was the only way he could tire himself out enough to put the nightmares out of his mind."

"So his exhaustion may be a blessing in disguise."

"You don't really consider him a suspect, do you?"

"Of course not, dear boy," Blakeley said much too breezily. That same question had caused him a restless night.

Nathan said nothing, but he didn't believe Blakeley. He was having difficulties accounting for Father Gorman claiming to have seen the crimes from the murderer's eyes, and he knew Blakeley wouldn't dismiss the matter so easily.

But as the two men entered the precinct house, they turned their thoughts to another problem: Victor had been arrested for blowing up theatrical producer Hermie Hinsky. Even though Lt. Hudson had called him the night before with the news, Blakeley had been too tired to worry about his butler. And when Hudson told him Victor's story of the deadly cigars, he was less inclined to help his servant. But despite his petty larceny, Victor had inadvertently

helped avert mayhem in the Blakeley household—
the source of which could only be Christopher Beecham. And so, Blakeley had asked a favor of a mag-
istrate in the Second Precinct, where Hermie
Hinsky had been blown to bits. As a result, Victor
was transferred to the lockup in the Eleventh,
where he would be kept under wraps by policemen
familiar with his particular personality foibles.

In the back of the lockup, Blakeley and Nathan
found Victor sitting on a stool, rocking monoto-
nously, his eyes fixed on nothing in particular. He
looked especially wretched with his clothing half
shredded by the force of the blast in Hermie Hinksy's office.

Fatzinger, standing guard outside Victor's cell,
tapped the bars with his nightstick as they approached. Because Blakeley had successfully had
Fatzinger reassigned to his duties in the precinct,
Hudson was once again at odds as to what to do
with him. The night before, Hudson had only too
gladly sent Fatzinger to escort Victor back to the
Eleventh, believing that not even he could foul up
such a simple assignment. Since that time, Fatzinger had camped out in front of Victor's cell, as if
the butler were his own private prisoner.

"No shleepin', you," Fatzinger said and tapped
the bars again.

"I'm not sleeping, you vile rustic!" Victor
snapped.

"You haff company."

"Oh?" Victor saw Blakeley and jumped up to
greet him. "Oh, sir, bless you."

Never had Blakeley seen Victor so fawning. He
was trying to reach Blakeley's hand through the
bars so he could kiss it, but Blakeley pulled back.

"Hello, Victor," he said. "How are our friends
treating you?"

"Unconscionably, sir," Victor protested and

pointed to a bunk near the wall where Bummy Rummel snorted, mumbled, rolled over, and mumbled again. "They have me sharing these despicable quarters with that vagrant. He smells like a garbage bin, sir."

"Dott's on accounta in der garbage bin outside Patsy Dowd's saloon he vuss shleepin'," Fatzinger told them.

"It's where he belongs," Victor said, waving his hand before his face.

"You should talk," Fatzinger said, sitting on a bench, "mit der pants all in rags."

Fatzinger bit into his shoofly pie and sighed. He was not in the best of moods. He had received a letter from Strawberry Knockelknorr, the passion of his life. She had written to tell him she was in love with Hausknecht the undertaker. There would be hell to pay when he went home to Ebenezersville. Strawberry had also asked that he return his favorite photograph, the one taken at the previous year's Essenfest. In the photograph, she was dressed in a pumpkin costume, Fatzinger liked it for the seductive way her bulbous legs protruded through the two holes at the bottom.

His face twisted with anger, he said, "Dott Hausknecht vuss alvays a veasel in der henhaus."

Having no idea what Fatzinger meant, Blakeley smiled politely and said, "He certainly was."

"I presume, sir," Victor said, "you've come to effect my release."

"No," Blakeley said, passing a bag of clean clothing between the bars of the cell, "but we did bring you a change of clothing."

Panic stricken, Victor gripped the bars. "But, sir, I must protest. I am an innocent man!"

"Oh, I don't know, Victor," Blakeley said ruefully. "You look damnably guilty to me. What do you think, Nathan?"

"Damnably, Dr. Blakeley," Nathan repeated.

"Must you make sport, sir?" Victor groaned.

"No one is jesting, Victor. After all, you did abscond with my cigars, did you not?"

"By which action I undoubtedly saved your life. Have you thought of that, sir?"

"I have. But, Victor," Blakeley said piously, "poor, poor Mr. Hinsky."

It was safe to say that no one truly mourned the passing of Hermie Hinsky, especially those who had had the misfortune of working for him. A joke was circulating around show-business circles that somebody had come to town looking for Hinsky and had asked a few passers-by if anyone had seen the producer. "Yeah," one said, pointing to the east. "There's Hermie." Then another had pointed to the west and said, "And there's some more of Hermie."

No one had mourned him except Emma Shmeckman, who had wept hysterically from the moment she regained consciousness until Hinsky's lawyer in New York had returned her wire and informed her that Hinsky had left her only his collection of French postcards and a recipe for stewed prunes. In her rage at the producer's posthumous slight, Emma's hatred of actors, even marginal ones like Victor, brought her to new levels of shrewish belligerence. Her voice as shrill and clear as a siren, she told her story to anyone who would listen, and she was determined to testify against Victor no matter what.

"This horrid situation, sir," Victor said on the verge of tears, "is not to be endured."

"Now, Victor," Blakeley said, "but for our friends here at the Eleventh, you'd be in some dungeon eating fish heads and mice."

"I suppose, despite your gross exaggeration," Victor sneered, "I should be most grateful for that."

"Well, it certainly isn't nice to abuse Lt. Hudson's hospitality.

When Bummy emitted a long, noisome burp, Blakeley and Nathan stepped a few feet back from the cell. With nowhere to go, Victor could only grimace.

"Gawd! I am like gentle Clarence locked in the Tower, waiting to be drowned in a butt of malmsey."

"Oh, really, Victor, it's not so bad," Blakeley chided. He took a piece of paper from his coat pocket and handed it through the bars. "Look, you're a celebrity. Rosie clipped this item from the gossip pages of *The Inquirer*."

Victor snatched the paper out of Blakeley's hand. Little smiles twitched across his mouth as he read. An actor who had suffered particularly grave humiliation at Hermie Hinsky's whim because he had gone to college had written a eulogy to be enjoyed by others in the trade:

They say a snake the other day
Bit old Herm Hinsky while in sleep he lay.
This is the truth, for nobody lied—
The snake, and not old Hermie, died.

But this time, gents, we'll hit the bar.
We'll drink a toast to a great cigar,
And the butler who works for the English
   bloke,
Who sent old Hermie up in smoke.

"I knew that would cheer you up," Blakeley said.

"You only brought it to me because they included you in it," Victor pouted.

"In a very small, humble way," Blakeley said. "Still."

"Now, Victor," Blakeley said, clearing his throat, "about the cigars?"

"You mean," Victor snickered, "the *Hoyo de Monterrey José Gener Excaliburs*?"

"Those."

"Personally, I think they're overrated, sir."

"Victor," Blakeley suddenly growled, "where did you get them?"

"Please do not raise your voice, sir," Victor pleaded. "I've a frightful headache. The smells in this place—dear Gawd!"

"Very well then," Blakeley said, trying his best to keep his temper in check. "I shall whisper. Where did you get the cigars?"

Victor turned his head in feigned contrition. "You know, sir."

"Yes, yes," Blakeley said, "I know that much. I saw the package under your arm as you took them to Hinsky, instead of leaving them where they belonged. What I want to know, Victor, is who delivered them?"

"Why, a delivery boy, of course."

"And?"

"Really, sir, I paid no attention. Good heavens, I was on the threshold of—"

"Was he young, Victor? Old?"

Victor turned his back, then sighed and said, "I don't know!" Then he turned around again and said, "Well, youngish. Twentyish, I'd say."

"That's better," Blakeley said. "Anything else, Victor?"

"Yes," Victor said. "He walked with a limp."

"So," Blakeley said to Nathan, his suspicions confirmed, "Beecham did injure his leg the night he shot Simeon Dorsett, and it has not yet healed. Determined little devil, that Beecham." He returned his attention to Victor and said with great sincerity, "Victor, old boy, I cannot thank you enough. I do hope you'll be comfortable here."

"You're leaving, sir?" Victor gasped.

"I must check the cigar box for something called fingerprints, Victor," Blakeley said.

"But, sir!" Victor howled. "What about me?"

"Oh, yes, I'd quite forgotten to say that Mrs. Snopkowski sends you her best. She's making some kielbasa and sauerkraut soup for you."

Victor paced his cell, wringing his hands. "Alas!" he cried. "I am truly undone."

"That's why we brought you the change of clothes," Nathan said.

He had been silent throughout the visit, because he felt no sympathy for Victor. But the butler's vexation so amused him, he would not resist at least one dig at his expense. "Your uniform looks really terrible.

"But, sir, I am innocent!"

"Now, Victor," Blakeley said in the same tone he used when lecturing Ralphie "you were caught with a box full of the murder weapons just after having had a heated exchange with the victim. The police can't just allow you to exit gracefully into the wings, so to speak."

Behind Victor, Bummy awakened and sat up, smacking his lips and trying to clear the cotton from his mouth. In the next cell, another vagrant, Happy Harry Arbuckle, was stirring. Bummy slowly noticed him.

"Hi ya, Harry," Bummy said. "Hey, Harry, I want ya to meet my buddy Victor. Hey, Victor, say hello to"—Bummy paused to belch—"my buddy, Happy Harry."

Happy Harry looked at Victor, yawned, and went back to sleep.

"That's nice," Nathan said. "Now you'll have someone to share the kielbasa and sauerkraut soup with."

"And Officer Fatzinger will take good care of you," Blakeley assured Victor.

"Mit all der fancy ladies I am fed up," Fatzinger said as Blakeley and Nathan left.

"He loves it," Nathan said as they walked back through the noisy corridor.

"He certainly does," Blakeley agreed. "It's Victor's best moment since he played the talking lamppost in *The Merry Butterfly*. Just listen to him."

Through the many noises of the lockup, they could hear Victor wailing in his best stage voice, "Oh, fie, sir! Fie, fie, fie!"

Chapter Nineteen

That night at dinner, Mrs. Snopkowski, ecstatic over Victor's humiliation, reached new heights of culinary genius. She first served a rich leek, potato, and bacon soup; next came oysters in a champagne hollandaise sauce; the cook finished her gourmet feast with London broil in Ravigote sauce, a dish she knew was one of Blakeley's favorites. For Ralphie, there was a bonus of little stuffed dumplings called pierogies, which she fried in butter with shallots and mushrooms. Ralphie consumed these delights by the dozen. Between courses, Mrs. Snopkowski disappeared to the kitchen and returned to the dining room with a sillier grin than she had worn before leaving, and everyone at the table readily understood that she was visiting the secret place where she kept her homemade dandelion wine.

Just as Ralphie, his mouth crammed with several pierogies, was about to whisper to Nathan his tale of the strange world he'd visited at Cassie Aimwell's apartment—which, unknown to anyone present except Nathan, was the place he had slipped off to so often of late—Mrs. Snopkowski put her ruddy, pie-pan face next to his father's ear and asked for the tenth time, "How long dey got-em dott yonko in jailhouse for?"

Grateful for the wonderful feast, Blakeley answered once again, "They haven't said, Mrs. Snopkowski."

She laughed with wild abandon. "Maybe for good?"

Actually, Blakeley knew all too well that the fingerprints on the cigar box involved in the Hinsky death were those of Christopher Beecham; so there was no reason to hold Victor any longer. But as Lt. Hudson had said after watching Victor become violently ill from the sight of Fatzinger eating pickled pig's feet, what Victor didn't know wouldn't hurt him. The memory made Blakeley smile, and he said, "We shall see, Mrs. Snopkowski. We shall see."

The cook erupted with a merry bellow, startling Sophia and Rosie, both of whom were quite shaken by Beecham's attempt to kill Blakeley. Don Orlando, whose physical health was still improving, while his spirit deteriorated at an alarming pace, rolled his eyes. Nathan and Allison paid no attention, their last misunderstanding over Pratt having been forgotten. Despite her resolve to keep Pratt on her side to help her career, Allison could tell that her involvement with the journalist might endanger her relationship with Nathan. And so, once and for all, she decided to build her name on her own. As he sat at the table, beaming at everyone around him, Nathan tried to keep himself subdued, but his joy doomed him to fail. And each time Mrs. Snopkowski burst out anew, he laughed heartily.

"To hell with sissy booze!" Mrs. Snopkowski announced to Nathan's amusement. She snatched the Chardonnay from the table and hurried off to the kitchen. She returned a minute later with a gallon jug of her deadly dandelion wine. "For diss, Snopkowski got-em good stuff!"

Not long afterward, the wine had caused the little gathering to glow. Ralphie and Nathan loosened their collars, but Don Orlando retained his dignified trappings, forcing Blakeley to do likewise. The ladies fanned themselves briskly. In a corner of the room, Mrs. Snopkowski slept peacefully, her snores drifting over the waltzes on the Victrola.

Blakeley watched Nathan and Allison with some satisfaction. He'd almost given up hope of their ever calling an end to their egotistical standoff. He was pleased that G. Lindsey Pratt was no longer a threat to their happiness—not to mention that their new rapprochement was exactly what Nathan needed to forget his silly idea of enlisting.

No one in the assembled company could have found fault with the dinner or the other guests. But one unfortunate exchange did take place that evening that would prove, in the end, to be a turning point in all their lives. And it was Nathan who unwittingly initiated the fateful conversation.

"Don Orlando," he said, tearing himself away from Allison, "I must ask a favor of you."

The Spaniard put down his glass of wine and dabbed his mouth with a napkin. "Anything in my power, young friend."

Nathan reached into his pocket and pulled out a neatly folded piece of paper. "My Spanish is very rusty," he said. "Well, to be more exact, it's terrible."

"I see. You want me to translate something for you."

"If you wouldn't mind."

"Not at all."

"It can wait until tomorrow," Nathan hastened to add.

"In this world," Don Orlando reminded him, "one can never be certain there will be a tomorrow. Let us proceed."

Don Orlando donned his eyeglasses and accepted the piece of paper. For a few seconds, his face retained the smile he'd been wearing for most of the evening. But something in the text before him caused the smile to disappear suddenly.

"Is something wrong?" Nathan asked.

The old Spaniard kept reading. His smile gradually returned, but its luster had faded. "It is nonsense, young friend. You should not waste your time on such things. It would be much better to think of great beauty and contemplate Miss Meredith."

"I wasn't aware that it was nonsense," Nathan said, not a little puzzled by Don Orlando's reaction. "In fact, I understand it is part of a scholarly work. My friend at Villanova College assured me that the volume that passage came from is an unimpeachable source on Indian legends."

Don Orlando raised his glass of wine. "Do scholars read fairy tales?"

"I really don't think Father Gorman would have—" Nathan stopped when he noticed the old man's hand shaking. Drops of wine ran down the old man's chin when he put his glass down. Not wanting Don Orlando to collapse as Father Gorman had the day before, Nathan relented. "I guess you're right. Sorry to bother you."

"Not at all. If I cannot do a small favor for a friend, then my days are truly of no use. But I assure you, this Father Gorman is mistaken. What you have here is a childish story concocted by the *jivaros*."

"*Jivaros*?" Nathan asked, and for an awkward moment, he wondered if he would have to ask Don

Orlando to return the piece of paper.

But the Spaniard suddenly realized he still had the paper. While he returned it, he said, "*Jivaros* are backward people who live in the hills or somewhere far from civilization. They have many superstitions." He lowered his voice, so as not to offend his hosts, and added, "If our friend Ralphie were from my culture, he might be considered something of a *jivaro*."

Nathan laughed as he pictured Ralphie wearing a sombrero and trying to do a flamenco dance. "Well, I told you my Spanish is terrible. Thank you for the lesson."

"An honor to be of service," Don Orlando said, rising. "Now if you will excuse me, I must retire."

"*Buenas noches*," Nathan said.

"Ah, *buenas noches*, young friend."

Sophia noticed Don Orlando standing and nodded to her son. "See Don Orlando to his quarters, Ralph."

"Immediately, madam," Ralphie answered in his best imitation of Victor.

"That isn't all he'll see to," Rosie muttered under her breath so that only Nathan could hear her.

She was once again referring to her brother's recent habit of seizing every opportunity to disappear for whole nights at a time. Although Rosie, in her attempts at seductive conversation with Nathan, had intimated that her brother was off for a night in the hay with the ever-willing maid Dumpling, Nathan knew better. For Ralphie, in his own unsubtle way, had told his friend he was seeing a mysterious woman of the world—one as dangerous as the Green Lorelei. And since the only woman Ralphie had met of late was Cassie Aimwell, Nathan hadn't been long in deducing she was the object of Ralphie's ardor.

As Ralphie escorted Don Orlando from the dining

room, he winked impishly at Nathan, who winked back in amusement and envy. Undoubtedly, Ralphie was off for one of his secret nights in the city. Nathan only hoped the night ahead held as much promise for him.

Shortly after midnight, Allison rested her head against Nathan's shoulder as they strolled down a gravel path behind the Blakeleys' house. It was a familiar route, one they had often taken on similar evenings after other large dinners with the Blakeleys. As they walked, Allison hummed a popular tune.

Nathan couldn't take his eyes off Allison. Her hair smelled of gardenias. Her dress was aquamarine like her eyes. The wine had released a familiar coquettishness. Almost instinctively, he kissed her ear. She, in turn, took his face in her hands and kissed him for a long time.

They stopped in the middle of a small bridge that spanned a narrow trout stream. They had oft times stood there to watch lilies float in the calm waters off the bank, where the stream widened into a pond. That night, a soft, soothing rush of water flowed over shallows. Nathan held Allison close, and she wrapped her arms around his waist. Both of them knew that, once and for all, neither would allow the other to stray from the best thing in either of their lives.

"How's your Spanish these days?" Nathan asked suddenly.

Allison stuck her face into his chest and growled. "That has to be the least romantic thing a girl ever heard."

"I'm sorry. I meant to ask you earlier, except Mrs. Snopkowski kept interrupting."

"Well, I don't think it's on a par with Don Orlando's."

"I know, but he was in his cups. And he became upset about the passage I asked him to translate."

"I don't think he feels much like speaking nowadays. The war has him down."

Nathan tickled her neck with light kisses. She tensed her muscles and giggled.

"I don't mind," he said. "I'd much rather work with you."

"I may charge a fee," she said, stepping back when he kissed her again on a ticklish spot.

"Whatever you say, as long as it's under a nickel."

Since it was dark on the bridge, they moved around in search of a brighter place and found a picnic table by the pond. The bench was relatively dry, and no branches hung over it, blocking the bright moonlight. Allison strained to read the passage, but it was no use.

"I'll have to wait until I get back to my room," she said finally.

"No fee until you do."

They were seated close together. The only sounds they heard were the chirping of crickets, the muffled croak of a frog across the pond, and the random squawking of some gulls, which had come up river from the sea and decided to tarry awhile at the pond.

Deep in Nathan's embrace, Allison had a brief recollection of Sister Mary Dolores, her lantern-jawed sixth-grade teacher who believed in public stonings for what she was thinking. She frowned briefly, then dismissed the nun to the dark recesses of her memory.

"I don't suppose you'd like to pay ahead, would you?" Allison asked as she pulled out of Nathan's arms and stood.

"You mean a whole nickel?"

"I mean how would you like to go for a swim?"

Nathan shook his head in mock disbelief.

"You heard me," Allison said, laughing at his comic expression. "How would you like to go for a swim?"

He started to speak, but nothing came out.

"Nathan, chastity doesn't become you," Allison said as she unbuttoned her dress. "So stop pretending. A swim will help digest all that food."

"Are you, uh, sure you—" He stopped in mid-sentence and watched her undress.

Allison stepped out of her dress, folded it neatly, and placed it atop the picnic table. "Nobody will see us, you know. If anyone comes along, we'll just get lost in the fog."

"I'd like that."

"Help me out of this corset, please."

When she turned her back, Nathan loosened the stays, thinking to himself how unnecessary a corset was on Allison's lovely, lithe body. Her corset undone, she removed it. In the moonlight her nakedness was breathtaking.

"You're spectacular, you know," Nathan whispered, gazing at her as if he had just unearthed a Greek statue.

Allison stepped forward, draped her arms over his shoulders, and kissed him. "A little while ago, after my third or fourth glass of wine, I decided that it was time to do what I've been dreaming about before something else gets between us and ruins it for good."

She stepped into the water, the sudden chill puckering her nipples. She waited until she knew he'd seen enough, then turned and slipped into deeper water.

"You know, you look absolutely stuffy," she said after wading a few yards out. When Nathan started to remove his clothing, she smiled. "That's much better."

* * *

It was almost three o'clock when Allison rapped lightly on the guest room door. It had been two hours since she and Nathan had sneaked into the house like two damp and disheveled felons. She should have fallen into a deep sleep and dreamed of things both primitive and sublime, of the many heretofore unappreciated uses of ponds and picnic tables, but the memories had only kept her awake. So she decided to translate the passage Nathan had shown to Don Orlando earlier, hoping that it would bore her to sleep. But what she discovered had so disturbed her she couldn't wait until morning to tell Nathan. And so she crept to his room.

Although Nathan was dozing, he rose immediately and tiptoed to the door when he heard a whispered voice saying, "It's me, Allison. Open the door."

"I can't be this lucky in one night," he said, popping a piece of peppermint-flavored chewing gum into his mouth.

"You're not," Allison said and pecked him lightly on the cheek.

She was wearing a silken robe over what looked to Nathan like a diaphanous gown. Her hair flowed over her shoulders and halfway down her back, and he longed to stroke it again. While he had dozed, his mind had entered that nebulous zone between sleeping and waking, and he had imagined that her body was still next to his as they stood half submerged in the water, locked in wordless communion.

"Oh," he said, disappointed by reality and Allison's reply. "Well, in that case, I hope you don't mind if I smoke."

"I didn't know you still smoked."

"Only when I'm desperate to find something to do with my hands."

Allison laughed quietly. "Very well. What I want

to show you is what I've made out of this passage you gave me. Where did you find it?"

"It was something I copied out of a book Father Gorman gave me. It had a few words I couldn't figure out, and I suspected they were important."

"May I sit on the bed and go over it?" she asked.

"Sure. I promise not to get fresh."

"Good," Allison said, laughing again.

She sat beside him and he smelled gardenias, which was a bit unfair. It would be far better, he mused, had she come in a flannel nightgown and nightcap.

"So what did you find?" he asked, snuffing his cigarette out after inhaling only once.

"It's about a legend from the Olmec period in Mayan history." She ran her finger across the page and translated the Spanish text:

"'At some time between eight hundred and four hundred years before the birth of Jesus, there arose among the Olmec savages a legend of a woman who mated with a jungle beast. Of this abominable liaison an issue resulted, the manifestation of which I have seen only in the form of clay figurines. It is a nightmarish entity the peasants call the *chan-ekal*—a baby with a gaping, snarling mouth, half human and half jaguar. Sometimes it appears in the form of a spotted animal resembling a tiger.'"

"*Chan-ekal*," Nathan said. "That was what stopped me."

"Where did Father Gorman get this, Nathan?"

"It's from the observations of a Spanish monk written over a century ago. He went mad. So nobody took him seriously."

"It's interesting, but very frightening," Allison said.

"As interesting as this?" Nathan said, kissing her neck and causing her to tense up again.

"I thought you were going to behave."

"Sorry."

"Apology accepted." She pointed out the last paragraph and continued reading:

"'The entity is considered the eager maidservant of *Ah Puch*, god of the Underworld in the service of whom it may take form of the long-haired harlot, *x-tabai*, the green-and-yellow serpent, *chay-i-can*, or in any other fashion appropriate to a werejaguar—'"

"Werejaguar?" Nathan said, interrupting Allison's translation.

"That's the word, Nathan. Werejaguar."

"Oh, God, do you mean Beef's been right all along?"

Chapter Twenty

"I dunno, Dad," Ralphie said, as his mother, his sister, and he inspected his father's costume. "I still think you ought to go as Henry VIII."

Blakeley could not dismiss the point Ralphie was making about his shape, especially since he was standing before the full-length mirror in his dressing room. "May I remind you, Ralph, that the period celebrated by the costume ball is the reign of Charles II? You're only off by a century or so."

"History was another course I flunked," Ralphie admitted without apology.

"I know," his father said. "In spectacular fashion."

"And stop boasting about it," his mother ordered.

Ralphie blushed and winked at Rosie. She stuck out her tongue, then helped her mother adjust a tall white wig. The long, brocaded gown Sophia wore fit her perfectly. She had decided to dress as the beautiful if notorious Nell Gwyn, celebrated actress and favorite mistress of the king. Her choice was unusually daring of her, since in past years she had attended the ball in prim Quaker costumes. But as she'd told her husband after a long period of indecision, she was risking her reputation for a worthy cause, and with all the danger in her life of late, she was feeling a bit intrepid.

Besides, with less than a week to go before the Restoration Ball, Sophia had found another worry to add to her fears about Christopher Beecham. For, because of the hysteria generated by Spector and his ilk over the Green Lorelei murders, she had reason to believe attendance would be down that year. If it was, she would never hear the end of it from the other members of the Tuesday Ladies. And if the upcoming ball was to be the last, Sophia was determined to enjoy her swan song, no matter how much she riled the closed-minded scruples of the city's elite.

Far from disapproving of her choice, however, Blakeley thought it a splendid idea. He had always enjoyed Sophia's sauciness, and if the truth were told, his vanity had always been bolstered by letting the world see the beauty he'd courted successfully in his younger days.

Sophia was truly beautiful in the pink-and-gray silken gown. And the powdered white wig and the beauty mark she had painted on her left cheek made her all the more bewitching.

As for Blakeley, his form was far more suited to the tweed coats and plus fours of 1898 than to the peacock finery of 1682. But, as Sophia said, the ball was for a good cause.

"Not exactly the stuff for which passionate love letters are written," he said, frowning at his image in the mirror.

"Daddy," Rosie proclaimed, "I think you look absolutely rakish."

"She just wants you to let her be courted by Ratty Rob Quimby," Ralphie said.

"Dost think Dr. Blakeley a gull, sir?" Rosie said huffily. "One easily cozened? A pox on your spleen, sir!"

"Huh?"

"Huh?" Rosie repeated. "You sound like a chimp."

"It's Restoration-period language, Ralph," Blakeley explained.

"And it borders on the obscene," Sophia said. "So I wish you wouldn't speak it."

" 'Sblood!" Rosie declared. "Would there were a physic to turn my Lady Blakeley into a modern woman."

"Odds fish!" Blakeley declared as he removed his velvet coat. "Yon wench has a biting tongue."

"Please do not encourage her, Ian," Sophia requested.

"Yeah," Ralphie said, "she gets carried away too easily."

"Perhaps you should look in on Don Orlando now, Ralph," Sophia suggested.

"I just did," Ralphie said, "when I helped him to his room after dinner."

"Perhaps a second look would be advisable," Sophia said flatly.

Suddenly, Ralphie remembered an assignation he'd arranged with Cassie Aimwell. Since checking on the depressed Spaniard would give him the cover he needed to slip away, he said, "Oh, all right, Mother. Whatever you say."

"That's a good fellow," Sophia said.

"Wouldst dally with the doxie?" Rosie chimed as Ralphie passed her on the way out. She giggled when he did not understand, then frowned when, instead of arguing, Ralphie started whistling and left.

Sophia looked at Blakeley, a little puzzled, a little concerned. When Blakeley only shrugged, she went back to studying her costume in the mirror.

At the top of the stairs, Ralphie met Dumpling, who had just come from Don Orlando's quarters after delivering a small snack of bread, meat, and wine. She stopped and stared angrily when they met.

"Hello, Dumpling," Ralphie said with false gusto. "How's our favorite Spaniard doing this evening?"

She passed by frigidly.

"Nice talking to you," Ralphie said as Dumpling went down the stairs, ignoring him.

Dumpling had been perturbed by Ralphie's recent lack of interest in her. She was so distraught, in fact, that Mrs. Snopkowski had threatened to fire her the day before because she'd eaten an entire *Schwarzwalder Kirchentorte* that had taken the cook an entire afternoon to bake.

Ralphie followed her with his eyes and noted how the anxiety was showing in her waistline. "Maybe another box of chocolates would help," he thought and chuckled to himself as he tapped on Don Orlando's door.

When a second knock brought no response, he put his ear to the door and listened. As he'd expected, the old man was saying his prayers. For someone who claimed to have lost all interest in his religion, Ralphie mused, old Don Orlando was certainly a religious man. At least, Ralphie assumed he was praying. Ralphie hadn't the slightest clue about the Spanish language, but Don Orlando certainly sounded as if he was praying. Sometimes, like at present, the prayers seemed desperate, as if they were impassioned pleas.

"He's probably praying for a victory in Cuba." Ralphie guessed and tiptoed away from the door. "It will take one helluva good prayer."

A half hour later, Ralphie was at the Fogwell Arms. He was met at Cassie's door by a man in a eunuch's costume. The man's gelatinous stomach covered the top of his yellow pantaloons. He remind Ralphie of a flour sack with a belly button.

"Are you Ralphie?" the man asked indifferently.

"Who are you?" Ralphie asked.

"I am Abdul," the man said.

"Really?"

"Really. And if you're Ralphie, the mistress awaits you."

"Abdul," Ralphie said, passing by the man in the eunuch's costume. "Sure you are."

Every time he'd visited Cassie, she had come up with a new gimmick. One evening she was Cleopatra. Another evening she was dressed as a lady out of King Arthur's court, and some poor slob had to wear armor in the heat all night, clanking around as he went back and forth from the kitchen to Cassie's bedroom. On Ralphie's last visit, she had assumed the identity of Robert E. Lee—gray uniform, white beard, and all. She wanted Ralphie to dress up as Ulysses S. Grant, but he refused. After several attempts, he'd finally told Nathan about their night together, and when Nathan stopped laughing, they'd talked about Cassie's eccentric games. Nathan suggested Cassie could be as uninhibited as she wanted only when she pretended to be someone else. And Ralphie had accepted his reasoning without argument.

That night, Cassie was seated on a large crimson cushion, surrounded by several tall candelabra and incense burners. The arrangement was reminiscent of the night she'd played Cleopatra, save for one detail: the green dress with red and yellow patterns around the neckline. Ralphie paused when he saw the dress.

On the long low table between her cushion and

his, cheeses, fruits, and wine were piled on several plates. The room was lit warmly by the flickering candelabra, and behind Cassie, conveniently situated as usual, was the brass four-poster bed.

"Good evening, darling," Cassie said, her voice as smoky as the scent of the incense burners. "You're late."

Ralphie didn't want to tell her that he'd almost forgotten the visit entirely. Nathan would probably say he was trying to talk himself out of the Cassie Aimwell fling, and Nathan would probably be correct. The whole thing was a bit too bizarre for Ralphie. Sometimes he felt like the pet monkey she'd rented for her evening as Cleopatra.

"That's a nice dress," he said.

"Green is all the rage nowadays," she said, "thanks to people like your father and gobs and gobs of publicity."

True to her word, Betty Jane Stamm had given a description of the Green Lorelei to any and all who would pay for it. Overwhelmed by the media's attention, Betty Jane had made the woman more grotesque with each interview.

Cassie's version featured more crimson than most, no doubt to complement the cushion. Her v-shaped neckline plunged down to her navel. It was only a fashion, Ralphie knew, but considering what the Green Lorelei had done to her brother, it struck him as beyond eccentric that Cassie would want to dress like the supposed murderer. Nathan might say she wanted to face her worst nightmares head-on.

"It looks nice on you," he said, sitting down on his cushion.

"Green is ubiquitous in Philadelphia," she said.

Ralphie knew what she meant. Cassie liked to play word games with him. He might have told her he knew the word, but he just smiled, selected a

313

piece of cheese, and poured himself a glass of wine.

"Let Abdul do that," she said.

"I know how to pour a glass of wine," Ralphie said.

The jug was almost empty. Obviously, Cassie had been working on it for some time.

"You sound cheeky, darling," she said. "Is something wrong?"

"No," he said, eating the cheese, sipping the wine. "Everything's fine."

She leaned forward and looked quite serious. "Is it Abdul?"

He laughed. "No, Abdul's all right."

"His name isn't really Abdul," she said. "It's George."

"I figured."

"I ordered him to change it for the evening to go with my costume." She popped a grape into her mouth and said smugly, "The market favors the buyer these days."

Ralphie ate some dates and started to refill his wine glass, but the jug of wine was empty. When Cassie clapped her hands, Abdul came into the bedroom.

"Get some more wine," she said, and when Abdul left, she looked at Ralphie with some consternation. Finally, she thought she knew what was troubling him.

"It's the green dress, isn't it?"

"No, no," he said, "I think it's—"

"Very well," Cassie said, jumping up. "I'll change it."

Before he could protest again, she disappeared into the next room. He looked over the fruits on the tray, although he recognized most of them, he was puzzled by a few. He picked up what appeared to be a black pear with a leathery surface. He was squeezing it gently when Cassie peeked through the drapes.

"Close your eyes, Ralphie," she said and winked.

"What do you call this thing?" he asked, holding up the fruit.

"Close your eyes," she insisted.

"All right," he said and obliged. He could hear her footsteps as she came into the room and sat on her crimson velvet cushion. A few seconds later, he said, "May I open them now?"

"One moment, please," she said. "All right, Ralphie, you may look at me now."

He opened his eyes and blinked. "You're naked."

"Very perceptive of you," she said and laughed. It was a very libidinous laugh.

"Jeez crumps."

Cassie wasn't entirely naked. She wore a red ribbon in her hair, a yellow one around her neck, and red and yellow ribbons around her ankles.

Abdul started to enter the room with a new jug of wine. He stopped abruptly when he saw Cassie, but she snapped her fingers and gestured for him to enter. He proceeded slowly and clumsily with his eyes closed. When he was at the table, he knelt on one knee, felt around with one hand, and deposited the jug with the other. With eyes closed, he couldn't see the two or three apples and the wine glass he knocked off the table.

When he got up, Cassie said, "The next time you return, Abdul, cover your eyes with a towel or something. My consort and I are having a naked supper."

"Yes, ma'am," Abdul said.

"Sensuous One," she reminded him.

"Yes, O Sensuous One," he said, turning and following his stomach out of the room.

She returned to Ralphie. "Is something troubling you?" she asked.

Ralphie should not have been nonplussed by Cassie's nakedness. He'd seen her in the nude often enough in the past. As he'd told Nathan, Cassie was clothed less often than a baby. Maybe it was having Abdul or George or whoever he was in the room with them.

Minutes passed as Cassie sat less than six feet away from Ralphie, her legs crossed Hindu fashion, challenging him with her half-open eyes to utter something bourgeois.

Finally, clearing his throat, he said, "Yeah, I was wondering what you call this."

"It's called an avocado."

"Can you eat it?"

"Of course," she said. "Let me show you how."

He rolled the avocado across the table. It passed through a lane between the wedge of cheddar and a basket of figs. She picked up the pulpy piece of fruit and looked at it appreciatively.

"They're hard to find," she said, "especially with the war on. They're picked in Florida and age as they're shipped up here. *Très cher.*"

She sipped her wine, allowing some of it to spill over her lip and run down her chin, then she licked it away slowly. Ralphie cleared his throat again.

She started to peel the black skin away to reveal the green pulp. "Oh, look," she said in the voice of a curious child, "it's green. What a coincidence!"

She removed the skin, held the avocado up, and squeezed it until the green pulp seeped between her fingers. "Have you ever heard of the Druids, Ralphie?"

"They were pagans, weren't they?"

"Yes, my darling," she said. "And do you know what Druid women used to do with their breasts?"

Ralphie's mouth opened. He tried to say something sophisticated, but all that came out was, "They, uh, jeez crumps, Cassie, how the heck would I know?"

"They used to paint circles around them," she said.

"Oh," he said. "Yeah, that was it."

"Only their circles were blue," she said, taking her left breast in her left hand. "I much prefer green, don't you?"

He nodded his head as she circled her left breast with green avocado pulp, then took her right breast in her left hand and drew a green circle around it with her little finger.

"There," she said, admiring her art work. "Isn't that beautiful?"

"It's different," Ralphie stammered.

"And here's a little trick I learned from a very forbidden book I read about Lucrezia Borgia. Do you know who Lucrezia Borgia was?"

Ralphie shook his head to show that he didn't, but he had a fairly good idea that Cassie wasn't referring to a saint. Cassie rubbed some of the green pulp over her nipples.

"Now, Ralphie," she said with a lascivious smile, "do you remember what you promised me last time you were here?"

James Aloysius Gorman hated idleness. He had lived his life according to an ethic more medieval than modern. He believed man was born to serve God—the same God who had given him talents and a sense of purpose. To fail to make use of those gifts was surely a grave sin. So, Father Gorman had no doubt Dr. Van Arsdale was a good man who did his job well. His order for bed rest was the proper prescription. But after four full days of lying abed, enough was enough.

Thus, when Father Capone asked him if he felt up to resuming his duties for a few hours, he answered eagerly that he was, though he knew in his bones that his body was still weary. Father Capone said he hated to ask him, but wartime emergencies had forced several of the priests to be assigned to parish duties around Philadelphia for the weekend. Two of the priests remaining at the monastery, including the provincial himself, were under the weather with a summer grippe, and there were many confessions to be heard.

To be truthful, if there had been other duties left undone, Father Gorman would have been happier performing them. He was distracted by his thoughts, and the sacrament was much too important to treat in any way other than quite seriously. The provincial had told him, however, that the men of the Twenty-eighth Armed Regiment were anxious to make their peace with God before going off to Florida in the morning.

A long line of penitents, mostly, but not all, men in uniform, awaited him as he entered the chapel at six o'clock. Father O'Toole, who had started at five, had not been able to last beyond a half hour before the grippe brought on nausea. So the line had grown longer in the time it took Father Gorman to dress hurriedly and walk down from the monastery. He sighed deeply when he saw the line snaking away from his confessional, around the back of the church, then up the aisle past the Stations of the Cross to where it finally ended by the votive lights near the altar.

It took Father Gorman over three hours to relieve the penitents of their burdens. By the time he'd heard what he thought was his last confession, he was exhausted. He massaged his temples and waited awhile to be sure no one was left in the church.

Five minutes later, just as he was about to leave, he heard someone enter the confessional and kneel. He opened the small wooden window that separated him from the penitent.

"Bless me, Father," the voice whispered through the lattice work screen, "for I have sinned."

It was a woman's voice. Father Gorman thought he detected an accent.

"It has been many months since my last confession," the voice continued.

The voice was pleasant but strange. The priest tried to place the accent.

He had no way of knowing that the woman wore green.

In the midst of his dreamless sleep, Ralphie heard the pounding; it was faraway, but persistent enough to awaken him. Because his head felt as though it was filled with broken glass, he didn't want to move. But the pounding continued, and he knew he had no choice. Although one eye opened quickly, he had to force the other to comply. As the pounding grew louder, he cursed, "All right, you son of a bitch, I hear you!"

In the early morning dark, made even gloomier by a sudden storm, Ralphie remembered where he was, and he hoped that Cassie hadn't heard him. But Cassie wasn't where she should have been beside him in the bed. All that remained of her was a few avocado stains on the silken sheets.

While Ralphie stared about him, the pounding stopped; then a man's voice cried, "Beef, goddamn it, wake up! It's Nathan."

His vision cloudy, Ralphie stumbled around, searching for his trousers and swearing at himself for letting Cassie talk him into sniffing ether. Once again he had learned a lesson too late: not all promises had to be kept, especially when they caused illness.

Another shout from Nathan roused Ralphie to hurry, but he wasn't going anywhere until he found his pants. At last he caught sight of them on Cassie's side of the bed. He stumbled and cursed again as he stepped into them, then gave up any hope of finding his shoes. Barefoot, he walked carefully through the dimly lit apartment. The thick scent of molten wax somewhat stifled the acrid smell of the ether, but the anesthetic's odor was still strong enough to turn his stomach.

"Jeez crumps," Ralphie thought as he realized he couldn't remember much of the previous evening—not even if he had enjoyed himself.

When Ralphie opened the door, Nathan stepped in and closed it behind him. The pouring rain had soaked his overcoat, and he dripped all over the vestibule. His bedraggled appearance had caused him trouble downstairs, where the burly night watchman had tried to deny him entrance. In the noisy fracas that ensued, Nathan succeeded in pushing his way past the burly man, and undoubtedly his shouts had roused several of the tenants who lived in the building.

"Nathan," Ralphie said, shaking cobwebs out of his head as his friend came into focus. "Don't tell me Dad figured out what was going on with Cassie and sent you here to break it up?"

"If he knows, he's pretending not to," Nathan said in a hushed voice, not wishing to disturb Cassie. He sniffed the air. "Ether?"

"Huh? Probably varnish," Ralphie said innocently, preoccupied with thoughts of his missing paramour. "What's going on?"

"The Green Lorelei has struck again," Nathan said, and for the first time, Ralphie noticed the melancholy in his eyes. "This time it was Father Gorman."

"A priest? That doesn't make sense. If Dad's theory is right, why would Beecham kill a priest?"

Nathan made a helpless gesture. "We'd better get to the monastery right away. When I talked to your father, he said he wanted you with him. I told him I'd keep an eye out for you. So move it."

"Sure thing, Nathan," Ralphie said, hurrying off to find the rest of his clothing. "Just as soon as I'm dressed."

Nathan wandered into the living room, glancing around at the spacious apartment. The walls were a bright garnet, decorated with portraits of nudes much like the one he'd noticed in the vestibule. The model was always the same, the naughty, narcissistic Cassie Aimwell. What he smelled was certainly not varnish, but there was no point pursuing the matter. Ralphie was old enough to know the price of exotic indulgence.

In the bedroom, meanwhile, Ralphie found one shoe and a pair of socks under the bed. The rest of his clothing—a wrinkled shirt, silk tie, and striped blazer—was in a pile on top of a chair. As he dressed hastily, leaving his tie undone, he looked around for Cassie. He wanted to warn her that Nathan was in the apartment so she wouldn't come skipping out as naked as a sprite.

"Cassie," he said *sotto voce*, "you anywhere around here?"

He looked into the overflowing closets, thinking she might have fallen asleep in one of them, then he checked the adjacent rooms, but there was no sign of Cassie. If he could remember what had gone on last night, he was certain he'd find her. As it was, he could only search on—under the bed, in a dark corner beside the dresser, behind a screen in front of the dresser. When he saw his messy image in the dresser's mirror he gasped so loudly that Nathan called to him from the next room.

On the floor behind the dresser, he spied the green dress Cassie had discarded a few hours earlier in favor of bare flesh and avocado pulp. The dress in hand, he stepped out of the bedroom and told Nathan he was worried. "She just disappeared. Poof! Like that."

Nathan took the green dress and studied it. He'd seen a few versions of the Green Lorelei costume in the past few days, but the glyphs on Cassie's were the most accurate he'd come across so far. But then, a woman like Cassie Aimwell could afford the latest, the best, and the most bizarre.

"She probably went out for a walk, Beef," Nathan said. "She'll come home when the party's over. Let's go."

Nathan tossed the dress on a sofa and Ralphie followed him out, but not before taking one last long look back. Outside, they entered a closed carriage that Nathan had hired, fearing the storm would make the roads too hazardous for his buggy.

It was close to dawn and raining heavily when they rode onto the Villanova campus. Although he was greatly distressed by the news of Father Gorman's death, Nathan had obliged Ralphie and helped him concoct an alibi.

"Do you think Dad will believe it?" Ralphie asked Nathan, who shook his head.

"I doubt it," Nathan said, "unless he's been sniffing ether too." Even though he had helped Ralphie think up the lie, it was one of the dumbest Nathan had ever heard.

"Well," Ralphie said, "it's the best I can do."

As they approached the college chapel, an ambulance drove by on its way to the morgue with Father Gorman's remains. They fell silent as it passed.

Blakeley and Father Capone were coming down the chapel steps on their way to the monastery when Nathan and Ralphie arrived. Both welcomed the shelter of the horse-drawn carriage.

"Father Capone has something important to show us," Blakeley said squeezing his ample girth into the small cab. Spotting Ralphie, he said, "Where the devil were you?"

Ralphie glanced at Nathan and answered lamely, "Fishing, Dad. I wanted to get an early start."

Blakeley glanced at Ralphie's clothing and frowned at having his intelligence insulted.

Seeing his father's response, Ralphie quickly added, "I left my boots and all down by the river and came running as soon as Nathan got me. Right, Nathan?"

Nathan was content to concentrate on the driver's maneuvering of the horse and carriage into a sheltered space near the entrance to the monastery. There they would be able to exit the cab and enter the building without getting too wet, which would have been inevitable out in the open since the predawn shower was picking up strength. Thunder rolled in the near distance, as if to signal the brunt of the storm was high.

Inside the monastery, Father Capone asked a young seminarian to bring them coffee, then led the others down a marble corridor to a corner office. "Please make yourselves comfortable, gentlemen," the provincial said, turning up a lamp and taking something out of his desk.

The seminarian appeared with the coffee as Father Capone placed a large book on his desk, loosened the leather strap, and opened it to a marked page.

The coffee buoyed Ralphie's spirits and warded off his ether hangover. He wanted very much to concentrate on the matter at hand like all the others, but he couldn't get Cassie out of his thoughts. He wondered where the hell she had gone. Had he done something so bad it had made her run off? Maybe she'd gone for help, thinking he was dead. Ether could do that, he'd heard. Or . . . no, that was just too ridiculous to think about. But what if he just hadn't been, up to it?

"Jeez," he thought, "could I have been that big a flop?" Of course not. Then again, for all that he could recall of the night before, he'd probably never know. He couldn't remember what happened after they'd gone to bed. He thought he could recall, vaguely at best, Cassie giggling hysterically and trying to rub an ether rag over his nose as he complained that he'd rather wait until their next tryst, knowing he'd never intended for there to be another. From that time on, he was going to come down with influenza or something whenever Cassie extended an invitation. But where the hell could she have gone? And why?

He gulped down the cup of coffee, hot as it was, and asked the seminarian for a second cup. Then he did his best to banish Cassie from his mind.

"Father Gorman had been translating something in this book," Father Capone said. "It's a manuscript that was written by a Spanish monk named Lorenzo Del Vaille late in the last century. Father Gorman told me it's considered questionable by pre-Columbian scholars, because the monk was obviously prejudiced against the Mayan religion, and because the monk went mad and spent his last years locked up in an asylum. Legend has it that he was under a spell of some kind."

"Father Gorman told us about the legend the last time we saw him," Blakeley said.

"The truth, according to Father Gorman," Father Capone said, "was that the poor fellow had been tortured by some Indians who resented his sticking his nose into their secrets. Ah, here we are now. The glyphs."

He turned the book around to show the others what looked at first like elaborate letters from an embossed medieval manuscript. But on closer scrutiny, they resembled the designs on the dress worn by the Green Lorelei.

"Now, that's curious," Blakeley said.

"Yes," Father Capone agreed and pulled out a small stack of papers that Father Gorman had been writing on before his death. "Father Gorman was very bored, as you can imagine. So he translated these pages to continue his studies. I don't know if he told you that the glyphs are called death's eyes. They are tiny red bells that jingle on the headdress of the Mayan god of death."

Blakeley and Nathan scanned the page of the manuscript and quickly perused Father Gorman's translation. But Ralphie was fascinated by the glyphs alone.

"How did Father Gorman feel about the author?" Nathan asked.

"He thought he was a fairly good source," the provincial said. "And as you know, Father Gorman was very knowledgeable in pre-Columbian studies. He told me Del Vaille was a specialist in Mayan writing. And since he had access to an account by another churchman who died a century earlier, he had the proper sources to investigate the Mayan myths. Padre Lorenzo was evidently onto something when the poor fellow lost his wits."

"And perhaps," Blakeley said, "Father Gorman was onto something just as strange before he lost his life."

Ralphie craned to get a better look at the glyphs. He spied a strange little figure standing upright with an ax in its hand. Over its head was a prominent closed eye. Ralphie pointed to the tiny bells on the figure's head, neck, wrists, and ankles. "Are these what the chambermaid described on the dress?"

"Yes," Nathan said. "They're death's eyes, as Father Capone said. The figure must be the god of death and, let's see, the eye overhead is that of a dead person. If they were in color, they'd be bright red." Nathan looked up at Ralphie and noticed his big grin. "What is there to smile about?"

"Listen," Ralphie said, leaning closer to Nathan's ear. "Those designs don't match Cassie's dress after all."

"Good," Nathan said, "I'm happy to hear that."

Some time later, the rain had let up, and the sun was starting to show through the dispersing clouds. Despite the frenzy of the storm, the heat wave had not broken; rather, it seemed to have become more oppressive than ever.

But not even the continued heat could alleviate Ralphie's happiness and relief over putting to rest his fears concerning Cassie. He could not stop smiling as he drove his father's cabriolet back to their estate, even though Blakeley and Nathan talked of nothing but death.

"I don't get it," Nathan said, echoing Ralphie's earlier comment. "If Beecham is committing the Green Lorelei murders, why would he kill Father Gorman?"

"I've been wondering that myself," Blakeley said. "And only one logical answer comes to mind: Beecham has nothing to do with the Green Lorelei. And if that's true, I dread to think how many more people will die before we stop both of these fiends."

"Maybe my theory isn't wrong, huh, Dad?" Ralphie asked. "Maybe the Green Lorelei is a werewolf."

Ralphie's suggestion reminded Nathan of the passage Allison had translated for him, and he shuddered at the possibility of having to destroy a supernatural being. But from Blakeley's frown, Nathan could tell his friend did not entertain any such idea. To save Ralphie from a torrent of parental abuse, Nathan waved a sheaf of papers Father Capone had given him. Father Gorman had been translating the prayers of the Mayans before his death; he had assiduously amassed a wealth of notes while working to understand the significance of the ancient people's religious beliefs.

"Do you think we might find any clues in Father Gorman's notes?" Nathan asked.

"Who can say, Nathan?" Blakeley answered.

Not finding much encouragement from his friend, Nathan would have given up his idea if the first sentence had not caught his attention. "Listen to this, Dr. Blakeley: 'On the fifth day, the merchant god *Ek-Chuah*, who appears as a serpent, reigns. And on the sixth day, called *Cimi*, it is believed that the god of death reigns.'"

"There's the sixth again."

"Right. Yesterday was the twenty-fourth—six days since the murder of Jack Hawthorne."

"That could be little more than a coincidence," Blakeley said, peering at the notes.

But Nathan would not give up hope so easily. On another piece of paper, he found a second Mayan prayer with the English translation immediately beneath it. It was evident that Father Gorman had had a difficult time with the prayer, because many words were crossed out.

"'Thrice be greeted when falls the word to the great *Chac*,'" Nathan read. "That's the Mayan rain god; he was supposed to be very powerful. I remember Father Gorman mentioning him in conversation. He said Christians could get along with *Chac*, but not with *Balam*, the fierce jaguar god. After invoking *Balam*, the worshipper would fill in the names of specific fears, desires, enemies, and so on."

"It's all very vague," Blakeley said.

"How does it sound in Mayan?" Ralphie said.

"Really now, Ralphie," his father said.

"Jeez crumps, Dad."

When Blakeley shrugged his shoulders in resignation, Nathan read the Mayan prayer aloud: "'*Ox tezcuntebac cu lubul than tu necte Chac, tu necte Balam tu can titzcaan, cu vantal in kubic nahi.*' Satisfied, Beef?"

To Nathan and Blakeley's amusement, Ralphie shook his head and frowned. "I've heard that somewhere before."

They spent the entire ride back to Blakeley's estate thus engaged, and Blakeley did not know what impressed him more: Nathan's reading and knowledge of the Mayan culture or Ralphie's uncharacteristic attentiveness. Nevertheless, the detective was not sure how the information would be of much use in his investigation.

"Here's another part of the prayer," Nathan said as the carriage started up the drive before Blakeley's house. "'*Yax, santo maben, cu yuntal in kati oltic zahuv cabob chan-ekal macal maubaal.*' Somehow I think the Mayans said it better."

"Yeah," Ralphie said, straining to place the words in his memory, "but it all sounds so familiar."

"Here's the translation," Nathan said, "'Herewith I offer before thy table bread, meat, and holy wine, and beg you to release the wild *chan-ekal* that he might slay my despised enemy.'"

"What's a *chan-ekal*?" Ralphie asked.

When Nathan paused uneasily, Blakeley said, "Yes, what is it?"

Since his night with Allison, Nathan had done some research on the creature. So he knew more than enough information to satisfy his friends' curiosity.

"The *chan-ekal* was believed to be a spotted animal about the size of a tiger. Apparently, Mayan priests could conjure the *chan-ekal* to kill their enemies. What's really interesting is that before they turned into the beast, the priests would turn into beautiful women. This ruse helped to trick their enemies into letting themselves become vulnerable. And when no one could save their victims, the priests became the jungle beasts."

Ralphie took in every word with growing interest, but Blakeley was less impressed by the myth. "I must say, Nathan, I can't see why a religious man like Father Gorman would have been so interested in such fantasies."

"He thought it helped him understand the people he served better."

"Say, Nathan," Ralphie said, unable to control his excitement. "What would you call a *chan-ekal* in English?"

Nathan paused again before saying, "A werejaguar."

"Ah, hah!" Ralphie said triumphantly.

Although ready to meet Ralphie's enthusiasm with his usual skepticism, Blakeley stopped short when he noticed an excited gathering ahead of him, just outside the door to the scullery. Mrs. Snopkowski and several maids were standing in a circle looking down as Sophia and Allison tended to a figure lying on the ground. Suddenly, two of the Welsh maids fell to their knees and started keening over the body. Alarmed by what they saw ahead of them, the men jumped from the carriage. But before they got very far, Allison rushed over to them.

"What is it, Miss Meredith?" Blakeley asked.

"It's the maid Dumpling. She's been poisoned."

"Oh, no!" Ralphie cried and ran to join the mourners.

Before Allison could explain that Dumpling was dead, Blakeley was kneeling beside the young maid's inert body, trying at first to find her wrist pulse, then to feel her heartbeat, and finally, desperately, to find a pulse at her carotid artery. At last, he shook his head.

As he rose, Sophia, white as death herself, threw her arms around him as far as they would go. "Oh, Ian, how terrible!"

The cook was so excited that no one could decipher the few English words she was sputtering as she tried to tell Blakeley what had happened. She waved her beefy arms and blessed herself again and again. It was a scene reminiscent of a madhouse as Mrs. Snopkowski prayed in Polish and the Welsh maids wailed behind her.

"Dumpling ate some poisoned candies," Allison said, showing Blakeley the box she'd picked up before anyone else could touch it.

"Thank heavens Rosie is off at her friend's," Sophia sobbed. "I dread to think how fearfully seeing all this would have affected her. The kitchen staff were making breakfast. I came down for a cup of tea because that horrible business at the college had me quite awake since you rushed out. Someone must have come by with the chocolates when poor Dumpling was outside hoping to avoid Mrs. Snopkowski. She took them and went off to that spot behind the bush for some privacy. No one knew anything was wrong until we heard the poor girl wailing."

"Who found her?" Blakeley asked.

Because Sophia was too distraught to continue speaking, Allison said, "One of the maids looked out the window and saw Dumpling out here acting strangely. Her eyes were rolling around and she was frothing at the mouth. She yelled something about a tingling in her lips, and suddenly she was writhing on the ground in convulsions. By the time Mrs. Blakeley and I got to her, she was dead."

As Allison finished the details of Dumpling's

death, Mrs. Snopkowski uttered a high-pitched mournful cry, which was echoed by the maids' banshee chorus.

Certain that any efforts to resuscitate the young maid would be in vain, Blakeley covered the corpse with his suit jacket and turned his attention to the living. He ushered Mrs. Snopkowski and the other domestics to the kitchen, where he ordered them to partake of suitable refreshments to soothe their frenzied bereavement. With a stern glance, he silenced Sophia's incipient reproaches—for who else but Christopher Beecham could have sent poisoned candies—and he asked Allison to escort his wife to her room for some rest. He sent Ralphie off to inform Don Orlando of the tragedy. And he set Nathan the task of investigating the area for any clues to confirm the homicidal deliveryman's identity. Finally, Blakeley called Lt. Hudson, reported the crime, and arranged to perform an autopsy at the city morgue.

It was only when a semblance of order was at last restored to the household that Blakeley realized he had been trembling for quite some time—an all-too-natural reaction to another brush with death. Not yet ready to face his wife, he sought the refuge of his study; there he would await the arrival of the ambulance Hudson was to send for Dumpling.

Not five minutes elapsed, however, before the ringing of the telephone disturbed his rest. It continued ringing for several minutes, and Blakeley shouted for someone to answer it before he realized his mistake. Victor, who considered himself the sole protector of the bothersome machine, was at present engaged in a limited run in the Eleventh Precinct's lockup. And considering the general agitation in the house, the phone might well ring far into the night before any of the servants would think to answer it.

Sighing wearily, Blakeley rushed down the hallway and, grasping the receiver with a grip meant to strangle, said, "Hello."

When no one answered, Blakeley forgot his solemn vow to refrain from profanity. "Christ blast it, hello!"

The only response he heard was a rush of air, as if someone had let out a deep, disappointed breath. The caller broke out with a string of angry, muttered vocables, then hung up.

As Blakeley stood by the telephone deep in thought, Nathan returned to confirm the obvious: the footprints he had found suggested a man approximately six feet tall who favored his left foot as he walked.

"Beecham, Dr. Blakeley," Nathan said and eyed his friend curiously. "Is something the matter?"

"He just called here, Nathan. And the bastard was quite upset to hear my living voice."

Before Nathan could say anything, Blakeley pounded his fist against the wall. "We have to stop him now, Nathan. I don't care if he's the Green Lorelei or not. We have to stop Beecham before he kills again."

Chapter Twenty-One

June 25, 1898, was a day that Nathan McBride would not soon forget. Judging from the brutal murder of Father Gorman and the poisoning of Dumpling, inexplicable dark forces seemed to be gathering strength to deliver a horrific coup de grace against all those he held dear. If Nathan had known about the violence to befall him and the others in the days to come, he might well have advised all to stay abed until the evil season had passed. Lacking such foreknowledge, however, he braved the unknown, relying on his professional skills and instincts to prevent more tragedy.

And so, not two hours after Blakeley's unnerving call from Beecham, he stood next to his mentor yet again in the city morgue. Both men were strained and distracted. For the corpse that lay before them was Dumpling. Hoping to ease the tension that filled the dim room, Nathan disagreed with Blakeley's assumption the cause of death was ingestion of aconitine.

He pointed a finger at Dumpling's gaping mouth, her blackened teeth more prominent than ever against her bloodless face. "What else besides sugar of lead discolors teeth so severely?"

"Nathan, please. Poor Dumpling's teeth were not good in the best of times. She had far too much candy in her diet."

"I'll say."

Cringing slightly at Nathan's irony, Blakeley held a beaker up to the light. He had taken a sample of Dumpling's vomit, to which he added some phosphoric acid and sodium molybdate. He poured the mixture into a vial and lit the Bunsen burner.

"I was with Scotland Yard," he said as the substance in the vial turned yellow, "when the Taylor woman poisoned poor Mr. Tregillis. It was the blackened teeth which put us on to her. I was at Maidstone the morning they hanged her. I shall never forget her cursing me from the gallows.

"On the other hand, Nathan," Blakeley continued while the liquid became brown, "I was also with the Yard when that Lemson fellow murdered his mother-in-law for the insurance. Terrible thing, that morphine. Lemson's addiction had him so heavily in debt that he was driven to poisoning one of the few friends he had on this earth.

"Lemson himself was a physician quite familiar with the pharmacopoeia. Since one milligram of aconitine is a fatal dose, he was able to carry out his scheme by poisoning a raisin in a Dundee cake." As Blakeley spoke, the color of the liquid started to change again. "Ah, here we are, Nathan, the color is now violet. What does that tell you?"

"Aconitine," Nathan said. He'd had no doubt that Blakeley was right all along, but his scheme had succeeded.

"Known variously as monkshood, friar's cowl, and mouse bane. And poor Dumpling ingested enough of it to kill the proverbial elephant."

Blakeley covered Dumpling's face and put away his instruments. A man from Harry Hackett's funeral parlor would soon take the body away for preparation. Blakeley had promised Sophia they would bury the girl somewhere on their estate, probably near Richard Petticord's grave.

"That poison is also known as wolf's bane, isn't it, Dr. Blakeley? It's supposed to ward off werewolves, right?"

"According to superstition, yes. But please don't tell me you've fallen pray to Ralphie's obsession."

Nathan didn't wish to discuss the strange thoughts that he had been harboring since Allison had translated the fragment Father Gorman gave him. He had almost convinced himself that the idea of a monster stalking Philadelphia was too ridiculous to be true. But coming across another reference to the *chan-ekal* had set him to considering the implausible again. Because of Blakeley's contempt for Ralphie's werewolf theory, however, Nathan chose not to raise the subject until he had firmer proof to substantiate the strange turn his thoughts had taken. For the time being, it was better to focus on the feasible.

They stepped out of the examining room, removing their aprons, and walked down the hallway. When they were outside, Blakeley took a piece of paper from his vest and handed it to Nathan. "I'd like you to take this list of names to the telephone company to see if you can find a match among their subscribers. I think that devil Beecham would be too vain to use a public telephone. So he must have had one installed wherever he's hiding."

Nathan scanned the paper. The names were all characters out of Greek mythology. From Aegysthus to Thyestes, they were names that Christopher Beecham would think suitable for an alias.

"What do you think of my idea, Nathan?"

"I'll let you know after I've checked into it," Nathan said, certain that it was the most logical way to track Beecham.

But Nathan soon discovered that even Blakeley's good ideas could try his patience to no end. The phone company's main offices were in a cramped, unventilated building a few blocks from Independence Hall. Arriving there already hot and irritable on that stifling day, Nathan was not in the mood for any arguments. No sooner had he stepped into the sweltering office, however, then he knew he was in for a long, hard search.

A double-bladed fan creaked feebly overhead, pushing thick, humid air into Nathan's face. The harsh blast was accompanied by the noisome stench of body odor. After his first whiff of the prevailing aroma, Nathan was glad he'd neglected to eat all day long. And the sight of flies battling over someone's lunch leftovers confirmed his feeling.

Several women sat writing assiduously into ledgers, their dresses soaked through. Their desks were piled high with papers, and the only break they took from writing was to move a paper or two across their desks. Shelves lined the walls, all bursting forth with files and papers. Indeed, the room was so filled with paper Nathan believed that the smallest spark would start a blaze that would cause more damage than the Chicago fire.

Glowering over the workers like an overseer, a burly man crept about, seemingly avoiding the few light rays that found their way into the office. He hunched over each woman and made sure none of them paused in her work even to wave away a fly. When he spied Nathan, he barreled toward him with a posture designed to threaten. But Nathan produced his badge—which, due to some slight oversight on Lt. Hudson's part, he still possessed— and the man kept his distance, making Nathan wonder briefly what he might be guilty of.

After a few tedious moments of poring over the company's records, Nathan was ready to run the office manager in for sheer contempt, and he still had several more hours of work ahead of him. The manager had informed him that over 1100 telephones were in service throughout the city, and Nathan had to check out every subscriber's name.

For all its monotony, the work did provide some solid leads and even stirred some memories that made Nathan laugh aloud. For although Beecham might be disguising himself behind a name like Electra Hammerschmidt or Hector Gonzaga, Nathan knew that the Reverend Mr. Menelaus Blore would cause no problems from his cell in Graterford, where he was serving a six-year sentence for fraud and attempted pandering.

And the listing for Cassandra Teagarden elicited such loud snorts of laughter from Nathan that a few of the working women joined him in his mirth. Even the manager's reproving glare could not check Nathan's hilarity. Miss Teagarden was the first woman he had ever arrested. Several years earlier, when he was new to the police force, Nathan had ventured into her Lonely Heart's Club on Fifty-fourth Street, posing as a recent immigrant who wished to meet someone of the opposite gender. Promising him the girl of his dreams, Cassandra Teagarden ushered him into a dirty back room and what he saw there prompted him to arrest her and all her girls. Those arrests earned him his first commendation.

As Nathan reached the end of the rolls, with a list of people that would take him days to investigate, the office manager burst into loud condemnation of a young clerk. Her blond hair straggly in the heat, the woman cowered beneath her boss's railing. When he waved a final, threatening finger, followed by a stream of unseemly oaths, and retired to his office, the clerk looked both cowed and rebellious, as if undecided whether to weep or to hurl a large rock at the man's back.

"Anything the matter, miss?" Nathan asked, mopping his sweaty forehead with a handkerchief. He knew the question was innocuous, but he also knew the girl had curly blond hair, big brown eyes and a cute little dimple on her chin.

"No," she replied shrilly. "These are tears of joy. I always sing and dance when I'm told to look for another job."

"Can I help?"

The girl sniffled. "Yeah, you could do me a favor and break somebody's arm, maybe." Then she broke down and wept.

Thinking she meant the manager, and knowing that breaking his arms was out of the question, Nathan returned to the subscribers' list. But the girl's continued whimpering made it hard for him to concentrate on the list. So he walked over to her desk.

"Besides breaking somebody's arm, is there anything I can do?" Nathan asked, offering her a piece of chewing gum.

Half crying and half laughing, she said, "You could lend me ten bucks."

"Maybe you should go back to your original suggestion."

"Maybe you should go back to work."

"I'd rather talk to you," he said. "My eyes are getting tired from reading the dull print. Do you think the telephone company could afford new typewriters one of these days?"

She chewed the gum and flashed a weak but

pretty smile. "The machines are okay. It's the ribbons. They're old."

"At fifty bucks a telephone, they can afford new ribbons."

"You sound like a smoothie," she said, looking him in the eye. "Listen, one more smoothie I don't need in my life these days."

"So, what's a nice girl like you need ten bucks for?"

She sobbed again and blew her nose gently. Then, after a dispirited sigh, she shook her fist angrily. "I cannot believe that at the age of twenty-one I still have to learn a lesson like this. Last week a guy comes in looking somewhere between a boy soprano and a guy on an army recruiting poster, if you can imagine. And not only that but he walks with a limp, as if his foot was hurt. So immediately my sisterly instincts are aroused. He limps over to my desk and asks—"

"Excuse me," Nathan said, his suspicion aroused. "He had a limp?"

"Yeah," she'd said. "A limp. So anyways, he wanted a telephone, but he didn't have the ten-dollar deposit, so I—"

"How old was he?"

"Early twenties maybe. So I ask him if he can put at least five dollars down, because sometimes the boss lets people do that if he figures they're good for the rest of it by the end of the week. Only the boss wasn't here. It was a Tuesday afternoon, and that's when his wife always plays bridge at her club. So he always goes home for some hanky-panky with the lady next door. And believe me, if I get fired his wife's gonna get a letter in the mail that will curl her hair fast. Anyways, I ask Mister butter-wouldn't-melt-in-his-mouth if he can put down even a one and he says, 'No, sorry, I'll have to come back later.' So, what's a girl to do? I took a chance.

I told him to be back no later than forty-eight hours from then with the money, and I put the order through. I could die."

She concluded her speech by blowing her nose again.

"What's his name?" Nathan had asked.

"Are you gonna break his arms?"

"If he's the man I'm looking for, I'd be glad to do worse. Is he on the list?"

"Yeah. Bring me that list and I'll show you." With the rolls before her, she ran her finger down the list of subscribers until she came to a name that had been written into a margin between "Overton, Samuel" and "Peterson, Harry." The handwriting was good but so small that Nathan saw at once how he had missed it.

"I wrote it in myself," she said. "The lists get retyped at the end of each month. It's probably not even his real name, the—pardon me. A lady shouldn't even think of a word like that."

"I have one more question, miss," Nathan said. "And if you give me the right answer, I can guarantee you'll get your ten dollars in a hurry."

"You sure?" she'd asked, wiping away another tear.

"Yes," Nathan said because he knew Blakeley would pay ten times that amount for a solid lead.

"So, what do I have to lose?" she said.

Gripping the corner of her desk, Nathan asked, "Was he missing a finger?"

Chapter Twenty-Two

Alexander Paris—Blakeley was right again.

Paris: the spoiled youth who stole Helen from her husband and carried her off to Troy, bringing on a disastrous war that meant little more to him than the woman. The Greeks knew him as Paris, but his own people called him Alexander. Blakeley was so pleased with Nathan's information he had donated the ten dollars needed to save the clerk at the telephone company from unemployment.

Blakeley's joy at finally having a solid lead on Beecham's whereabouts was tempered by the sudden appearance of G. Lindsey Pratt, Philadelphia's newest celebrity. Tipped by a paid informant at the morgue, Pratt arrived at the Blakeley residence sometime after the detective had returned from performing Dumpling's autopsy. He sat with Blakeley and his wife in their parlor, pretending to want to make peace and to offer Sophia last-minute help with the ball. But when Sophia rebuffed him for his less-than-gentlemanly behavior concerning Nathan, he dropped his facade and angrily demanded an exclusive interview. If the Blakeleys refused him, he threatened, he could easily publish a front-page article that blamed the police, and Nathan in particular, for the maid's death. He laughingly assured the Blakeleys that such a story would end their friend's career forever.

It was onto this scene that Nathan burst, enthusiastically shouting his news about Beecham. Although hungry and overheated, he had gone straight to Blakeley after hearing the clerk's tale of woe. Too excited to stop himself, Nathan blurted out most of the important details to his friend, who had risen to warn him to hold his tongue. Only when he realized that Blakeley did not appear elated with the information did Nathan spot Pratt. Then his smile faded and his teeth started to clench. Despite his better judgment, his hands tightened into fists.

"Hello, McBride," Pratt said, grinning wickedly. "I'll bet you're glad to see me."

Considering Pratt's threat to Nathan, and his knowledge of the clerk's story, Blakeley had no choice but to include the reporter in his plans to trap Beecham. He feared if he did otherwise, Pratt might attempt some bungling scheme on his own in order to secure his fame; in doing so, the reporter would ruin what might be Blakeley's last chance at ending Beecham's murderous spree. So, with Ralphie, Nathan, and Pratt to assist him, Blakeley went after his enemy. Despite his wife's nervous entreaties to let the police pursue the madman, Blakeley firmly insisted that he would never be free of the man unless he himself was the one to stop Beecham's attempt for revenge against all those he hated.

The West Philadelphia address Beecham had

given the clerk was, as Blakeley expected, not where he lived; it was only the place where he wanted the telephone installed. The men found that out quickly when they broke into an empty office in a building on the corner of Lancaster and Thornhill. Blakeley was not upset by this setback; he strongly suspected that Beecham was close at hand.

A quick sweep of the neighborhood showed that someone who wished to could easily be anonymous there. The neighborhood was agreeable enough, with yellow-brick streets, shade trees, and gas lamps lining the sidewalks. Largely residential, the area had several parks where children could play safely; and it was close to the shops on Lancaster Avenue, yet removed from the hucksters and street noise.

Thornhill was crammed with identical brownstones, all of which had six stories and whitewashed steps. Black wrought-iron fences protected steps that led to the basements beneath each brownstone. Greenish gutters jutting from the common roof were decorated with gargoyles and fleurs-de-lis at even intervals across the horizon.

It was late afternoon and the sky had turned leaden yet again when a sassy little know-it-all named Libby had, for a quarter, identified an apartment in her building as the place where a weird guy with a finger missing was living. Her building defied the military uniformity of the rest of the street by sporting two large flowerpots on each side of the main entrance. According to Libby, Beecham's rooms were on the fourth floor.

Immediately, Blakeley mapped out their strategy. Ralphie would crash through the door to surprise Beecham, Blakeley would follow with his revolver ready, and Pratt, as long as he had to be there, would stay below to cover the stairway. Nathan, meanwhile, would cover the roof, in case Beecham should try to escape by that route.

To all concerned, the plan made sense—until the storm came. As raindrops started to stipple the ground, Libby and her playmates scattered, and three young mothers holding infants ran for cover. A loud roar in the east startled several horses leading carriages down the street.

"Well, gentlemen, it's as good a time as any," Blakeley said, glancing at Nathan apologetically.

"Give me five minutes to climb the fire escape," Nathan said.

"Of course. Sorry about the weather, old boy."

"I won't melt," Nathan said, his lack of enthusiasm heightened by another explosion in the sky that signaled the beginning of a downpour.

After Nathan left them, the others ran up the steps into the vestibule of the brownstone. There they waited as Blakeley counted the minutes. Residents passed, eyeing them with mild curiosity when they noticed Pratt jotting notes in a pad. But since the residents were more interested in getting into dry clothing, their scrutiny was short lived.

At last, Blakeley closed his pocket watch and nodded to his son. Before he followed Ralphie, Blakeley warned Pratt not to leave his post, but the reporter merely snorted. As he climbed the stairs, Blakeley could smell liver and onions cooking. Ralphie gestured toward his stomach and silently reminded his father that dinnertime was drawing near. But since Blakeley hadn't taken a meal at all that day, and prospects of eating were not at that moment great, he had little sympathy for his son's hunger.

On his way to the fourth floor, Blakeley felt more like an intruder than a protector. For the building was clean and quiet with its polished railing and rose-pink wallpaper. It was not the sort of place where people customarily crashed through doors and wrestled villains to the ground. But Blakeley could not help being part of the fight he anticipated. So he pushed those thoughts aside as he and his son cautiously approached Beecham's apartment.

In front of the door, Ralphie tapped his father on the shoulder and whispered, "I didn't want to ask in front of Pratt, but do you want me to pick the lock? It wouldn't be as messy as breaking down the door."

"No, Ralph. Beecham might hear you. I don't want to give him any warning."

Ralphie nodded and paced his steps to the landing. Finding enough room to build up a good head of steam, he prepared to ram the door. But before he did, he muttered under his breath, "I sure hope that kid wasn't a practical joker."

"Eh? What do you mean?"

"You know, what if this isn't really Beecham's place? What if the brat took your two bits and sent us to some retired schoolteacher's apartment?"

"Good Lord, Ralph."

"Stranger things have happened, Dad."

The building was suddenly still, and the noise of the storm raging outside grew clear. In the silent corridor, Blakeley thought about Ralphie's suggestion, then shook his head and gestured toward the door. They would just have to take a chance and assume the little girl had told them the truth.

After his father's signal, Ralphie aimed his shoulder at the door and flew into it with the same abandon that had made Princeton's flying wedge so fearsome in his one semester there. The door splintered on its hinges and landed flat on the floor with a slam that rivaled the thunderclaps outside. They dove in, spreading out, crouching, surveying all corners of the front room.

"Give it up, Beecham!" Blakeley demanded. "We have you now!"

The only answer Blakeley got, however, was the

pelting of the rain and the ticking of a clock.

"Doesn't look like anybody's here, Dad."

"Perhaps, Ralphie. Perhaps."

Gradually, they relaxed and stood upright. Blakeley sheathed his revolver and wondered if indeed they had made a mistake, or if they'd been hoodwinked by the little girl, as Ralphie had suggested.

"This could be an old schoolmarm's flat," he agreed, as he searched the uncluttered apartment.

"Hello, what's this?" he said, picking up a volume titled *The Collected Works of Eurypides*. Next to it lay a thin volume of Sapphic odes. On a table beside an easy chair, he found Shelley's translation of *The Cyclops*. "It's Beecham's flat, Ralph," he said. "I've no doubt of it."

"He lives pretty well for a guy on the run," Ralphie said, picking up a jar filled with dried flowers. "He even smokes opium."

Blakeley opened the jar and felt the leaves. He smiled when he realized what they'd found. "It's not opium, Ralph," he said. "It's called aconitine. We'll hold this jar as evidence in Dumpling's death."

"If that's the case, we'd better be careful," Ralphie said, recalling Hermie Hinsky's fate. "There might be dynamite here too."

Another loud thunderclap made them flinch.

"We better let Nathan know it's time to come in," Blakeley said. "We'll just have to wait for Beecham to come home."

As Ralphie left, Blakeley started checking into nooks and crannies. The next room, separated from the first by a wooden archway, was a small dining room with a table, four chairs, and a china closet. The furniture probably came with the apartment, he presumed, but the china and silverware and expensive-looking wine glasses were probably stolen. There was a canopied bed in the next room, which he looked under, and a rolltop desk, which he opened just in case Beecham had been able to squeeze into it.

The kitchen was in the back of the apartment, facing a narrow alley that separated Thornhill from Landsdowne Street. Through the window, Blakeley could see into an identical kitchen, where a housewife was taking some bread out of her oven. Beecham's stove had not been used in some time, but cheese and wine were chilling in the icebox. There was no sign of Beecham in the kitchen either.

Passing through the dining room on his way back to the front room, Blakeley stopped in his tracks and felt for his revolver when a grandfather clock chimed five o'clock.

Letting out a sigh of relief, Blakeley chided himself for acting so foolishly. Then he noticed something very unusual in such an orderly place.

"Would someone like Christopher Beecham leave his grandfather clock with only two of three weights pulled up?" he wondered.

He stepped over to the clock and considered the situation. Sometimes the summer humidity caused the weights to stick. So it was possible that only one of them descended normally. But a clock with a problem like that wouldn't keep very good time. And that one was perfectly in sync with Blakeley's pocket watch.

He started to draw his pistol, certain that Beecham was in the room. He could feel him there. The devil must have been rewinding the clock when he and Ralphie had entered the apartment.

"Beecham," he shouted. "We have you surrounded."

Suddenly, the beautiful clock crashed into Blakeley with a hellish clang and shards of glass flew everywhere. Trapped on the floor by a crushing weight on his chest, he felt something digging into

347

his leg. Blood ran from a cut on his forehead, blinding him in one eye. He tried to squeeze the trigger of his gun, but his wrist was pinned to the floor, and the revolver dangled uselessly from his fingers, which were quickly turning numb. He heard heavy footsteps and saw Ralphie dash into the room and stop suddenly.

"Beecham—don't do it!" Ralphie shouted.

Blakeley felt the revolver being pried out of his hand. As a shot rang out, Ralphie dived for cover.

"You know when it's time," Blakeley thought. That was what he'd heard somewhere long ago. But it wasn't his time to die. "Too soon. Too damn soon...."

Then Beecham was standing over him with a look that he'd never seen in human eyes—a feral, lupine stare. The madman was atop the grandfather clock that had Blakeley pinned to the floor. Blakeley was still blinded in one eye, but through the other, he saw Beecham aiming the revolver at his head. He tried to move, but nothing seemed to give. He tried again and Beecham slipped a little.

Catching himself, Beecham squeezed the trigger and Blakeley saw a flash of light. He heard only a small part of the terrible blast that accompanied it. The blast was followed by the noise of something hitting bone.

"Get back!" Ralphie yelled at Pratt, whom Blakeley spied peering into the room.

"Great Scott." Pratt said. "Look at your father on the floor."

"I can see him, Pratt," Ralphie said. "Just keep your head down."

As Pratt ducked behind the doorframe, Beecham turned toward him groggily, rubbing his cheek, prepared to fire at anything that moved.

From his hiding place, Ralphie watched Beecham blinking his eyes and prayed that the large volume of Eurypides that he'd hurled at the madman's head had landed before Beecham could fire directly into his father's face. He also prayed that Beecham didn't realize he was unarmed.

"What's he doing now?" Pratt said from the hall.

"I'll let you know as soon as he shoots me," Ralphie said.

"Please do."

Beecham fired at Ralphie, who ducked behind the archway, and quickly realized it wasn't shelter enough. A second bullet shattered the wood, and Ralphie dived into a small niche between the wall and the china closet. Another shot hit the glass, and the pieces of china along the top shelf fell out one by one. Beecham tried to fire once more, but nothing happened.

"Hey, Pratt, he's out of ammunition," Ralphie said, when he heard the impotent clicking of the revolver. "Let's get him!"

"You get him," Pratt said from the hall. "I'm busy writing this down."

Ralphie glanced at Pratt and made a mental note to replace Pratt's black eye as soon as the one Nathan gave him faded away. Then he charged at Beecham. He had wanted to attack in that manner when he was in the army, but he had been sent home before he had the chance. And Beecham did just what Ralphie had expected the Spaniards to do: he met Ralphie with everything at his disposal. He stunned Ralphie by striking him with the empty gun, and Ralphie sank to his knees. He aimed a kick at Ralphie's head, but his injured ankle kept him off balance. Ralphie got up and was back into the fight quickly, shaking off the blow like an undaunted prizefighter. He tackled Beecham, slamming him into the wall.

"Now you're really gonna get it," Ralphie promised, swinging wildly as Beecham got to his feet.

The punch missed Beecham and hit the wall, causing a picture to fall to the floor. Beecham picked up a small but sturdy table and swung it right into Ralphie's solar plexus. Ralphie groaned and doubled up.

Free of Beecham's weight, Blakeley slowly shoved the grandfather clock aside and saw Ralphie on his knees with Beecham hovering over him in the doorway. Blakeley tried to get up. Then dizziness came on, and he was once again on his back, the blood from his wound blinding him completely.

"Ralph," he warned as his son tried to catch his breath, "don't underestimate him."

Attracted by the sounds of the struggle in Beecham's apartment, a crowd had gathered on the stairway. The curious spectators pulled back in fright when Beecham burst through his door, practically foaming at the mouth. Unbeknownst to the onlookers, however, their presence was equally disconcerting to Beecham. For they blocked his exit to the street. With no other exit open to him, he scrambled up to the roof, his injured ankle forgotten in his frenzy to escape.

The storm was still full-blown when Beecham stepped onto the roof and ran toward the fire escape. If he could make it down to the street, he could get lost in the maze of streets and alleyways thereabouts. Soaked to the skin, Beecham laughed wildly. He was certain that he had at last succeeded in killing the great Dr. Ian Blakeley.

All the time the battle raged inside, Nathan sat on the leeward side of the roof, facing the rear of the building. Though little was visible in the rain, he'd be able to see anyone coming onto the roof. He was glad he couldn't see the street below. For, unknown to any of his friends, he had a terrible fear of heights. He had been loath to object to his part in Blakeley's plan, but his phobia had caused him some trepidation as he had climbed the fire escape.

Ten minutes passed, and just as Nathan was giving up hope of any action, a clap of thunder shook the rooftop and Beecham dashed through the door, taking him by surprise. As Beecham laughed and hurried across the roof, Nathan gave chase. But he slipped to his knees in a puddle and Beecham, aware of him for the first time, descended upon him. Unlike Ralphie, however, Nathan knew how strong Beecham was from past experience. So, rising quickly, he stepped out of the maniac's reach, but not before Beecham landed a glancing right.

Beecham tried to follow the right with a left, but Nathan moved his head just enough to make him miss, and while Beecham was off balance, Nathan landed three neat jabs and a right cross to Beecham's jaw. Boxing was the young policeman's milieu; he had never lost a fight.

But soon he could tell that Beecham also knew a thing or two about fighting. Beecham struck a boxer's pose and started counterpunching. When Nathan moved in, Beecham countered with a flurry of body punches and a good left hook. Beecham stepped back and laughed derisively as Nathan felt his jaw for missing teeth.

Nathan went into a crouch and answered with a flurry of his own, which stunned Beecham and sent him reeling backwards. They fought in that manner across the rooftop for several minutes until Nathan sensed that Beecham was running out of steam. He caught his adversary coming in and landed a solid right to the jaw.

"All right Beecham," he said. "Enough?"

Beecham was on his knees, spitting out blood, struggling to rise. Nathan knelt and handcuffed

Beecham's left wrist to his right, then helped him to his feet.

Out of breath, he swore he'd smoked his last cigarette ever. "Nice fight, Beecham," he acknowledged when they stood up.

Beecham, however, was obviously not interested in compliments. His face, marked with welts and bruises, showed no emotion at all as Nathan looked into it briefly before starting to lead the other man to the rooftop door.

"Let's go, Beecham," Nathan said, wondering what had become of his friends. "I hate rooftops."

Beecham didn't move when Nathan tugged at his handcuffed wrist.

"All right, Beecham," Nathan said. "You can walk or be dragged away unconscious. Take your pick."

Beecham stared at him for a second. Nathan should have known by the suddenly mad look in his eyes what Beecham intended to do, but Nathan's mind was on getting off the roof. Without warning, Beecham let out a strange scream, and a second later, Nathan felt himself taking flight. He realized too late that Beecham had jumped over the side, taking him along.

Nathan had ugly visions of his body being scattered across the street and sidewalk, of being gawked at by some pedestrians, while others turned away to retch. He reached out for anything to stop their flight and saw one of the decorative gargoyles staring him in the eye as he grasped the side of the gutter. He groaned loudly when Beecham's weight tore at the handcuff around his wrist, and seemed to pull his body apart.

Up on the roof, he heard someone calling his name. He believed for a moment the voice was calling him to the next life, it was so far away.

"I'm here," he grunted desperately.

"Where the devil is he, Ralph," Blakeley said. "I can't see with all this blood in my eyes. And I can't hear anything in this rain."

"I can't hear anything either, Dad."

Beecham's screams were maddening. Nathan tried to shout over them. "I'm here! Over here. Look over the side!"

He kicked at Beecham to shut him up, but the effort only caused his grip to loosen. He felt the cuff cutting his wrist as Beecham writhed in the air, trying to take Nathan with him. The gutters were blocked in spots, causing water to overflow into his face. When Nathan tried to call out again, he took in a mouthful of slime. He spat it into the face of the gargoyle that was staring at him.

"Nathan! Are you there?" Blakeley called, his voice nearer than before.

"Over here, Dr. Blakeley! Over here!" Nathan shouted, then looked down. "Beecham—shut up!"

"Did you hear something, Ralph?"

"Just the damn rain, Dad."

They were walking along the rooftop, near the edge, sloshing through puddles. Beecham's howls were maddening, but at least they might draw attention, Nathan thought. If his arm didn't come out of its socket before they spied him, they'd be able to save him.

"Jeez, Dad," Ralphie said, "did I ever tell you I'm afraid of heights?"

"No, you didn't," Blakeley answered.

"So am I, Beef!" Nathan hollered. "So am I!"

Ralphie stopped. "Dad, I just heard something."

"Nathan?" Blakeley said.

"Here! I can hear you, Dr. Blakeley. Look over the side."

As he screamed, he felt his grip coming loose.

"Dad," Ralphie said. "Look—a hand!"

"Where?"

"Here," Ralphie said, his voice coming still closer to Nathan. "Listen to that racket."

"Shut up, Beecham!" Nathan demanded, but Beecham only screamed louder and tried harder to pull them to their deaths.

"Nathan, thank God!" Ralphie shouted. He reached over the roof and tried to get a grip on Nathan's wrist, but the rain made it difficult. "I'll have you up in a minute. Hold on."

When Beecham saw Blakeley standing next to his son, he started to kick the side of the building frantically and to yank even more desperately. Tired of Beecham's struggles, Nathan took aim, and knocked him out with a well-placed kick to the side of his head. All at once, Beecham went limp.

"Good shot!" Ralphie exulted. He tightened his hand just as Nathan's started to slip away from the gutter.

"Hold onto him, Ralph," Blakeley said, grasping his son by the back of his coat. "I hope your coat is well made."

"Double stitched, Dad," Ralphie said, grimacing as he struggled to drag Nathan up over the gutter. "Only the best."

They began the slow, painful effort to hoist Nathan and his prisoner over the gutter. There were grunts and groans and curses. The first time Ralphie joked about his father's weight, Blakeley took it good-naturedly. The second time he ordered Ralphie to desist. It was hardly the time for frivolity. Finally, Nathan and Beecham were over the gutter and on the roof. Nathan lay on his back, letting the rain wash the slime off his face. Blakeley and Ralphie sat for a moment, catching their breath.

Then Blakeley, blinking through the blood and rain in his eyes, checked the deep cuts on Nathan's wrist.

"Good," he said.

"Good?" Nathan asked.

"The artery isn't severed."

"Oh," Nathan said, still trying to catch his breath. "Good."

"You're a lot tougher than you look, chum," Ralphie said.

"So is Beecham. Believe me."

"I found out," Ralphie said, shaking his head.

Beecham was still unconscious, most of his body lying in a deep, slimy puddle. Nathan thought for a moment, then moved Beecham's head away from the water to save him from a strange form of drowning. He sat up and felt his shoulder to be sure he still had an arm attached to it. Suddenly, he realized everything that had happened and how close he'd come to finding out if there really was a heaven or hell or all the rest. He started to laugh then, partly out of relief, mostly at the absurdity of life. He noticed the blood running from the gash on Blakeley's brow where Beecham's bullet had grazed him. It was dripping off Blakeley's nose and onto Nathan's jacket.

"I'll thank you not to bleed on my clothing, Dr. Blakeley," Nathan said. "Remember, I'm unemployed."

"Terribly sorry," Blakeley said and laughed with him.

They looked up and saw Pratt stepping out onto the roof, shielding his hair from the teeming rain.

"Let me punch him, Dad," Ralphie said as Pratt started to walk across the roof.

"You've had enough adventure for one day, Ralph."

"Jeez crumps."

Pratt arrived and quickly glanced at the inert form of Christopher Beecham.

"Dead?" he asked.

The others shook their heads.

"Hmmm," Pratt said and jotted a note. "It looks like undue force to me."

Before Blakeley could stop him, Ralphie reached over and showed Pratt the true definition of undue force. Nathan laughed heartily at his friend's punches, and Blakeley raised a hand to cover his own approving smile.

Chapter Twenty-Three

Nathan's convalescence was wonderful while it lasted. The overpowering stench of phenol and coal tar that pervaded his private room notwithstanding, his four days at Good Samaritan Hospital were—to a suspended, and therefore unpaid, member of the Philadelphia Police Department—virtually halcyon. Not even a hatchet-faced nurse named Sister Remegius, who was unpleasant enough to make his sutures fester, could spoil his stay.

But G. Lindsey Pratt was proving to be more harmful than the proverbial swarm of locusts. For, after Blakeley, Ralphie, and Nathan had dragged Beecham off to the Eleventh Precinct, the reporter sneaked into the madman's apartment. Therein, he found wallets and other personal effects of several local playboys. Most damning of all was a pocket watch that bore the inscription, "Happy Birthday, Reggie. Love, Cassie." With that evidence in hand,

Pratt had written an exclusive article in which he declared that he alone had discovered the man responsible for the Green Lorelei murders.

Despite the fact that the reporter could not produce the infamous woman in question, no one could deny that Beecham was capable of committing the savage killings. Civic officials praised the reporter for his service to the community. And the general populace was so enamored of Pratt that there was talk of erecting a statue of him behind Independence Hall.

Of course, Commissioner MacDonald was outraged that, for all the manpower and time invested in the case, Blakeley had failed to solve it. Despite his earlier inclination to believe Beecham the most likely suspect, Blakeley did his best to convince the commissioner that Pratt was wrong. But MacDonald refused to accept his argument that no one had shown Beecham to have plausible reason for slaying Father Gorman, and therefore, the police should not conclude their investigation until either a probable motive was established or, better yet, the real murderer was jailed. Since MacDonald could do nothing to Blakeley, he went after Nathan. The morning after his arrival at the hospital, Nathan awakened to the delivery of a letter from the commissioner that threatened to extend his term of punishment for another six months because he had violated his suspension by working on official police business.

And to make matters worse, Nathan realized that in the frenzy to capture Beecham, he had not taken time to mourn the passing of his old friend Father Gorman. More than once in those four days, his thoughts took a decidedly melancholy turn. But he was never alone long enough to be overwhelmed by his gloom. If Allison didn't drop by with baskets full of delicacies cooked by Mrs. Snopkowski, Blakeley came around to discuss the Green Lorelei case. Although they had strong doubts that Beecham was the murderer, both Nathan and Blakeley agreed that they'd rest easier if, on the sixth night after the last murder, all was calm. Until that time, they could do little but study the evidence they had and wait.

Despite the fact that the Restoration Ball was looming over her like the shadow of death, Sophie dropped by Nathan's room every day to show her appreciation for the great service Nathan had done for her family. To repay her debt of gratitude, she insisted that Nathan should stay at her home from the time of his discharge until she was firmly convinced that he was fully recovered. On each visit, Sophia brought greetings from Don Orlando, and either Rosie or Ralphie accompanied her. Although her crush on Nathan was more pronounced than ever, Rosie was becoming more bold in their intercourse. And on the pretext that she wished to improve her Latin over the summer, she elicited a promise from Nathan that he would help her study while he was recuperating. As for Ralphie, he had little to say except that, after his experiences with Cassie Aimwell and Dumpling, he was staying clear of women for a while. So, all in all, Nathan's brief respite was the best holiday he'd had since the weekend the summer before when Allison and he had slipped off to Atlantic City.

But all too soon, Nathan was getting dressed to leave. He could have used another week of bed rest, but the doctor said he was strong enough to leave the hospital. And so, the last day of June was the last day of Nathan's brief and joyful rest from the daily grind.

He had Allison to thank for the clothes he wore, because she had braved the wrath of his landlady, the widow Allcock. Although the widow was known to keep a loaded shotgun in her apartment, Allison had slipped into Nathan's rooms and selected a light blue blazer to match a pair of white trousers and white shoes. What made Allison's gesture even more gratifying to Nathan was that the expensive finery had been given to him by none other than Lillian Russell, for whom he'd performed body-guard duty. The clothes were only a gift for services rendered, but Allison had always acted jealously other times when he had them. Those days, Nathan hoped, were gone forever.

After leaving the hospital, he headed straight for the precinct house. There, he had to endure the good-natured howls of his friends as they admired him in his finery. But his pleasure was short-lived, for Blakeley had asked him to perform a favor. And true to his word, Nathan found himself following Lt. Hudson down the long, stuffy row of cells in the lockup.

"Tell Dr. Blakeley I really hate to do this to him," Hudson said apologetically, "but I'm outa space. Besides, now that we have Beecham, we have no excuse to hold the sap."

"I'm sure Dr. Blakeley is grateful for all you've done," Nathan said, certain that Blakeley had not missed Victor while he had been a guest of the Eleventh Precinct. "He'll make a contribution to this summer's clambake and picnic."

"Fortunately," Hudson said, "all Victor ever reads is the show-business section of the paper. So he still doesn't know we've caught the guy who murdered Hinsky."

When they passed Christopher Beecham's cell, Nathan stopped and backed up to have a look. The state was still trying to decide where to keep him while he awaited trial for the murders of Cybel Ash-baugh, Judge Magwood, Simeon Dorsett, Hermie Hinsky, and Dumpling, not to mention the men he was accused of killing under the guise of the Green Lorelei.

When he saw Nathan, Beecham howled and salivated. Nathan and Hudson had to get out of the way quickly when Beecham spat through the bars.

"You bring out the best in him," Hudson said.

"Down, boy," Nathan said, when Beecham roared so loudly that he could be heard two blocks away. "You want to tell the world you're nuts, right? That way you might escape the gallows again. Good luck."

Beecham was still howling when Nathan and Hudson arrived at Victor's cell. Fatzinger unlocked the cell, inside which Victor was seated as far from his cellmate Bummy Rummel as was possible.

"Hiya, McBride," Bummy said, smiling toothlessly as the officers went in.

"Bummy, what're you doing back?" Nathan said. For the vagrant had been released from protective custody the day Beecham had been jailed.

"He was caught relieving himself on Preacher Gridley's porch," Hudson said.

"When ya gotta go, ya gotta go," Bummy said matter-of-factly. "I'd a aimed the other way only the wind was blowin'."

"I don't know who is more disgusting," Victor said, pointing first at Bummy, then at Fatzinger. "He with his foul morning smells and his constant scratching at his private parts, or this inbred fellow with his diet of pickled oysters."

"Vunst I told you," Fatzinger said, "und fifty times more it musta bin, dese here ain't oysters. Dese are piggled bull's balls!" He reached into the jar and pulled out a specimen, which he then dropped into his mouth. After swallowing the delicacy, he burped and said, "Clean yer ears oudt!"

"Oh dear Gawd," Victor said.

Hudson tossed a satchel at Victor. "Time to go,

Primrose. Somebody just confessed to blowing Hermie Hinsky's head off.''

The satchel bounced off Victor's chest and fell to the floor. "What?" Victor sputtered. "But you can't release me. It's unfair!"

"What're you talking about, Victor?" Nathan asked.

"Oh, sir," Victor said, "could you not wait until I know that I will return to the stage?"

"I think you've milked it for all the publicity you're gonna get," Hudson said.

"Come along, Victor," Nathan said, helping him stuff his few possessions into the satchel. "Dr. Blakeley says Mrs. Snopkowski misses you."

Hudson started to pick up a small pile of papers that were arranged on the bunk. Victor snatched them away hastily.

"Your memoirs, Victor?" Hudson said, trying not to smile.

"They are not for your perusal," Victor said, holding the papers to his breast. He turned to Nathan. "Come along, Sgt. McBride."

Nathan smiled and followed Victor out, like a footman in the wake of a star's triumphant exit.

"So long, Victor," Bummy said and passed gas noisily. "I'll miss ya."

A few cells down the corridor Nathan again passed Beecham, who approached the bars to snarl and salivate. Victor yelped and jumped back in terror. Nathan paused to study the prisoner.

Beecham bore the satisfying cuts and bruises Nathan had given him a few days earlier. Most prominent was a black-and-blue mark on his forehead, which Nathan had given him when he kicked Beecham into unconsciousness. Nathan smiled when he saw it.

Beecham roared, causing Victor to flee down the corridor. Hudson decided it was time to have Beecham put in a straitjacket.

Standing at the door, Victor nervously demanded that Nathan take him away before Beecham tore the bars away from his cell. But Hudson shook a mocking finger at the distraught butler, then took Nathan aside and said, "Take heart, chum."

"Easy for you to say," Nathan joked.

"I mean it," Hudson said under his breath. "I pinned a tail on the commissioner. Remember the first lady you ever arrested?"

"Cassandra Teagarden." Nathan said.

"Yeah, she's the one," Hudson said with an impish grin. "Well, guess who visits her for strange favors?"

Chapter Twenty-Four

"Good Heavens, cleavage, no less," Blakeley thought, gazing at the low neckline that revealed his wife's bosom, which was so white it was in imminent danger of sunburn.

What wouldn't Sophia do for her favorite charity? Blakeley wondered, as Allison, Sophia, and he prepared to board the four-horse carriage he had rented especially for the ball.

"Hold! For shame, sir!" Rosie whispered, when she caught him staring. "My lady Blakeley is an honorable woman. Thou shouldst not look upon her person thus."

It had been a mistake, Blakeley knew, to praise Rosie's understanding of seventeenth-century idioms, and he hoped her mother had not heard that. Evidently, she hadn't, preoccupied as she was with preventing the hired footman from looking too closely at her plunging neckline.

"I want you to keep an eye on Don Orlando,

Rosie," he said, in an attempt to keep the girl from annoying her mother.

"But, Daddy, isn't that Ralphie's job?"

"It is, but . . ." Blakeley's voice trailed off, leaving his thoughts unspoken.

They both knew that Ralphie had been acting quite oddly for several days. Perhaps it was the Beecham business. Perhaps it was the death of the maid Dumpling. Perhaps it was the apparent disproving of his werewolf theory. He had not even responded to Cassie Aimwell's telephone calls.

"I quite understand," Rosie said loftily.

"And please see to it that Victor doesn't tie up the telephone. It must be free for Nathan to answer in the event we have an emergency."

"I shall," Rosie promised. "Nathan is a dear boy; I would do anything for him."

"Eh? Well, as to Don Orlando, it won't be much of a task. The old fellow will no doubt imbibe some Madeira and go to his room early. When you no longer hear him reciting his prayers, he is asleep. Ralphie usually looks in on him to be certain, or so he tells me."

"I am your servant, sir," she said, curtsying and returning to the house. Blakeley would be pleased to see all the seventeenth-century business over and done with.

As Rosie entered the house, Blakeley called after her, "Do try to keep Victor away from the liquor cabinet!"

He climbed into the carriage and sat next to Sophia. Across from her sat Allison, dressed in a gown of green silk and lace. It was true that green was to be seen everywhere, but the color became her better than most women. Allison smiled sadly as they drove along, and Blakeley knew it was because Nathan wasn't escorting her. But, gallant as ever, Nathan had insisted she attend the ball, while he helped Rosie study her Latin.

In her seat, Sophia fidgeted nervously, waving her fan and tugging at her neckline, unconsciously trying to hike it up. Hoping to calm his wife, Blakeley touched her hand gently.

"My dear," he said softly, "at the risk of being misunderstood, were this truly the court of King Charles, and not a harmless masquerade, I would approach the evening with great trepidation. For I am certain the king would find you enchanting, and he was notoriously successful with the ladies."

"Ian," she said, "please tell me you don't think I'm—"

He touched her lips with his finger. "I think you are simply the most beautiful creature I've seen since the day I beheld the Venus."

"You don't think I'm brazen then?"

He smiled and kissed her hand. "Chastity is to my lady," he recited in the tones of a courtly poet, "what wit is to the poet, civility to the statesman, grace to the—"

She interrupted him with her fan and shooed him away playfully. "Oh Lud, sir, methinks thou art a rogue, a rake, a scoundrel who would turn a lady's head," she protested in the voice of a blushing maid.

"Foh! I protest! I would but rally my lady, not seduce her."

She laughed and kissed him on the cheek. "Consider her rallied then."

"Good. Now we may cease this silly language until we get to the ball."

The carriage, with its costumed driver and footman, drew some attention as it clopped past pedestrians on their way home from work. It was warm inside the cab, and the costume Blakeley wore was uncomfortable. No wonder, he thought, the court of Charles II was so libertine; it was certainly the sort of clothing one preferred to be out of. The curled wig he wore was also hot. And he had balked at having to shave most of his beard to fit the style of the period, but he had at last relented for Sophia's sake. With the bruises from his encounter with Beecham still fresh on his face, however, he looked more like a highwayman than a courtier. The only part of the costume that he truly appreciated was the handkerchief he had tucked inside his lace cuffs and used to swab his brow. Blakeley only hoped it would last the entire evening.

"Yeah sure, Rosie," Ralphie said, his mouth crammed with food, "with dollies like Miss Meredith and even Lillian Russell to keep him company, Nathan's just bound to get goofy over you. Ha!"

"Don't babble with food in your mouth, brother dear," Rosie fired back. "You'll slobber all over your shirt again."

"You said that before."

"Yes, and you got gobbledegook on your shirt anyway."

Ralphie chewed the mouthful of meat loaf and gulped it down. He and his sister always engaged in verbal free-for-alls when their parents were away. Despite Don Orlando's presence, they continued their mutual barrage of insults unchecked. Rosie's crush on Nathan was too good a target for Ralphie to pass up, and Rosie was not about to let her brother get the upper hand on her.

"Besides," Ralphie said, preparing to shovel more food in his mouth, "I don't think it was a good idea to borrow Miss Meredith's gardenia water. You smell like you went swimming in it."

"You wouldn't know gardenia from pigweed," Rosie said. But her brother's remark struck close to home, and she pushed her plate away.

"I dunno, Rosie," he said between mouthfuls. "I

think you've been reading too many of those dumb romantic books."

"Well, reading too much is something no one will ever accuse you of," she said.

"That's Miss Meredith's dress, too, isn't it?" Ralphie asked, as he broke off a piece of bread and dipped it in gravy. "Bet she doesn't know either."

"No, it isn't Miss Meredith's dress."

"Well, it isn't yours."

"Not that you deserve to know, but it's Mother's dress. And now you have gravy on your tie. Cassie Aimwell must like men with flies buzzing around them."

"Mother's dress. Oh, yeah, that's right," he said, flushing at his sister's reference to the recent target of his youthful lust. "You'd need a couple of potatoes to fill out Miss Meredith's. Ha!"

"Hedonist."

"Anyway, what does your boyfriend, Arnie or Ernie or what's-his-name, think about this great big crush you have on Nathan? Or haven't you told him yet?"

"Arnold—" she sought a proper explanation— "has acne. He's really just a child."

"Ha!"

Although he watched the brother and sister argue, Don Orlando was too preoccupied with his own thoughts to intervene.

"What do you think, Don Orlando?" Ralphie asked suddenly, as if just realizing the Spaniard was at the table. "Maybe when you get back home you can get some Gypsy lady to cast a spell on Nathan and make him fall for Rosie."

Don Orlando nodded noncommittally and finished his glass of wine. Although he had shown a good appetite of late, his dinner was untouched, which was something the young people would have to conceal from the sensitive Mrs. Snopkowski.

"Forgive me, please," Don Orlando said, rising, "but I must retire now. I am most fatigued. Please tell Mrs. Snopkowski once again that her cuisine is excellent."

"Would you like us to bring something up to your room in case you get hungry later?" Rosie asked.

"That would be most agreeable. Perhaps some bread and meat and, of course, some wine."

"Help him Ralphie."

"I am well," Don Orlando said. "I assure you I can certainly climb the stairs unassisted."

"Help him, Ralphie," Rosie repeated.

"Rosie, you heard the man say he doesn't need any help," Ralphie said irritably. "Trust him."

"*Buenas tardes*, my young friends." Don Orlando kissed Rosie's hand and left.

"You can sure be a boor, Ralphie," Rosie said.

"Pass the potato cakes."

Nathan entered just then and apologized for having missed dinner.

"It's all right, Nathan," Ralphie said. "You can eat Don Orlando's."

"Nathan," Rosie gushed, "it's so terribly good of you to offer to help me."

"Help her with what?" Ralphie asked.

"Her Latin, Beef," Nathan said, surprised by a sudden whiff of gardenias.

"Don't you have to take something up to Don Orlando's room, Ralphie?" Rosie said with a cheerless smile.

"Huh?"

"You heard him say he'd like some bread, meat, and wine, didn't you?"

"Yeah."

"Well, take it up to him."

As Ralphie prepared a tray for Don Orlando, mumbling to himself all the while, Rosie poured Nathan a glass of wine. "Tonight we shall explore the magical world of the past participle."

"What?" Ralphie asked, raising the tray from the table.

"Nothing you'd understand, brother dear." Rosie helped him with the tray, making sure that Nathan caught a good glimpse of her dress as she passed him. "Don Orlando asked for bread. Give him half a loaf. The poor man looks as if he might starve to death overnight."

"He looked all right to me," Ralphie said.

"Nevertheless, Father said we should see to him. So run along. Nathan and I have serious work to do," Rosie said, taking a Latin text from the windowsill. She sat next to Nathan, who started sharply at the strong scent of gardenia, and gazed deeply into his eyes. "I suggest we begin with the verb *amare*."

Ralphie laughed at his sister as he left the dining room. Ever since he'd discovered that Cassie had left him in the middle of their last night together for the man she'd called Abdul, he'd almost lost his sense of humor. He felt so humiliated he wanted to have as little to do with women as possible. And when he knocked on Don Orlando's door, he repeated his pledge to steer clear of any member of the fair sex who dared to flutter her eyelashes at him.

Upon entering the room, Ralphie was surprised to find the Spaniard standing in his open window. In his hands, Don Orlando held a small, leather-bound prayer book. His mind full of bitterness, Ralphie didn't wonder long at his guest's behavior.

"It is very good of you children to show such concern for an old fool," Don Orlando said ruefully. "Please put the tray on my dresser as usual."

"I don't see any fools around here, do you?" Ralphie asked as he followed Don Orlando's instructions. "Except maybe Rosie if she thinks Nathan's going to fall for her."

"Thank you, my friend," Don Orlando said, ignoring Ralphie's joke. "*Vaya con Dios.*"

"Yeah, same to you," Ralphie said, watching curiously as the old man arranged the bread, meat, and wine on the dresser. "If you want anything else, just pull the old ringer."

"That will not be necessary," Don Orlando said as Ralphie left his room. "I have all that is required."

The estate of millionaire Giles Abercrombie was the perfect place to hold the Restoration Ball. There, the elite of Philadelphia's society could roam for hours around the large Tudor mansion and the sprawling gardens, which were decorated with neoclassical statuary and fountains, and they would never visit the same spot twice. Abercrombie had made his fortune in copper after the world went mad for electrical gadgetry. Standing in the spacious doorway to his mansion, Abercrombie received the Blakeleys with visible approval for their choice of transportation, and Allison with open admiration for her choice of costume. But his wife took unspoken exception to her husband's flirtatious behavior, and she departed hastily to seek out the nearest gaggle of gossips.

Although Blakeley wished the charity hospitals well, he dreaded the evening and wanted it over. He had no more interest in sporting about with drunken imbeciles acting as members of the royal court than in attending a hog-calling contest. And because the four-horse carriage was too large to maneuver through the narrow streets, the ride to the Abercrombie estate had taken twice as long as it should have. As a result, by the time Blakeley stepped out of the carriage, he felt like a steamed clam.

Besides being physically uncomfortable, he re-

called the many conversations Nathan and he had
had in the hospital. If they were right about the
Green Lorelei, the ball would be a perfect opportunity for her to strike. And the fact that the ball
took place on the sixth night since the last murder
worried Blakeley too. He would have to be vigilant,
but green had become such a popular color that
summer he might not know he was looking right at
the cursed woman until it was too late to act.

For Sophia's sake, Blakeley did his best to hide
his thoughts. After her horror over Beecham, and
all the toil she had endured to plan the ball, he did
not want to strike a new chord of terror in her. As
he escorted Sophia and Allison around the patrician
gardens, he could not stop complimenting his wife,
much to her embarrassed amusement, on the wonderful job she had done with her preparations.

The garden was lit by pitchblende torches, which
cast a surrealistic light on the statuary whenever a
breeze broke through the heat. Everywhere, guests
milled about in the spirit of the time. Some early
arrivals had been at the wine cask a trifle too often,
and their laughter betrayed them. Several young
women in red half-masks portrayed famous London
prostitutes, and a portly woman in tights pretended
to be Mistress Bracegirdle, the actress famed for
her shapely legs.

"Do you feel a little less conspicuous now, dear?"
Blakeley asked.

"Yes, oh yes," she replied through a clenched
smile, as they acknowledged a passing couple in
distinctly unflattering pirate garb.

"Funny how a masquerade brings out the hidden
self, isn't it?" Allison said.

"True," Blakeley observed. "I believe that fellow
is an attorney."

"Just think, Ian," Sophia said, a mixture of teasing and relief evident in her voice, "if you hadn't

372

caught Christopher Beecham, you probably wouldn't even be here."

Wisely choosing to tread lightly over the subject that had so lately vexed his wife, Blakeley smiled and asked, "Tell me, dearest, how many new fools will we have to suffer this evening? Or are they all familiar ones?"

"Now, dearest darling, it's all for a good cause. Try to remember that and keep a straight face. Besides, I do realize how miserable you are tonight, and I love you all the more for it."

"It's unfair of you to speak like that."

"I know. As for the new faces, I suppose there will be quite a few. Giles Abercrombie loves to show off his popularity. He will trouble you, Allison. I could tell by the look in his eyes when he saw you."

"Wonderful," Allison said to Sophia and Blakeley's amusement. "I do so love gentlemen with hooked noses and bowed legs."

Inside the mansion, servants in costumes were distributing ale, red wine, and other libations of the period. A small orchestra played carefully selected music, and some of the guests who had taken lessons for the occasion were dancing a minuet. It was all quite well planned, Blakeley had to admit, all the way down to the tidbits of lark and venison served as appetizers. Sophia had done herself proud. Dinner would be roast boar with the traditional apple in its mouth. There were gaming tables and card games, where the stakes were deliberately inflated to aid the charity hospitals. Aware that the Tuesday Ladies expected her to contribute liberally, Sophia had ordered her husband to lose a few hands at the tables of his choice.

Blakeley accepted a tankard of ale from a serving wench and suddenly muttered to himself.

"Ian? Did you say something?"

"It's probably nothing, dearest."

"What's probably nothing?"

He laughed absently. "It's just that I've already counted eight women in green dresses."

"It's very popular," she said, waving at a ridiculous fellow in fop's clothing. "You're responsible in part for it, you know."

"Who is that man? The dandy in pink silk?"

Sophia covered her face with her fan and whispered, "I don't know. He's bowing to everyone so I thought I should acknowledge him. Oh, look, I know that fellow over there."

Blakeley noted a gentleman across the room where Sophia had gestured with her fan. He looked especially awkward in the dress of a dandy. The man noticed the trio and toasted them with his flagon of wine.

"I believe I've seen him somewhere," Sophia said. "What's his name?"

Blakeley strained to picture the man behind the false beard. "Oh, my God," he said suddenly, "it's Spector."

"*Amatus est*," Rosie said for the third time, gazing into Nathan's eyes with unsettling intensity. Ever since they had retired to the parlor—which had better lighting than the dining room, Rosie claimed—the girl had been drawing nearer and nearer to Nathan as they sat together on a sofa.

"I heard you the first time, Rosie. What does it mean?"

"He is loved."

"That's right. You're catching on, but there are other words on the list."

"Who cares?" Rosie asked, leaning forward.

"Who cares?" Nathan said, his surprise evident when he felt the overly eager adolescent's breath on his lips.

"There is also *optatus est*," Rosie whispered. "He

374

is desired, because he is *pulcher*, oh so beautiful."

Nathan swallowed nervously and sought the most diplomatic way out of the embarrassing situation. But Rosie had him cornered on the sofa. The only way to escape would involve moving her physically, perhaps by taking hold of her shoulders and giving her a gentle push. Of course, Nathan could also put his foot down and tell her that she was behaving inappropriately, but he was unprepared to deal with a heartbroken teenager.

"*Pulcher* is an adjective," he said instead. "We aren't studying adjectives."

"Then let's get back to *amatus* and *optatus*."

"Maybe you should look in on Don Orlando."

"That's Ralphie's responsibility," Rosie said, forgetting her promise to her father in the heat of the moment. "My responsibility is to pass Latin. You do want me to pass, don't you?"

"Rosie, all I want right now is for you to back off an inch or two."

"Why, *magister pulcher meus*, are you afraid of me?"

"No, it's just that you're giving your beautiful teacher a crick in his neck."

Rosie pulled back slightly, the romantic look in her eyes changing into the scowl of a frustrated brat. "Nathan McBride is very *crudelis*. And that makes me very *demens*."

"You're not *demens*, Rosie," Nathan said, hoping that by sticking to tutoring he could escape Rosie's wrath unscathed. "You're *irata*. *Demens* means mad in the sense of insanity."

"I don't care! I hate Latin." Rosie stormed off the couch and picked up Thomas Aquinas, who had been sleeping peacefully before the girl's outburst. "I don't frighten you into muscle spasms, do I? Come, Thomas, let us visit our friend Don Orlando."

Nathan breathed a sigh of relief when she left.

Rosie was attacking her teen years with frightening ferocity. But he could not help noticing that her mother's skirt was too long for her and that the big, fluffy Thomas Aquinas hid her entire chest as she held him in her arms.

"And this too shall pass," he said hopefully.

Rosie found Ralphie in his father's study, stretched out in a chair with his feet propped up on a stool. A magazine covered his face. Rosie shook him, but got no response; so she kicked the sole of his shoe. Ralphie gurgled, but did not move.

"All right, I'll check on Don Orlando," she said and headed upstairs. "All men are wretched dogs, present company excepted. Right, Thomas?"

The cat purred, as if he understood her. Pleased with the cat's apparent loyalty, Rosie hugged him to her. She walked carefully across the landing, hoping not to disturb Don Orlando if he was resting. A few feet from the Spaniard's door, Thomas's muscles suddenly tensed. Rosie stroked him, but he wouldn't calm down.

"Now, Thomas, it's only Don Orlando in there. He's nothing to worry about," she said to soothe the cat. But when she stopped at the door to the Spaniard's room, the cat growled and his fur started to rise. "It's all right, Thomas. Really, I don't know why you're acting so silly."

As she listened to hear whether Don Orlando was asleep or not, the cat screeched and tore at her dress. Breaking Rosie's grasp, he jumped out of her arms and bounded down the stairs.

"Gee whiz, Thomas," Rosie said, "if you tore Mother's dress I'm going to be one very unhappy maiden for a long time."

She checked for damage, but the dress was unharmed. The cat had, however, left a few scratches on her forearm. She would have to be careful not to get bloodstains on the dress. And it would take her hours to clean off the fur Thomas Aquinas had shed while in her arms.

"Nutty cat," she said, putting her head to the door again. "*Felix demens.* Stupid Latin."

Blakeley had taken a seat at a table with a group of people who were playing ombre, a card game similar to bridge whereby many seventeenth-century fortunes were won and lost. Blakeley hated bridge. He also hated having to lose at it, especially to fools who exclaimed "Pshaw!" and "Odd's fish!" after every move.

But lose he did, and Sophia rewarded him with a smile as he deposited five dollars into the pot. "Wouldst breathe some fresh air, milord?" she asked.

"If my lady will breathe it with me."

They stepped out onto the veranda, where a cool breeze was drifting through the potted shrubs. The heat inside the house had driven several other guests to seek comfort there. Blakeley excused himself to dab his brow with the already damp handkerchief, and Sophia fanned herself briskly.

The orchestra was playing a sprightly gavotte, and several couples danced a few yards away. True to Sophia's prediction, Giles Abercrombie had approached Allison, who could find no graceful way of refusing to dance. The Blakeleys watched her in particular.

"I wish I'd taken some lessons now," Blakeley said.

"I can teach you in two minutes if you'd like."

"I doubt that."

She reached out a hand and struck a stately pose. "Take my hand and I'll prove it."

"If you lose, you'll have to put some money in the pot."

"Alas, milord, there's not a penny in my purse.

Now, when I step this way, you do the same."

As they moved to the rhythm of the harpsichord and strings, Blakeley did indeed begin to catch on. But suddenly he stopped.

"What is it?" Sophia asked.

"Down there," he said, unhappily pointing at a path that led up to the house through the roses and statuary.

G. Lindsey Pratt, dressed as a king's musketeer, was being carried in a sedan chair—a mode of transportation he no doubt thought appropriate for the city's newest celebrity. Beneath their burden, two burly bearers were beginning to wilt in the heat. When Pratt stepped out of the chair before the house, one of the bearers lost his grip. The chair lurched sideways and Pratt fell on his face. Blakeley applauded the mishap quietly.

"Oh, for heaven's sake," Sophia gasped, but soon she laughed too.

Pratt was on all fours momentarily as he picked up a feather that had fallen from his musketeer's hat. When the reporter stood, one of the bearers tried to steady him, but he listed anyway.

Blakeley wished to avoid Pratt. Failing that, he would certainly lose his temper and cause a scene. After the grief Pratt had caused Nathan, Blakeley had built up a great deal of animosity toward him, which, once ignited, would explode with all the force of a fireworks display.

"Do you know what I've been thinking, darling?" Blakeley said as he watched Pratt.

"What, Ian?"

"I think Don Orlando was right from the start. I doubt Pratt ever set foot on Cuban soil. I dare say he made all his stories up—especially since he fabricated the whole story about Beecham being the Green Lorelei without anything more than the slightest of circumstantial evidence."

Nodding her agreement, Sophia tugged at her husband's arm nervously. She knew her husband couldn't tolerate frauds like G. Lindsey Pratt, and she wanted to prevent a scene from taking place. "Do stay away from him, won't you, Ian?"

"I shall do my best," Blakeley said, leading Sophia across the veranda. "Come, let us promenade."

"As you wish, milord."

Behind them, Pratt argued loudly with the bearers, and Blakeley wondered whether the reporter would soon have more bruises added to those Ralphie and Nathan had administered.

Nathan was putting away the textbook and notes when Rosie ran breathlessly into the parlor, almost tripping over her mother's skirt.

"Nathan, come with me, please."

"Rosie, once and for all, I'm—"

"Please," the girl said again.

Without another word, she pulled Nathan behind her. As they headed upstairs, they woke Ralphie from his nap. Blinking in confusion, he rose and followed them, curious to see what all the commotion was about.

As Rosie dragged him along the second-floor landing, Nathan said, "What's the problem, Rosie? You're white as a ghost."

"I'm not sure. When I went to check on Don Orlando, I heard him chanting something. So I knocked to ask if he needed anything. When he didn't answer me, I looked inside. I think he's in some kind of trance."

"That's just his prayers," Ralphie said as he joined them outside Don Orlando's door.

"No, it's not," Rosie insisted. "He's speaking in some language I've never heard before, and he looks as if he's going to die."

When Rosie started to open the door, Nathan

stopped her. If Rosie was wrong and the old Spaniard was only saying his evening prayers, he would be very embarrassed by their intrusion. Before they went crashing in, Nathan would determine if their intrusion was warranted.

When Nathan put his ear to the door, Rosie asked, "What's he chanting?"

Nathan gestured for her to remain silent and tried to concentrate on Don Orlando's words. Even though he could not decipher them, they sounded very familiar.

"He's just saying his prayers, isn't he, Nathan?" Ralphie asked.

"Quiet, you galoot!" Rosie said.

Before the brother and sister could break out into a full-scale argument, Nathan put his fingers to his lips. He listened to Don Orlando's murmurings for another minute, then shook his head. "I don't know what he's saying, but I know I've heard it before."

"I hear it every night. It's only his—" Ralphie broke off suddenly and listened closely. "Holy cow, his prayers! I knew I'd heard those words before!"

"What are you blabbering about?" Rosie asked.

"Listen, Nathan. Aren't those the words from that Mayan curse we found in Father Gorman's things? You know: *Ox texcuntebac cu lubul than tu necte Chac.*"

"*Tu necte Balam, tu can titzcaan, cu vuntal in kubic nahi,*" Nathan said, finishing the line. "It is the Mayan curse. He's trying to conjure the *chan-ekal* to destroy someone, but I can't make out who."

"We have to stop him," Rosie said.

"I wish it were that simple, Rosie. But we could be endangering all our lives just by listening," Nathan said as he strained to understand Don Orlando's words.

"Maybe we can save the guy he wants to kill," Ralphie said. "Can you hear a name?"

His ear to the door, Nathan said, "It sounds like rat or bat or or...."

Pratt had spied Blakeley and Sophia from across the veranda; they had no chance of escape. Pratt's stride was confident, despite his being fully aware that the people he was advancing toward utterly despised him. As if they were all the best of friends, he kissed Sophia's hand and offered Blakeley a firm handshake. If he noticed that neither was accepted with good cheer, he gave no sign. Only at close range did Blakeley notice the injuries Ralphie had inflicted were still visible. The sight of them buoyed his spirits.

"Of all the beauties here, Mrs. Blakeley," Pratt said, "you are truly the crown jewel. And I must say you've done a wonderful job with the ball."

"You're too kind, Mr. Pratt," Sophia said, nervously waiting for her husband's anger to flare.

"Is Miss Meredith with you?" Pratt asked.

"She is," Blakeley said.

"And McBride?"

Before Sophia could give the game away, Blakeley squeezed her hand. "He's lurking somewhere about."

Pratt shrugged. "I guess there's no accounting for taste." When neither Blakeley nor Sophia responded, Pratt changed the subject. "Some day soon, Dr. Blakeley, when you have an opportunity, I'd like to pick your brain for a while. There are very few Renaissance men left in the world, and I think you'd make a fascinating story."

"Like your tales of war, Mr. Pratt?"

Blakeley slipped his cutting remark into their dialogue so smoothly that Sophia hadn't seen it coming. But when she heard it, she cringed.

"I beg your pardon?" Pratt said, blushing.

"I asked if you thought a story about me would

381

be as fascinating as the tales you invented about the war."

"I didn't invent those stories," Pratt sputtered, his jaw dropping.

"Come now, Mr. Pratt, it's all too clear to me how you work. You fabricated your articles about the war the same way you did your story about Beecham and your ridiculous leg wound. I just pray that your lies don't cost another innocent man his life."

Pratt glanced from Sophia to Blakeley, then said, "Excuse me, I need a drink."

"Try the spiced rum. Don Orlando tells me it's quite good," Sophia said, her voice cracking.

As Pratt started off, he said through clenched teeth, "It's a job, Blakeley. I do what I'm told."

"Pratt. That's what Don Orlando's saying," Rosie said after she and the others had listened to the Spaniard for several minutes.

"Good Lord, it is Pratt," Nathan said. "Beef, can you knock the door down?"

"Practice makes perfect."

As Ralphie stepped back, Don Orlando's chanting grew louder. It seemed almost too strong to be coming from such a frail man.

"Damn," Ralphie said as he bounced off the door. "Dad buys only the best."

As the pitch of the chanting grew higher, and Rosie covered her ears in terror, Ralphie charged again, but the door gave only slightly. Ralphie backed up a third time, taking a few extra steps. He skewed his face into a study in concentration and rushed forward unchecked. He hit the door at full steam, and it slammed against the wall inside.

Ralphie and Nathan rushed into the room, while Rosie hid at the top of the stairs. The men looked around, and to their dismay, there was no sign of

Don Orlando. Nathan rushed to an open window, knowing even as he did that it was a futile gesture.

"We're too late, Beef," Nathan said. He moved over to the dresser and inspected the makeshift altar Don Orlando had laid earlier. Inside the prayer book, he found the Mayan curse.

Without waiting another moment, he ran out of the room and down the landing, startling Rosie as he flew past her. Seconds later, he was in the alcove where the telephone hung. Much to his annoyance, Victor was about to use it.

"Victor, give me the contraption."

"Didn't anyone ever tell you how to say please, Sgt. McBride?"

"You can call your bookie later," Nathan said, grabbing for the receiver.

"Don't let him hit me, Miss Blakeley!" Victor cried as Rosie came down the hallway.

"I know how to handle this, Nathan," Rosie said, taking a chain from around her neck. "Here you are, Victor, the key to the liquor cabinet."

Victor huffed, snatched the key, and dropped the receiver. Immediately, Nathan jiggled the arm and turned the crank, hoping the central operator would answer quickly. If he wasted too much time, G. Lindsey Pratt would soon be making headlines, instead of writing them.

After his encounter with the Blakeleys, Pratt took a flagon of wine from a tray and winked at the tipsy serving wench. Then he sought refuge on the veranda.

"What a jerk," he thought, hiding in the shadows. "I didn't cause the war. How the hell could I cause a war? Christ, I'm getting peanuts out of it. If Blakeley wants to get sanctimonious, why doesn't he go after the big boys? Let him holler at Hearst or Mellon, not at me! Goddamned stuffy Englishman. As if nobody ever got rich in England from a war. Damn it, he burns me up."

"You look sad, sir," a woman's voice said, interrupting Pratt's thoughts. "Might a lady offer comfort?"

In no mood to flirt, Pratt waved his arm at the dark-haired woman in a half-mask who had crept up next to him. Like so many others that evening, she wore green. Having had enough of that particular shade, he moved a few steps away.

"Perhaps a promenade in the garden?" the woman said, following him. "We could tarry awhile."

When Pratt sipped his wine and said nothing, the woman slipped her arm around his. "Don't you think my person agreeable, sir?"

"Look, lady, I'm really sick of all this seventeenth-century garbage," Pratt said. And as he pulled away from her grip, he felt the unmistakable warmth of a breast.

"All the other gentlemen found me agreeable, sir," the woman said, her voice full of a controlled, breathy urgency. The lady had prepared her charade well.

"They have a name for what you're doing," Pratt said.

"Oh, fie, sir," she gasped and covered her face with a red fan.

Regarding the sensuous young woman closely for the first time, Pratt liked what he saw. But his mood was still darkened by Blakeley's accusations, and he preferred to be alone. "Why don't you run along and play cards or something?"

"I would rather stay with thee, sir," she said, clasping his arm tightly to her chest. "And I can be as civil as a gentleman would desire."

Through the mask, Pratt caught a glimpse of the woman's eyes. Like her voice, they were impossible to dismiss. "Who knows?" he thought, dismissing all memory of Blakeley's rebuke. "This could be just what I need to cheer myself up."

"Do you mind if I tarry, Mr. Pratt?" the woman asked, her eyes fixed on his.

"You know me?"

"Everyone knows you," she said, her eyes growing more intense.

"Do you have a name?"

"Just think of me as an agreeable trollop." Satisfied that she had his undivided attention, she started to walk away.

The woman's body was somehow too lithe to be human. She moved with slow, languorous movements that might turn quick and lethal on a whim. Her dress plunged low in the back, revealing flawless olive skin over subtly toned muscles. After a few paces, she smiled at Pratt, and he could not look away from her eyes. He felt like a child as she drew him close to her with a wink.

"When I drink I like to frolic," the woman said.

Pratt looked around for a serving wench, but the only one he saw carried an empty tray and danced drunkenly by herself. Not wanting to leave the woman, for fear of missing out on a special treat, Pratt offered her his flagon. "I'll share my wine if you'll promise to stop speaking that silly old language. It's bad enough we have to wear these stupid costumes."

"As long as we're breaking the rules, will you pardon me if I remove my mask?" she asked, accepting his flagon, then raising her mask. "I have a hard time drinking with it on."

After she had sipped the wine, tiny drops rolled off her lips like beads of blood. They were the same color as some of the strange glyphs on the neckline of her dress. Her eyes riveted on Pratt, she smiled and licked the wine from her lips with delicate snakelike flicks of her tongue.

"Maybe we should go in," Pratt said as a soft rain started to fall. But neither of them moved, and Pratt could not take his eyes off the woman's.

When she drank the rest of the wine, the woman again ran her tongue over her lips and savored the drops that had fallen there. Then she pulled the mask back over her eyes. "I've a better idea, Mr. Pratt. Why don't we find our own shelter?"

While the woman in green was leading G. Lindsey Pratt down the garden path, Nathan was hanging up Blakeley's telephone and cursing under his breath. When the operator had put his call through to the Abercrombie estate, some drunken fool had answered the phone and hung up before Nathan could ask for Blakeley.

"What now?" Ralphie asked.

"I guess I'll have to go to the ball, Beef."

"Nathan, if what we think is true, Pratt will be gutted before you get halfway there."

"What else can we do?"

"Give me the telephone," Rosie said. "We can save Pratt if we can get to Daddy in time."

"Try to smile, Ian," Sophia said. Since their run-in with Pratt, Blakeley had grown more and more irritable. As they stood with Allison among the revelers, Sophia tried to improve her husband's mood.

"I am trying," Blakeley answered, but not very sincerely.

"Does he look as if he's trying, Allison?"

"Admirably," Allison said, wishing she could take off her shoes and rub her feet. She had just finished dancing with Giles Abercrombie, who had trod on her feet more than the floor.

"I'm afraid I ate too much of that roast boar,"

Blakeley said. "Tomorrow I shall begin a program of temperance. Until then, I believe I shall enjoy another tankard of ale. Will you excuse me while I look for a serving wench?"

"Of course. Just keep smiling."

"I shall, dearest," he said. "And please do not tell Spector where I am."

The last thing Blakeley wanted at the moment was another tankard of ale. As the evening wore on, it began to taste like bile. What he wanted was to breathe some fresh air and to forget about Pratt. He walked outside, where a thin mist drifted across the veranda. Beyond the duck pond, lightning flashed. When he caught a sudden chill, as if a foreboding of doom, he decided he'd had enough air and returned inside, where a pair of acrobats were entertaining a crowd.

"You look dour, Blakeley. Doesn't the glittery life appeal to you?" Giles Abercrombie asked, his curly wig tilting unmajestically. To emphasize his remark, he slapped Blakeley's back with feigned heartiness.

"Not at all, Abercrombie. Deep down, I'm a bon vivant."

"In that case, we'll find you a cooperative wench for the night," Abercrombie said with an affectedly dirty laugh. Nudging Blakeley in the ribs, he added, "That Miss Meredith is quite the little lady. You should bring her around more often."

Blakeley had heard Abercrombie's silly hailfellow-well-met line too many times to enjoy it. So, not wishing to defy propriety by insulting his host, he smiled weakly and walked away in search of his wife and Allison. In his haste to abandon Abercrombie, he almost didn't hear a serving wench address him.

"Are you named Blake?"

"Blakeley."

"There's a telephone call for you. Some young girl it sounds like, and she's real excited."

"Thank you. Where is the telephone?"

"I'll show you for a dollar," the serving wench said, folding her arms defiantly.

Not at all amused by the young woman's behavior, Blakeley frowned, but paid her anyway. Stuffing the bill between her breasts, the serving wench led him to the scullery.

"Hello," Blakeley said, totally unprepared to hear Rosie's voice and the strange story that was to follow.

At the very moment Blakeley was taking his call, Pratt and the woman in green were sitting together on a dry spot in a secluded arbor. The rain had begun to fall heavily, but it did not bother them.

When Pratt took her face in his hands to kiss her, the woman said in mock protest, "A lady needs a moment of reflection before giving in to her lust."

"Why? Do you have a husband looking for us with a shotgun?"

"That should be the least of your fears, Mr. Pratt," she said and pushed him back on the ground, covering his body with hers.

The woman weighed heavily on Pratt. He tried to shift her body, but he could not budge her. The longer she lay atop him, the more difficulty he had breathing. As they groped in the dark, Pratt could not help thinking that the sounds she made were more like rattles of death than cries of pleasure.

At last, he had to get her off him. But before he could tell her to move, a flash of lightning lit the arbor. To his horror, Pratt discovered that the woman in green had turned into a vicious beast with massive jaws. Screaming for help, the reporter tried to free his pinned arms and legs, but to no avail. As the catlike creature pawed at him with its savage claws, Pratt's cries changed to whimpers for mercy. But the creature's feral eyes blazed forth with hunger, not compassion.

In the scullery, Blakeley gripped the telephone receiver, too stunned by what Nathan had told him to comprehend it. "It all sounds so absurd."

"I know, Dr. Blakeley, but it's true. I only hope we're in time to save Pratt."

"I shall do my best, Nathan. But you must do something too. If I miss him here, I don't want Don Orlando to get back into the house. Go down to my laboratory and get the aconitine we found in Beecham's apartment. Put it in every entranceway to the house."

Without another word, Blakeley hung up and rushed back to the revelers to search for Pratt. Nowhere did he see the man in the musketeer costume, and no one he asked had seen him for quite some time. As he raced about, Blakeley's mind tried to fathom the truth about Don Orlando, but his thoughts only became more jumbled as he dashed out of the mansion, ignoring his wife's anxious voice calling to him.

Outside, the rain fell furiously and a strange wind whipped the flowers and bushes, practically uprooting them. Blakeley shouted out to Pratt, but the only people he roused were illicit lovers who had taken refuge from the storm in the several bowers throughout the garden. Suddenly a scream rose over the howling wind; it continued for several seconds before fading away. Blakeley rushed toward the piercing screech. But as he reached the arbor from which it had come, he smelled the strong stench of burning flesh, and a gust of hot air blasted his face. Blakeley caught a fleeting glimpse of a strange beast as it hurried away, and he knew he was too late.

He stepped carefully into the arbor as the wind died down, and there he found the gutted remains of the once-famous reporter G. Lindsey Pratt.

Down in Blakeley's laboratory, Nathan pried open the cabinet in which he found the aconitine. After he raced back upstairs, he handed Ralphie a handful of the poisonous leaves. "We have to put these in all the entranceways to the house, Beef. It's our only chance to keep Don Orlando from getting in. Rosie, you stay down here."

The girl did not protest; rather, she stood at the bottom of the stairwell and held on to the bannister, as if for dear life.

Nathan and Ralphie rushed about the house, dropping aconitine in all the doors and windows. In their frenzy, they didn't notice the bewildered looks and shouts the servants gave out when they invaded the kitchen and pantry. The first floor completed, they made tracks for the bedrooms upstairs, heading for Don Orlando's room first.

Although ready to drop a handful of the poisonous leaves on the window frame, Nathan stopped short when a movement outside caught his attention. With his free hand, he pulled at Ralphie. "Beef, get away from the window!"

Ralphie gasped at the strange, cloudy face of a huge jungle cat poised just inches away, apparently floating in the air. He yelped and backed up. "What the hell is it?"

"It's Don Orlando. Throw the leaves at him, Beef. They're wolf's bane."

Despite Nathan's urgent instructions, Ralphie stood mesmerized by the cat. Seeing Ralphie entranced by the creature's hypnotic eyes, Nathan grasped him by the collar and yanked him backwards. Aroused by the jarring movement, Ralphie threw a fistful of aconitine at the window. As the *chan-ekal* roared its outrage, Nathan and Ralphie heard Rosie's screams rising from the floor below.

Nathan took what was left in the container and poured it over the bread, meat, and wine that Don Orlando had offered to the Mayan god. When the *chan-ekal* roared again and tried to enter the room, the men dived into the hall, a great blast of warm air following them.

"Where'd that wind come from?" Ralphie asked. "It feels like something from a blast furnace."

"That's the wind Petticord and the others heard," Nathan said. "It must be an evil wind that accompanies the *chan-ekal*."

"What do we do now?"

"Pray that we were in time to stop Don Orlando from getting in," Nathan said.

The wind blew through the open door with gale force and knocked pictures to the floor. Unanchored odds and ends flew around and shattered against the walls and ceiling. As the violent wind reached its peak, Ralphie and Nathan held their breath, trying to remember prayers learned long ago. And in the midst of the turbulent disturbance rose the wild cry of the *chan-ekal*. But when the wind started to die down, the feral growls began to fade, then they changed to the pathetic murmurings of a man before disappearing completely.

At last, Nathan and Ralphie traded wary looks and crept carefully into Don Orlando's room. Everything was in great disarray, very much like the crime scenes they had investigated over the past few weeks. The odor of burnt animal flesh hung so heavily about the room that it unsettled the men's stomachs, but they could find no sign of the old Spaniard.

Rosie, who had run upstairs the moment the wind stopped, entered the room. Sickened by the stench, she walked over to open the window farther. When she did so, she let out a piercing scream. For, far below on the stones of the walk, lay the broken body of Don Orlando.

Chapter Twenty-Five

For days after the fatal Restoration Ball, headlines around the country featured the news of G. Lindsey Pratt's brutal murder. Hailed as a hero in the war against Spain, Pratt was also honored for leading the investigation that ended the Green Lorelei's bloody spree, which was exactly what Blakeley and the authorities wanted.

No one was having a harder time accepting the truth than Blakeley. But damning evidence, in the form of a journal Don Orlando had kept, sealed the case against the dead Spaniard. For each entry detailed his murderous rampage. In language more suited to a monk of the Inquisition than a modern diplomat, Don Orlando damned his victims, one by one, to perdition for benefitting from the war that was sounding the death knell for his beloved empire. He wrote no entries on the nights of the killings, but the days afterward, he recorded his sensations during his shape-shifting experiences along with his joy at succeeding in his aims.

Blakeley read the journal with great interest. But he burned it when he was done to destroy any link between Don Orlando and the Green Lorelei. Although the entire journal upset him greatly, the entry that cut him the deepest was the one in which Don Orlando told of his conversation with Nathan about Father Gorman. For it was after their talk that Don Orlando resolved to kill Father Gorman before the priest helped Nathan figure out that a *chan-ekal* was lurking in their midst. Despite the detective's efforts to spare Nathan any guilt, however, he could tell his friend had already made the connection and was greatly distressed by it.

The truth about Don Orlando shocked Allison and the rest of the Blakeley family as well. Indeed, Rosie was hysterical for two days before she calmed down, and Sophia was not much better. But to Blakeley's great surprise and relief, Ralphie handled the situation with great maturity. No doubt the nervous conditions of his mother and sister inspired his behavior. Whatever the cause, Blakeley appreciated his son's help caring for their womenfolk—and also his good grace to avoid rubbing his father's face in the fact that he had been right about the Green Lorelei all along.

Allison too might have fallen victim to nerves had Blakeley not put her to work. From the first, Blakeley believed that revealing Don Orlando's story would have a devastating effect on the public. What with the lingering war fever, and the media frenzy documenting the Green Lorelei's crimes, the detective could only imagine the acts of cruelty that righteous indignation might lead the general citizenry to commit against anyone who appeared to be of Latin descent, should the truth be revealed.

So with the cooperation of Commissioner MacDonald and Governor Stone, Blakeley invented an explanation for the death of the Green Lorelei. The murderess, his story went, was a disturbed young woman. She suffered from a deep-seated personality disorder; as a result, she was a wanton temptress one moment, and a violent shrew who hated men the next. It had been the first few victims' misfortune to meet her when she was acting the vixen; only after their sexual encounters with the woman did those men discover her split identity. Father Gorman had apparently been slain when the woman had gone to him to confess her sins. But fear of what would become of her must have released the murderous side of her personality. Pratt had printed his article about Beecham being the Green Lorelei to lure the real murderer to come after him. Thus, he had lost his life while serving the public that so adored him—but not before stabbing the woman several times and causing her subsequent death.

Blakeley had Allison write up the story and give it to her editor, who was less than pleased to perpetrate such a hoax until a telegram from Governor Stone quickly changed his mind. When the papers were off the presses, G. Lindsey Pratt was hailed as a champion of the people—an accolade that in death, as in life, he never deserved. But Pratt did at least provide Allison the opportunity to make her name for breaking the story. Her newfound fame was a hollow victory for Allison, but she was determined to make the best of it.

The public's hunger for the lurid details of Pratt's death was satisfied by Spector and his brethren. And within a few days, even the most colorful accounts were given little space. To Blakeley's satisfaction, the attention the papers paid to the Green Lorelei's last victim served to obscure the obituary of a certain Spanish diplomat. The old man had apparently committed suicide because he was despondent about the war in Cuba.

Soon the Green Lorelei would be another footnote in the city's history, and Blakeley eagerly looked forward to that day. Until then, he and his family and friends would have to heal the deep psychic wounds they had suffered. And there was no better therapy than the Blakeleys' annual Fourth of July picnic.

The air that day was blessed with the smell of fried chicken and roasted hot dogs. Over one grill a pot of clam chowder was simmering, over another the most savory bean soup Mrs. Snopkowski had ever concocted. In another hour or so, the servants would start to carve up the suckling pig that had been roasting on the spit since early that morning.

Conducted by a little fellow in an oversized commodore's hat, a band from the Sacred Heart Orphanage down the river was playing Sousa marches on instruments Blakeley had purchased for them last Christmas. The orphanage was Blakeley's favorite charity because it was Nathan's first alma mater.

Nathan couldn't be there to enjoy the festivities, however. He was spending the Fourth of July in Fairmount Park, hiding in the dense bushes, hoping Fatzinger, disguised as a young lady, would attract the attention of the masher who had been terrorizing the maidens of the Eleventh Precinct for several weeks. Had the commissioner not caved in so quickly to Governor Stone's demand that Nathan be taken off suspension at once, he might have had one more day in the sun with Allison. But since the commissioner knew he'd been caught playing in the mud with several of the soiled madonnas in the employ of Cassandra Teagarden, he was more than willing to grant Det. Sgt. McBride an Independence Day pardon. And so, Nathan's life was back on its surly course. But with Allison by his side, he was willing to take on whatever came his way.

Despite Nathan's absence, Blakeley was in excellent spirits as he watched the 50 children from the orphanage play everything from badminton to crack-the-whip.

He was sitting on a bench with Governor Stone, who had come in from Harrisburg for the city's annual parade. They were smoking cigars of the kind Blakeley favored—which was, of course, without dynamite. In the near distance, Sophia and Allison were teaching some little girls how to mount Gladstone, Sophia's favorite horse. Farther away toward the riverbank, Ralphie was letting himself be blocked, tackled, and roughed up by a gang of the smaller boys.

Blakeley and the governor watched the goings on with great amusement until Blakeley noticed a certain uneasiness in the governor's manner.

"Don't tell me you have to leave so soon," Blakeley said. "I was hoping you'd say something to the gathering. The little chaps in the band have been practicing a drum roll for you."

"Not at all, my friend," the governor said with forced joviality. "I never miss an opportunity to get on the soapbox."

"Hmmm." Blakeley's cigar had grown a long ash, which he flicked off with his finger. "Is it next year's election?"

"No."

"Am I meddling?"

"No."

Governor Stone cleared his throat, stood, then removed his hat to fan himself. He was a tall man, at least an inch taller than Blakeley, and thin.

"Then?" Blakeley said.

Stone looked around and said in a low voice, "It's about Beecham."

"Beecham?" Upon hearing the dreaded name,

Blakeley looked around, as if the madman's name itself were too obscene for the ears of the children. "What about Beecham?"

Stone paused, wishing he could find a better way to telling his friend the bad news, than said bluntly, "He's escaped."

Suddenly, Blakeley was very warm. He waved his hand in front of his face to chase away a persistent fly. Then, he stood hastily and kicked a tree trunk.

"*Damn*," he said. "Damn him!"

"I'm terribly sorry, old friend," the governor said. "There was a message waiting for me when I got off the train an hour ago. You should get the official word at any minute."

Blakeley closed his eyes and weighed the situation. Perhaps it would be best to send Sophia and Rosie off to England for a while to keep them out of danger while he hunted the bastard down. Perhaps Allison would like to go along with them.

"How?" he asked after a moment, not that it mattered all that much.

"Well, it seems that Commissioner MacDonald has a niece," Stone said. "She's the apple of his eye."

Blakeley nodded. He had often heard Hudson cursing the young woman because, among other things, she had somehow been responsible for the hiring of Bones Fatzinger. "I know of her."

As the governor started to explain how Beecham had escaped, Victor interrupted. There were mustard stains on his apron and bean soup on his shoulder. He was sweaty and furious.

"Sir, I must protest," he said. "I am a celebrity's butler, not a hog slopper."

Blakeley recited multiplication tables in his head, bit his tongue, and said, "Go away, Victor."

"But sir—" Victor whined.

"Go away, Victor," Blakeley said again, his voice almost a growl.

Victor huffed, made a gesture of great despair, and marched back to the barbecue pit, where Mrs. Snopkowski had assigned him to the pot of boiling corn cobs.

"You were saying?" Blakeley said.

"Well," the governor began slowly, "it seems MacDonald's niece wants to be a journalist like your friend Miss Meredith. So he had Beecham transferred from the Eleventh Precinct to a lockup in the suburbs, where his niece could interview Beecham more conveniently. That was only a few days ago. I don't suppose I have to tell you what a devil Beecham is with the ladies."

Suddenly, the little Sousa band struck up a march and the tuba player hit a loud, discordant note.

CEREMONY IN SCARLET

FRANCIS JOHN THORNTON

"Thornton writes with meticulous attention to the period detail that matches E.L. Doctorow's flair in *Ragtime!*"
—*PITTSBURGH PRESS*

THE TIME: 1898
THE PLACE: Gaslit Philadelphia
THE CRIME: Mass Murder

Someone was killing vagrants throughout the city. Not only killing them, but mutilating their bodies, ripping out their hearts for some unspeakable reason. Under tremendous pressure from city officials, the police were only too glad to enlist the aid of Dr. Ian Blakeley, former Scotland Yard detective and pioneering criminal pathologist. Confident and cerebral, Blakeley little realized that the trail of victims would lead him from the slums of Philadelphia to the elegant Main Line, where he would encounter an evil more diabolical than he could ever imagine.

__3010-1 $4.50 US/$5.50 CAN